PENGUIN BOOKS

After Robert

Sarah Quigley is a New Zealand writer who has won numerous awards for her short stories and poetry. She has a PhD from Oxford University and recently held the Buddle Findlay Sargeson Fellowship.

AFTER ROBERT

Sarah Quigley

PENGUIN BOOKS

PENGUIN BOOKS

Penguin Books (NZ) Ltd, cnr Airborne and Rosedale Roads, Albany,
Auckland 1310, New Zealand
Penguin Books Ltd, 27 Wrights Lane, London W8 5TZ, England
Penguin USA, 375 Hudson Street, New York, NY 10014, United States
Penguin Books Australia Ltd, 487 Maroondah Highway, Ringwood, Australia 3134
Penguin Books Canada Ltd, 10 Alcorn Avenue, Toronto, Ontario, Canada M4V 3B2
Penguin Books (South Africa) Pty Ltd, 4 Pallinghurst Road, Parktown,
Johannesburg 2193, South Africa
Penguin Books India (P) Ltd, 11, Community Centre, Panchsheel Park,
New Delhi 110 017, India

Penguin Books Ltd, Registered Offices: Harmondsworth, Middlesex, England

First published by Penguin Books (NZ) Ltd, 1999

1 3 5 7 9 10 8 6 4 2

Copyright © Sarah Quigley, 1999

The right of Sarah Quigley to be identified as the author of this work
in terms of section 96 of the Copyright Act 1994 is hereby asserted.

The assistance of Creative New Zealand towards the publication of this
book is gratefully acknowledged by the publisher.

Designed by Mary Egan
Typeset by Egan Reid Ltd
Printed in Australia by Australian Print Group, Maryborough

For Martin O'Connor
for his unfailing emotional and editorial support

and my sister Rach
for being there

Acknowledgements

Love and thanks must go to my family and friends who have taken an interest in this book, and have encouraged me when it mattered most. I am especially grateful to Margie, Rach, and Martin, whose close and continued readings and incisive comments helped me more that I can say. Thanks also to Hilary Wilson for her belief in my writing; to landlord and artist Stephen Gleeson who shared the daily grind; and to Michael Sinclair for his constant friendship and inspiration.

My especial appreciation to Anna Rogers, whose editorial expertise and intelligent insight carried this book to its final stages. Many thanks also to everyone involved at Penguin: particularly to my publisher Bernice Beachman, and to Geoff Walker, Philippa Gerrard and Callum Hayes.

I am grateful to Creative New Zealand for their generous financial assistance towards this project; and to Buddle Findlay and the Sargeson Trust for partially funding me through the writing process. Special thanks must go to Graeme Lay, Kevin Ireland, Bernard Brown, and Stephen Stratford for plying me with lunches and good humour during my time in Auckland.

Finally my love to my father, the memory of whose love for me keeps me writing.

Before

There is a Soho in London, and one in New York. But not many people know that there is also a Soho in the sky. You can't see it well from a city—that's the irony. You have to go far away from the orange glow to get the best view.

Most comets are named after their discoverers, resulting in obscure forgettable names like Hale-Bopp and Swift-Tuttle. Cynics and astrologers see this as proof of our arrogance, or maybe plain stupidity. Because, when it comes down to it, scientists have no power at all over the science of the stars. Some comets will return to our skies in 76 years, some in two and a half thousand years, and some keep their orbits a mystery from us altogether. Human lives come and go while the comets wheel.

Unlike most other names, Soho is an easy one for a comet, being colourful, short, with cosmopolitan overtones. Soho is a thoroughly modern comet, even though it has been around for thousands of light years. Perhaps it reincarnates itself on each journey from the deep-freeze of space into our tiny solar system.

This is a story of one comet and a small group of people who watch it arrive into their sky. In particular, it is the story of Halley and Claudia, living on opposite sides of the world but born under the same astrological influence. As Soho enters their orbit, so their lives seem destined to collide.

Do they have a choice? Perhaps every choice, perhaps none. It's impossible to tell. A comet's tail always points away from the sun so in effect it's racing backwards. And humans often travel in the same way. We think we're good at navigation, but can we really only do it in hindsight? Our heads, preoccupied with the present or the past, are turned aside from our future, so sometimes it's impossible to tell if we plan where we go or if we just drift there.

This is the story of a long traverse, by two very different people. One journeys across the world, following tragedy and the Soho Comet, from the Northern Hemisphere to the South. The other person is already there, yet although she appears stationary she is traversing where she stands.

Both are looking for something and find something quite different.

And this is the way it so often goes. We don't see what's right in front of us until we crash into it. Maybe we're blinded by our own expectations—or maybe it's just comet dust in our eyes.

December

Introducing Halley

The first sign of life in Halley is that her body grows a little smaller. Although this could be a quirk of nature, it's more likely that it's a premonition. Because by the time she starts to grow, by the time she knows what's happening to her, Robert is dead.

After she's told this, the world is never quiet. She doesn't find this strange—it would have been much stranger if things had stayed the same. It's just that she never knew there was so much sound in the world. Now she sits in concerts with empty seats on both sides of her and still she hears fingernails on nylon skirts and nylon skirts on nylon stockings. The drop of a programme is a branch crashing, or a falling body, and two rows back someone is swallowing.

Now she understands the Camden murder case she read about in the paper. She understands the guy watching a movie who shouted at the couple behind him to be quiet. She understands the couple who followed the guy after the movie finished and finished him off too, with a knife, in an alleyway.

Yes, now she understands rage and noise. She hears it all around her.

Movement, however, is something else. She has started to wonder at how much people move. (*How can they be arsed?* she hears Robert say.) Arses on seats in buses on trains; feet on steps, footsteps; hands in hair, fingers in eyes. These days Halley even finds it hard to blink because her eyelids scratch her dry eyes. Down and up, up and down, it's a constant effort and it's risky because, with every move Robert doesn't know about, she moves further away from him.

The tears she isn't crying have settled in her stomach like a sickness. She can't eat much because she feels constantly unwell. After she undresses and lies down in bed, she waits for some physical manifestation of her grief. She waits to see it spill over the edges of herself, expects blood to seep from her nose and mouth and the soles of her feet, arteries to split and veins to rupture. But none of this happens. Her body remains swollen and sealed.

Time swells, too, like grains of rice; it bulges against the sides of every day. Every morning Halley must prepare to wade through the heavy hours until her joints crack, and her skull creaks with fatigue. But she knows this is fitting. Because, in its slowness, time is imitating Robert.

Robert. His face is the slowest Halley's ever seen. Expression doesn't happen in his face for thirty seconds after it should. Then, half a minute later, he'll laugh blink swallow open his eyes. (No, this is wrong, he *would*, he *had*, he is in the past tense.) Halley wonders what Robert's face was doing while he was falling. Did it have time to register surprise?

✿ *And Claudia*

Claudia, pronounced like Cloud, is a heavenly being. But she doesn't feel blessed.

Her body's a perfect 10, in shop fitting-rooms and in the eyes of others. But her life? Well, the way she sees it, her life is less than 10 and less than perfect. In fact, as her story opens, Claudia's life seems to be diving into negative numbers, out of the black into the red.

Life. It's been described as a balancing act. In general Claudia is good at acts, but she is finding this particular one a struggle. She looks ahead, hopes it won't be a lifelong one. At times she thinks it'd be a relief if she could bow out before 21.

At the thought of this—at the thought of youthful potential cut short, the thought of the key Diane will buy for her birthday, which would then become redundant—Claudia's beautiful eyes fill with tears. Though she's not sure if this is because she can envisage her coffin or because she can envisage it topped with paua-shell tack. She imagines, she laughs, she cries.

Yes, Claudia's life is one version of tragi-comic. It walks the knife-edge of duality and is at times hard to reconcile, even for herself. She has the presence of a tragedy queen, and a sense of the ridiculous.

The difficult dichotomy of her personality could be blamed on the universal resonance present at her birth. It was the first dawn of a bold August, the Southern Hemisphere was crackling under new blue frost. Jupiter, king of the planets, surrounded by fifteen ambivalent moons, was in the ascendant. Little wonder, then, that Claudia's small vibrating body absorbed an excess of emotion. Her lifesong was set before she emerged, a tiny perfectly formed golden Leo with a fierce appetite for love and life.

Is it preordained, then, that Claudia is used to ruling? Certainly, she has the lion's share of:

1) love. This is the way with one-child families—and for that matter can she and Diane even be considered a family? For they have nothing in common. Diane, all too aware of this, has fed

Claudia the consequences of her guilt for twenty years.

2) life. Diane is a midwife and, although her profession holds no interest for Claudia, she has witnessed some interesting facts in her time. Looking at seven-week scans, for instance, she has seen twin foetuses curled together like pretzels; then, a month later, there is only one. Diane tends to view life domestically so thinks of the womb as a room too small for two. After the battle for maternal resources, the cells of the loser are absorbed back into the mother, and the winner is free to stretch out in a newly spacious amniotic sac.

Claudia has stretched out all her life. She is addicted to attention and will go to any lengths to get it. She swims in the warm fluid of others' approval.

Diane has named her observation the Vanishing Twin Syndrome.

Halley

London is clamped between an iron sky and an iron earth. Dusk closes in almost before morning has been dispelled, and the only bonus is that the Comet Soho—topic of much conversation and many newspaper articles—becomes visible by the middle of the afternoon. As the sun struggles downwards through a grey pall, 25 degrees to its right the smudged comet appears. It provides reassurance to the Northern Hemisphere that heat and passion still exist, that somewhere flames leap and warm gas bleeds behind the dark clouds.

Apparently Soho is moving, will shortly be disappearing to southern skies. Yet with that strange, simple human conviction in permanence, Londoners believe that Soho will always be around. They emerge from offices and look at the white body, the milky tail, with proprietorial eyes and complacent mouths.

Life on earth is connected to stardust

Halley also looks at the comet. She also watches it appear nightly in the north-western sky, its yellow sodium glow triggering the sodium-vapour street lamps. But with her vision recently peeled by tragedy, her eyes stinging with the onion-knowledge of loss, she knows that Soho isn't here to stay. Like everything else, it may appear to be a fixture but in fact it is racing away at more than 27 miles a second. She watches its deceitful, apparently static form with a slight sneer, but also with understanding. Because of Robert.

Yes, because of Robert and his leaving, Halley knows more about the Comet Soho than any scientist. She knows it has more human characteristics than astronomers could ever pick up with their powerful infra-red telescopes. For example:

1) It is moody. Its surface is dynamic, ever-changing, has vents that turn on and off as it rotates in the flattering attention of the sun. Icy one minute, it can turn to angry gas the next. It is a complex and unpredictable body. It is both beautiful and terrifying, mysterious and utterly explainable.

2) More than 80% of its mass is composed of water. Like a woman's body, it has rhythms that call silently to the moons and the tides. Like a man's body, it contains the organic molecules necessary for the genesis of life. Where it falls, where it spills, it sows the precursors for new life.

It is both female and male. It is capable of creating life.

3) It may be a giver but it is also a taker. Because when it disappears, no matter how many other stars may continue to shine, the sky will appear unbearably empty.

This last point is what makes Halley look most ambivalently upwards at night. Soho is moving away to the Southern Hemisphere: by New Year, the London dark will once again be unbroken. Unless Halley also moves, she will be left behind, bereft.

She has started in on sleepless nights. Sandra calls them white nights, though she doesn't know where the expression comes from. Does Halley?

—No, Halley tells Sandra.

It is a lie. She has been to St Petersburg in an Arctic mid-summer, when the night sky is bleached into a semblance of day. It's just that she is too tired to explain (so it is only a white lie).

—No, Halley lies.—I've never heard it before.

White lie white night white knight. Robert—teeth laughing, dark face—would appreciate the irony. Irony was a favourite with him, he picked it up the way others pick up money on the street, and he would share it with Halley afterwards like sharp and shining treasure.

So Sandra goes away unenlightened. And every night Halley lies spread-eagled like a Russian city and longs for the falling of complete darkness. The inside of her head is like a room without curtains. Light glances off surfaces, there is nowhere to go, no cupboard to crawl into and close the door. Her dreams are no more than hallucinations

she is in the unknown room of an unknown drug-dealer, hears the police at the door. what to do? quickly throw bags of cocaine out the window which burst in mid-air scattering dreams on the heads of pedestrians. late evening, dreams falling on heads like snow, white nights, nightmares

Sleeplessness has become an addiction. Halley refuses sleeping pills; she has had more than enough contact with oblivion. Besides, the more she sleeps, the more she forgets. *That way madness lies.* She lies in bed, the blackness pressing on her open eyes, and numbers her dead. Her terrier, two grandparents, her half-cousin David, and now the partner she had intended to have forever. Can she also include herself, she wonders? Because, despite the foetus growing inside her, she feels lifeless. She lies, she lays out her dead in neat rows and does head counts.

She has heard that mental illness can begin this way: by keeping constant tallies in your head. Still, she does it purposely. She counts sheep because she knows this never works. (If she goes to sleep, Robert may slip away when her eyes are closed.) She takes a perverse satisfaction in counting Sandra's toilet trips in the middle of the night and knowing that none have slipped by her.

She is vigilant in the extreme, she is a vigilante whose law enforcement has failed only once: in letting Robert fall. He has fallen, from scaffolding from grace, through the November air, through her fingers. She did not keep him safe and is paying now for her inattention.

—Well, if you won't take Imovane, says Sandra practically, —why don't you give herbal pills a go?

Sandra is always practical, and never more so in the face of death. She deals with grief all day at the clinic, points out the bonuses of population control to pregnant teenagers. Even now, when trauma has barged into her own home, she is not thrown.

—Nothing, says Halley firmly.

Her eyes are bloodshot and she reads in *Time* magazine that rats deprived of sleep die within two weeks. Sandra looks disappointed and puts lavender oil on Halley's bedside table.

Halley can feel her limbs becoming heavier, and her head creaks on the pillow. She feels far, far older than twenty, but she reads fiercely that giraffes only need four hours sleep and cattle sleep with their eyes open. She comes to know her body too well and finds there aren't enough possibilities for positioning it. Right side left side and she can't lie on her back because that was how Robert was found, staring at the sky.

She lies inert in her bed through nights that stretch out like cats. She simulates movement by constant writing, though the decision to switch on the light is too hard to make, so her writing crawls in the darkness. She writes like a blind person, leaving extra-wide spaces between the lines, using scraps of paper laid alongside her pillow. In the morning the paper and sometimes her sheets are covered in words like a tabloid but there's nothing current about them. Black and white trash, overly familiar. They read like Halley's mind: like history. One morning she finds words on her hand and her wrist but the skin has already sucked most of the ink out of them. She reads

wait

she reads *nowhere*

—words that are blanks in themselves. By the time each

morning creeps along, she is sick with anticipation, like waiting for a phone call that never happens but still she stays on the edge every night, ears and temper strained. She used to read all the time, even in the shower, book held out of the water on a stiff arm like a European newspaper-stand. Now other people's words irritate her, so she must write her own.

As December limps on, she writes more and more. Even in the car. Words demand to be written to Robert, about Robert, and if they don't get put down it's like turning her back on him.

As she is heading towards Tower Bridge, it happens again. She knows she should pull over but inertia keeps her moving, and her left hand

(after ten weeks in the womb, it is already decided if the baby is right- or left-handed)

moves over the pad like a sleepwalker while her right hand crosses over to the gearstick, back to the wheel, trying to cope with the car and the rest of her life. Because her hands are fully occupied and her mind doesn't work properly any more, it takes her a while to stop and the police officer keeps his siren screaming alongside her until she does.

—What the hell do you think you're doing! he says.

—Sorry I was writing sorry, Halley says.—Sorry.

—Writing! he says.—Why the hell d'you think there are rules against hand-held phones?

—I didn't sorry think I just sorry, says Halley.

—You were all over the bloody road, the officer says.

—I'm left-handed, says Halley lamely.—It makes it harder.

—Even worse! he says.—Put the pen and paper away. Now!

Halley puts her memories of Robert away in the glove box. She has a rule: no crying in public, and she looks sternly at herself in the rear vision mirror. Her eyes remain impassive.

The officer is also impassive, and hands her a ticket for 20 quid.

—Try concentrating on what's important, he says.

Halley almost laughs for the first time since Robert's head splintered on the curb.

Robert's legacy

Primrose Hill, 2 July, sunny with quick clouds. This is how their conversation went:

Robert: You know how Sandra isn't your mother?

Halley: Well, she is really, she brought me up.

Robert: Yeah, but since she isn't really, does your stuff automatically go to her?

Halley: What, you mean if I'm killed?

Robert: Yeah. (Sorry.)

Halley: (That's OK.) Don't know actually.

Robert: I've only got one asset.

Halley: Me, right?

Robert: (You're a liability.) I meant my flute.

Halley: (Thanks for the compliment.) Don't forget your sunglasses!

Robert: Oh yeah. My only two assets. My flute and my sunglasses.

Halley: And your phenomenal memory, you should insure that.

Robert: You want it? I'll leave it to you.

He might have meant to

but he obviously hasn't because, after the police officer leaves, Halley realises she's forgotten how to drive. The more she tries to think about it, the less she knows. Which pedal for her left foot? What's the pedal in the middle for? Which foot which hand? She sits on the hard shoulder with her hazard lights on. Her mind's indicating everywhere except forwards. She stares out at the grey London Tuesday, the fog, and feels as if she is looking at the interior of her own head.

It is the ticket on the dashboard which finally tells her what to do. The officer has long gone, not realising the significance of what he has handed to a pen-wielding, line-weaving lawbreaker.

Halley has been handed escape. It has taken her some minutes to recognise it, some minutes of looking at her own scrawled name and address on the careless driving notice. Because of her constant writing

(Robert: *irony again!*)

she has become a skilled interpreter of words. So accustomed to rows of letters, in fact, that she can now read between the lines.

This is the truth. That the name and address on the ticket don't actually refer to her. They are no longer her, she lost that identity on another, past, Tuesday when dead Robert thrust a new and unwanted identity upon her. Unwanted, and unnamed—until now.

She sees. She sees that she can exist in the blank spaces between the accusations, and around the edges of Halley Barbaud, 12 Ainger Road, NW1. Her head stirs.

She keeps the Raybans because whenever she sees Robert's face it's always wearing these. Also she's heard stories of a hole in the sky, and a fierce sun that can bleach even the darkest eyes. So she keeps the Raybans but she sells Robert's flute. With the money she pays the driving ticket—she thinks it's only fair—and puts the rest in Lloyds Bank ready to take to a travel agent. She doesn't know exactly when she'll go, but she knows it will happen. Her departure has the inevitable approach of a freight train towards a tunnel, and she waits for the rush of air to displace her.

Low odds

A person would have to fly once a day for 19000 years before becoming involved in a fatal accident. Still, Halley reads frequently of plane crashes and, yes, infernos have been known to set her sleep alight. There has been the odd time—as with most dreamers—when she's been trapped in steaming jungles. She has occasionally wrestled with crocodiles, has taken a few poisoned arrows in the back, has spent nights pinned in trenches by the amputated stumps of bodies. It is true that these are all possibilities, but they don't worry her unduly.

No, the odds that worry her are more specific and sometimes slow her feet so that she stops in the middle of the pavement. What are the odds, she asks herself, of finding (for the second time) a flute-playing carpenter with a photographic memory and a love of numbers? What are the odds of knowing that the phone will ring before the number's even been dialled at the other end, or of listening for someone singing a certain song before the shower's been turned on? These odds are not great, she thinks. No book-maker would take bets on these odds.

(Robert: *I once bet on a horse that came in so late it had to tip-toe!*
Halley: *Your jokes are so bad you could be a stand-up comedian.*)
Now? She would give anything to hear a very bad joke again. Instead, she is living one.

Since time has slowed down out of respect for Robert, Halley feels she must choose her destination in an equally appropriate way.

This is how she does it:

1) By going into Dillon's on the Kings Rd after her five o'clock lecture, and buying a large map. (What she really needs is a globe but they're far more expensive, and Robert was never extravagant.)

2) By carrying the world home in a dark blue paper bag, under her arm, on the tube.

3) By going to her room, shutting the door, and getting on with it.

Apparently Halley knew the alphabet before she was four (Sandra has told her this several times, with pride). Latitude and longitude, however, still baffle her. Struggling with the map is an effort—an effort worth making only for Robert, whose limbs are outstretched to all corners of the world, whose face is turned always to the sky. Yet even as he free-falls through eternity, even under the strata of her grief, Halley feels the guilty stirrings of a desire to give up.

She forces herself on, bundles the map into an approximate sphere, holds it together at the bottom like a balloon. Starting from London, she draws an imaginary line through the creased paper, through the void in the middle, and comes out the other side. Her finger ends up in the middle of the sea, somewhere near the Campbell Islands. But Robert always liked volcanoes, so just a quick waver north and Halley's finger is in Auckland, which she knows has many extinct volcanoes.

(Robert: *Good work, Hale!*
Halley: *Glad you approve.*

Robert: *Especially appropriate now I've joined the ranks of the extinct too!*

which makes Halley smile.)

He used to lie in bed at night and divide her face into planes. A plane, B plane. His finger draws lines on her skin, eyebrow nose ears and the cleft in her top lip, and he names them as he draws. Radius, diameter, axis.

—I think my lips would fit pretty well just there, he says.

—Don't go off on a tangent, she says. (Being a word person, this is the only line she identifies with.)

He's right, his lips always fit well under the arc of her cheekbone. The bones in her face are big like the bones of her body. Other people call her hands huge but Robert calls them long like a line—his favourite shape.

—A line? A line's not a shape! Halley says.

—You want a shape then? he says.—H-H-H.

He only ever stammers when he's lying down, and only in the dark. He's the inverse of other stammerers, the exception to the rule of bright lights and metaphoric spotlights and too much attention and—

—Hexagon? she offers.

—Nope, he says.—Halley-shape.

In Halley's experience, based primarily on bed with Robert, when guys talk about the bones in your face they love you.

Certain oddities

Once Halley decided to skewer through the centre of the earth, she began to feel more than a general nausea. She felt tiredness, irritability, impatience, all of which were foreign to her. Although she was a Leo, child of the sun, she usually tried not to burn people. Now she just didn't care, would flare up or flash out without warning.

Her breasts hardened along with her nature, but her stomach stayed small, not much bigger than when it had rested quietly against Robert's back. Because of this she would get glared at on the tube for being young, healthy and sitting down. This didn't bother her. With the anticipated inversion of her body came an inversion of character, so she could sit for forty minutes on a dirty London Transport seat, looking impassively at blurry walls darkness blurry walls darkness. She didn't necessarily like her new self but just as it had been proved she had no say in the matter of death, it seemed she had no choice in life either.

Like her nature, her body also decided to change of its own accord. Often she found herself losing her balance, stumbling against other people whose own bodies seemed somehow to be the wrong way up. She didn't know a lot about what was happening to her, but she knew an alien body was upside down in hers, and so it felt fairer to lie with her head at the foot of her bed and her bare feet on the pillow.

Sandra, trained in the art of unconcern, always practised hard to be professional at home. But when she saw Halley upside down on the bed, her light unconcerned voice became so unconcerned that it was obvious—she was deeply concerned about Halley.

—Are you OK darling? she said. Her pretend voice floated to the ceiling, caught and swayed in the fringed light-shade.

—Yeah, I'm OK, said Halley.

—Are you sure? said Sandra.

—For God's sake Sandra! said Halley in her newly irritated capacity.—Just stick to cross-examining your patients, why can't you.

—Sorry hon, Sandra said. Her voice was quick: airy like the cloud passing over the sun during the twenty seconds in which the father of her adopted daughter's baby fell to his death.

—It's just that I'm pregnant, Halley said.

—You're what! Are you sure? Sandra cried.

—I am, Halley said.

—Halley, hon, Sandra cried.—My honey hon!

—Go away, Sandra, said Halley tiredly. She wanted no endearments, or at least not from anyone still living.

Can you handle the truth?

The truth is, Sandra has a lot to do with Halley having to leave. Robert and his lines are part of the reason, but Sandra is the rest of it. Because even though Halley thinks she has prepared for Sandra, even though she has expected it in her head and the tiny internal swelling of her stomach, Sandra's liberal attitudes take her by storm and hasten her departure.

The first manoeuvre is so gentle that Halley doesn't recognise it as an assault. That it takes place on a Tuesday—from now till eternity a black day—should have been enough to warn Halley, but it is early and she is dulled by nausea. She sits at the table, letting black decaffeinated coffee trickle down her closed throat, and doesn't see it coming.

Seemingly innocently, Sandra is reading the *Guardian*.

—Thirty people killed in the West Bank, she says, shaking her head.

—That's awful, says Halley.

Pause.

Unenthusiastically, Halley picks up her toast.

—God, the violence that's happening in Zaire! says Sandra, looking shocked.

—Yeah, it's terrible, says Halley.

Pause.

Quietly, Halley puts down her toast.

—And it's no better here! says Sandra, flicking back to the front page.

Halley can't manage a response to this one. She burps.

—You feeling sick, hon? says Sandra.

Halley is, so much so that she has to leave the table and run for the bathroom. When she comes back, her nose and eyes are running. Sandra looks majorly unconcerned, smooths the paper into casual folds.

—There's too much suffering in this old world, she says.

—You're right, says Halley.

(She thinks: *This is a redundant comment—Sandra is always right.*

She thinks: *I know all about suffering. What I know about suffering would fill a hundred* Guardians.

She thinks: *How selfish I've got. I've started relating everything anyone says to myself.*)

But in fact, it happens that she is right. Sandra's comments, which appear so universal, prove to have a very personal slant. The struggles taking place in other countries have leapt off the printed page, have entered their own house.

As the days go by, Sandra begins dropping facts on Halley like conversational bricks.

—Did you know the Americans have a five-year moratorium on human cloning? she says.

—You can't ban science, says Halley.

—The penalty's two and a half thousand dollars, says Sandra.

—You can't punish progress, says Halley.

—But think of the staggering implications! says Sandra.—It's a real moral and ethical dilemma.

Halley looks wary. When Sandra starts talking morals and ethics, she knows the focus will soon swing her way.

—There are too many unwanted lives in the world as it is, says Sandra ominously.

—Well, some scientists say cloning will actually save lives, not just create them, Halley says. Doggedly, she sticks to the bigger issues, though she knows this won't buy her much time.

—That's justification for morbid curiosity! argues Sandra.—God knows I'm liberal, but it's not natural.

—It is! objects Halley.—Twins are a type of cloning.

—Twins! says Sandra, as if she's never heard of them before. Sure enough, the focus swings in Halley's direction as if in the face of a sudden wind change.

—D'you think you might be going to have twins? asks Sandra.

—I'm talking about genetics, not me! snaps Halley.—I'm just saying that whenever cells divide, even naturally, that's cloning.

—I guess so, Sandra says. She shuffles her patients' files in front of her, feeling her way to her next line of attack.

—A pregnant woman in Britain has a one in eighty-four chance of having twins, offers Halley as a ruse.

—Yes but *you*, persists Sandra.—Do you have a feeling that there might be two on the way?

—It's far too early for that, says Halley in a resigned way.—I hardly think of the baby as a person, let alone two.

—Exactly, darling, says Sandra meaningfully.—But they grow alarmingly fast.

Halley looks down at her lecture notes, looks away at the TV. She knows but doesn't want to see where they are headed.

The next day, Sandra comes home from the clinic loaded up with her own statistics, opens her bag straight away, heaves them at Halley.

—Did you know there are between 1.3 and 1.5 million abortions in Britain each year? she says.

—No, says Halley.

—It's a positive thing really, says Sandra in a musing way.— People taking responsibility early on instead of realising later they can't cope.

By the end of the week, Sandra has armed herself with even heavier ammunition. Her attacks are becoming less subtle and her key in the door sounds like the whining of approaching bombers. Halley braces herself.

—We had a seminar today from a Swiss gynaecologist, Sandra says brightly.

—Yeah? says Halley noncommittally. She thinks, stupidly, that if she lies low the conversation might sweep over her head.

—Apparently early-term abortions take far less time, says Sandra.—Most doctors can do about ten abortions a day if they're early ones.

—Fascinating, says Halley, coldly, distantly, from her trench.

On Monday, Sandra comes home from work with all guns blazing.

—Halley! she says. Her voice has a new machine-gun directness to it: Halley's chin goes up in alarm.

—What? says Halley. She has known the moment for action has been getting closer, but now it's here she'd do anything to put it off. Tiredness pulls at her extremities like lead sinkers, anchoring her in the present. With a supreme effort, she gets up from the sofa.

—Tea? she offers, flicking on the kettle.

Sandra flicks it off again—red herring thrown back into the sea.

—Halley, hon, about this baby, she says.—Only one per cent of all abortions are done after twenty weeks.

—So? says Halley.

—So, I think we should really get moving, says Sandra.

—What on *earth* are you talking about, Sandra? says Halley. She works hard to inject surprise into her voice and surprises herself in the process. No one would know she has been anticipating this conversation, gathering sandbags of strength around her for the final showdown.

—I'm talking about talking, says Sandra in her wisest, lowest voice.—We must start talking about it so you're mentally prepared.

—Firstly, I'm nowhere near twenty weeks, says Halley.

—I know, darling, says Sandra.—But we could get you to a doctor, maybe visit a clinic so you see it's not so frightening after all.

—Secondly, says Halley,—are you really suggesting I have an abortion?

Again, she strives for genuine incomprehension. She doesn't mind appearing slow, it is all part of her stalling for time.

—Isn't that what we've been planning for? says Sandra. Her face is as amazed as Halley wants her own to look, but Sandra's is real.

—You amaze me, Sandra! says Halley (completely untruthfully).

—I'm not giving it up, she says.

The words ricochet round the kitchen, bounce off the corners of the fridge, and Halley moves swiftly to back her advantage.

—There's no question of giving it up, she says. Now that the subject has finally narrowed, moving from vague statements on the entire female race to focus on herself—well, now she finds it surprisingly easy to make statements of her own.

—Halley, you can't have thought about this! Sandra cries.

—Thought about it! exclaims Halley in disbelief.

(*Irony!* crows Robert somewhere in her head.)

—I've done nothing BUT think about it since the goddam blue line appeared in the goddam wrong window! cries Halley.

—Darling, the D and E method is perfectly painless nowadays! urges Sandra.—Less than point five per cent have any kind of difficulty!

Her hand strays towards her briefcase, as if wanting to check on her statistics, then reaches out for Halley instead. Halley can hardly bear it.

—Letters! she shouts, sidestepping.—Letters numbers percentages! You sound just like Robert! Only he'd want me to keep it!

—Do you really think that's what he'd want? asks Sandra carefully. Her hand falls without making contact, floats at her side waiting for another opportunity to touch.

—Well, he's not here to ask, is he! shouts Halley.—So I'm deciding for him!

—Let's at least talk about it, pleads Sandra.

—No! Halley shouts.—NO MORE TALKING!

After the roaring that has gone on in her ears for the past weeks, there is a strange pleasure in making a noise herself. She finds she can hear herself perfectly. She thinks of an open-ended air ticket to a place with space

a pregnant woman in Britain has a 1 in 84 chance of having twins. a New Zealander, oddly enough, has a 1 in 56 chance, which might have something to do with the people of that land's excessive craving for space

Sandra's mouth opens and shuts. Superimposed on her face, Halley can see wide seas and a vast mountain floating in the blue, with a crater on top. She narrows her eyes against the sun and there is a figure there, dark against the dazzle, with what could be a flute or maybe a spirit level in his hand.

She can't hear Sandra's arguments
(Robert: *Silent protest! ha ha*)
but, almost, she can hear her heart beating again.

Background research

In fact, although she appears to have been doing a lot of lying on Sandra's sofa, Halley has been quietly organising her exit. She has avoided her friends, has stopped answering the phone, in order to concentrate on the task in hand. Her deft method of approach is worthy of Robert: it's all a matter of addition, subtraction, and coming up with the right set of numbers. But the approach itself is partly due to her creative mind

(Robert: *Mathematicians are masters of imagination too!*)

and partly to a chance meeting with a woman who is a registrar by trade but who could also work part-time as a guardian angel.

Halley is walking in Regent's Park. Sky: grey. Mood: darker. She has been driven from the house by Sandra, whose silent looks have needled Halley's guilty stomach, whose comments have goaded her into flight.

(Halley has just skimmed *The Sun Also Rises* for the third time and, as you can see, her head is full of bullfighting imagery. The trumpeting of elephants rising over the zoo walls sounds to her like bloodthirsty crowds. She longs for some Spanish sun but December hangs sulkily around her head. Instead of hot white dust on her feet, she has mud.)

On her way to the park, everything has spoken to her about her decision. Car bumper stickers loudly congratulate her:

Choose life! Your mum did!

and

Everyone deserves a birthday. Don't abort!

But she doesn't want pious approval any more than she wants pious disapproval. She just wants space. She walks moodily over the bridge, swaying slightly, towards her angel.

Gabrielle is not only named appropriately, but she is pregnant: an outward manifestation of an internal link with Halley? Wedged into a swing in the children's playground, Gabrielle isn't reading, or eating, or doing anything other than sitting. It could almost appear that she is waiting.

Halley sits on the bottom of the slide. She smiles at Gabrielle: Halley, who rarely talks to strangers, who gets told to smile for the camera when she thinks she is already.

Yes, there is something strange about this particular day, sunk in the belly of a dark December. The air, touching Halley's cheek with a clammy hand, suddenly lifts at the sight of a heavily pregnant blonde woman sitting on a swing. The grey fog is suddenly streaked with the lightness of possibilities.

Gabrielle is suggesting coffee, although the two of them have only just met. She has the afternoon off work. Where does she work? At the Registry of Births, Deaths and Marriages. In fact, Halley feels as if she has heard this information before, but she dispels the sense of déjà vu by telling Gabrielle about the degree she is doing in archaeology.

In a café nearby they drink weak tea and, under the guise of general conversation, Gabrielle imparts the following valuable information to Halley:

a) You don't need any form of ID to order a new birth certificate.

b) There is no cross-referencing between birth and death certificates.

c) The Maida Vale Registry Office is open from 8.30 to 4.30 five days a week.

When the early evening begins to breathe on the window, Halley and Gabrielle know it is time to part. While Gabrielle extracts herself from the booth like a cork easing from a bottle, Halley pays for the tea: a token gesture only, since Gabrielle has just handed her the key to both anonymity and motherhood. Not to mention sunshine in the middle of an iron-fisted winter. When Halley turns away from the till, she half-expects to be alone. In fact, Gabrielle is still there waiting to say goodbye in the conventional way.

She is not, however, at the registry office on the subsequent trip Halley makes there—which does not surprise Halley.

Perhaps Gabrielle has given birth already and is lying in a Guy's Hospital bed.

And perhaps not.

In the local library, Halley finds what she needs. In the crumbling pages of an ancient borough newspaper: a girl, born in the same year as Halley, who ended her life aged two in a goldfish pond in Primrose Hill Road. Her name: Haley (with one L) Purcell.

Once again, Halley with two Ls is unsurprised. She hears Gabrielle as she reads the first name of the girl (*Might as well make it easy for you*), and Robert pronouncing on the second (*Purcell is Purfect!*)

Although she appreciates the preordained nature of this task, Halley does not conduct this part of her research without personal payment. As she reads the death column, she feels a pain high in her chest which might be water filling her lungs. She sits on a library stool and breathes with difficulty through the cramps, breathes in the smell of the homeless and the bereaved. The light is greenish, seeping in through the weed of trees pressed against the windows. Staff move with the quick suddenness of fish. There is a woman who could have lost a child eighteen years ago weeping silently over computer records.

When Halley B. closes her own records and stands up, it is with more knowledge of Haley P. than the facts of her short life and shorter extinction.

And so it is with a sense of rightness and without guilt that she goes to the Maida Vale Registry Office and lies to Gabrielle's colleague. She supplies date of birth (not her own), mother's maiden name (not Sandra's), and childhood address (North London: there is an air-bubble of truth in even the densest of lies). To this litany of untruths, she adds a tale of an unlocked suitcase left unattended in the middle of an Italian railway station, and an opportunistic thief. Her tale is convincing in its carelessness, shaming in its stupidity.

—You should always keep important documents on your body, says Gabrielle's colleague reprovingly.—Especially in those foreign places.

Halley bows her head meekly, hands over her pride and 25 pounds. In exchange she receives the birth certificate of a stranger. It is eggshell-coloured with a texture like new-born skin.

On the way home, Halley sits on the top of the bus, folds and opens and folds the certificate for three blocks. She sits on the front seat and feels as if she's piloting a ship, a sea of traffic parting around her. The paper crackles like a short-wave radio, as if trying to contact its previous, rightful owner. But Halley thinks she has a right too, and a similar purpose: for she is also hoping to get in touch with the dead.

Robert.

She puts the birth certificate in and out of Robert's old document wallet several times, sits on it, whacks it on the vinyl seat beside her. She picks up a half-empty polystyrene coffee cup lurching on the floor, and stamps the certificate with a brown ring. By the time she's navigated the bus as far as St John's Wood, her new identity looks battered, old, lived-in, authentic. By the time she disembarks at Chalk Farm, she feels as if a significant part of her journey has already been completed.

She and Robert take the boat down the Thames. It's a humid London day, moisture beads Halley's top lip and makes Robert's hair frizz. They pass the Globe Theatre, backed by tower blocks. With a single blink Halley removes the glass and chrome, and substitutes white houses, criss-crossed with beams, toppling over narrow streets.

She tells Robert what she's done.

—What about all those lawyers and accountants? says Robert.

Halley strips them of their suits and redresses them in doublets and hose.

—Much better, says Robert.

They get off at Greenwich under the bows of the Cutty Sark. The grass in the park is browning and by the time they reach the top of the hill Halley is sweating behind her knees, under her breasts. While they wait for the timeball to fall, they stand one on each side of the meridian line.

—You're too far away, says Robert from the eastern side.

—No, just a step, says Halley from the west.

They hold hands across the hemispheres, jump from one side of the world to the other. Robert talks about the scientific revolution, while Halley watches the way his mouth moves.

—I think I must be descended from William Lilley, finishes Robert.

—Who? says Halley guiltily.

—The astrologer, repeats Robert patiently.—He forecast the Great Fire of London.

—What's the point of forecasting large-scale disaster? asks Halley.—Can't do anything about it.

—Guess they could've laid in a few buckets of water, says Robert mildly.

The timeball is rising. They fall silent and watch it slip snakewise towards the grey sun. When it falls, they feel as if they've lived through history.

—But this happens every day, says Robert.

—No, I don't believe it happens when we're not here, says Halley.

—You mean the old 'tree falling in the forest' thing? says Robert.—It's not real unless someone's there to see it?

—Exactly, says Halley.—Robert and Halley, manufacturers of reality.

—*And mankind cannot bear very much reality*, quotes Robert.

Halley has borne too much in her life and now she feels as if her hold, like the timeball, is slipping. Inevitably hope rises, inevitably it falls, within the space of an hour or even a minute. Her mind tries to close itself to these fluctuations; she slams doors in her head, tries to lock them but fails, as in a nightmare when intruders cannot be kept out.

In the days before she finally discards her old identity, London begins to oppress her. This, too, is unwelcome, unfamiliar. She has always been fuelled by the city but now it slows her down and drags at her back. She feels its streets rotting in her blood vessels, swelling her reluctant limbs like gangrene, reeking of decay. Its buildings are covered with the grids of scaffolding and plastic sheeting like shrouds. Sometimes she looks up and sees boots through the boards, waits for them to slip, waits for a body to fall like a bruise against the yellow sky. She shuts her eyes and her mind moves forward to New Zealand, where the buildings come second and it's the mountains that claim lives.

And so she followed red tape, hand over hand, with the ease of the long-term blind. Her false birth certificate led to visa application forms. For these she required the signature of a referee: more specifically, a professional who had known her for two years or more. She looked for a shiny suit on the street and a hunger in the eyes, selected a middle-aged man with a receding hairline loitering on the platform at Victoria.

—I just need someone to sign it, she said.—I'm in a hurry to get to the immigration offices.

—Who do you want me to be? he asked shiftily, obligingly.

She tells him a Justice of the Peace and a long-term friend of the family. She gives him a tenner and carries away her form, bearing his undistinguished mark.

This part was swift and easy, because she could deal with it herself. Her passport followed more slowly, reliant on an unwieldy bureaucratic system, delayed for days in toppling piles of application forms, churned through sluggish hands, but finally birthed and sent home to Haley Purcell, c/o Halley Barbaud.

She lay, in the skin of her new persona, on the sofa and replayed the entire sequence of events. Its progression may have appeared tenuous, but in fact it had the logic of a Bach prelude. And now it was done. She had reinvented her past to save her future. Halley was Haley, and was ready to leave.

Claudia

Sun, rain, windy showers, shreds of clouds that might be imagination catching in the top of palm trees. Auckland is Claudia's home, and in its changeable nature is an accurate portrayal of her inner life.

Her light head, hardly weighted by her long light hair, turns this way and that. She holds an entire galaxy behind her shining eyes, she can traverse the outer solar system and beyond in a day. Sometimes, she loses her way.

She carries with her, through the streets of her childhood, dramatic images of newly born stars. She walks past the old brick railway station and sees a dying planet surrounded by red moons. As she passes the sturdy museum planted on the hill, galaxies collide around her. Most of the time she emerges unscathed.

It can be an exhausting journey existing as Claudia, however. She moves through her twentieth year like Io around Jupiter: changing shape as she comes close to people, changing back as she whirls away. The flexing in her shape inevitably causes friction, leads to high temperatures and a rocky surface. Colourful, at times exhilarating, but not always comfortable.

After certain eruptions, she lies on the sofa or sits on the bus, and reflects in this way:

—that she needs someone other than herself to interpret her.

—Another.

—The Other?

But this is usually temporary. Although she occasionally thinks she would like a centre to her universe, she is in fact better at dealing with constellations. She is happiest burning brightest, she is the star of her own story.

A still point in Claudia's orbit

She will, however, permit satellite characters. One of them is Adrian.

If horoscopes are important (Claudia is a golden lioness in an urban jungle) then names are equally so, and Adrian is not a good name. But he carries it off. In fact he carries it with such aplomb that, if Claudia didn't know him so well, she'd probably be losing sleep over him. She gets on so well with Adrian that she sometimes forgets they're boy and girl—a rare occurrence for Claudia.

She's been friends with Adrian since their souls collided over a pair of trousers. Both were in a second-hand shop, eyeing up some maroon velvet flares. Claudia thought they were overpriced, Adrian couldn't fit into them: both coveted them, both shrugged, both left.

Half an hour later, having walked different routes to the same coffee bar, they were both ordering double espressos with hot water on the side. They pretended not to notice each other. Not until they ended up in the same queue for the same afternoon movie session did they acknowledge there was some kind of coincidence here. They sat together, talked, and here they have ended up. Friends.

—I think it was karma, says Claudia.

—I think you trailed me, says Adrian.

—Did not! says Claudia indignantly.

—You always bite at that line! says Adrian.

They not only admire each other's taste, they also know each other's dislikes. For instance, they both loathe what the generation before has done to the world.

—Stuffed the environment, says Adrian morosely. Recently he has stripped his wardrobe of all animal products, has started wearing fake fur coats and canvas shoes.

—Stuffed the economy, says Claudia. She has never forgotten, and never stopped regretting, having to abandon the maroon flares.

Even if Claudia did want something less platonic with Adrian, he now knows far too much about her for anything to happen. Claudia has a strong belief in the aphrodisiac of mystery, and she knows once this has dissipated there's no going back. For instance, Adrian knows that:

a) she can't define irony and

b) she doesn't know how to use it.

She has always taken herself very seriously, can't get out of the habit, and keeps taking Adrian seriously too. Which is unfortunate, because Adrian is a king of irony, a prince of pastiche—a trait that even extends to his clothes.

At the moment he is in a phase of wearing collars to his elbows.

—Not a phase, he corrects.—I don't have phases, I just evolve.

But the huge collars have been around for a while now, seem definitive enough to be called a phase. The shirts are narrow, and are secured to his narrow body by lurex vests. The head is currently, constantly, covered with berets. He's evolved into a young Auden crossed with a young Gary Glitter: a look that is tasteless to the point of obscenity.

Could this be his first fashion blunder? It's possible, but unlikely. It is far more likely that this lapse is exactly what he's aiming for. Sometimes Claudia likes to believe that the whole thing is a deliberate ploy to catch her off guard. But in the very early morning, before Claudia is distracted by people, she knows the truth.

Even for Claudia, radiating at the centre of Claudia's universe, it's a stretch to believe that Adrian selects his daily clash of oranges and pinks because of a desire to disarm her.

Adrian has witnessed other things about her which make romance impossible. He has seen her looking up the phone book, and consequently knows that she has to say the alphabet through from the beginning every time to get it right. He has seen her inhale cigars and then kneel with her head down toilets. He has heard her story about being adopted, has listened to her cry because she wants a mother but instead has Diane, with whom she has nothing in common.

—And never will have, weeps Claudia.

—But even blood relations can be bastards to live with, comforts Adrian.

Adrian and Claudia. Their names may sound good together but it's all right as it is, and Claudia is an opportunist—knows enough to snatch this and keep it close, unchanged. And so she continues to share with Adrian many platonic loves: velvet, caffeine, slamming the older generation. Romance is for others.

And then, Ben

Ben. Satellite # 2, but a player in his own right. He steered himself into Claudia and Adrian's universe one night, entering their flight path so quietly that they didn't see him coming. He has no obvious radiance about him. But now, sometimes, Adrian and Claudia can see in the dark because he is there.

Ben is asked for ID wherever he goes. He has the face of a 14-year-old: it's white and after a few drinks it doesn't keep its shape very well. Although his face is 14, however, his brain is at least a hundred. Claudia thinks Ben could join Mensa if he was a joiner, which he isn't.

—Follow the herd, end up a nerd, he says.

He could easily be mistaken for a nerd: a skinny scientist, shorter than Claudia, with floppy hair and spaniel eyes. He has one green and yellow rugby jersey which he wears everywhere. Claudia and Adrian have frequently helped him in the direction of style, have donated to him excellent op-shop finds for which he thanks them and then wears, politely, under the rugby jersey. The doormen at Utopia never let him in without a reference to the All Blacks and an invitation to arm wrestle.

The three of them have spent many nights of their shared lives clubbing at Utopia. Inside its gates, Claudia dances sexily with whoever she picks, Adrian dances colourfully with colourful groups, and Ben dances in a strange flailing way, usually with himself. Strangely, the red shadows are as fitting a backdrop for him as the science lab where he works. Their celestial antics are often enhanced with bright plastic-coated capsules provided by Ben and his after-hours chemistry.

On nights when Ben socialises, he throws off his white lab coat and dons a huge velvet jacket. From its vast grid-iron shoulders, his white neck emerges like the stalk of a delicate flower. The jacket is a pre-ritual ritual: he must put it on before dancing, and always before picking up a bong or a joint, which he does regularly.

—It's my smoking jacket, he says, stroking the collar.

Through soft marijuana mist he rolls the sleeves up over his thin twig wrists, ready for action.

—I grow old, I grow old, he cackles.—Pass the joint to Prufrock, children.

Although he is the youngest, there are times when his eyes look through walls. He is wiser than Adrian's psychotherapist parents, and more practical than Diane. He has seen everything and expects nothing. Claudia and Adrian flare, flicker, explode, and occasionally collapse. Their natural environment is the nebula, they live and lose their way in a massive cloud of swirling gas and dust. Ben is a very small, very dense star, circling its own sun. The temperature of his surface is difficult to determine.

And he talks and he is silent

If Adrian embodies irony, then Ben is a paradox. He shines like a child, yet he is a creator of amphetamines. He reads Sartre but works in a lab and sometimes smells of bleach. He has legs like toothpicks, which end in steel-capped work boots. But the most paradoxical thing about Ben is his verbal facility, which sometimes inverts to a verbal inability.

Very often, and more often than not when he is off his face, he talks in complete paragraphs. His mouth is large in his small face, it can reel off pages of facts like an encyclopedia, can spin fantasy and spellbind with fables. At these times Adrian, Claudia, all surrounding listeners, are left for dead.

Or else Ben can stand like a standing stone, with his tongue weighted with boulders, and preserve a most complete, most daunting (for other people, and probably for Ben himself) wall of silence.

Claudia, quixotic, has no patience with other quixotics. After all, who does not prefer to believe themselves unique? So when Ben retreats, Claudia's brain picks up the corrector pen and whites Ben out. He is written back in only when he has something to say. Claudia's silences are quite different from Ben's. Hers are as dramatic as soliloquies, and therefore acceptable. His, she thinks, are just irritating hitches when the curtain sticks. But Ben never resents her casting him like this, even after he has emerged.

By contrast, faced with the stone-face of Ben, quixotic Adrian becomes less so. As Claudia storms away from the blanks, Adrian fills them in. He becomes a master crossworder, moving deliberately, divining and defining Ben's thoughts which refuse to come into the light. His tongue becomes forked and he speaks for two. It is understood that Ben appreciates this, though he cannot say so until later.

Yes, even to his friends Ben is a paradox. But the most paradoxical thing of all is the way in which, pulled in opposite directions by headstrong Adrian and Claudia, he manages to join them. With Ben in the middle they become a unit: they are ABC. When Adrian and Claudia spark, Ben grounds them. His skinny legs straddle the gulf that sometimes yawns between them; he is the lightning conductor that brings them to earth.

The tragedies that compose Claudia's life

In keeping with her dramatic nature, Claudia often thinks of her own life story as a tragedy.

Part the first: She only has one parent. (This looms very large when she has had a few drinks.) The relationship between a girl and her father is very significant, she thinks: a father is the first man a girl falls in love with, and after that nobody quite measures up. So who is Claudia supposed to use as her measuring stick? It is no wonder that she avoids love.

This one-parent syndrome burns a hole in the back of her throat when she tries to swallow it neat.

Part the second: The one parent she does have is a constant source of irritation to her. Diane is level-headed flat-footed down-beat and straight up: all traits that are anathema to Claudia. Diane espouses the virtue of sense continually, not only by her very behaviour but aloud in clichés—another thing Claudia abhors. The phrase *Look before you leap* has the power to make her jump through metaphorical windows of opportunity, the phrase *Sleep on it* has her dancing through the night with impatience.

Part the third: Claudia has no real sisters or brothers. She has a stepbrother called Giles, seen seldom and looked at wonderingly as a different kind of species. Is it any wonder, then, that she cries when she watches family sitcoms? Is it surprising that, when it comes to time and possessions, she is slightly selfish?

The backdrop

At the time of our entry to her life, Claudia is living in Mt Roskill with Diane. Indeed she has lived there for all of her twenty years. She has no particular liking for this part of the city. A long time ago Diane unthinkingly dumped herself and Claudia here, in the dullest part of dull Dominion Road, in a straight neighbourhood on the straightest road on earth leading north and south forever without thought of deviation.

Often in this month of December, Claudia waits for the bus with afternoon grit in her eyes and compares this road to her life. No foreseeable end, no possibility of seeing back to where it all began. Just a few predictable blocks of present seen through a suburban summer haze.

She has tried to find an escape route, has given a couple of wild veers to the side in the past couple of years. Fashion design, architecture, homeopathy. They're all compatible with her interests but nothing quite fits.

—Sweetheart, you must decide on something, says Diane. She has poured her overtime savings uncomplainingly into Claudia's whims, but is tiring of it as her arches fall.

—Diane how can I know whether I like something until I've tried it? says Claudia reasonably.

—That's life, hon, says Diane, reasonably.—How do you know you can live with someone till you've moved in with them? How do you know you want a child till you've had one? How can you know you'll want to go out for dinner next Saturday? It doesn't stop you accepting an invitation.

—But you can minimise the risk, argues Claudia,—by not committing until you're sure.

She knows she likes sashimi, for instance, but she ate some of

Adrian's before she ordered. To make sure. She says this to Diane.

—Committing to Japanese food is a bit different from committing to a career, says Diane drily.—You'll find out.

Claudia sighs. She hates it when Diane pulls the life-experience card on her.

—Why don't you try social work? says Diane, without a trace of sarcasm.

—Might as well put your head on the governmental chopping block, says Claudia. She kicks the leg of the table and thinks grimly of unemployment, disillusionment, apathy, lethargy, and violence.

—Want a poached egg, hon? says Diane, heaving herself off the sofa. She can never talk on theoretical issues for long, always brings it back to the worst of mundanities.

—God no, says Claudia, watching in horror as Diane concocts a stringy white mess in a pot of water.

Silence, apart from a hissing element.

—You know what I heard the other day, says Claudia.—That eating an egg is like eating the mucus from your fallopian tubes.

—Is that so, says Diane placidly. She fishes out two sloppy hunks of hen mucus, slops them on bread, shakes half the salt container over them.

Claudia should have known that a midwife can't be phased by talk of reproductive organs, even when she's shovelling the equivalent into her mouth. She looks objectively at Diane who's looking passively at the TV. She marvels at it, still: how she has ended up entrenched in the life of someone so incompatible.

—At least she's kind, says Adrian reasonably.—She's not your archetypal wicked stepmother.

—She's not a stepmother at all, says Claudia.—She's an adopted real mother.

—Don't get pedantic on me, says Adrian.—Whatever kind of non-mother she is, you can't deny she's kind.

Surprisingly, Adrian is big on kindness. For instance:

1) He always reads literature that he's given on the street.

2) He never asks anyone to explain a joke he's just told.

3) He never quizzes them on a book when it's obvious they've only read the inside cover.

4) When he can see that Claudia is indigo blue, he'll talk for hours about an orange Whitefriars vase he's found in some desperate garage sale.

Yep, Adrian's OK.

His parents are OK too, as far as Claudia and Ben can see, but Adrian's kindness evaporates faster than laughing gas when he talks about them. He despises their bourgeois work ethics and their bribes of a sports car if he'll study commerce. (Claudia and Ben, seeing personal advantages, say Just Do It.) He despises their large Remuera house with green-striped awnings and neo-classical white pillars.

—Neo-everything, he says.—Neo-nauseous.

He makes a point of kicking the pillars with his pointed shoes every time he enters or exits the house. Which is fairly often because, like Claudia, Adrian lives at home.

—Why don't you move out then? asks Claudia. She doesn't mind Chris and Gerry, but she's appalled at the attention they lavish on Adrian. They're both psychotherapists and they seem to spend a lot of time at the kitchen table discussing Adrian's lack of motivation. Always (Claudia notices when she blunders into an impromptu Adrian session) in low and reasonable voices. In fact, it might be this which most appals her about Adrian's parents. Surely, she thinks, if a situation is worth getting serious about, it must also be worth extracting melodramatic mileage from it? She has always been scared of noise vacuums, and black holes of emotion.

—Or have Chris and Gerry begged you to stay? she says.— Doesn't that happen with real families?

—What are you talking about, real families! scoffs Adrian.— Ours is like something out of a PC comic strip. Chris'n'Gerry Cherry'n'Gris, even their names are interchangeable.

He laughs bitterly.

—Here sits the product of a pseudo-sound environment, he says to Claudia.

Her strange and simple rules

Claudia is making her own changes. New Year is approaching, as is the need for life decisions, but in the meantime it's time for her to pay Work and Income a visit so they can pay her.

Surprisingly, Adrian is down on the idea.

—You know you could walk into any bar or shop in the city and they'd hire you on sight, he says.

—But why? I'd work my butt off and go nowhere, says Claudia accusingly.

—You're going nowhere right now anyway, says Adrian, raising his elegant eyebrows.

—I need time to think about career choices, says Claudia with dignity.—Even Diane agrees.

—Well speaking of Diane, says Adrian slightly meanly,—I thought you wanted to be independent, and that means earning.

—Like you are! says Claudia.—The Shrinks are financing your summer so why can't the government finance mine?

—I happen to have plans up my sleeve, says Adrian darkly.— Involving work.

—You know what, Aids? says Claudia.

—Yes, I know what, says Adrian.—I know I don't like you calling me that.

—You're dumb, that's what, says Claudia.—Don't you see in a few years it'll be the other way round? We'll be supporting the parents and the politicians.

—Whatever, says Adrian peaceably.—Idle away your summer if you want. Feel free to come running when you get bored.

—You're insane! says Claudia.—Four months of uninterrupted Utopia sounds like, well, Utopia.

—Oh, you're funny, says Adrian.—Just don't look too over-privileged when you go to sign up or they won't give you nothing, kid.

But it happens that Claudia knows more about it than Adrian. Diane has been in and out of work, on and off benefits, for as long as Claudia can remember. For years, yellow forms and file numbers have drifted round their house like leaves, to be raked over with resignation and kicked through with deserving feet.

No, in Diane's house there is no shame in queuing with your hand out. The only shame Claudia will feel is if she fails to get what she is entitled to.

Claudia enjoys dressing for the challenge, takes her time over it.

—Wear something sort of flowing and messy, instructs Adrian from her floor. He has been lying there for a couple of hours eating Tim Tams, and now he eyes up the curtains with sartorial interest.

Claudia sings herself around the room, opens and shuts drawers, tilts mirrors, flits like a bird. She appreciates having a pre-performance audience but for once she doesn't believe in Adrian's vision. Her instincts are unerring and realistic, and she chooses a sick-yellow shirt that used to belong to Diane.

—Neat and tidy, she says.—I'm making an effort.

She teams this up with some mistake trousers from a street-fair and scrapes her hair back into a sensible pony-tail. She has a weakness for her feet, however, so she indulges herself by putting on a fantastic pair of silver slingbacks she picked up from the Red Cross.

—My feet tell the truth about me, she says in a satisfied voice.— No money but style to spare.

Adrian sighs pointedly, disappointedly, and throws back another Tim Tam.

—You'll get bored, he predicts.—You will.

She has a full afternoon of queues. Work and Income is mostly filling in forms, but the Employment Centre requires forethought. She must appear willing to jump through any hoop asked of her.

She scrawls her name and address in large confident left-handed letters, and happily discloses how low Diane's income is. She is then swept off into a cardboard booth by a huge blonde woman called CJ to be quizzed on her special talents.

—No I'm not very good with numbers, she says.

—Or keyboards, she says.—Left-handed, you see.

—Actually I'm computer illiterate, she says.—Virtually.

—Well probably not shopwork or caregiving, she says biting her lip.—I'm impatient and a bit of an introvert.

—I have Grade 6 in flute, she says proudly.

—I love literature, she says.—My knowledge of Shakespeare is huge.

—Baroque dance, she says.—I'm quite talented at that.

To keep indifferent, to keep cool

She is also, obviously, talented in entertaining others. By the time CJ has finished asking about Claudia's ideal job, CJ is roaring with laughter and Claudia is smiling wistfully. CJ's bulk shakes the desk and Claudia waits for the cardboard walls to fold flat.

—Good luck with finding something, CJ says when she stops laughing.—It's extremely unlikely we'll come up with anything for you.

Claudia looks despondent. She shrugs at CJ, leaves the booth, and flies off down the empty corridor with wings on her slingbacks. Outside it's a glinting day. The harbour throws its arms open to Claudia, welcomes her to summer.

She shakes out her pony-tail and strides along K Rd, down Queen St. She's feeling so buoyant, is so on the apex of a sharp bright world, that the gods intervene. In the most appropriate of ways, too, aiming for Claudia's Achilles heel. One minute she's striding, the next she's flapping. The sling bit of her slingback has detached from the rest of her shoe, and is hanging on by a thread.

—Oh fuck, she says. She flaps into a phone box to ring Adrian. He's at home but powerless, because both the Shrinks are out in their cars.

—What a bastard! he says.—You paid so much for those shoes! Three dollars wasn't it?

—Yeah, she says.—So much for designer labels.

—Demand a refund, darling, says Adrian.—Consumers have their rights after all.

They cackle down the line at each other and then Claudia hangs up and rings the lab, but Ben's either got his head in a fume-hood or his hands in a cauldron because he isn't taking calls. Claudia forgives him on the assumption that his labour will supply them with a good Friday night. She thinks briefly of Diane, discounts her, and slides carefully out of the phone box. She steps and slides, steps and slides, for two lamp-posts until she reaches the taxi stand.

(—*Newly-signed Beneficiary Catches Cab!* headlines Ben.

—*Dole-bludger Masquerades as Duchess!* trumpets Adrian.

Claudia shrugs.

—MPs take cabs to the corner shop, she says.—And they have shoes, even.)

✌ *Haley*

Bangkok airport. The floor is as hard as any floor, and Haley has six hours on it. The only place she can lie flat without getting trodden or trolleyed on is behind a pillar, next to the door of the male toilets. She smells sour piss and old carpet.

She has left her steely serenity behind her, in London, along with the extra L in her name. Now her eyes are like faulty blinds—they stay shut for ten twenty forty seconds but snap open at footsteps boarding calls or the displacement of air around her head. After a temporary peace, brought about by concentrated action, the world has become loud, unstable again. The airport is composed of badly cut fragments, a montage of sounds and shapes inadequately pasted together. Haley's scalp flinches, tightens, waits for collapse. She moves closer to the pillar. The desire for sleep burns in her bladder, like an infection she cannot get rid of.

It's her first night in this room, this room of Robert's. She's been here before, so often that there are Halleys layered on Halleys, reflected back in endless lines like opposing mirrors. She's read newspapers in this room, has drunk wine eaten crisps talked big felt small. She's told jokes in this room, been made a joke of. Has been angry, been the cause of anger. She's had grids tattooed on her back from the woven floor matting. She's touched Robert's cock here, watched it grow here, held it in her hands her mouth and felt her limbs fall into instinct. She's had Robert inside her, on the bed, on the floor, in the chair. But she's never slept here.

As it turns out, she can't tonight either. Robert's arm is under her neck like the edge of an incompetent hairdresser's basin. Halley's head leans backwards but can't reach the pillow, her throat is stretched so that every swallow becomes a major manoeuvre. But she's been thinking about rearranging herself for so long now that any movement seems like a marathon effort. She lies there thinking, *next breath I'll move next breath I'll move next*, until the anticipation of movement gives way to a certainty that she'll be lying like this forever.

By swivelling her eyes sideways, she can just see Robert's face. Without a smile it looks more masculine, less Robert. She's suddenly hit by shyness. How the hell did she get here? If he wakes up she won't know what to say to him. She turns her head very slowly to get a better look at the person whose unknown naked body is hip to hip with hers.

—Hrmm eh? he says.

—What? she says nervously.

—You OK, Hay?

—Yeah, I'm OK.

—Darling Hay.

And he's back into sleep without being out of it.

She lies, feeling his heart rock the bed, feeling it beat through her like the engine of a boat. He leaves his arm under her for four five seven hours. The rest of his body moves, sometimes he mutters, but his arm stays hot and heavy under her neck. The skin gets sweaty and when she turns her head she has to unpeel her cheek from him.

Light moves across the walls, sliding like butter, from cars leaving places she's never been and going to places she hasn't heard of. The freedom of staying in a room that isn't hers is enormous. She thinks of hotel dark, bed-and-breakfast dark, different-from-home dark. Of when she was six, or ten, and unfamiliar street lights shone through net curtains, made spider-webs on floral wallpaper. Of holiday wakings, of not knowing what she'd have for breakfast.

By 6 am she's relived her life several times over, feels immeasurably different, but at 6.14 when Robert opens his eyes he still seems to recognise her. He smiles (suddenly she recognises him) and then moves his arm.

—Fuck! he says.—Pins and needles.

He turns his back to her without turning his back on her, and his breathing goes from surface to deep again so she knows she'll have another half-hour by herself. The soft clutch of the pillow under her head is unbelievably luxurious but she misses the arm too, so she has to put her hand on it very lightly to maintain contact. In the confident morning, though, she knows the arm's here to stay.

At least, she thought it was.

The plane from Bangkok to Sydney is full. After dinner, flight attendants walk the aisles like teachers in a dormitory, pulling down blinds and dimming lights.

But Haley Purcell asserts her rights. Once the uniformed watchers have disappeared, she becomes a watcher herself. Slyly, she slides her blind up again. The Chinese woman next to her sighs. Haley doesn't care, she is sick of accommodating others.

She looks out. And there is all the sky for her.

She has a waking vision

the comet and the crescent moon are flaunting themselves. the moon is making the most of the comet's glory, its dark side steals some of Soho's light and it becomes striped. it drifts into the horns of Taurus and comes to rest there, low in the north north-western sky

but Soho is racing with the plane. its tail is longer than the Milky Way, brands the sky from horizon to horizon. when the comet comes level with Haley's shoulder, it slows down and free-wheels around the moon. it knows it won't be back for another two thousand years and it's not ready to leave. Haley laughs at it, wryly. she knows all about lingering

—so come with me, she says—*come to the Southern Hemisphere for a while*

she watches it keeping pace with the plane, following her to a land of smoking mountains. when the stars begin to streak into each other, egg yolk mixed into white, she closes her eyelids for just a second

when she looks again, all she sees is deep blue nothing.

At Sydney, at Immigration, she gets told that she has to clear Customs.

—But I'm not staying! she says.

—You're here for longer than six hours, says the woman with the crisp-packet face.—That's staying.

—Only because the connection's delayed, argues Haley.—I won't even be leaving the airport.

—Doesn't matter, the woman says. Although her screwed-up mouth is still talking, she's already forgotten about Haley.

There's some confusion about Haley's bags. They've been taken off the plane: no, they haven't been taken off the plane. She stands by the carousel and finally sees her suitcase sail towards her, but she waits a lot longer before realising her pack has gone solo to Auckland. By the time she straggles tiredly to Customs, all other passengers have gone and so the officers are at a loose end. They scrutinise her face. She blushes. She gets searched.

She's OK through the clothes stage, and she's all right when they open her toilet bag. She stays expressionless as they open tapes, CDs, hunt under the covers of books and through their pages. She would never have imagined such hiding places; these people are better than clairvoyants at predicting the way people's minds work.

But then it starts. They pick through her photos, see Robert wrapped in a towel, see Robert making faces, saying *You can only take this photo if you promise never to show anyone*. They flick through her diary page by page. They see her angry black writing, see her exclamation marks her vanity her felt-pen flowers, her past twelve months.

They come upon Robert's letters: only five, because one week was all the time spent apart over two years together. With clumsy antipodean fingers, they touch the delicate French stamps. They prise open the peeling flaps, they frown at the illegal lavender stolen from a purple Parisian garden and smuggled onwards across the world.

Haley watches Robert's handwriting fade under the stares of two gorgons who no doubt have their own tragedies but would never bring them to work. Under their impersonal stone-eyes, Robert's French stories falter. His jokes fall flat under the flat fluorescent light. And now Haley is losing him. She can't hear him say *ma cherie* or *ma belle Hallee* in a very bad accent. She is losing him, fast. She must do something before he vanishes, so she breaks two rules she's spent a lifetime upholding: lets herself cry in public, and cashes in on physical weakness.

—You're pregnant! one of the gorgons says.—God, why didn't you say so!

Quickly, she becomes womanly and she gives the uniformed guys angry stares.

—It's all right for you, she says.—You don't have to put up with obstetricians and sore tits.

She takes Haley to the staff toilets and reels out handfuls of paper towels, tenderly scratches Haley's face with them. She asks when it's due, and does Haley want a boy or a girl, and has she picked out names yet.

Haley is not used to weeping in front of people and the unfamiliar attention, the rough-gentle sympathy, make it harder to stop.

—Don't know don't know, is all she can say.—Can't just can't know.

—You take a minute, sweetheart, the woman says.—Take all the time you want. Wash ya face brush ya teeth, and you'll feel better.

Robert wakes up at 7 am on weekends, and on weekdays it's 6, and he never needs an alarm clock because that's the way he is. He has his smooth black back to her but she can tell when his eyes open anyway, so that when he turns over her own eyes are open too.

—Did you sleep well? he says.

—Hardly! she says.

—Well, did you sleep at all? he says.

—Not really, she says.—I'll be Halley from Hell all day.

He gets out of bed by straddling over her and then jumping for the floor. (Did he always sleep next to the wall?) He walks to the basin. His arse is unselfconscious.

He comes back and stands in front of her and cleans his teeth. He scrubs diligently but his eyes are intent on her as she lies. His cock is beautiful and makes her ache so that she has to turn into the bed, curl into herself, watch him from under her arm. When he's got toothpaste all around his mouth and down his chin, he heads off to the basin again.

—Did you bring your own toothbrush? he says.

—I didn't want you to get the wrong idea about me, she says.

—Too late to say that now it's the morning after, he says.

She can hear water running, him breathing.

—Your turn, he says.

She sits up and he's back with the toothbrush and toothpaste, and a cup for her to spit into. He applies the toothpaste carefully.

—A pea-size, he says.—That's all you need.

Even though she hasn't slept she has the taste of night in her mouth. She opens up and tries not to laugh. Robert takes his job very seriously.

—Don't laugh, he says.—It's forbidden to laugh.

—And next time, he says.

(There will be a next time.)

—Come prepared, he says.

Dante and destiny

Haley sits for six hours with her packed and repacked suitcase. She has no Australian coins so can't get a trolley, and is forced to drag the suitcase with her wherever she goes. To the coffee shop, to the bookshop, and then to the toilet, where she takes it into the cubicle because she doesn't trust anyone any more. She sits on a disposable toilet-seat cover with her jeans round her ankles and feels more despair than she thought was possible. Despair fills her, presses on her lungs and against her ribcage like a tumour. She takes shallow breaths and feels as if she's going to suffocate.

Back in the departure lounge she comes close to panic. Something has happened to her memory; and now the journey is all she knows. She can't remember her friends' faces or the texture of Sandra's voice, she can't remember which bus she used to catch in the mornings or what season it was in London. She looks at her watch and sees that it's 1 am, but is that past, present or future time? She can't remember enough to work it out.

Her head is crumbling, and she puts it between her knees, holds it with both hands. Will Auckland even be there at the end of the curved flightpath? It could easily happen that the plane will begin its descent, that the pilot will look down through rags of cloud for tarmac, lights, and will see only creamed golden beaches and black-green bush. Then they will pull sharply up, almost vertically, the wind screaming in their ears, and Haley will have to leave behind that land of silence and echoes and re-enter the noise zone.

Yes, this might very well happen, she thinks. The others on the plane will break into excited talk: their destination has been snatched away but they are not devastated, they will just have to retrace their path back through the clouds to their homeland. But Haley, unlike everyone else on the plane, has nothing behind her now either and will spend the rest of her life circling the earth, caught between two names, not belonging to either. She will remain in limbo.

The Customs officer walks past. Her face looks tired, but she smiles when she sees Haley.

—Meeting up with the dad in Auckland, then? she says.

—I don't think he'll make it, says Haley.

—Well, you'll soon be there, says the woman comfortingly.

At Auckland International Airport Haley walks the gauntlet of peering heads like a lone cheetah. Her skin pulls tight over her cheekbones as she walks towards no one she knows, her face hardens like one of the oatmeal masks used by—is it Sandra? the woman she lived with some centuries ago? Yes, Haley Purcell appears to walk with purpose but this is only because otherwise she will sink onto the purple and red carpet and will never get up again.

Claudia

Claudia and Ben are barefoot, because it seems like a good idea. The time? That sliver between night and early morning. Neither of them wears watches. Both are higher than the bright anticipatory sky.

They have bounded from club to club not noticing the stars wheeling and then fading. Now they are en route for breakfast at Adrian's.

—Why didn't he come with us? asks Claudia wonderingly, ten hours too late.

—He's changing, says Ben with foreboding.—Seems to have things on his mind.

They enter the Domain carrying their shoes. The wet grass welcomes their ankles, and they wade through glittering ponds. Under the surface they see small insecure tracks made by the human instinct to follow.

—Who first walked this random way? says Ben, weaving along one.

—And who second-walked it? says Claudia dreamily.

The old-man trees are still hung about with mist, wisps trail from their chins and shoulders. Ben begins to prance. He high-knees it through the knee-high undergrowth, rushes up the hill towards the museum. By the time Claudia has caught up with him he is engaged in dialogue with a small branch.

—Oh hello, Claudia, he says politely.—Meet my new friend, the twig.

—Hey there, twig, says Claudia.

She twirls above the slanting harbour, Rangitoto tilting like a plate on a careless arm. Ben dances with his small branch, strange waltz-like steps.

—You move divinely, he says bowing to the stick.—Ever tried looking for water?

Some joggers power into view: for them it is the start of a day, not the middle of something running with its own rhythm. Ben looks at them and begins to caper. Carrying his woody companion, he rushes after the joggers, whips at their neon Nike feet, flicks wildly at their escaping white cotton ankles with a sound like fast-flying wings.

The joggers are alarmed, horrified. Claudia shrieks with laughter. Ben cackles wildly.

—I am the Imp of the Twig, he cries.

—Fuck off, cry the joggers. They look once, desperately, behind them as they sprint away.

Ben and Claudia sink down on the steps of the museum, lean against each other, feel the air get warmer. Then they remember Adrian, who is their destination. Their stomachs are hollow and they think of Remuera fridges, big as lighted ships, floating on red-tiled floors, loaded with cool white cargo. They head for the road. Concrete grasps their feet roughly.

—Pre-day, my favourite time, says Claudia.—Anything is possible.

—Claudia, says Ben reprovingly.

He is standing by the pedestrian crossing. There is no car in sight.

—Come over here, he says.—Cross here.

Claudia looks sideways at Ben. The smoky gloss of Utopia still hangs about his head, his purple eyes still whisper of LSD, speed, ecstasy.

—No point in breaking the law, says Ben. They walk primly across the white lines, holding hands.

The father thing again

Claudia keeps coming back to it. It's worse on the days when she wakes with a hangover, which are many. She wakes at ten eleven or twelve o'clock to an acid blue head and the realisation that the world has started without her.

From her hot tangled morning she looks back on the night before: three floors of smoke, funk, glitter. From her hot twisted sheets she looks ahead, hoping that someone new will appear at her bedroom door. But it never happens and all she ever hears is Diane in a pre-work fluster, or the dull thud of an empty house.

She invites Ben over for middle-of-the-day soaps and Indian food, offloads her woes on him.

—It's unhealthy, she complains to him,—two females living alone, together.

—Unhealthy how? asks Ben from the depths of a beanbag.

Claudia sighs. If it were Adrian he probably wouldn't be listening and would agree anyway, at least making her feel affirmed. But Ben—well Ben always requires analysis of a complaint, even while stuffing his face with onion bahjees.

—You know, all those hormones rushing around the house, she says. She hopes Ben will retreat at the mention of hormones. He doesn't.

—If you had a father here you wouldn't really want him, he says wisely, turning his full attention to her problem.

—I would so! says Claudia indignantly.

—Well, think about it, says Ben.—Likely as not he'd be some hangover from the stockmarket era, know what I mean? Brainwashed by the cult of the self, trained to go for the jugular, masquerading as a caregiver?

—At least I'd have an anti-hero, says Claudia,—to help me define myself.

—Role models are way overrated, says Ben.—Parents are overrated.

He crams some naan into his mouth and looks at the TV. Claudia looks at him.

—You never talk about your parents, she says.

—What's to talk about? shrugs Ben.—Broken marriages and collapsed investments.

—At least they do things, says Claudia.—Life with Diane's got all the excitement of an empty fridge. It's like two-day-old salad without dressing.

—Like curry without a kick, says Ben.

—Like Marlboro Lights without a light, says Claudia.

There's a metaphoric pause, then

—Diane owes it to me to get an interesting lover, Claudia says plaintively.—There must be someone out there who wants a midwife with big hips.

—Miaow, says Ben.

—Oh, she's OK, says Claudia.—She's just fixated on work. She probably just needs a good lay to loosen her up.

She turns the volume up and they watch mothers husbands cousins and great-aunts indulge in feuds, struggle with unemployment stress disorders safe and unsafe sex.

—See? Role models are extinct, says Ben from his throne of polystyrene balls.

—I guess so, says Claudia wistfully.

—Don't know why you're so worried about it, says Ben comfortingly.—You fit in anywhere, you're the ultimate chameleon.

—You think so? says Claudia, brightening up.

—I do. You're the definitive version of undefinable, says Ben.

—Diane just calls it unfocused, says Claudia.

—Mother talk, says Ben.—Fuck the family stick to friends.

He loops his arm through Claudia's elbow. They sit side by side in companionable silence and split the last beer.

—OK, I've got it, says Ben, credits and empty bottle rolling in front of him.

—What it? says Claudia.

—The ideal father figure, says Ben,—who can show you how to live.

—Yeah? says Claudia, licking curry smells off the tin-foil lids.

—Samuel Beckett, says Ben.

—That Irish writer? says Claudia.

—Yeah, he said all he wanted to do, says Ben,—was sit on his arse, fart, and think of Dante.

—He sounds perfect, says Claudia seriously,—but I don't know if Diane'd go for him.

The thing is, Ben can't be there all the time. When the lab calls with a voice like a siren, curry loses its seduction, daytime TV is lacking, and his soul isn't Claudia's for the taking. Then she's on her own to face herself.

Yes, the depression's worse after a drunken night. It grabs her with its claws and leaves scars on the back of her smooth neck. All she wants, she thinks, is some authenticity. Something anything anybody to look up to.

Diane doesn't really notice Claudia's sadness. She does most of her living when Claudia's sleeping and, just as Claudia livens up, Diane's heading for the sleeping pills. This is one addiction that Claudia sees as a complete waste of time, and she says so to Adrian.

—What's the point of taking drugs that get in the way of living? she asks him.

—I guess for some people they actually enhance living, Adrian says drily.—You know, get rest, have energy, will earn?

Claudia looks sharply at him. He's always off on mystery missions these days, to see a man about a dog, and she's started to worry that he's dabbling in some kind of work ethic.

—I'm worried about you, Adrian, she says abruptly.

—Pourquoi? says Adrian, who adopted French with his beret look.

—So is Ben, invents Claudia.—We want to know what these secret meetings are about.

—I've told you, work, says Adrian.—I'm working on work.

—Tell me more, says Claudia, putting on her most disinterested face.

Adrian knows her far too well.

—Nope, he says.—You'll get overexcited and it might never happen and we all know disappointed Claudias are a bitch to live with.

Because of Adrian's growing responsibility, she's seeing less of him. So she hears his verdict on the father-deprivation crisis second-hand.

Apparently he's told Ben, who tells Claudia, that soon Claudia will be eyeing up older men.

—No good being our age, old son, he tells Ben, who tells Claudia.—She'll be heading for forty-plus.

Claudia is repelled by the thought. She confronts Adrian.

—Don't slap some syndrome on me! she says.

—So call me a shrink's son, shrugs Adrian.—Insult me all you like but it won't change facts or fate.

—It's so clichéd it's crap, says Claudia.

—You might be perfect, Claud, says Adrian,—but you're still part of the human race.

Claudia doesn't know if this is a compliment or an insult, so she looks half-flattered and half-disgusted.

—You'll see, says Adrian.

He's using these words too often to be good company these days.

Claudia sees

He's right. It's annoying, but at least there is not only truth in his words—there is also the perfect out. This is how Claudia excuses herself:

—if what she's doing is a predictable behavioural cliché, then she doesn't have to blame herself, she can blame human nature.

—Yeah! Go for it! Abdicate! approves Adrian.—It's an important skill and could save your generation.

Her inverted Oedipal complex

She's started sleeping with the family doctor. Her *family* doctor— she's amazed to remember how reluctantly she used to undress for him. Now she steps out of her jeans for him without a thought. Once the skin on her chest blotched when his hands went any- where near her, now it stays a self-possessed caramel under his mouth. And her breasts disclaim any memory of former stetho- scopes on her (formerly) concave nipples.

The affair is made easier by the fact that she doesn't care about the doctor's wife. Doesn't care about her, doesn't care for her. Vivienne is the wife's name, and she's a kitset woman. She shops regularly in the quiet rooms of renovated houses, relies on murmuring assistants to supply the latest parts for her model. And so she has the put-together look that Claudia despises. Claudia herself spends a lot of time in front of mirrors, but pulling herself apart instead of putting herself together. In other words, Claudia begins with perfection and works down with dexterity. Considering this, she should feel sorry for Vivienne but, although she has the unblemished face of a Madonna, pity isn't part of her make-up.

So this is how it began.

A Tuesday afternoon at 5 pm: the most soul-destroying of times, when shadows fling themselves onto the road, wanting to stay at any cost. Not only does Claudia have no pity, she also has no patience for obvious desperation. So the shadows fall under her definite feet, and she steps into the medical centre onto dull carpet that also asks to be trampled on.

God no, on a Tuesday, at 5 pm, Claudia has no mercy for the meek.

She kicks a scornful hole in the magazines on the waiting-room floor. She has brought Hemingway with her. Sitting ankle-deep in other women's problems, she launches into *The Sun Also Rises*.

Soon the blood is pumping faster through her smooth limbs. By the end of the second chapter Lady Brett is her best friend. They have so much in common! They share the desire for a kindred, they are justified by their nature in cutting swathes through male ranks. Theirs is a kind of beautiful hubris plainly headed for beautiful tragedy.

Interrupted by the flat voice of a flat-chested nurse, she walks to meet Dr Heath through narrow corridors delicately scented with bull-blood. When Heath enters the ring, he has an air of ruthlessness about his smooth head. Under the glamorous fallout of Hemingway, he has become larger than his usual 5 foot 11 and his shoulders have expanded to fill his clean white shirt.

There is the possibility of violence in the air. How has Claudia never noticed this man before? And is he thinking the same about her? His speculative look at his one-time child-patient almost amounts to blood-lust.

—What's the problem, Claudia? he says. His voice rolls around the arches of the room and she thinks she hears the crowd roar.

—Oh, a tampon, Claudia says demurely.

—A problem with insertion? he says.

—No, the opposite, says Claudia.—I forgot about it, left it in, other things on my mind.

Heath, too, looks as if he has other things on his mind: things that are definitely associated with her.

—Let's have a look, he says, and he proceeds to lay her.

No, not yet! For even in Claudia's story events do not happen this fast. Today Heath simply lays her *out*, on a high couch, white sheet under her apricot buttocks. At this point in time, he slides only a speculum expertly inside her.

The patient lies composedly studying the doctor's gloves. His hands are striking, she thinks. Long-fingered, no double-joints, masculine hair on a masculine wrist. Perhaps the moment he extracts the foreign body from her own newly foreign one is when she decides. Or he decides. Or was it decided long ago by Hemingway, pausing between chapters to give Brett space for another love interest?

Claudia abdicates (and may be right to do so)

She reads the paper every day. Horoscopes? They're as relevant to real life as any reportage.

Starwatch: Your Day Today

Do we have free choice? It's impossible to answer that. In a universe governed by the laws of physics, scientists assume that our freedom is limited. But astrology assumes that, by understanding ourselves and anticipating the future, we can begin to choose for ourselves.

Claudia reads such suggestions carefully. She finds that the more she knows about astrology, the more difficult the issue of free will becomes.

—Horoscopes are crap, states Adrian.

—They're modern-day riddles, says Claudia.—You have to take time to figure them out.

—Time I haven't got, says Adrian, confirming her growing suspicions that he is leaving the realms of dreamer and idler.

—If people had listened to William Lilley, says Claudia,—they wouldn't have died in the Great Fire of London.

—Who's Willy Lilley? says Adrian.

—An astrologer, says Claudia,—who made predictions like that.

—A lucky guess, dismisses Adrian,—based on observations of wooden buildings and too many candles.

—Well, Nostradamus saw the rise of the Nazis hundreds of years before Hitler, insists Claudia. (She has spent quite a bit of time reading old *Reader's Digests* in Heath's waiting room.)

—You don't say, says Adrian, humming an irritating tune.—History, all history.

—OK, did you know that financiers consult astrologers? challenges Claudia.—Did you know the Dow Jones index has been related to the movement of Mars? Did you know *that*?

She half-hopes Adrian will also scoff at this. Instead, to her dismay

—Really? he says with sudden interest.—Is that right?

He sits forward and takes the newspaper from her.

—May I? he says, with entrepreneurial politeness.

Is anything accidental?

As observed by Adrian, Claudia does have a passionate and personal belief in the stars. Often she credits or blames them for her life happenings, particularly in affairs of the heart.

For, according to Diane, Claudia had dramatic astrological beginnings. Her birth coincided with an astrological event of world importance. As she emerged with her face screwed up, fighting against the light, a massive eruption occurred on the face of the sun.

The facts

That solar eruption, which took scientists by surprise, resulted in the violent birth of a vast gas-bubble. Launched by the sun's energy, this super-heated sphere flew like a missile towards Earth at 2 million miles per hour. Its flare caused worldwide blackouts, halting international contracts of supreme importance, inconveniencing thousands of city-dwellers.

Traffic lights became uninformative, families cooked over gas, illicit lovers made illicit love by candlelight (though perhaps they would have done so anyway). Computers spewed out unsaved knowledge, cable communications were interrupted for hours. Once again, nature was asserting its dominance over technology. Yes, the disruptions to human life twenty years ago were considerable.

And so it is hardly surprising that Claudia has disrupted her own life and the lives of others for the twenty years since. The energy inside her has catapulted her in and out of situations, has allowed her to spearhead her way through life. But even the most forceful of departures eventually loses momentum, as she will discover. Heath's radiance is phosphorescence in a dark cave, temporarily dazzling. As his light flickers and wanes, Claudia is to feel less fortunate, even ill-starred. But this, too, is in the future. For now, Heath and Claudia are fated to travel together through time, for a time.

The explosion that is Heath and Claudia takes place not long after Hemingway struck the first match. Minutes after the receptionist and sundry patients have cleared the site, ignition occurs on Heath's large unblotted blotter pad.

He has ordained a check-up

—purely to discount internal infection, he says.

He rubs his hands

—purely to warm them, he says.

He slips on some gloves, begins his examination, and chats about the stars. Claudia is amazed, affirmed, and can't wait to tell Adrian.

—If I were a medieval physician, says Heath gently,—I'd pray to the stars before starting this.

—I don't think any praying's necessary, says Claudia persuasively.

—I'd consult the sky and then prescribe you nettles, herb of Mars, says Heath.

—Sounds painful, says Claudia flirtatiously.

—Or thistle, herb of Jupiter, says Heath.

—Ditto, says Claudia.

—So what *are* you going to prescribe? says Claudia.

—This, says Heath and, finishing his preliminary work, begins what Claudia really came for.

First, and symbolically, the gloves must come off again. Turning them inside out, Heath throws them on the floor. This is to become one of his trademarks. In fact, in a post-modern world this would anticipate, summarise, and conclude the character of Heath. Ten empty digits lying carelessly on the ground: they symbolise a man of four times ten years, who still discards objects without thinking.

Over the course of this affair, the consulting room floor will be littered with trousers, socks, boxer shorts. All will be inside out. Claudia is no tidier by nature but, by nature, she is wiser. Even during the first exploratory launch, she realises the danger of this trait, knows the importance of a quick getaway. When required, she sloughs her own clothes off right way in, like a lizard. Twenty years younger than Heath, she is always ready for the shadow over the sun.

That pair of gloves. The material possession in all tragedies indicating that no good is to come. The gloves are the first intimation that Heath is flawed, and once again it was written in the stars. He was destined to be less than perfect, although initially Claudia thinks he may fill the recent void inside her.

Now that she comes to think of it, however—now she has identified that breathless, restless feeling as something missing— well, now that void doesn't seem so recent. It has been with her for most of her life.

The peculiar habit of rightness

Claudia, Adrian, Ben. They move through life as one; as complementary, supplementary parts. Yes, they argue. Occasionally they decide they can't stand one or the other or the other. There are days when they won't approach the phone to make their point. But they operate as a unit: they are their own self-created self, bound by the sinew of common bonds. Their veins run with the same rhythm, they are moved by the same things.

If Claudia were asked, this is what she would say. They are one body. Ben is the intellect, Adrian is the style, and she is the inspiration of their three-pronged body. But she is beginning to realise that Adrian possesses a certain wisdom hidden until now by his sartorial impact. Under his beret is a brain, under his lurid shirt beats a serious heart.

And so he proves to be right not only about her Freudian tendencies but also about the more mundane issue of boredom. After a very short time, Claudia has become hugely, monumentally bored with life as a beneficiary. Heath absorbs some of her growing restlessness, but Heath is married and employed, has to go home go to work go home go to work. Every time Claudia leaves the surgery straightening her clothes smoothing her hair, she can feel the unused portion of her restlessness churning inside.

Sometimes she finds herself running for no particular reason. Not many people run for nothing: they will do it for exercise, or to catch the bus. But Claudia flies down the steepest of streets towards the big harbour. Her long legs grab the black footpath and throw it behind her, her hair is straight out in the backdraught. Why is she running? To escape the terminal boredom that is overtaking her, rolling down the hill after her, just dying to crush her. When she stops people stare at her but she can still smell its stale breath hanging around her head.

—Yes, I know what you mean, says Adrian when she tells him.—I've been bored for most of my life.

He is too kind to say, *I told you so.*

Divisions

So it's 3 am in Remuera and the Shrinks have removed their tolerant selves to the south, leaving Adrian's mind to go west. He has cracked open a new bottle of Black Label and has served up massive quantities of cannabis in a bong. Although he now looks as if he's staring at a crack in the pine table, he is in fact contemplating the chasm.

—It's down there, he says frequently and darkly.—I'm down there with it.

Ben and Claudia recognise the warning signs. But they're both floating. They're so at peace that they can't even contemplate postponing Adrian's journey into the dark. Besides which, Claudia's interested. Adrian's a lot more open when he's stoned and despairing, and she hopes she can remember later what he lets out now.

—I'm not going to put up with them any more, says Adrian to the table.

—Hope he's not talking about us, says Ben unworriedly.

—Gris and Cherry, you dumb bastard, says Adrian.—They're driving me fucken insane.

His eyes narrow, look green and take on the shape of marijuana leaves.

—At least you didn't have a choice, says Claudia.—You were born to them.

—Yeah yeah, says Adrian impatiently.—Did you have a choice aged two being adopted by Diane? I don't think so.

—I just meant you don't have to be driven crazy by the 'what if' question, says Claudia dramatically.

—I am so! says Adrian.—Every day. What if they went on sabbatical for a year, what if they retired to the Coromandel and left me the house.

—You could move out, says Claudia, as she is supposed to. (The conversation is reassuringly circular, her responses are almost programmed.)

—And lo! says Ben, out of the blue.

—Lo what? says Adrian, looking up almost hopefully.

—Lo, a mighty hunger strikes, says Ben irrelevantly. His own eyes are red and curve like new-born fingernails but, as always, he can see enough to blunder to the cupboard and start foraging for food. The Shrinks, both over six feet, have built their kitchen to match. The sight of Ben's ant body half-climbing into the pantry is as familiar as the conversation.

—I need cash, says Adrian.

—What about your legacy? says Claudia.

—Saving it, says Adrian shortly.

—What the fuck for? says Claudia, sweetly.

—Just something, says Adrian.

—Just tell us, says Ben.

—Yeah, says Claudia.—Enough with the secrets.

—If you must know, says Adrian,—I'm going to open a shop.

The words seep slowly into Claudia's consciousness. The particle of anxiety raised by Adrian's uncharacteristic ambition is quickly swamped by the cannabis cloud in her head. She starts to laugh.

—What sort of shop, she says.—A hemp shop?

She and Ben manage to focus on each other and scream.

—Real funny, Claudia, says Adrian, not smiling.

—I thought so, she says. She tries to stop laughing but she can't.

—It probably won't come off anyway, shrugs Adrian.—Anyway, that's what I need the money for so I have to stay here.

—Coffee, Claud? says Ben the Provider.—Coffee, Adrian?

—You're a natural, Ben! says Claudia.—You too could enter the service industry!

She looks sideways at Adrian.

—Quit, says Adrian moodily.

—Joke, says Claudia.

—You're the one who needs a job here, says Adrian slightly meanly to Claudia. He stares at himself in the side of his empty glass.

—Hey yeah, Claud! You could work for Adrian! says Ben.

Normally acutely sensitive to context, his senses have been blunted by Adrian's earlier generosity.

—In his drug store? says Claudia, coolly.

—I wouldn't trust you with drugs, says Adrian,—or anything else.

—Here's coffee, says Ben hurriedly, dumping two cups in front of them and knocking over the sugar bowl.

—Exactly what did I do to deserve that? says Claudia directly to Adrian.

—Well, you're not the most responsible human being, are you? says Adrian.

Claudia takes a deep breath.

—I'm out of here, says Ben quickly.

—Go then! says Adrian. He stares at the table and rakes the spilt sugar into coke lines.

—Well, OK, yeah, bye, says Ben, looking slightly hurt and even more hurried.

He closes the door quietly behind him, leaving Claudia and Adrian with coffee but without an intermediary. The kitchen table suddenly becomes a vast prairie, a bleak windswept expanse scattered with misunderstandings.

—What the hell's the matter with you? says Claudia, shading her eyes so she can see Adrian.

—Nothing's the matter with *me*, says Adrian significantly.

—And there is with me? says Claudia.—You're the one who just snapped at Ben.

—Only because you provoked me, says Adrian, provocatively.

—Christ you can be a moody jerk, says Claudia, swinging back to anger.—You never used to be like this.

—So there's a new Adrian and you don't like him, says Adrian.—Have I got it right?

—I just think, cries Claudia.—You just seem—

—Stoned? says Adrian.—That's all I am and now I'm going to bed.

—No! says Claudia.—Don't!

But Adrian is lurching out the door and she sits on angrily at the table, alone. To take her mind off the fight she looks for something to read but all she can find are cookbooks and an article on obsessive-compulsive disorders. She sits for a long time. Anger gives way to unhappiness. Pride stops her going upstairs to find Adrian.

It's 6 am. The yellow kitchen suddenly looks dirty. She lets herself out into the clean yellow morning. It's early but she might as well go to bed.

January

Haley

London was cold as a fridge, Singapore was air-conditioned, Auckland is warm wet breath from a warm stale mouth. That first week of that first New Year without him, Haley feels as if she's slowly suffocating. Every time she leaves the hostel she dives into the tepid street, waits for her lungs to fill with moisture. She chokes at traffic lights, here where the air is the cleanest in the world. The sky is hot but it's the colour of lead. Here, where the sun is supposed to always shine.

She takes a bus along the waterfront and walks slowly back towards the city. St Heliers, Mission Bay, some name beginning with K that she doesn't attempt to pronounce even in her mind. The grass is like some kind of sinister watercress. It's so coarse to the touch that it reminds her of Robert's hair and she has to walk faster to leave it behind. But it's in front of her as well, it's all around.

It's the trees that really make her realise this is some place he's never been. They're like something out of the jungle. They're spiky, they stretch out sharp fingernails to stab at the sky and hold the hills back with stiff fingers.

She has found a place to stay by picking up a flier at the airport. She's realised that bodily survival is not so difficult, just a matter of getting on a bus and going somewhere.

(Sandra, brightly: *Life goes on.*)

It goes on, in fact, frighteningly constantly; it's keeping afloat emotionally that causes the problems.

—You a long stayer then? the hostel woman says.

She throws a glance at Haley's passport and calls her Helen. Haley doesn't mind, she doesn't feel like Haley with one L or Halley with two. Which she supposes is what she wanted.

—Until I get a job I expect, she says. Instinctively, she cringes at the sound of her closed vowels. They don't fit here, mark her out as a snob.

—Yeah, well, here's the rules, the woman says.—No visitors after 10 no phonecalls after 10 no baths after 10.

No talking or laughing or breathing after 10, thinks Haley angrily as she takes her key to promoted Paradise. And no living at any time. She picks up her reunited luggage and trips up the stairs because the matting has holes in it.

—Watch that, Helen, says the woman. She shuts the office door and Haley opens hers.

It's a room, nothing more or less. Just a room with no memories and a Diet Coke can under the bed. She has no stuff to make it hers, has deliberately brought no memorabilia. She's not looking for a home, she just needed to escape one.

What price recognition

And she walks. She walks everywhere. Her back is starting to ache but she walks grimly, forcing the streets to get to know her. She cannot be accused of apathy, lethargy or laziness. She is searching hard for Robert, for some small path that will lead back to him. Her feet are loud on the new roads, tramp heavily as if they are weighted with lead dust.

But strangely, she is sealed. Sealed like the roads, closed off to the elements and to the outside. Most days she feels nothing, and she looks forward to childbirth all those months ahead as a connection to what Robert felt when he hit the ground. The explosion of pain will come as a relief, will allow her to share in the cracking of bone and the parting of flesh from flesh.

The dichotomy of it all is exhausting. She wants to feel, she can't feel. She walks, she is getting nowhere. And physical exertion doesn't bring rest. Her mind has followed her doggedly, anxiously, to the other side of the world. She remains caught in the vast jaws of insomnia, which shake her every night until her eyes are loose and aching.

So she lies in a narrow alien bed in a crumbling house. Pieces of the wall fall quietly on her in the night, so that in the morning her pillow is covered with plaster, and her hair is full of dust as if she has been lying on a pavement. The difference is, there is no one to pick her up. There is a bruise under her fingernail, but nobody there to see it fading.

She needs food. There's something called a superette a few blocks from the hostel. She passes swaying rows of high-rise apartment blocks with gates that open like silent mouths expelling shiny cars. She realises she's in an upmarket area. Sandra would love it. (Sandra will never know.) The hostel is incongruous: peeling turrets, gaps in its teeth, straggling garden planted out with beer cans. It's like a fallen woman, an ex-aristocrat who's lost her looks and money but still lingers on familiar territory.

The people on either side polish their door knockers and look away when Haley walks out the gate.

On her first foraging trip she steps around a car parked on the footpath and bangs into a guy coming the other way, but much faster. He doesn't look like other Remuera dwellers, he's pulling a beret down over his eyes even though it's 30 degrees, and his psychedelic shirt hits Haley with as much force as his body.

—Sorry! he says.—My fault.

He's the first person that's looked Haley in the eye since she arrived.

—It's OK, says Haley, almost smiling.

She dreads navigating her way round different food, she's too tired. Outside the superette are vegetables that, in England, are seen only at Halloween or fed to the cows. On the shelves are tins of things that in England are never tinned, and in the freezer are huge hunks of animals. Having seen the facilities in the hostel kitchen, Haley searches for pre-cooked meals and post-dirt veges. She feels desperate, but her public crying day—that airport emergency—was a one-off. She looks stern and buys baked beans and a Moro bar: the closest she can get to British comfort food.

The guy in the shirt's walking back the other way. His turquoise and pink diamonds shift in front of Haley like a hologram. His steps bring him out of focus, in focus, out of focus, until her eyes protest and she looks at his face.

—Hiya, she says.

—How's it going, he says.

—Fine, she says.

—Fine, thanks, he says.

They both realise that neither question needed an answer and stride on past each other. Haley trips on a tree-root and takes the end off her toenail. She steps off the footpath onto the damp steaming earth, crouches down and watches the blood form a perfect globe on her toe. She squeezes the graze and more blood comes, and more.

—Ow, shit, she says.—Fuck, ow.

Her toe bleeds for the next three blocks. She feels slightly better.

A job. She gets one without days of newspaper ads and buses, without a visa. It's time she was lucky. Though Sandra wouldn't think of it as luck. Her favourite joke was (well, probably still is):

Q: What do you say to a person with a PhD in McDonald's?

A: A Big Mac and fries, thanks.

This was always followed by a shake of the head and a

meaningful face that even now makes Haley cringe. Sandra has brought her up to be a big fish in an any-size academic pond. And now here she is in the land of opportunity working in a shop. The ring as she crosses the shop doorstep every morning sounds defiant.

The shop? It's called, it has to be called, Kiwi Krafts. And it's here that Haley, stumbling in looking for a toilet, finds a temporary life.

—Excuse me, she says to the blonde.

—Don't tell me! says the blonde.

—Sorry? says Haley.

—You're South African no Scottish no Irish, says the blonde.

—No, says Haley.—I'm English. From London.

—Oh my God! says the blonde.—Why'd you come out here?

—I like it here, sidesteps Haley.

—But London! says the blonde.—The clubs!

—I suppose they're OK if you're into that sort of thing, says Haley.

She wouldn't be able to name one club if she was held at gunpoint, but she looks polite as the blonde—whose own name is Kelly—reels off a list of them. She has to wait for a break in the London entertainment guide before she can dart in with her request for a toilet.

It turns out there isn't one, but there is a job going. Does Haley need a job? Once Kelly finds out that the answer's yes, she hands over the key to the staff cubicle.

Haley's entry is legitimised on her exit because, walking back out into the shop, she bumps straight into Kath, the manager. Haley's lucky stars have arranged it so that Kath is tired, overworked, and not wanting to interview a list of potential workers. Haley is hired, no questions asked, and will be (under)paid, under the table.

—Great! says Kelly. Her instant attraction to Haley becomes more explicable when Kath leaves to go to the bank and Haley is filled in on how mean Kath is and how much Kelly wants someone else to work with.

Sure enough, Kath is mean. This at least allows Haley to remain silent on the pregnancy issue, and guilt-free about her silence. She has heard enough of Sandra's stories about prejudiced bosses to want to disguise her condition. And so Kath remains uninformed, and Kiwi Krafts is the first place (though certainly not the most beautiful) to become familiar to Haley's new-hemisphere eyes.

In fact, although she's stuck in a smoked-glass shop in a smoked-glass street, she gets to see a lot of national beauty spots. The only thing is, they're on tablemats, postcards, paper-weights, and always in technicolour. Mitre Peak, Mt Cook, the geysers at Rotorua: she carries them home in her head, walking carefully so she doesn't drop them. Lying in her hostel bed, she diligently strips away lurid greens hot oranges hot pinks egg-yellow. Once the icons are reduced to outlines, she stacks them behind her eyes for easy reference. They are beautiful in their photo-negative simplicity. She can wait for the real thing.

The comet has arrived with the New Year. While Kelly keeps a wistful eye on the streets of Soho, London, Haley watches the sky. She can't decide if it's comforting to see a reminder of the past or if it makes her lonelier. Because her Soho is now surrounded by strange, bright, alien stars. The huge Southern Cross tilting like an anchor. And Orion the hunter lounging upside down.

—Haven't you got any work to do? Haley says to him severely, as she lies with aching feet and waits, hopes, for sleep.

Work. First a godsend, then a necessity, then, very quickly, a drag. Haley gets annoyed with people from her own country whinging about the heat, she gets annoyed with Americans complaining about how small everything is. If they wanted to be cold, she thinks, why didn't they stay in Yorkshire; if they wanted to be overwhelmed, why the hell did they leave Phoenix, Arizona?

But Kath, who's unfailingly rude to her employees, insists on politeness to customers. So Haley smiles when she feels like spitting, takes it out on the Sellotape instead, rips brown paper so ruthlessly that sometimes she almost frightens herself. She thought pregnancy was supposed to make you radiant and peaceful, but then perhaps she has upset the course of things by traversing the globe.

However savage she feels, she drops phrases like *Have a nice day* loudly into the conversation. These are bait for Kath, who is always listening. Such politeness will keep her in work, will lead her out of the hostel and into a room of her own. So Haley keeps her eyes expressionless and smooths sheepskin rugs and tourist tempers like a professional.

No mail arrives at the hostel for her, and that's the way she wants it. She knows Sandra won't have accepted her written plea for a quiet disappearance, will be combing ex-holiday sites on the South Coast and phoning Barbaud relatives in the South of France.

—As if! thinks Haley, scornfully.

She has lived with Sandra long and closely enough to know how Sandra thinks. Sandra may pride herself on knowing how everyone else thinks but really she doesn't. For instance, she would never dream that Haley must journey so far to see if Robert is findable. So far! Sandra herself has been all the way out here many years ago, has seen this land of green volcanoes with her own eyes, but then Sandra never looks back, strides on towards new experiences with assertive legs.

—Change is always positive, she says.—Regret is a wholly negative emotion.

She has trained those around her in the art of moving on, and it would not occur to her they might disobey. Despite this, Haley initially cringes when she hears the hostel phone ring in the middle of the night. Which it does often, for this is a sanctuary of the dispossessed, but it is never for her and after a while Sandra's shadow shrinks, diminishes.

Sandra becomes a needle in a haystack, searching for a needle in a haystack.

Grounded

After only a few days at the Double K, Haley can work the till without looking. After a week, she can convince Japanese tourists that the sheepskin rug at the top of the pile is exactly the same as the one at the bottom. She can subliminally dissuade Germans from systematically removing every key-ring from its case to ensure regularity of paua patterning.

She has acclimatised.

Soon she is presented with a name badge. Ki-Kraft Haley. Obviously, although Kath looks at Haley as if she's a particularly poor stock sample, it's easier to keep her than to look for someone else. Besides, without a legitimate work permit, Haley has no rights and can't cause trouble.

—Welcome to the family, says Kath. Her voice is as stiff as her hair, frightened into immobility by onslaughts with a can of hairspray.

Haley looks silently at the badge. She would rather have KK tattooed on her arm than wear a name badge, but by now she has zero tolerance for the hostel bathroom and meals of cold baked beans. She submits, pins her new identity on her collar where it perches on safety-pin legs like some monster insect.

—Haley's a bit of a weird name, isn't it, says Kelly, looking critically at the badge.

—I guess so, says Haley. She unpacks a box of paua and gold tiki brooches expressionlessly.

—Wasn't there a comet or something called after you? Kelly says.

—That's Halley with two Ls, Haley says, keeping her head down.

—Oh, says Kelly blankly, obviously seeing spelling as a thing of the past.

—Anyway, she goes on,—your parents must've been rapt when the scientists picked your name for the comet.

—Actually, I think it came a bit before me, says Haley. She starts arranging the tikis in rows according to expression. Despite the fact they've come straight off a production line, she can definitely see degrees of scowl.

Kath comes in the front. Kelly goes out the back. Haley stops assessing the emotional state of the tikis and starts polishing the cabinets with newspaper because Kath approves of clean glass, doesn't approve of emotion.

Haley's own emotional state? Well, that's a different ball game, as her old American archaeology professor used to say.

Actually it's no game, it's more like a long-division exercise and she tries obsessively to solve the problem. But within every emotion are smaller fractions of other, conflicting emotions that seem to have no relation to each other. Her mind is so full of Robert that her scalp stabs, aches as if she is permanently coming down with the flu.

—Get the hell out of my head Robert, she says.

She is intensely angry that she has been forced out of England, and angry with him for leaving her a new life to look after. Just as her belly is stretching, so her soul must now stretch to accommodate unlimited futures: because this baby will have babies will have babies. Thanks to Robert, Haley has become infinite when all she wants is to stop.

Master of grief

Although better, her sleeping patterns are still sketchy. Consciousness clings to her with its fingernails, whining monotonously about leaving the one place where it knew Robert. It drags her eyelids up again and again, forcing her to look into alien antipodean darkness. When exhaustion finally takes over and Haley can step unencumbered into her sleeping head, there is the promise of something bigger

she is wandering towards the harbour bridge. it draws her night after night, with its cool iron smelling like blood, and its breath of water. she approaches it with a fatalistic relief; fear is there but she walks lightly on the floor of her dream. this is her escape. three hundred feet, a hundred feet, and sometimes she gets as far as feeling the rust under her fingers and the space swinging under her feet

but always, always before she can let go, the promise of relief lets go of her. before the quiet waters can close over her shadowy head, she's returned to her bed

and she wakes, and her back and legs are running with wetness. Rivers of disappointment, distress, dislocation, staining the stained mattress. Her one thin sheet smells faintly musty and although she showers the smell follows her round all morning.

In her lunch-hour she walks down Queen St, past Cin-Cins to the waterfront, trying to recover some sense from the dream. She looks past the café-dwellers and the people-watchers to the bridge, which turns slightly away from her. Arching its back towards the North Shore, it pretends not to know her. She buys a roll filled with egg or warm tinned beetroot, feeds her stomach without thinking or caring. She sits on a bench and watches the curve of the shadow-bridge on the water. It never reaches all the way from one side to the other, always falls short or gets distracted by boats, cut across by other shadows.

When she walks back to work, there's something hard, knotted, inside her. It could be the embryo but it feels like betrayal.

Kelly worries about Haley's solitary lunch-hours, decides Haley needs a social life. Friday night is designated as the launching pad: Haley will be catapulted into fun. She dreads it but is too tired to resist.

She wakes to a closed day. The evening is a long road away but the signpost is in stone: 9 pm will arrive, and Kelly will be waiting at the corner. There is no exit.

—Feel my arms, Kelly says.

She rubs her kitten arm against Haley's.

—Smooth, don't you think? she says.—I waxed them last night.

There's no friction but Haley's own hairs stand on end. It is a long time since anyone touched her skin deliberately and she moves away.

Kelly's arm looks unreal under her unreal gold bracelet. Skin without texture, two-dimensional magazine skin. From the bracelet dangles a cracked heart. Kelly's heart has been cracked, too, by a bass guitarist called Todd whose band is playing tonight at Kelly's favourite club.

—Can't wait, can you? says Kelly, who thinks she might recapture Todd's attention.

Haley can, could wait forever, but she agrees mildly. She thinks the baby can take another lie, as long as it's white.

All day the sheepskin rugs are twice as heavy, and the vacuum cleaner drags behind her like an overweight dog. Kelly leaves at lunchtime, using up a precious afternoon off to get Todd-worthy. Haley watches the clock and her longing for bed becomes a craving, becomes all she can think of, like vodka for an alcoholic or cream sponge for a bulimic. If she goes back to the hostel before going out, she'll give in. So she goes to McDonald's, orders a plastic burger and synthetic fruit pie, and gets changed in the toilets. It's early, she has all the time in the world to make herself look like a clubber, but no instinct, imagination or desire. Especially no desire.

Queen St has stretched. It's longer than it's ever been, and Haley walks on automatic. She's emptied her head of all thought and only just remembers to meet Kelly on the corner of Vulcan Lane. Even in the semi-dark she sees Kelly's slightly pitying look: Haley's clothes are too loose and not shiny enough, and her hair is too natural. But Kelly's sense of duty is well developed and she doesn't renege.

(*You see? Some people don't let other people down*, says Haley to Robert.)

Haley gets asked for ID at the door. Kelly doesn't. Haley's left her driver's licence in her locker at work.

—It's all right, just this once, the bouncers tell her.—Have a good night, OK?

Haley tries to look grateful. She follows Kelly's gold heels up the stairs.

—Drink? shouts Kelly.

—Lemonade, shouts Haley.

—What? shouts Kelly.

Haley doesn't know if Kelly can't believe her ears or if she just can't hear. She knows she's already a massive disappointment to Kelly so she repeats herself.

—Lemonade, straight, she shouts.

Kelly looks at her as if she's said something shocking. She opens her mouth, says something or not, ploughs off to the bar. The guys standing beside their table turn their backs on Haley and make the most of Kelly's disappearing curves. Haley looks at her watch. It's 9.15.

It's 12.15 and late enough for Haley to leave but now she can't because Kelly is a mess. The band has finished, Kelly's life is finished. Todd has been sighted leaving with someone younger and blonder than Kelly
(*Impossible!* says Robert
You've never met her, reminds Haley coldly)
and Kelly is in despair, in the toilets.
—What the fuck'm I goin to do? she says.
Tears stand on the end of her endless eyelashes and Haley tries to wipe them off but Kelly jerks away because her mascara isn't waterproof and Haley is smudging her eyes.
—Why don't we just find a cab and go home? says Haley. She knows this is stupidly optimistic but she can't help saying it anyway.
—No! says Kelly. She straightens up angrily and nearly takes her head off on the hand-dryer.
—I'm gonna have a good time, she says, swaying.—Let's go to Utopia, sposed to be good there.
—Kell, says Haley,—don't you think you should get some sleep?
—Todd'll be there, says Kelly menacingly. It's not clear if she's aiming her menace at Todd or at Haley for obstructing her from Todd.
Haley realises with a despair approaching the depth of Kelly's that it's going to be easier just to go to Utopia.

It's Haley's idea of hell. It's even worse than where they were before, because there are twice as many people and they're twice as intimidating. Even Kelly, riding on the wave of severe anger and many Malibus, seems intimidated. Her gold shoes look out of place, sparkle with less certainty.

—Jus one drink, Kelly says.—Jus to show Todd.

She's quietened down but Haley has heard about Kelly's previous fights (fingernails, teeth, and once she ripped a camisole right off a girl's shoulder). She doesn't particularly feel like pointing out that Todd isn't even there.

—OK, Haley says.—I'll have a water.

She gets a non-alcoholic sangria for Kelly, who doesn't notice the difference. Anxiously, Haley watches her pick out the glacé cherries but instead of hurling them about Kelly just eats them, savagely.

They sit on the floor against the wall and drink and don't say anything because

a) they've run out of topics and

b) they wouldn't be able to hear anyway.

Haley's watch fills up with sweat and heat and then stops, but that's OK because she'd really rather not know. A guy comes up and offers them a smoke. Haley says a curt no—she's starting to feel sick—but in fact he's the best thing to have happened all night. Kelly's recovery is miraculous, and miraculously swift. By the time Haley has swallowed the last of her water, Kelly is radiant and looks like staying till the sun comes up. But

—Hey Haley, she says,—I'll come with you.

Haley recognises this for what it is: token female solidarity. She gives the solidly female answer expected from her: she's fine. She can't tell whether she is or not, she can't assess anything with her head full of music shouting dry ice lights, but she hopes she is.

Heading for the door, she is almost felled by a girl with straight glossy hair who's flying off a table. Haley would fall, but a guy standing by the table reaches out and grabs her and holds her upright.

He says something. He is small and pale, is wearing a velvet jacket that is too big for him.

—What? she says.

He says it again, he waits. He's wearing a rugby shirt under the jacket, which even at this odd moment strikes Haley as odd.

He waits, she's supposed to answer. She shakes her head, he

looks concerned. She nods, he smiles, and pats her on the shoulder. The glossy girl swoops from the table again and again.

Haley goes to the toilets. She locks herself into a cubicle and lies down flat on the floor. Her hair lies around the base of the toilet and the floor is smeared with piss and dirt and paper, but she doesn't care. She looks up at the ceiling panels, peeling like an old blister off a heel. The fluorescent strips flicker fast enough to keep up the pretence of light.

She can feel dance music through the floor and her shoulder blades are still colliding with the soaring glossy girl and the earth is spinning.

That was how it happened. She remembers exactly which night it was. And earlier, the roof of the world was spinning.

She's fallen off her bike. Walk tube and another tube but at last she's at Chalk Farm. Polluted November air has been circulating through the underground tunnels, through people's lungs, through the hot carriage. Halley has forgotten her gloves today and her hands are mottled red and purple from abrupt changes in temperature. They lurk at the end of her arms like reptiles, try to withdraw into her sleeves.

It is so cold outside the station that her fingers strike, refuse to undo her bike lock. She coerces them. It's like trying to pick up a pin with mittens on. She fishes out a packet of crisps from her backpack and has to split it open with her teeth. She rides on thinking of coffee, thinking of Robert, thinking of how she can't feel her extremities. She puts one hand in her pocket, one on the handlebars, holds the crisp packet in her teeth—and hits ice. Her nose and mouth are immediately full of salt-and-vinegar grit, her already thin jeans give way at both knees, her knees swiftly gather up gravel, glass and whatever else they can scavenge during a three-feet skid.

Time always stretches out a moment of impact, milks it for all it's worth. So there's time to think: it isn't going to happen, it can't happen, it is happening. It has happened. Then, treacherously, time quickly moves on leaving Halley on her side with the bike on top of her. She hears a few laughs, looks through the spinning spokes, sees the grey sky free-wheeling above her, sees some kids sitting on the railings having a smoke.

—Excellent! they say.

—Do it again, they say.

—Could've seen your cunt, they say.

Halley is covered in crisps. They are mashed into her coat and crumbled into her hair.

—What flavour are you then? say the kids. They laugh.

—Get fucked, Halley says.

—Phwarr! they say.—Yes please.

She knows they're not worth it but she's so pissed off and the whole of her body hurts so much that she gives them what Robert calls a Halley look. It has the power to turn people to stone (Robert says) but with these kids it just means they mutter things about her instead of shouting them. She gets up and pedals off without looking at them again. Blood traces the legs of her jeans like a map, cold tears make roads on her cheeks. She's riding on the footpath so when she meets Robert on the last corner she nearly falls off again.

—Hale! he says.—Just coming to see if you—what the hell have you done to yourself?

He says he'd like her to cry once in a while, but this isn't the once. She just gets off and hands her bike to him and goes into the kitchen to thaw. Emotionally as well as physically. Sandra's still at work so the ordeal doesn't get any worse. Halley pulls her jeans round her ankles and sits on the edge of the table while Robert tortures her legs with Dettol.

—Fuck, she says.—Ow ow that hurts.

—Want to sit down on a chair? he says.—Feeling funny? Feeling faint?

—No, she says.—No, and no.

—The Maori people don't let you sit on kitchen tables, he says. —Anywhere you eat, they say, you can't put your arse.

—Where the hell did you pick that one up? says Halley crossly. She's always cross when she's in a vulnerable position, like sitting in her knickers with blood on her knees.

—From a guy on the construction site, says Robert.—From Auckland.

—Well, we're not in New Zealand, says Halley.—So I can sit on the table.

She quickly winces a tear away, which luckily Robert doesn't see because he's rinsing the cloth.

—Want a plaster? he says.

—No, says Halley.—Just blow on it.

The calm air from his lungs is like a cobweb, lying on her broken skin, holding back the welling blood. Why does the blood stop so fast? For no reason that would satisfy medical science, but Halley knows. Later that night in the Slug and Lettuce the same Robert-breath is on her neck, behind her ear. His breath is warm, they are drinking warm, flat beer and competing for the worst day.

—I smacked Darryn in the head by accident with a five by two, says Robert.

—My cunt was talked about on the street, says Halley.

When 10.45 reels around, they have a good line-up of glasses. The barmaid screams 'last orders', and then they help each other back to Halley's place. Robert is planning to ride her bike home to his place but

—The wheel's fucked, he says.—How the fuck did you get home on this, Hale?

—D'you know how much you say fucked when you're fucked? says Halley.

Robert gets off the bike.

—Was going to give you a deep-throat goodbye kiss, he says.

—Well, give me one hello instead, says Halley.

They go inside twined around each other and end up on the kitchen floor. They're still at the shirt stage when they hear Sandra upstairs in the bathroom.

Halley pulls her shirt down and her jeans up. Robert pulls his shirt down and his mouth down.

—The Sandra is around, he says too loudly.—No sex in the kitchen.

Right above their heads Sandra shuts the bathroom cupboard, which sounds like reproof.

—Shut the fuck up! hisses Halley.

—Halley! says Robert.—Don't talk to Sandra like that!

They laugh so much they have to lie there for a while and wait for the room to stop spinning.

—Rob, says Halley.

—Hmm? says Robert.

—I've got a lecture at 8.30 tomorrow, says Halley.

—So you wanna make it quick? says Robert.

—So I need some sleep, says Halley. She stands up in a dignified way and clutches at the bench. Unfortunately she grabs the handle of the built-in chopping board, which pulls right out and flies to the floor, covering her in parsley left over from an omelette-making session two days earlier. The crash is enormous.

—Sorry Sandra! says Halley.

Robert laughs, leans on the bench, misses. His arm catches the edge of Sandra's baking tray and cooling biscuits fly at Halley like planets.

—Seems to be my day to be covered in edibles, she says.

—Glad I'm around, says Robert. He eats parsley off her collarbone.

—Aphrodisiac, he says.

He finds a chocolate chip in her hair.

—Aphrodisiac, he says.

They make it upstairs to Halley's room. In bed they find they have no condoms.

—But, Hale, you always have some in your tin, says Robert. He shakes her empty tobacco tin upside down.

—The magic tin, he says.—Letting us down at the crucial minute, the fucker.

—But the minute's always crucial, says Halley.

They laugh until they get too hot to laugh and then they get serious. Seriously responsible. Robert gets out of bed.

—Where're you going, says Halley.—The shop?

—You're hopeful, says Robert.—The spare bed.

—Oh Rob, says Halley.—Don't be a spare I mean square.

She lies and laughs to herself until she realises Robert means it.

—You can come back, she says.—I promise I won't seduce you.

—Not worried about that, he says from the other bed.—Worried I'll seduce you.

—But Robert, it's safe anyway, says Halley.—It's a safe time.

—Hale! says Robert.—No it isn't, it's the optimum time.

—Opt for optimum, she says.—I optimum in favour of sex.

—That means the worst time, silly, he says.—The pessimum time, silly Halley.

—Not silly! says Halley.—Just not very good at counting.

She used to pretend to count the days, though she was never very good at it, but when she met Robert she gave up pretending and left it to him. The only equation she can think of now is Number 1 = Robert.

—Can't I just give you one kiss? she says. She gets out of bed and sways across the room.

—Fuck this floor's unstable, she says.

She makes it to the other side and lies down with relief.

—Absolutely no kiss, says Robert.—Kissing is forbidden on this side of the room.

Halley kisses him with her eyelashes. She aims for his eyelid, gets his nose and pretends to herself she was going for that all along.

—Butterfly kisses don't count, she says.

—It all cunts, says Robert.—I mean counts.

—D'you want me to cross back over the border? says Halley.

—Absolutely, says Robert.—I will absolutely stay here and you get back to your own territory.

—D'you know how much you say absolutely when you're pissed? says Halley.

—Absolutely I do, says Robert seriously.—D'youthink the room would stop spinning if we turned on the light?

—D'youthink you could stop talking, says Halley even more seriously.

Her fingers move into Robert's mouth. They trace his teeth.

They find his fingers and persuade them into movement too. His fingers trace the curve of her thighs, the curve of her arse, start to move inside her.

—Hey Hale, he says.

—Hmmm? says Halley.

—Nothing, he says.

—We shouldn't, he says.

—But what the fuck, he says.

—It might stop the spinning, she says.

She doesn't regret it. If she had Robert in her spare bed again? She'd still cross the dark floor to get to him.

Claudia

Diane has given up on Claudia being gainfully employed. She's usually too hassled to be interested in what Claudia is or isn't doing, but she must have picked up some Heath vibes hanging around Claudia's smooth and innocent head. Because suddenly she seems to realise that her daughter's drift could be supported by someone other than herself.

—There're some nice young doctors started at the hospital, she says conversationally. The iron hisses in her hand conspiratorially.

Claudia laughs. She already has a doctor, thanks. Though the classifications of 'young' and 'nice' are debatable. Claudia is beginning to wonder if she's made yet another foolhardy foray into that minefield of romantic mistakes. The Hemingway Heath lasted less time than it took to read the book and his real-life character has been revealed. He is—she has to admit—flatter than a page, more two-dimensional than typeface, as bland as an uninscribed cover.

—Why's that funny? says Diane mildly. She irons on: pillowcases, sheets, nighties, stuff that no one but she will ever see. This thought sobers Claudia instantly. Perhaps a dull middle-aged doctor is better than an empty bed?

—Actually, she says,—it's not.

Walking down a new road

It is partly her desire to start writing her own story. It is partly to annoy Heath, whose capitalist leanings/middle-class snobbery are annoying. It is partly to disconcert Diane, who has now made up her mind that Claudia is unemployable and should probably just marry Adrian.

(—Is she crazy? says Adrian. He falls about laughing.

—You are living with a crazy woman, he whoops at Claudia.

—Me? Good marital material? he shrieks.

—Diane thinks you're a nice boy, says Claudia mildly.—Which you are, of course. But marry you? My prospects would be better if I washed dishes.)

It turns out that with this last line Claudia is speaking prophetically. Because this is exactly what she is about to do.

In Vulcan Lane is a notice on a window, which she has walked past unseeingly several times. It is the shoes in the next window along that draw her, daily. They sing out to her in pink, yellow, and turquoise suede voices: impractical songs to which Claudia's feet know they could dance.

But today, she is thinking of more than new shoes. She is thinking of a new identity: more than a married doctor's lay, more than a party girl, more than a pretty lost child in a life-sized playground. She may decide to retain some of these characteristics but, if so, this will be entirely her choice. Once she has been pigeon-holed by other people, you see, Claudia has a perverse desire to fly.

Her senses help her without being asked: her head decides to notice the notice, her eyes decide to read it, her brain decides to assimilate the letters into an offer for her and only her.

Waiting staff wanted. Experience preferred but not essential. Apply within.

The words are straight from a black-and-white movie, could be forty years old, and this reassures Claudia. Some things, at least, stay the same. Sure, it is a chrome café, not an elegant old hotel. Lattes are served instead of tea, biscotti instead of lamingtons. But the concept is the same. People must eat and drink, other people must carry. Serve and be served, from the Romans onwards. And she goes in.

—Full- or part-time? she asks serenely.

—Full, says the woman, looking at her hard. She is called Myrtle, is under five foot and makes Claudia feel like a tall, very graceful wading bird.

A nine-to-fiver! Claudia flinches but only internally. This is exactly what everyone thinks she can't do, so she'll do it.

—And some weekend work, says Myrtle.

Christ! Claudia thinks of mornings after Utopian nights, grits her teeth.

—I can do it, she says, inclining her bird neck graciously.

Myrtle looks at her piercingly, head on one side, searching beneath Claudia's presentable surface to see if there is a born waitress lurking there.

—You've done this type of work before, have you? she says.

Has she! Has she! Well, actually, Claudia hasn't. But she knows that any good actress can make a good waitress, and after all she has been acting since the dramatic night of the solar flare.

—Have I what! she says, avoiding a direct lie, hoping the gods will reward her.

—Monday, says Myrtle significantly.

—I think it's Tuesday, says Claudia, feeling like Alice in Wonderland.

—No! says Myrtle.

Claudia jumps.

—Monday you start, says Myrtle.—Leave your phone number, I'll call you.

—OK, says Claudia smartly and Myrtle is gone.

Claudia looks around at the shining glass shining white china shining chrome, with eyes that have been newly cleaned. Everything looks suddenly different. The furniture faces a different way, the sliding doors open onto a different Vulcan Lane. Inside and outside, all is changed. Because this is now her workplace. Her place of work. She tries it out carefully in her head.

Sits down suddenly feeling oppressed.

Can't order a coffee because she's staff not a customer.

Looks at the red-haired waitress's apron critically. It's not tied right. Feels better.

Decides she'll visit the shoes next door, and immediately the sun comes out. Yes! The scarlet pair has been looking particularly entrancing, and she is employed and earning now. Wedge heels, straps to enhance slim ankles. Suede poems, scarlet songs, money to buy them with. She leaps to her feet.

—And Claudia, bellows Myrtle, anticipating her exit.

—What? says Claudia in an irritated voice. She doesn't appreciate being bellowed at, it isn't Monday yet.

—You'll be on your feet all day, says Myrtle with a sharp knowing look.—For God's sake, wear sensible shoes.

Between a rock and a hard place

Of course, one of the main reasons Claudia became a waitress was to show other people. Now she remembers: plans to show other people usually end up backfiring.

She does show Heath, but only in a low-key unsatisfying kind of way. He is astonished, but only slightly, that she would voluntarily take on a job when she could be kicking her pretty heels around the surgery. He is disconcerted, but only slightly, that he is now screwing a waitress instead of a potential—

—A potential what? says Claudia, curiously. She too would like to know what she is going to be.

Heath loses interest in her future before he can finish his sentence.

—Bet you look cute in your apron, he says.

Claudia looks dismissive. Heath doesn't seem to realise that this is her stand, obviously sees it as a whim which will fade like an unfortunate hair-colour.

—How long are your lunch-hours? he asks hopefully.

And Diane's reaction? Well, this is also a let-down. There is a strange deluge of twins at work, and the only times Diane surfaces is to emphasise the importance of contraception.

—Because one unplanned baby is hard enough, she says darkly,—and you've got to remember it can turn out to be two.

—Then you just adopt one out, says Claudia sweepingly.—There's always a solution.

—It's not that easy, says Diane, surprisingly sharply.

—I guess not, says Claudia, taken aback.

—Then again, if you had a partner who loved you, says Diane with a wistful look in her eye.

Claudia waits for a complaint about Garry, father of Giles, ex-husband of Diane, who has left a trail of children in his careless wake. But no, not this time.

—Well, then it would be a different story, says Diane.—Then a woman could cope quite well with twins or even triplets.

—Thanks for the warning! says Claudia in horror.—I'll aim for a guy with a low sperm count.

Diane smiles wisely, shakes her wise head. Clearly she persists in believing that very shortly Claudia will be ready for Adrian's hand or anyone else's.

—So how long is this waitressing phase going to last? she asks.

Claudia suddenly sees why Adrian objects to the phase word so strongly.

—Why the hell are you so keen on marriage after your past experience? she says angrily.

—Well, it's as good as the alternative, shrugs Diane.

Is it? Claudia looks round at the kitchen, imagines a man sitting at the table or standing at the stove. Would Diane be more or less tired if she still had a Garry in her life? Claudia can't decide.

—Want an egg, hon? asks Diane.

This Claudia can decide on without a thought.

—No! she says.—NO GODDAM EGG!

—But thank you anyway, she says.

And her friends are no better

Ben is dismayed. He'll miss her, she won't be creatively fulfilled, and worst of all is the location.

—In Vulgar, sorry, Vulcan Lane! he says.

—It's OK actually, says Claudia defensively.

—Which café is it? asks Ben suspiciously, although they both know he doesn't know one from another.

—Quel Fromage, says Claudia with a dashing French accent.

—Whatever, it's a pity, says Ben.—Or should I say, Quel dommage.

He looks a little happier for having an outlet for bad wordplay. But the writing's on the wall. He is not at ease with café people, nor does he approve of them.

No, he will not be coming to see Claudia, much as he'd like to support her in her new venture. He can't stand those kissy types. Sorry, Claud.

And Adrian. He can usually be relied on to give a horrified, pitying, or generally over-the-top reaction. But when he hears that his best friend is adopting a new persona—perhaps forever—he just raises one eyebrow.

—Way to go, Claudia, he says laconically.

—Is that all you're going to say? says Claudia argumentatively. She has prepared a row of ammunition to fire at objections: her chin is up, her blood is up.

—Each to their own, shrugs Adrian.

This is so un-Adrian that Claudia's artificial adrenaline leaks out of her, leaving traces of anxiety. Is Adrian losing his identity just as she's gaining one?

—Are you OK, Aids? she says concernedly.

—Of course, he says.

—You don't seem yourself, she says.

—And why should I be? he says.—You're moving on, so why shouldn't I?

Claudia is taken aback. Her lips part but no words come out. She realises with annoyance that this is all the wrong way round: Adrian's supposed to be disconcerted by her, for Christ's sake.

As it happens, she feels they should all be very concerned. As her flat shoes wear in, she feels her personality flattening. She becomes too skilled at frothing milk, remembers too frequently how Fromage regulars take their coffee. But she can't leave because this is what Heath/Diane/Ben/Adrian are expecting. She is tied to her apron strings by pride.

It's OK, it's not OK. She could go on forever, she wants to stop tomorrow. It's dull, it's secure-making. It's life. It's her life.

Every day seems like Tuesday
but it really does happen on a Tuesday. This is when Claudia finds another, newer focus for her energies. Now that she's found a job, you see, she wants more, and more. Change works like this on people, becomes addictive. Once you see that you can alter your life just by reading a notice, it's difficult to stop looking around.

And so Claudia stares into her life and sees areas that could do with attention. For instance, she is ready to live somewhere other than the house where she has spent her entire life so far. She is ready for love of the heart rather than lust. She is open to possibilities on all fronts and as the number of coffees she makes climbs into the hundreds, she becomes increasingly impatient.

She begins renovations by sweeping through her past: wardrobe cupboards and under the bed. Clothes fly like confetti, old shoes lie over the floor like discarded lizard skins. Monday night is spent sitting with her back against the mirror, rereading and discarding old letters. Sheets of paper slice the air, falling with a swift grace never achieved by those who wrote on them, those who once defiled them with clumsy biro love for Claudia.

This phase between phases is slowed by indecision: a rare emotion for a Leo. Claudia does much pulling out of boxes and putting in the bin, much pulling out of the bin and putting back in boxes. This is because she realises that she is throwing away glinting fragments of herself.

Suddenly she is overwhelmed with nostalgia. Not for the boys she knew (indeed she can hardly remember their faces) but for who she was when she was with them. Her heart flashes like a malfunctioning traffic light, she falls in and out of love several times over the course of the evening. But not with the letter-writers—no, with herself. With the Claudias who were, those Claudias created by the needs of others who have now gone to Taiwan or America or could be living unseen just a few blocks away.

Tears stand in her eyes. She was so goddam colourful back then, and then, and then. She misses the excitement of her old, inconsistent self. Now she wears a predictable drab apron and pours eight faithful hours of coffee every day.

It is complicated, this issue, but she understands it although it flickers in her head like a prism turning in the light. This is the essence of it:

1) She wants a return to herself, but it must be a renovated self.

2) She wants someone to help her fashion and decorate the new self.

3) She wants it soon.

Sitting on the floor, narrow back reflected back on itself, Claudia may look motionless. But inside she is fermenting, is ready for transformation. Is ready for the next day—or does she herself create that day, simply by the latent yeast of her desires?

The leavening of Claudia's life

He's far too nice and she knows it the first time she sees him, standing there in the thin kitchen with his thin arms. But because she prefers anticipation to actuality, she glows under the fluorescent light. She is the candle flame and the moth at the same time.

—Hi there! she says.

—Hey, he says.—I'm Leif.

He is part-Maori, has flour on his T-shirt and flaked almonds in his hair.

—Hi Leif, she says. Her stomach dances: Leif Garrett, disco king of the seventies! But she squeezes demurely past him to the apron cupboard. They'll always be bumping into each other from now on; the kitchen's a galley and she's—

—I'm Slave Number One, she says. The strobes are whirling

inside her but she lets only the occasional gleam escape from her demure eyes.

—And what do they call you off duty? he says.

—Claudia, she says. She picks up her loathsome apron with reluctance, ties it over her secret, sparkling navel, her narrow hips and her slightly convex stomach. And with that, her shining self becomes beige. She drags the apron to the sink with her as if it's an iron lung.

—Where've you sprung from, Leif? she says.

—What, originally? he says.

—Yes, says Claudia greedily. She wants to know all about him, instantly.

—From Granity, originally, he says.

He speaks with the rhythm of a Beat poet and he looks serious as he kneads his rhythmic dough.

—Interesting! says Claudia airily. She has no idea where this is but there are more important things to discuss than geography. In the meantime she keeps her uncertain back to Leif and deals with what she knows: dishes.

—The West Coast, Leif explains, interpreting her back.

—Oh right! says Claudia.—You're a mainlander then.

She turns to smile at him and suddenly, in the beautiful angle between his chin and his neck, she sees the kitchen walls start to change colour. The change spreads rapidly and within seconds the entire room lightens from streaky grease to the clean colour of sand.

—Pass me that cloth will you, Leif, she says, standing transfixed in the unfamiliar kitchen.

—Sure, he says, and he puts one hand out and back again smoothly so as to accommodate his kneads.

—D'you like Auckland? she asks. She takes the cloth reverently and dips it in holy water. She's put too much dishwashing liquid in, as usual (she veers towards excess in all things). The bubbles shimmer lightly, sway like her heart.

—Yeah, I guess, he says, sounding slightly surprised.

—A bit of a change from the Coast, says Claudia, hurling china carelessly around the sink.

—I guess, he says again.—Though I've lived here almost all my life.

—Oh, says Claudia. She smacks a plate against the tap and it cracks.

—Well, we should go out one weekend, she says, rallying fast.

—Sure, he says politely.—Though I'm in a band, so I don't get many weekends off.

—What do you play? Claudia asks, throwing the broken plate in the direction of the bin.

—Guitar, he says.—And I sing.

—Must be the name, says Claudia.—It's all in the Garrett.

—Huh? Leif says. He sounds even more surprised than when she assumed he had just arrived from the West Coast.

—The seventies disco man, says Claudia.—You know.

—I don't think I ever heard him, says Leif.

—But I'm sure he was good, he adds kindly.

Claudia goes out to clear some tables. When she comes back to her sink, she sees the smashed plate has been wrapped in newspaper and is sitting quietly back in the bin.

—Thanks Leif, she says.

(Two days later, she sees one of his pay slips lying on the bench. She sees that his name is Leith.)

Alternatives

Of course it happens that sex on the office floor becomes a place of carpet burns. And it happens that soon Claudia begins to think of Leith instead of Heath. She finds this mildly disconcerting when Heath is pounding diligently above her for an average of twelve minutes. (He is, after all, an ex-med student: a textbook man.)

—*Heath, Heath!* appears to work well for him, but increasingly less well for Claudia. What would happen if she cried out Leith, Leith at the eleventh minute? Would her history be rewritten? But the stars have decreed that she remains in ignorance on this point, for even in orgasm Claudia is self-contained.

Leith remains kind, polite, and seemingly unaffected by her, though sometimes he laughs at her as she sparkles and dances at the sink. Since reading *The Sun Also Rises*, Claudia is struck by the optimistic thought that Leith, like Jake, might be emasculated. What other reason could there be for his imperviousness to her shining self? But even as she speculates, she knows this is a fiction.

And so her epic trek through the landscape of love continues. Endurance and tolerance have never been among her talents. But she tolerates the medic and his attendant thorns in her side because, every time she leaves the surgery after what she intends to be the last encounter, the carpark becomes a vast desert. Dull sexless hills of tarseal undulate before her. Claudia is a child of Iliad and Homer; she believes in the journey and believes, moreover, that any journey is preferable to staying at home. So she brushes the Heath-dust out of her eyes and hangs in there for an oasis, never losing her bearings.

Her bird-wrists may appear frail but wishbones are deceptive, are strangely hard to break. Her star-sign: Leo, symbol of strength.

Ben is only a part of his name

Although Ben hasn't been to lectures for a term and a half, he spends a lot of time in the university laboratories. His initials (he is Ben Marvin Kestrel) are the same as his favourite chemical: benzylmethylketone, or BMK. Although he himself is sometimes forgotten, the BMK he requests from the lab stores is a restricted chemical and always in demand. For, in skilled hands, it becomes amphetamine: in the language of Utopia, it translates to speed.

—You ever thought of making a bit on the side with that? Claudia always asks when he appears, red and yellow capsules on the narrow palm of his hand.

—Not interested, Ben always answers.

And it's true, he isn't. He doesn't have Adrian's entrepreneurial edge or Claudia's skywards vision. He just enjoys the process and wants his friends to enjoy the results. He is both a true intellectual and a true friend.

—Wanna watch me make it? he says to Adrian.

—You bet, says Adrian.

Ben knows Claudia has no scientific curiosity but he also knows she hates being excluded, so

—You'll have to come to night class too, he says to her, kindly.

They enter the lab under cover of darkness. The equipment looks prehistoric: dinosaur necks rear above benches, dinosaur mouths clamp around flasks. The air is weighted down with heavy moonlight and a sour smell. Ben begins to rummage in drawers and Claudia's nose starts to run.

—Hurry up! she says.—Remember this is all in the name of speed!

Ben's eyes shine behind his huge safety glasses. He gives glasses to Adrian and Claudia too.

—Wicked! says Adrian.

He puts them on and looks even more sixties, the heavy black rims emphasising the black golf motifs on his white shirt. Claudia is less keen, puts them on the top of her head like sunglasses and then gradually slides them down onto her nose.

—Lab rules, says Ben approvingly.

Once he begins, he is swift. His thin hands seize up bottles, and light bunsen burners with zeal.

—First, take the ammonium formate, he instructs.—Mix and heat.

He looks like a mad cooking-show host, stirring enthusiastically over his gas flame.

—This is called the Leuckhardt reaction, he says.—Look hardt.

He cracks with laughter and nearly drops the test tube. Adrian, who has been hanging over the bench hoping for an early effect, shies away.

—Christ, Ben, he says.—I'm hoping for speed, not a lifelong handicap.

Ben hunches over his motley collection of glassware, inscribed with felt-pen. BEN'S BEAKER FUCK OFF! one says. Keep Your Lecture-rous Hands off my Wares! orders another.

—Anyone would think he gives a fuck, observes Adrian.

—And how! says Ben, in very bad American.

He lunges for the sulphuric acid and Adrian sidesteps hastily.

—This is my grande passion, Ben says Frenchily.

He shakes the tube violently.

—My grandiose passione, he says in make-up Italian.

—Like my business-to-be, says Adrian tantalisingly.

—Like my, umm, says Claudia desperately.

She thinks of Leith's forearms pouring beans into the coffee machine.

—Like my talent for macchiato, she says.

—Oh puh-lease, says Adrian.—Whatever happened to a coffee is a coffee is a coffee?

Claudia looks sideways at Adrian the Ambitious and Ben the Brain. She looks ahead to a career of frothing milk. She sticks her lip out.

Ben notices. Quickly, he holds out three boxes of empty capsules in front of her.

—Wanna choose the colour, Claudia? he says kindly.

Swings and roundabouts

You remember that night in the Shrinks' kitchen, back in December? When Adrian gave his two best friends a sneak preview of his project only to be laughed on his way to bed? Well, since then he has been busy—perhaps partly, it has to be admitted, out of defiance. He has taken the seed of his idea, has nurtured and coaxed it and grown it in the secret dark cupboard of his head, and now that it is full-grown he has transplanted it into a room above a bridal shop at the top end of Symonds St.

Despite their initial negativity, Claudia and Ben are invited over to view it.

—It will soon become known, Adrian tells them modestly,—as the greatest pop art store in New Zealand.

The sign is easy to spot. It stands orange and blue on the footpath, shouts at them like one of Adrian's shirts: RETROPOLIS! It directs foot-traffic past grimy plastic brides, up some dingy stairs, straight to Adrian who is sitting behind a lime-green Formica table.

Although it is opening day, he already looks as if he has been there forever. When Claudia and Ben arrive, he is staring impassively into the mouth of a glass fish. He doesn't say anything to his visitors, though he lets his pale eyes flick over them before re-engaging with the pale glass gaze of the fish.

The potential sellers of the fish are watching Adrian with strained obedient expressions, standing at his counter like failed disciples. Claudia looks at them dispassionately, sure of her own taste; then looks around.

Outside she can hear sirens and horns; inside, heavy breathing and concentration. Outside meters are running fast towards late afternoon. Inside time is heading purposefully backwards. Claudia feels the twinge of alarm that is becoming familiar when she contemplates the changes in Adrian.

All other eyes are fixed on the fish. The Brylcreem guy who has brought it in has sweat on his top lip. He licks it away. The girl holds her sequin handbag at stiff arm's length, as if it's an electric eel.

—So? she says almost aggressively.—Is it worth anything?

Adrian looks at her gravely, though as he takes in her bobby-socks he gives a faint wince. He clears his throat and takes one last, long look into the gaping mouth in front of him.

—By God, he says darkly,—it's seen a bit of use.

Claudia looks at the blindingly obvious scratches on the glass scales. If this is all it takes, she thinks, she too could be a pop art expert. But Adrian's assessment hangs weightily in the damp air and the couple stand in respectful silence. Ben is standing on one foot, looking up at a red Chopper bike hanging from the ceiling on nylon fishing-line. Is he remembering his childhood or thinking about dinner? Claudia can't tell. Why are both her best friends so goddam opaque?

Finally Adrian stirs, swims upwards, breaks the thick surface of respect.

—I'll give you fifteen, he says.—No more.

The boy looks stricken.

—It's as much as you'll get anywhere, Adrian says carelessly.

He really doesn't seem to care. Is this an act too?

—That's fine, says the girl hurriedly.

Money changes hands, the couple bow and scrape, the girl swings her pony-tail.

—Fab shop! she says brightly.

Adrian winces again, looks at her, looks meaningfully at the door. Too soon, Claudia relaxes. On the way out, the boy pauses to look at something. A silver wine-cooler bag emblazoned with *Grape Ideas!* Adrian twirls sardonically on his swivel chair but says nothing. Carefully, the boy holds out the bag and studies it with his head on one side. The silence stretches like bubble-gum.

Suddenly Adrian bursts into shouts of false laughter. The boy goes red, drops the bag and knocks over a purple plastic goblet which dominoes down a row of them.

—You don't want that crap, do you? hoots Adrian.

—Of course we don't! hisses the girl savagely to the boy.

—No, I guess not, mate, says the boy. He now seems filled with the uneasy conviction that his taste is somehow flawed, stumbles after the girl. His disappearing back is hunched with haste and embarrassment.

—OK, mate, says Adrian clearly.—See ya round, mate.

Claudia listens to the shoes rushing down the stairs, then

—Fuck Adrian, she says,—that was a bit rough.

—I don't think so, says Adrian airily.—Christ! The way they pussy around you'd think I was selling the bloody Crown jewels.

He lies back as far as it's possible to lie in an upright swivel chair. His hands are behind his head in a way his parents would immediately classify as assertive bordering on arrogant. He looks at Claudia and Ben with the glow of battle still in his eyes.

—There are always people around with no taste and too much money, he states.—You just have to tell the bastards what they want.

—But is that really right, Adrian? says Ben. He stands on his other foot and his sneaker taps against the wall anxiously.

—'Right'? What the hell is 'right'? says Adrian.—This is retail not right, Ben.

—What you're doing is intimidating people into wasting money, says Ben.

—No, I'm not *intimidating people*, says Adrian. He copies Ben's voice but picks up the disapproving note and amplifies it. Ben blushes slightly.

—In fact I tell them like it is, Adrian says.—That design shops may sell this stuff for less, but it's not genuine.

—You mean it's pseudo-tack, says Claudia.—As opposed to genuine tack.

—It's still tack, says Ben disagreeably.

—Exactly, says Adrian.—And if they don't have a sense of humour about the whole thing, then they deserve to be taken for a ride.

He takes a long, slow look around his domain, which resembles a cross between a psychedelic *Avengers* set and a graveyard for crockery. He gestures at it, and then at the controversial fish lying in front of him.

—I mean, he says, looking hard at Ben,—you're a fucken square if you don't see that this stuff is funny.

Ben fidgets noticeably. His mouth has gone into its straight line, as if someone started to saw his head in half and got bored when they reached his ears. He looks at Adrian. Adrian shrugs. The clammy air gets clammier with tension.

—OK, Ben, says Claudia.—We're out of here.

She can't understand how they got to this point but she's not going to let her two best friends come to blows over a stupid glass fish. She raises her eyebrows at Adrian, heads towards the door feeling uncommonly like a jaded mother. On the way out, she picks a mood ring up from a tray on the counter.

—Just a borrow, she says to Adrian over her shoulder,—to check I'm still myself.

The ring goes bright green on her finger (her nature is still passionate and vital). She steps into the 5 pm dust and heat feeling affirmed, but there is a sour taste on her tongue which she hopes will wash away with a Coke.

They wait in line for their vege burgers. Ben is only slowly recovering his speech, so Claudia orders for both of them.

—And a large kumara fries, she says. She puts the mood ring on Ben's little finger. The stone goes black.

—Change, says Ben, looking morosely at his hand.—Christ, it's overrated.

The slide

He's right. Adrian is changing. The Shrinks are around less and less, but Adrian doesn't seem to be equivalently happier and happier. The words conference circuit used to have him rolling his eyes with anticipation rolling a cigarette rolling a joint. But now? He just shrugs.

—Shall we come round? offers Claudia.—Friday night, after work?

—If you want, says Adrian.—But I might not be here.

—Where will you be? demands Claudia.

—I don't fucking know, do I? says Adrian.—How do I know where I'll be before it happens? Might be in bed, I suppose, might be in the bath.

—Christ, you're a lot of fun these days, says Claudia crossly.—It's like being friends with Karen Carpenter or something.

—Look Claudia, I've offered you free run of the house, says Adrian.—Get pissed on the Shrinks' wine, get off your face on whatever stuff Ben gets hold of, just don't ask me to account for every minute of my fucking time, OK?

After this, Claudia follows Ben's example and stays away, waits for Adrian to call her. He doesn't.

—I told you, says Ben when she complains.—There's something wrong with that boy.

—Yes there is, says Claudia.—He's turning into a self-centred son of a bitch and he deserves to know.

It is easier to be angry with someone than to acknowledge the unease working in your stomach every time you think of them. Claudia works on her anger overnight and by the next day she is ready to storm Retropolis.

The shop door is closed even though it's the middle of a Saturday. This makes Claudia even angrier; she has made a special trip to point out Adrian's faults to him, she's used up all her change for the parking meter, and now it doesn't look as if he's even here.

She bangs on the door with her fist. The stone falls out of her (borrowed) mood ring, reminding her that she's never taken it back and now it's too late.

—Cheap shit! she says.

She picks up the stone and posts it through the letter slot in the wooden door frame, then puts her ear to the slot. A voice is mumbling inside.

—Adrian? says Claudia sharply.—Why the hell aren't you open?

—What? Is that you, Mum? the voice says.

—No I'm not your mother, thank God, she says angrily.—It's Claudia. Remember me?

A blurry figure approaches the frosted glass, running blurry hands through blurry hair. Closer, blurrier, then the door opens and Claudia sees what used to be Adrian.

—Adrian! she exclaims.—What's the matter with you?

He looks like Worzel Gummidge on acid. His stubble, which is usual, has no style, which is unusual. He is wearing a lime-green polyester shirt (reassuring) but it's on backwards and inside out.

—You look shocking! says Claudia, still a bit sharply. Now that she's seen him she's seriously worried but it's hard to throw away accumulated anger that fast.

—Well thanks, darling, he drawls.—You look ravishing, as always.

A month ago Claudia would have believed him but she is no longer certain of anything.

—Why haven't you rung me? she demands.

—Things on my mind, says Adrian. He shrugs, stands back for her to come in.

The shop looks as bad as he does. Junk is piled around the floor, and it still looks like junk rather than desirable accessories. Adrian sees her looking.

—Got a few dealers coming in this week, he says dismissively.—Just haven't had time to sort it out yet.

He pulls a chair out from under a squid-like mess of telephones.

—Have a seat? he offers.—Original Bertola, going for big bucks in Paris you know.

Claudia looks at the stained cushion and decides to lean on the counter instead. How to start? Since concern is always easier to express in someone else's voice—

—Ben's worried about you, she says. (After all, this is no lie.)

—Oh really? Adrian says looking bored.—Sweet of him.

—He thinks you might be having a spiritual crisis, invents Claudia.—Or maybe an incestuous relationship.

—In my dreams! says Adrian.—The mundane nature of my life startles even me.

—It's no more mundane than it's ever been, says Claudia.—And anyway, now you've got this place.

—Exactly, says Adrian.—So my life just got worse. I mean, look at this useless shit!

He sneers around at his cartoon shop.

—Boring, he says.—Dull. Tedious as hell.

—But you really wanted this! says Claudia, startled.

—Yes, I thought I did, agrees Adrian.—It would appear I've made a mistake.

—Well, give it time, says Claudia. She can hardly believe she is saying this, since she herself hates this particular piece of advice. It doesn't appear to work for Adrian either.

—It's me as much as the shop, shrugs Adrian.—I just don't interest myself any more. It's like I'm living out the parts of TV soaps that happen during the ad breaks.

—So you've just found out how most people feel most of the time, says Claudia, wisely.

—I beg to differ, says Adrian.—Most people have an abnormal interest in themselves. I have none.

—Sex? enquires Claudia.

—God no, says Adrian exhaustedly.—I'd rather have a cigarette.

Claudia thinks of Heath and can identify with this; then thinks of Leith, and can't.

—So if Uma Thurman walked in? she says.

—I'd sell her a lava lamp, says Adrian.

Claudia roams through her mind wildly for something to combat this crushing apathy.

—Coming to Utopia tonight? she says, without much hope.

—Staying in, says Adrian.—As my ole momma used to say, only bad things happen to you outside, honey chile.

Claudia sighs. She's sorry that Adrian's zest for life is running out fast but she's aware that so is the time on her meter.

—What's the time? she asks.

Adrian shrugs.

—Dunno, he says.—The clocks have all stopped.

And they have. This disturbs Claudia as much as anything. The shelf crammed with clocks, which last time was chattering, is now completely silent and strewn with chrome corpses.

—Oh, says Claudia, biting her lip. She sinks into a black vinyl beanbag, which sighs under her.

—The attitudes in this country suck, Adrian is saying irrelevantly. His eyes are red and fixed on the far wall, and he seems to be stuck in some mind-groove of his own.

—They suck, he repeats.—Man eats dog, look after Number One, private enterprise rules, and you know what the worst thing is?

Claudia doesn't.

—I've gone and bought into it, says Adrian, waving his hand at the shop.—Those bastard politicians have got to me.

He holds out three copies of *Streetwise*.

—Have to buy it every time I see someone selling it, he says,—and I never even read it. It's just such an effort turning the pages. How's that for hypocrisy?

Claudia sits back slightly desperately. She feels as if she's sinking, into the beanbag, out of her depth.

—The twentieth century is completely ghastly, says Adrian.—Ginsberg knew it, Timothy Leary knew it, hell they all knew it.

Claudia is starting to feel that every step of this conversation is like walking deeper into a swamp.

—And now, says Adrian,—I know it.

He is looking straight at her for the first time. There is no glint of a smile behind his eyes.

He's back

To Claudia, Adrian's decline seems set to stay. But just as the skies are unpredictable, so too is Adrian. For almost immediately after Claudia begins mourning his loss, he returns to her life. With a vengeance.

Ben, having a scientist's faith in natural cycles, credits the moon and tides. Claudia doesn't know what to credit but is first happy and then dazed. Because Adrian bursts back on the scene like a dazzling meteor, and hits the earth scorching.

His inventiveness soars, along with his energy levels. He comes up with new playthings for his friends, buys purple packets of herbal ecstasy and scatters them around like confetti. He dances through the nights, sells harder and talks faster.

He buys transport so that he can move around more quickly. Not a car but a skateboard with handlebars and a bottle of fuel strapped on the back. A petrol-powered retro-scooter on which he stands like a boy from the 1950s. Holding the long handlebars, he takes the corners with massive aplomb. His body leans, he whips through the traffic, the wind sweeps through his hair and he wears wrap-around shades. He is very cool.

Although his engine is only 5 cc, and his top speed 20 ks per hour, no one can catch him.

The Leith project

Now that her friend's life looks like being restored, Claudia can work on her own. Which means, working on Leith.

—Call me, she says to Leith. She flings off her apron and it billows through the air like her airy words, coming to a floating rest in the pan. Apron strings mingle with strings of egg-white, escaped from the shells because she hasn't bothered to prick them.

Quietly, Leith fishes her apron out of the eggs with a ladle. He hangs the apron to dry on the drumstick of a rotisserie chicken. (Quietly.) Then he turns back to his quiet éclairs.

Claudia notices that the apron is drinking up the chicken fat. Leith doesn't notice this sort of thing, just as he doesn't notice other people's unrequited passion. The grease continues to make inroads on the cotton, maps out the dull trip of the next dull day, but Claudia is too highly strung and too artistic to fuss about laundry. She leaves the apron adorning the chicken.

—Call me, OK? she says again. Should she say, *call me tonight?* Probably, but her easy mouth gums up around Leith.

—Sure, Clawd, he says.

He always says sure, and he always says her name like Claw with a D on the end, which she hates. (He always says sure but he never calls.) Claudia's told him many times how to say her name but he's so vague. It drives her crazy.

What she hasn't told him is how his teeth grab and cling onto his bottom lip when he's concentrating on using the cream-bag.

This drives her crazy too, but in quite a different way.

He has a Friday night off the band. She knows, with a girl's instinct, that it's up to her. (He never calls.)

—Come out with us! she suggests.

—Yeah? he says, looking faintly surprised.

—Yeah, come drinking with me and Aids and Ben, she decides.

—OK, he says agreeably. He doesn't look excited but he doesn't look reluctant. Has Claudia just been too subtle in the past?

—I might bring my flatmate, he says.—It's his last weekend in town.

—Great! says Claudia enthusiastically. She doesn't believe in stage-managing events to the final degree. She has faith in her magnetic personality, has faith in its ability to draw all disparate elements together.

The girl with glitter in all the right places

She knows it will be a good night, can feel it in her high cheekbones and the thrumming bones of her bird-wrists. Leith is waiting on the footpath. He looks the same as he does at work: peaceful, easeful, only minus the apron.

—And the flatmate? asks Claudia.

—I'm gonna meet up with him later, says Leith.

Claudia doesn't fret at the promise of eventual desertion. She has no belief in later, is a child of the present, knows that the future might never happen. She glows in the cavernous entrance, a firefly between two rocks of doormen.

Adrian is babbling by the time they track him down. He is splayed at a corner table, long arms long legs, long hands wrapped around a Guinness. The music: deep funk that fills Claudia's slight body and she's home.

—You made it, Adrian's lost it, says Ben calmly in her ear. He is sinking a Guinness too, and four more are lined up in front of him because a trip to the bar is hazardous for someone as small as he is. He offers one of the bottles to Claudia.

—No thanks, I'm in a schnapps mood, she shouts.

—You want one? Ben shouts politely to Leith.

—Hey there, Claudia, bellows Adrian.—Hey, Claudia's friend.

—Watch him, says Ben.—He's away.

—You've arrived just in time, says Adrian loudly.—The little men are here.

Although his mind is working overtime, his body appears to have turned to stone. He sits motionless in his corner chair, only his head flying back and forwards.

—Claudia, he says urgently.—Come here.

—What is it? says Claudia, shimmying down beside him.

—See this little red elf? Adrian says confidentially.—He's going to take us to a parallel universe.

—He's got your elf syndrome, says Claudia to Ben, remembering the dance with the twig.

—Yeah, but he paid a couple of hundred for it, says Ben.

—That much for a wrap? says Claudia, admiring, appalled.

—Looks like it's worth it, says Leith.

Adrian begins talking loudly. He is clearly having a conversation but it's impossible to make out where one word ends and another starts.

—Mental elf warning! says Ben, whose wit works at top speed when fed on Guinness.

—Listen, he's saying something! says Claudia.

—The matrix of life! says Adrian slowly and clearly.

It takes a couple of hours before Adrian's eyes focus on things which other people can see.

—What the hell did you take, Aids? asks Claudia curiously.

—DMT, says Adrian, who has now returned to the English language. Red veins map out the whites of his eyes like cracks on dry earth.

— DMT? says Claudia.

—That's diemethyltryptamine to you guys, says Ben conversationally.

—You gotta try it, slurs Adrian. His face has the waxy look of the newly returned.

—Looked pretty heavy duty, says Leith. He has slotted in almost too easily which, Claudia thinks, is both good and difficult. Versatility she likes, but Leith is so versatile he is impossible to capture.

—Man I tell you, slurs Adrian.—Ginsberg, Burroughs, they all used it. Best stuff around.

—Are you still on your Beat poet trip? says Claudia.

—Talking of trips, says Leith,—gotta take one to meet my flatmate.

—Great to meet you, man, says Ben seriously. Even after pouring pints of black beer into his small self, his manners are impeccable. Claudia looks at his throat—his thin pale throat weaving upwards from the collar of his rugby shirt. She feels a fierce possessive love for him.

—Ditto, dude, waves Adrian.—Are you going or staying, Claudia my good wench?

Claudia wavers, Leith anticipates.

—I don't think the next pub's really your scene, Clawd, he says.

Claudia glows, feels schnapps-coloured, peach-coloured. Yes! Leith knows her enough to identify her scene. And so she is quite happy to stay.

—See you tomorrow then, she says radiantly.

—Back at the mill, says Leith.

—I'll be the one with the apron on, says Claudia.

—C'mon, Claudia! cries Ben. He is gearing up to dance, his

runty arms and legs are beginning to tap and wave randomly.

—C'mon, he cries.—Let's groove, my friends, my friendly groovers!

Claudia is energised by smoke and happiness, she can go all night.

—Adrian, get off your arse and dance, she says. She weaves invitingly beside him.

—Dance yourself, says Adrian, who looks as if he is about to slide under the table.

—I intend to, says Claudia. She makes a face at Ben and they comet onto the dance floor. Tails of laughter flare behind them.

—That boy, he is uuuup and he is dooowwwn, says Ben.—UP! and then DOWN!!

Claudia jumps onto a table, flies from it, flies and flies again. She is a bird, a glittering beautiful silvery bird with exotic thoughts in her head. She feels a slight bump in her landing but her crested head is floating well above ground level.

—Are you OK? Ben shouts.

Claudia doesn't know what he's talking about, she's fine and she just wants to fly.

—YOU OK? Ben bellows.

Claudia vaguely notices a dark girl who has stumbled against Ben. Could it be that the Claudia-bird's wings have grazed the dark girl? This is what Ben is implying. The dark girl looks vacant, says something, disappears in the direction of the toilets.

Claudia has no time for blank nameless people. There is soaring to be done. She swoops and soars, she sees Adrian slumped at the far end of a telescope and Ben beginning to flail.

She swoops, she is beautiful and she can fly.

Disintegration

Retropolis is open at spasmodic hours.

—So? says Adrian sweepingly.—It's not like it needs constant attention. Plastic doesn't go off, you know.

He gets out a hammer.

—You renovating? says Ben absently. He has been preoccupied

lately and says he has family pressures, though no one believes Ben really has a family. Claudia has always imagined Ben growing in some petrie dish in a lab and springing up one day, tiny but fully formed, his baby forehead already creased with thinking lines, his miniature rugby jersey already smelling of chemicals.

—Renovating? I don't think so! says Adrian.—That's a dirty word in a retro shop.

He reaches under the counter and extracts a long cardboard box.

—Be prepared for a trip back to childhood, children, he says. From the box he extracts a long metal pole with a spring on the end.

—Swingball! Claudia says with delight.

—That's right, my observant little friend, says Adrian.—Don't need a memory like an elephant to remember this sensation.

—It's sweeping the nation, chorus Ben and Claudia.

Adrian starts hammering the pole into the middle of the wooden floor. Splinters of floor fly. Ben and Claudia look slightly alarmed, slightly admiring.

—You sure you wanna be doing that? asks Ben.

—All in the cause of having a good time, cries Adrian.

Soon the swingball is planted, stands proudly like a branchless tree. Adrian gives it an experimental smack with the bat. The ball flies like an angel up the spring.

—Yesss! Adrian whoops.—We have movement, we have entertainment.

There's a tiny tap at the open door. A woman stands there in a pink nylon trouser suit.

—Hey! Fab suit! says Claudia reverently. Too late, she realises the woman is wearing it for real.

The woman smiles uncertainly. She sees the swingball planted in the middle of the shop and her eyes flicker in a small, diffident panic.

—I'm from the shop downstairs, she says in a wavering voice.

—Of course you are! cries Adrian.—You're Betty's Bridal Boutique!

He advances towards Betty and starts pumping her hand.

—What can we do for you? he asks expansively.

—Part of my ceiling is crumbling, says Betty apologetically.

—Just doing a bit of interior decorating, beams Adrian, waving towards the entertainment centre.

—But is it safe? says Betty slightly breathlessly. Her small body is shaking, not so much from anxiety as because Adrian is still vigorously and absentmindedly pumping her hand.

—Safe? It's as safe as houses! beams Adrian, dropping into Betty-speak.

—Hey Adrian, says Ben quietly.—You could probably let go of her hand now.

—Oh, yeah! says Adrian. He places Betty's hand almost reverently back at her side. It hangs tiredly beside her pink nylon hip, recovering.

—No more hammering, I promise! says Adrian jovially.—Back to your shop, fellow shopkeeper!

—You don't think the city council will mind about, umm, says Betty. She gestures to the silver stick plummeting deep into Adrian's floorboards, into her plaster ceiling.

—Nah! says Adrian.—They couldn't give a fuck about old buildings, want excuses to build new ones anyway!

—I suppose so, murmurs Betty.

—Away with you, Betty Boo, says Adrian jovially.—Betty Boo or is it Blue something borrowed and something new!

Claudia winces. Betty turns for the door with a faint scratching of nylon slacks.

—Come up for a game sometime, cries Adrian graciously.

Ben and Claudia collapse on a sheepskin rug. They are not sure whether to laugh.

—Boy, she really rained on your parade, didn't she? says Ben.

—No time for lounging around, says Adrian.—Get up, you laggard, we have serious sport to attend to.

He dances in the middle of his mutilated floor, flexing his muscles, jabbing dancing flexing jabbing, eyes narrowed competitively.

—Life is a fight against mediocrity! he proclaims.—Sharpen up or lose!

Ben jumps up and spars with the air. Dust from the floor is still floating in the sun, the windows are streaked and bright, Ben floats like a butterfly in small boots.

Adrian grabs the bats.

—Blue or red? he cries.

Claudia lies in a meadow of long musty wool, watches the lime-green ball fly back and forwards creating a luminous circle. She falls into a trance.

Adrian is that ball, eye-catching, still orbiting but always seemingly close to wild anarchic flight. Ben is the cord: pliable, slender, hard to see at times but nonetheless firmly grounded. And what is Claudia? Well, she is the bright displaced air, moved by other forces, impossible to define, capture, or hold. Free, definitely. Formless? Perhaps.

But watching Adrian and Ben through half-closed eyes she is aware of something else, outside of this room. She feels, she exists in, a state of grace: she is conscious of some small centrifugal force, giving stability to her insubstantial disturbed existence.

Haley

Thinking back, she remembers Robert as too clever for her. It wasn't apparent at the time but in retrospect, she has nothing to say to some of his comments.

When she lies in her hostel bed at night, listening to the Germans playing pool underneath her, her mind always takes her back to the British Museum. She might want to remember Robert on the beach at Brighton with shiny plastic windmills stuck behind each ear, but somehow it is determined that as long as she lies in a hostel bed in Remuera, Robert is standing in front of the mummies in the Egyptian room.

—I saw this documentary this morning, he is saying.—About archaeologists taking scrapings from the fingernails of mummies.

They are in a museum, they are talking about archaeology.

Halley with 2 Ls, student of archaeology, should not only be on solid ground but higher ground. Instead of which Robert is at the top of the hill and she is still climbing. But this is what she likes, as well as resents, about Robert. He can move onto her territory, make it his own, without even realising it.

—Yeah? she says.—What for?

—Cell samples, says Robert.—Clues to finding cures for modern diseases, HIV TB CJD.

—I guess, says Halley,—that the world moves in cycles.

She realises as she says it that this is hardly an earth-shattering observation.

—You're absolutely right, says Robert seriously. He listens to all her comments as if they're her discoveries alone, instead of universal truths discussed by scientists, philosophers and poets over many centuries.

—So all we have to do is follow the circle back, says Halley, gratefully.

—Yep, says Robert.

—And we find the answer to the present in the past, says Halley.

She stares at the leathery cheek of the closest mummy. It's a particularly small body. She feels sorry for it, displaced and stared at by monster people out of its time.

—The marriage between modern biology and archaeology, muses Robert.—To unlock the matrix of life.

The matrix of life. The phrase has a beauty to it, though Halley could never attempt to explain it. This, too, is quintessential Robert. Always, he has fused number-talk and poetry in a way she can't reach. At night he talks of quadratics vectors ciphers and surds, with a shape to his voice that sings Halley to sleep.

She wonders what matrix means to him. Does he first think of mathematical patterns in rows and columns? Or does he think of a deep mould, receiving and shaping and accepting and giving back an image of itself?

—What do you think, Robert? she says.

—What, Hale? he says, turning towards her.

—Nothing, she says, because as soon as she sees his eyes again she knows him and what he is. He is everything. He is columns and curves, he is receptacle and producer, and negative and positive.

—Want coffee? he says and he smiles at her.

—Sure, she says.

They walk to the café under the vaulted ceiling and Halley's feet meet the newly laid floor with certainty, sole to solid lino, because now she knows how Robert's head works.

This is the thing that keeps her awake long after the Germans have laid down their cues. What was Robert thinking as the quick ground flew to meet him? Was he thinking of her? Or was he, so soon after pacing out the lengths of boards, still cradled by the certainty of measurements?

Haley lies in her narrow bed and holds the sheet so that her fingernails slice through into the palms of her hands. She hopes against hope that Robert had no thought of her as he fell, so that the moment of impact was nothing more than the solution to a long and complex equation.

Falling into an answer. That is what she hopes for when she thinks of the death of Robert.

February

Claudia

Even the sight of Leith's calm hands working his dough can't calm her. She's feeling edgy, is wearing the world like a scar, doesn't want to be at work at home in bed or in the world at large.

—Excuse me! I didn't order this, calls a business type. His gut hangs threateningly over his belt: danger! approach at own risk!

Claudia doesn't want to approach so she hums around an empty table and pretends she doesn't hear.

—Excuse me! Excuse me! says the business-gut.

Claudia raises her eyebrows in a cool questioning kind of way, distances herself from the whole situation by pretending there will be no outcome. (She will not have to talk to him, he will not complain, she will not have to apologise and trek back to the kitchen for another order.)

—Excuse me, girl, he says.—This is NOT eggs benedict.

Delicately, Claudia stands away from the table, inspects the plate from a distance. There is an egg-like mass on one side and the whole dish makes her stomach heave but it doesn't look quite as sickening as eggs benedict, no.

—You're right, she says after a deliberate pause.

—So get me my eggs, says the man.

His companion laughs in a disbelieving, patronising way. She has been talking on a mobile about the state of her shares; she also has a mobile on the table, and one in her bag over the back of her chair. Now she snaps her conversation shut and enters the fray.

—For Christ's sake! she says.—Not exactly the best of service is it!

She is a hard blonde with none of Claudia's natural advantages, but she is well aware of her one major advantage: she is the customer. Yet Claudia remains undaunted, for she is only playing at the role of waitress, after all. She advances towards the table, swinging her narrow hips in a nonchalant way.

—Do you have a problem too? she says politely.

(—Apart from the obvious, she adds in her head.)

—Actually I do, says the blonde.—This long black is cold.

—Well, that could be, says Claudia slowly,—because I brought it to you fifteen minutes ago.

The blonde goes red.

—Roger! she says angrily.

(—Roger! mimics Claudia scornfully in her head.)

—Just get us the correct order and another long black, says Roger embarrassedly. Having entered the ring so assertively, he now looks as if he is fading.

—Certainly sir, says Claudia.—The customer is always right, or so they say.

She picks up the mess of eggs and the cold cup, whisks over the table-top with her cloth, sending little flecks of food back and forwards. Food over Roger, food over Roger's companion, food over Roger.

—Anything else, sir? she says demurely.

Roger waves her away. His neck is mottled. Claudia glances

down at her own smooth chest, flicks her smooth hair over her shoulder.

—And for you? she says to the blonde.—Another mobile phone?

The blonde laughs angrily. Her table phone rings and she has to pick it up. Claudia smirks her way into the kitchen where she is also summoned by the phone. With the adrenaline of battle in her veins, for a moment she has forgotten her unexplained edginess. She asks Leith for complimentary bacon on the side, to rub salt in her customer's wound. Then

—Hello? she says triumphantly.

—Claudia, did you know that? she hears. She hardly recognises the voice.

—Adrian? she says uncertainly.

—Yes it's me, the voice says.

—Can it wait? says Claudia. She wants to get the eggs benedict back to the table while she's still winning.

—NO! says Adrian emphatically.—I have to tell you something, important it is and I tell you.

—He's raving, she mouths to Leith.

—Two minutes, warns Leith, flipping bacon.

—Why aren't you at the shop anyway? asks Claudia.

—Don't feel too well, says Adrian.—Head's a bit spinny spinny head today.

—So what is it? says Claudia, monitoring conversation-time by the colour of Leith's bacon.

—The Carthaginians, mutters Adrian.—Did ya know, the Carthaginians sacrificed their kids in times of national stress.

His voice, although babbling, is slow, drags through the sentence like a stretched answerphone tape.

—Really, says Claudia uncomprehendingly.—Well, that's interesting, Aids, but I gotta go wait tables now.

—Wait! says Adrian.

—Yes wait, that's what I said, says Claudia.—Waiting's my job and I have to go do it.

—Wait listen understand why can't you! says Adrian.—The

burden on youth, it's crushing, understand, why don't you?

—Eggs are up, calls Leith.

—Believe me, Adrian, I understand, says Claudia.—I myself feel quite burdened right now.

—Burden on youth! says Adrian loudly.—Undeserving youth doesn't deserve that!

Leith shoves a plate of steaming food under her nose, mouths NOW at her.

—Eggs, says Leith.

—I'll call you tonight, OK? says Claudia.—We'll do something.

—Please! says Adrian.—Please!

—Bye, says Claudia.—Bye now.

She dumps the vile plate in front of the vile Roger, gives bitter coffee to the bitter blonde. She doesn't say anything, keeps her eyes down. Suddenly her stomach is churning again and she's lost her appetite for insults.

The day spins faster and faster on its axis, threatens to disintegrate. The lunch rush starts. Stella the redhead gets her second migraine of the week and Claudia is coerced into working late, reconciled by the fact that Leith has been similarly coerced. By the time she remembers Adrian and gets to a phone, it is dark outside and Adrian isn't answering. She calls Ben at the lab.

—Haven't seen him all day, says Ben.—He was gonna come in this afternoon but he hasn't showed.

The uneasiness, queasiness, in Claudia's stomach twists like an unfamiliar road.

—Need a ride home, Clawd? says Leith, grabbing his helmet.

—Well, somewhere, says Claudia.

They arrow into the night traffic. At each corner Claudia feels as if gravity is going to betray them. Clinging to Leith's back without even thinking *this is Leith's back!* she waits to be flung off the edge of the world. She tries to focus, plans her way back to security.

1) She will get home, there will be a message from Adrian telling her to meet him there, wear this, bring this, at this time.

2) If there is no message (but there will be) she will borrow Diane's car and go round to Adrian's. He will be watching reruns

of *Gilligan's Island* and raiding the Shrinks' wine cellar (they are away conferencing). He will try to discuss world issues with her, she will flick through back numbers of *Vogue* to annoy him, they will plan where to go in a few hours when their faint hangovers from last night have disappeared.

3) If she can't find him . . . No, this is not allowed to be part of the plan.

—I'll wait till I see your light go on, says Leith.

She runs inside in the dark, runs to the phone. The red eye of the answerphone blinks at her. She waits for Adrian's voice, hears only Marcus of Marcus Motors telling her that her car won't be ready until Tuesday. Where is Diane in the dark house? Diane has left a message too, saying she has gone out to dinner and won't be back till late.

End of messages.

Ignoring the sharp pains in her stomach, Claudia runs onto the dark street where Leith is still sitting on his bike, having a conversation with a cat.

—To Adrian's? Sure, hop on, says Leith. He doesn't try to talk her out of it or ask her to explain, he just unhooks the spare helmet from the handlebars again and hands it to her. (There have been times when his passive acceptance has annoyed her but now she is deeply grateful for it.)

A variation on Scenario # 2. (This is still possible.) Claudia is swept through the Remuera streets on Leith's motorbike instead of in Diane's car. But still she arrives at Adrian's, and Adrian is still there as he is supposed to be, clashing with the floral sofa.

Might be, must be.

Isn't.

They go next to Adrian's shop. Claudia stands by the window full of eyeless hairless brides and rings the bell. She is sharpened by the night and the feeling inside her. Everything is louder, more raw, strikes her in the eyes or the nose or the stomach.

The street is as dirty as anywhere in the world. The footpath is streaked with dried vomit and the doorway smells of piss and alcohol. There is a dim light upstairs in the window of Retropolis, which could be one of Adrian's sixties lamps or could be a reflection from the XEROX sign across the road. No one answers the bell.

Where now? At the Alex Evans bridge Leith slows down. The traffic lights are hidden by other, more important, flashing lights. Although Claudia's urgency is at his back, Leith has to stop.

There's a cop with a torch. There's a cop car parked on an angle. There are a few people hovering around trying to look purposeful and concerned, but the reek of curiosity hangs in the night air.

—You can drive on slowly, sir, says the cop to Leith.

Leith crawls along in second but now the pain in Claudia's side stabs so sharply that she feels as if she might topple from the bike, and she issues other orders. Leith pulls into the side, off the bridge. They look down on surreal orange motorways and the aftermath of a tragedy.

—Shocking thing, mumbles the old woman next to Claudia.

—What is? demands Claudia.

—It's a terrible world, says the old woman, rustling her parka in an ominous way.

—I know that, says Claudia,—but what's happened?

—Well, it's the boy isn't it, the old woman says.—He jumped.

There's a slow avidity about her like a hawk hovering round a road kill.

Claudia stares at her. The woman's mouth is slack, it hangs down at one side and moves slowly, slowly, but it can't be stopped.

—They say he was just young, Claudia hears from far away.

—Just a young man, she hears.

—Jumped to his death, she hears.

The world cries in Claudia's ears like the wind down an empty pipe.

A human skull is surprisingly tough, but when something is travelling at great velocity (the head, the surface, or both towards each other) and there is a collision, a skull cracks as easily as an egg. The giant palms of speed and gravitational force press together, there is a moment of anticipation before the laws of science make their effect felt.

This is the crux of it: anticipation. The actual moment of impact is not, contrary to belief, important. As in all endeavours, it is the anticipation and the aftermath that are significant. Life and death have this in common: the moment of consummation is so supreme that it cannot be recognised. It is gone before it can be apprehended.

Men and women leap or fall through the ages. The air is never what they expect because it is unimaginable, this full release. Soft and tangible against limbs and faces, the air gives the illusion of comfort. But when hands reach out in blind instinct, they find only treachery. There is, after all, nothing there.

There is little or no time for despair, however. Despair is for the other people, those who must deal with what is left behind. Those who must clean up skulls which, like eggshells, have cracked: sometimes not fully open but still damaged beyond repair. Those people must mop up leakages of a substance that minutes before held mystery and now is only matter.

—We don't know it's him, says Leith.

—The police station, says Leith.

—First place to start, says Leith.

—Then I guess the hospitals, says Leith.

Claudia cries. It's all she can do. She is crying because she and Ben have lost their best friend, she is crying because the stars are still wheeling overhead while human breath grinds to a halt all around the city.

She can't stop.

The police station is like some kind of club where everyone except them knows the rules. People are striding around, even ones with blood pouring from their heads, as if they have some appointment to keep. Claudia is buffeted by other people's purpose. But then they have one themselves, and Leith is a rock.

He's winding his way towards the front desk, she's following in his wake, when he stops.

—Are you OK? he's saying, but not to her.

There's a girl standing by the water-cooler. She doesn't look too good—but Adrian, Adrian.

—Leith, let's go, Claudia says, but her voice is so tiny it slips down among the legs of all the walkers and rolls away across the shiny floor.

The girl is swaying, sitting down. There's some kind of hassle with a water cup, but Claudia must not look outwards because she must not see someone else's problems. She is holding herself up in her head, with both hands and all her strength. If she lets herself drop who knows what will have happened to Adrian, something far worse than clambering onto the rail of a bridge and submitting himself to the dark. She holds onto him and her on the slippery rail, and if she loses her balance here in the police station his death will have been a violent and not a welcome one. And it will be her fault.

—Sometimes we just know, she hears Leith say to the girl.

She stares hard at Leith's back. If he knows so much why didn't he tell her to listen to Adrian? Why didn't he tell her to keep Adrian on the phone instead of distracting her with plates of eggs? Why didn't he point out that Adrian wasn't always right, that Adrian's laughter was sometimes more of a question than an answer? Why didn't he? Why?

Leith is still helping the girl. His back is wide, and his arms are muscly though they are thin. There is a lot of strength under his stretched T-shirt, and Claudia puts out a hand but pulls it back before she touches him. The air behind him must make a little kind of rush, though, because he turns around. He puts a hand on her hair.

—We don't know it's him, he says.

How does her hair feel to his hand after the rough leather of his gloves and the hard corners of the visor? She breathes in the scent of her own hair and to her it smells of blood. She is roughened from the night streets, she wants her smooth and shiny self back but the past two hours have rubbed her like sandpaper.

—Polish me, she cries to someone.—Take me in your hand.

—You sure you're OK then? says Leith.

She is not OK but he is not talking to her. The girl he is talking to instead of Claudia looks over his shoulder. She looks directly at Claudia as if she wants to make some kind of connection, but Claudia is severed from all people and she turns away.

Rewind

After the police station, after they have established that Adrian may be lost but he is presumably still alive, after Leith has dropped Claudia off with offers of help the next morning, she doesn't know what to do. Near-tragedy is harder than tragedy, she thinks. No one has written the rules of behaviour for someone who has seen their friend kill himself, and then seen him snatched back. She's at a loss, a feeling that used to be alien to her but is becoming disconcertingly more frequent.

Diane is in bed, oblivious to Adrian's death and resurrection and continued absence. Claudia has no desire to wake her and talk to her, nor does she have the energy. She is wrung like a rag, her eyes stinging with past salt. She has seen the sand stretching forever grey, unrelieved by gaudy shirts or colourful conversation.

Red light blinking on the phone. A new message. She crawls on her hands and knees towards it, can hardly be bothered to listen to it.

It's from Adrian. He has rung while she and Leith have been searching the city for him, he has reached out to her while she has been ripping him—feeling him ripped—from her head.

He has not been in a hospital or a morgue.

He is not in a cell lying in his own vomit breathing whisky bleeding from his head.

He is alive. And drunk.

This is how his live, drunken conversation with her answer machine goes:

It's probably extremely good that actually you're not there because I am—hah! extraordinarily drunk as you can probably tell. It's appalling, isn't it, I'm appalling, but I was hoping you would talk to me and I could listen and sober up but you're out . . .

where are you, treacherous harpy?

I'm not supposed to drink right now for various reasons but you can't get better all at once can you . . . I just wanted to share with you that I'm getting better and also that I've just walked home from the shop at midnight in nothing but my boxer shorts . . . hah! inexplicable but true . . .

it may sound extraordinary, Claud, but I have to tell you that there's very little to compare with walking home at midnight in the summertime, in the light of a comet, in your boxer shorts . . .

I shall sign off here but I tell you one thing this life is extraordinarily good and extraordinarily bad and there's very little else to say about it, Claud . . . It's just the most extraordinary thing and don't let anyone tell you otherwise.

Although she takes herself to bed, she is so angry that she can't sleep. At 3 am she gets up again, takes Diane's car and drives on roads as black and deserted as graveyards towards Adrian's door, where she leans on the doorbell and then on the neo-pillars because her legs are about to give way.

When he answers the door in his old man's pyjamas, she can't stop hitting him. He pulls her inside, into the hallway, where she hits and hits him. And then she is crying too much to do anything except sit on the floor.

—Calm down, for God's sake, says Adrian.—Claudia, just calm down.

Claudia cries at him: the motorbike, the orange lights, the mosaic road, the ringing the knocking, the night the night and the bridge.

—I was in the shop the whole time, explains Adrian.— Drinking, with my headphones on.

They move from the hall floor to the kitchen floor, which is slightly more hospitable. Adrian says she always overreacts, but he sits beside her on the red tiles and holds her ankle for a long time. When he gets up to make coffee, she can still feel his hand on her foot, his fingers have held her flesh too hard but it was necessary and they both know it. There is some shred of comfort in their shared knowledge.

There is always a next day

Yes, Adrian is alive. Yes, Claudia had rushed needlessly into a world with no walls, turning and turning in the black wind. But she was right about one thing: Adrian had been in that world too, is still there periodically.

—I'm manic, he says with a shrug.

He has opened Retropolis, though he has a hangover big enough (he says) to fell a team of All Blacks. He leans on the counter, tracing a pattern with his pen.

—Manic? says Claudia.—As in depression?

She is surprised but not surprised, realises as soon as he has said it that she knew this and just hadn't faced it.

—As in bipolar, as in mentally ill, says Adrian. He barks like a dog. Claudia jumps.

—Barking mad, he says with a forced laugh.

—But why didn't Chris and Gerry—? Claudia asks.

—Did you ever hear the old saying about cobbler's children running barefoot? says Adrian.

—Well, no actually, says Claudia.—But I get the gist.

—Let's just say it was left to someone else to diagnose me, says Adrian. He starts roaming round the shop, winding every wind-up toy, starting a fantastic plastic dance.

—Useless, my parents, he says.—Can't spot a dysfunctional even in their own home.

—Too easy and too hard? says Claudia.

—Whatever, says Adrian.—Crusading off to cure the rest of the Western world and they leave their own offspring to fend for itself.

He kicks a penguin on a unicycle which has stopped pedalling by his left foot, looks at Claudia defiantly, expectantly.

—I guess it's like a mirror, tries Claudia.—You know, when you stand so close you can't see your own reflection.

Adrian looks at her as if she's mad.

—I guess you know what you're talking about, he says dubiously.

—I'm talking about losing perspective, says Claudia earnestly.

—Like having your face so close to someone else's that they've got three eyes.

—Well, the Shrinks have four and they haven't used any of them, says Adrian, wilfully, obstinately.

—And now? says Claudia giving up on trying to be fair.

—Now they're a pillar of prescriptive strength, says Adrian bitterly.—Ha! Never happier than when they're tinkering around with drugs.

—Like parent, like son, says Claudia.

—Ha! says Adrian again but there is a gleam of appreciation in his tired eyes.

—Haven't got it quite right yet, of course, he says.—And it doesn't help when I drink, as they tell me ad nauseam.

—So you've known for how long and you haven't told me? says Claudia. She is indignant but more than that incredulous. Mostly, she would choose attention over secrets any day.

—Not everyone can wear their pain on their sleeve, Claud, says Adrian.—You have a special gift for that.

He lies flat on his back on the floor, ankle-deep in whirring, marching, rattling toys. He is a magician who orchestrates a hundred lives, only not his own.

—Stick with the uppers, he advises wearily.—Lithium's not great for the energy levels.

Claudia picks up Road Runner and watches its legs go nowhere. Pedalling thin air in true cartoon style.

—Aids, promise me one thing, she says, not looking at him.

—Maybe, he says.

—Promise me you won't jump, she says, very quickly so that she doesn't fall through the surface of Saturday night again.

There's a silence filled only with whirring clicking and humming.

—Aids! she says, desperately skimming.—Please!

—I don't make promises I can't keep, says Adrian in black-and-white movie style. Claudia looks at him, hoping to see a stage persona. She sees from his profile that he is Adrian, and he is serious. Her heart gives a small creak.

—How's this? says Adrian.

—Yes? says Claudia, holding her heart together and hoping.

—I promise I won't jump without asking you first, Adrian says. He turns his head sideways to look at her and there are tears in his eyes.

❧ *Haley*

Life can't stay monochrome forever, even if that's its usual state. Haley finds that the sun does sometimes shine, that it picks up water from the harbour and threads it on needles and weaves light through even her closed vision. People on the street, she notices, ignore her only if she keeps her eyes down, London-underground style. If she looks at them, she gets

—Hey, hi, gidday, and

—How's it going?

and she finds she can answer.

Her hostel is as grey as ever, people move in and move on, and she does not decorate her walls. But if she stands in the corner of her room and presses her head hard against the wardrobe door, she can see Rangitoto floating in the harbour. Looked at through narrowed eyes, the line of the window-frame could be a person on the rim of the crater; with a blink, the person could almost be waving.

—Haere mai Rang-i-to-to, she practises. But when she's in a hurry,

—How's it going, Robert, she says hopefully.

Can it be called irony or is it fate

Queen St. It baffles her. It's at the heart of the city but its footpaths, which seem as wide as motorways to Haley, are almost empty. Life doesn't happen here—the nerve-centre has shut down, leaving a semblance of life in the outer limbs. On pedestrian side streets, ant-workers swarm to money-machines, feed, file back into offices.

South Auckland, Kath tells Haley, is like another city in itself. There you can find street kids, skateboards, cheapskates, crime. Kath shudders: not her cup of tea. Haley looks at Kath's smooth face and wants to put deep scratches in its half-inch surface. Meanly, shamefully, she longs for violence to shatter Kath's complacent life the way it has her own.

Irony is a buzz word these days. It is used to mean sarcasm, or a pun, or some sarky comment thrown by a gameshow host. But, as the classical playwrights knew, true irony is dramatic irony. When the gods listen to human desires and turn them on their heads. When the watching stars deliberately misinterpret human intentions and point fumbling feet in a different direction altogether.

(*This is not what I meant!* characters cry when they get what they have wished for aloud. *This is not what I wanted!* as they tumble through the thin and mocking air.)

And so, when violence does arrive in Queen St, it is not Kath who bears the brunt. Haley has internally voiced the desire for violence and so it is Haley, who could already qualify for the lead in a Greek tragedy, who is tested once more.

It's a Saturday evening: long birdsong, long shadows, long day. Haley is sitting immovably at the counter with Hemingway's *A Moveable Feast*.

(Robert: *I might have deserted you but Hemingway has staying power!*)

She maintains a fierce look that has so far been successful at warning off customers. Kath has forbidden Haley to read at work, even when there is nothing to do; apparently it is imperative to look busy at all times. But Kath the dictator is not there, so Haley reads.

Saturday night, 7.30 pm. The door opens, closes, opens, closes. Haley reads Hemingway's description of the *death loneliness* which comes at the end of every wasted day. She thinks of the words that were in her head that morning, which she will be too tired to write down when she gets home. The desperation of the souvenir-hunter presses on the back of her neck. She feels the weight of useless clutter. Knows the oppressive nature of knick-knacks, the compulsion to spend money on them, the dread of returning to a room without them. Hemingway's words ring both true and irrelevant. Haley bites her lip.

The door opens, closes, and there is a new presence in the shop, a sharp smell of ammonia.

Haley breathes through her mouth, keeps reading.

—Hey! a voice says.

Haley hangs onto her fierce concentrated look, reads on.

—Hey! she hears again.

She looks up.

There's a woman standing at the side of the counter. Her hair is bleached to the colour of bone, she wears a bone pendant shaped like a fish-hook round her neck. (Haley has sold ten, twenty, sixty of these pendants since starting work here.) And what else? There's a gun in the woman's hand.

The room lurches. Haley's stool sways underneath her. An earthquake? But the woman hasn't moved and her gun is completely steady. Completely, steadily, aimed at Haley's head.

—This is a robbery, the woman says.

Haley stops thinking about crawling under the counter, starts thinking about lying under it instead. Lying dead. She opens her mouth but has no idea what to say, wishes she was the type to scream or cry because this would seem appropriate behaviour. Of course Kath's training manual, with its useful pages on fire, floods, and armed hold-ups, is out of reach, wedged under one leg of a wobbly table in the staffroom. Of course Haley hasn't read it.

Her smarting eyes refocus but the woman's still there.

—I don't want to hurt you, the woman says.—But I will if I have to, so do what I say.

There doesn't seem anything to say to this, either. Reflex action: Haley looks at her book. She sees that Hemingway is drinking Martinique rum and eating oysters, and she feels as if she might throw up.

—Open the till, the woman orders. Her collarbones are as sharp as her voice, and she hunches her thin shoulders around the gun.

Haley reaches inside her shirt for the key chain round her neck.

—Don't fuck with me! the woman says.

—I'm just getting the key, says Haley. She can hardly hear her voice over the loud swell in her ears, a tidal wave of blood.

—OK, the woman says suspiciously.—Open the drawer.

Haley opens it. She knows what she's going to see but still she looks, and hopes.

—Sixty dollars! the woman says in disbelief.

—I'm sorry! says Haley.

—Sixty fucken dollars, the woman snarls. She moves the gun so that it touches the skin behind Haley's ear.

(—The skin behind your ear is like paper-skin, says Robert.

He scratches it very quietly with his fingernail. All Halley's feeling rushes to this one place behind her ear.

—Halley's paper-skin, I'm leaving messages on your paper-skin, says Robert.

—Robert, help me

—Am I scratching too hard?

—Robert save me)

The gun is scratching on her thin, paper-skin. Its cold mouth searches along Haley's hairline and she waits for her skin to tear, for the contents of her skull to spew red on the glass counter.

—Where's the rest of it, bitch? the woman says. Her voice is getting louder, and the gun moves back and forth restlessly. Is it the woman's hand or Haley's head that's shaking? Haley can't tell.

—Kath, she did a pick-up, Haley says faintly.—Two hours ago.

—Don't fucking lie to me! shouts the woman.—Where's the rest of the fucking money?

—None, nowhere, Haley whispers.—The bank.

—What's that then? the woman says, looking towards the computer.

—Just the sales records, whispers Haley.

—Open it! the woman orders.—Open the fucking safe or I'll really hurt you.

—Please, it's a computer, Haley says.—Please.

—All this for sixty fucking bucks, the woman says. She grabs the hair at the back of Haley's head, pulls it back so far that Haley's throat creaks.

—Don't you ring the cops, the woman says. Her voice is hot on Haley's cheek.

—No, Haley says.

—Don't ring any fucking body, OK? says the woman.—If you do, I'm going to shoot you and anyone else out there, got it?

—Got it, whispers Haley.

Her head is let go, snaps forward. The woman strides to the door, looks right and left, and the door closes behind her. There is a sudden silence.

Haley doesn't know what to do. She feels as if she's in a bad melodrama, and that there should be a cut to another scene, but life keeps on running. She's at a loss. Any kind of action seems too much or too little. Would it be too, too strange to tidy the rugs after she's had a gun at her head? She looks to Hemingway but, left on the same page, he's had no choice, has just kept on drinking and smoking.

The stool is suddenly very high and too narrow, so Haley sits on the floor and lets the wall support her head. After some time, she looks up the front of the phone book because she doesn't know the emergency number, and she dials 111.

She gets taken up Queen St in a police car. People look sideways at her at traffic lights and she feels like a criminal. Suddenly handcuffs are cold on her wrists, and she hears the boom of a cell door. The red taste of panic sears her throat.

—You OK back there? the police woman says.—Not in shock?

—I'm fine, says Haley.

—Thanks, she adds, grateful for kindness. She holds on hard to the door handle with her left hand and sits on her right hand, but both hands still shake, exposing her as a liar. She is not OK at all.

They sail up the hill in the police car, but slowly because it's a Saturday night. Drunks, drugs, brawls, gay bashings. Haley is an island drifting in the middle of an alien weekend. She floats her head against the window. Even through her hair, the glass feels very hard and cool and suddenly the gun's there again. Quickly, she sits upright and doesn't lean back until they're at the police station.

How does she get inside? She doesn't know: just remembers warm outside air scented with jasmine, and then the chill smell of bureaucracy.

(Robert: Define the smell of bureaucracy!

Halley: Computer printouts, old filter coffee, uniforms, and an undertone of intimidation.)

She has smelt bureaucracy so often in the past few months that it almost makes her feel nostalgic. Concentrating hard on her breathing, she sits on a hard orange plastic chair. And after what might be half an hour, or a day and a night, they call her into an office.

—And you're sure that's everything you can remember? the guy says.

Haley looks at his moustache and wonders if he grew it to fit in, or if he was the moustache type before he joined the force.

—Oh, and a bone pendant, she says. She hesitates. Was the pendant in the cabinet in front of her, or around the neck behind the gun?

The cop is alert to minimal pauses.

—You positive about that? he says. The cords in his throat are fat with law-abiding blood. In a sickening flash, Haley remembers a pulse in a white throat, yellow hair, and a scroll of yellow-white bone.

—Yes, she says.—Definitely a carved bone pendant.

Her accent sounds precious after his thick vowels, marks her out as a prim foreigner in a bastion of Kiwiness. She looks nervously at him, waiting for **him** to mimic her.

—Anything else? he says **matter-of**-factly. His pen writes with sturdy upright strokes.

—No, that's all, she says. She feels so grateful to him that she drops her bag and her daily life cascades over the floor. Keys and Chapstick skid on lino. Bank statements and scraps of writing float more gently on the breath of gravity. Haley bangs heads with the cop, who's spotted something between his boots. He holds it out to her but his fingers are so big that she can't even see what it is.

—Film canister, he says.—Don't want to lose your memories, do you?

He smiles, drops the plastic container into her hand and his hand is dry and hard. She wants to ask him if she can sit there for a while and learn from him because he's impassive, unemotional, and he just goes on with his job as if it isn't born of disaster, violence, accident, and near-death. But

—Thanks, she says, and she stands up.

She walks out into the corridor holding her empty polystyrene coffee cup. Again, she doesn't know what to do and she despises herself for weakness. Behind her, she can see her past mapped out like an erratic sonar path. All she seems able to do is lurch from dilemma to dilemma. Around her are purposeful people who surge towards her and break like waves on the rock of her indecision.

Should she go back to work? Will Kath be waiting impatiently at the door with her keys in her hand?

—*For God's sake, Haley!* Kath is mouthing angrily.—*It's not like you've been hurt or anything.*

Is she expected to return? Is she expected to go home? Is an armed hold-up regarded as nothing in this land of rugby-heads and stoics? Or is she expected to be in shock?

She's expected to want to see Robert. Ostensibly, she's been given a choice, but she knows she's expected to say yes. In fact, the prospect scares her so much that her stomach twists. Yet she's on the train heading towards Robert's dead body so fast that it's too late to put the brakes on the whole thing. Her grey dread blurs with the drab countryside.

There's no one there to meet her at the station. Robert was always—was notoriously—late. Late to be born, late to mature, late to ask her on a first date.

—*Blame my parents,* he'd say

and it was quite possibly justified. The Lilleys are the type whose entrance is always preceded by an usher's torch. When Halley was invited to Edgeware for her first in-law dinner, she arrived at seven and the soup arrived at the table at twenty minutes to midnight.

Was it naive of her to think, as she did once, that events could be unique? That incidents occur once and once only, that change is implicit in their unreadable faces? She is much wiser now and, as clichéd as it sounds, sadder. All events are generic, she realises now, and so Robert's parents are late to the station. Why should it be any different just because there is now a permanent gap where their son used to be? Halley stands by herself, by a pillar, for twelve minutes. In other circumstances twelve minutes can be negligible: now they stretch so far, are so accommodating to her imagination, that she starts to shake. She will soon see the dead body of the only person she has ever really belonged to. She shivers—from cold? from fear?—and shrinks inside her coat.

Robert's parents may not have changed their long-term habits, but physically they seem altered. They look diminished, from internal or external cold. They sink into their car seats, talk in voices Halley can hardly hear.

He is there at home, waiting for them where they left him. In the piano room: new carpet, green-grey smell, scuff marks leading to where he lies, as if he has walked in there and laid himself down to rest. The setting seems appropriate: Halley has always associated grand pianos with coffins. Robert would have liked it, though this is almost certainly not why his parents have put him there. She'd like to have the energy to joke with him about it but she knows humour lies damaged, steeped in its own blood, somewhere in her past.

The chill aching in her throat, the germ-laden wind through the station, Robert's parents who are too dull with grief to talk to her. These things have taken her away from herself. She is a blank, she has nothing to say to Robert. Walking towards him, dragging her shoes like club feet, she just wants to get it over with.

She's heard the clichés: it's not the person you knew, there's nobody there, it's a husk. But when she looks between the insultingly unreal wood and the cheap satin, it's definitely Robert.

He's strangely pale, his eyelids are wrapped over pregnant eyes, there's a mutilated area on the left side of his head, which must have meant difficulties for the funeral assistant, but it's him. And now she does want to talk to him.

—Fuck you, Robert, she says.—Fuck you fuck you, you fuck.

She looks at his hands, which knew their way around a guitar, a curve of wood, her own hips, but were blasé, unfriendly, to a ladder of scaffolding last Tuesday morning at 10 am. The hands don't look apologetic or different, would probably do the same thing next Tuesday and leave her again.

—You stupid bastard! she says. She'd like to shock him into waking up, let him know how careless he's been. She's so angry at him for not changing beyond recognition, for still being there but no use to her.

There's a line of make-up on his chin like a thin smear of varnish, but his fingernails are clean. Alien.

—Thanks a lot, Robert, she says.

She stands for a while and feels so annoyed with him that she doesn't really feel like touching him. Finally, she touches his forehead with a grudging finger and realises. It's true, she's been talking to nobody. The head is concrete in the shade of a fence, it's the thick rubber of a glacial wetsuit. She had been planning to kiss him goodbye but too bad, he's already gone. She strides to the door without looking back, her shoes squeak in the hall, she strides to the kitchen.

Robert's father is making instant coffee.

—Want one? he says.

He takes the kettle off the stove and pours. He gives the cup to her and she sees that there is no coffee in it, he has forgotten the coffee so she drinks hot water.

—Want something to eat? Robert's father says. There is food on every surface, so much food that it looks like the set for a cooking show. Rock-cakes, scones, sponges, sandwiches. Although she's sure she's not supposed to want anything, she feels hungry. She's sure she's supposed to be feeling altogether different, but who can she ask? There's only one person who could help her with this, and he's given up on her.

—Yeah, OK, she says.—I'm starving, actually.

She cuts butter so thick it could be cheese and eats two date scones and an egg sandwich and feels sick.

Is New Zealand a particularly violent place? While Haley stands at the water-cooler and drinks cup after cup of indecision, the Saturday night city splinters around her. There is so much blood, more than she thinks could be visible on arms and legs that are still moving.

Haley is not used to dealing with bloodshed. After all, archaeologists need to deal only with the dried skeletons of the past. Both the large scale of her subject and its reserve had appealed to her. In the endless white deserts of history, around the huge pyramids, she had found space to roam, while the great width of years between that world and this prevented uncomfortable intimacy. England, country of her childhood, is one of subdued moist grey flesh; but her ideal country is ridged with dry bones and leaves only clean dust on her shoes. And now? She is standing by the water cooler in a primal country of aggression and visible destruction. She looks into blue water, sways before a red tide.

—Are you OK?

It's a Maori guy, or part-Maori. She can only just see him through the bloody haze in her eyes.

—No, she says.—Not really.

For the first time she has admitted it: she is not OK. It is as much of a relief as a blister bursting on her heel; she feels the infected fluid of solitude begin to weep out of her.

—Here, sit, he says.

And then she's sitting and he holds her cup on a slant so water falls on her knee.

—Sorry, he says. He's not at all awkward though.

—Feeling any better? he says.

—Yes, I think so, she says.—I just felt a bit faint.

—You're pregnant, aren't you? he says.

His hand touches her belly, lightly. She sees his finger as clearly as if it's been captured in a photo, dark skin with a row of little white notches like knife-marks along the edge of his nail.

—Well, yes! she says.—How could you tell? I'm not even showing.

—Old Maori instinct, he says with a smile.—Sometimes we just know.

Haley's eyes are no longer glazed with red, she can see white, brown, blue again. Behind the guy, she sees someone else standing, waiting for the return of his attention. A small slim girl, with eyes like the sea, and she's crying completely silently. Glossy tears, slipping over her high cheeks. Her bones are like a bird's

(Robert: You have bird bones too Halley!)

but this girl's are delicate, sparrow-bones, whereas Haley is a hawk.

—Oh God, I'm sorry, Haley says.—I'm holding you up.

—He's killed himself, the girl cries.—I didn't help him I didn't help him and now he's dead.

—We don't know that yet, the guy says. But he puts a hand— that same white-scarred, quick finger—up to her shiny hair.

—We know it probably isn't, he says, smoothing her, calming her.

—Now, you sure you're OK? he says to Haley.

—Yes, go, says Haley.—Go and find out about your friend.

The girl gives Haley one incurious look and then looks away again, at the back of her own tears. Her eyes are full of her own certain tragedy, have no space for other people's.

No space and no inclination, Haley thinks. She watches the quiet guy and the glossy girl go, watches them weave towards the enquiries desk through the battlefield of an average Saturday night. And suddenly anger is sweeping up her throat, filling her mouth with bitterness, startlingly strong. Because Haley doesn't believe in accidents any more. After Robert, she has come to believe in carelessness and stupidity, and so she doesn't see victims walking past her, all she sees are avoidable casualties of car chases, gang warfare, bigotry and intolerance.

She's furious at people who gamble with their bodies. She's furious at the girl for rushing towards tragedy without even knowing if it's coming for her. Most of all, Haley's furious at Robert. What was he doing leaving her in a world where she gets guns pointed at her head?

Her fury is fuel, gets her out the door and onto a bus to the suburbs. Kath's probably deducting time off her wages right now but Haley is furious and is going home.

She's angry, she's very angry, but it's nothing compared with Robert. He is so angry that he keeps working while he speaks to Halley, which is a rule he's never broken until now.

—You what? he is saying.—You what?

—You're repeating yourself, says Halley coldly.

—Because I can't believe it, I can't make myself believe it, says Robert.

—Well, believe it, says Halley angrily.—I read it, OK?

—But you knew how I'd feel about that, says Robert quietly.

—Yeah, well, I had to find out, shrugs Halley.

—And now you have, says Robert.—Feel good, does it?

—Of course not! shouts Halley.—It makes me feel like fucking shit, OK?

—I'm not going to apologise, says Robert.

He keeps carving but his blade is moving all over the place, scar on scar on scar.

—But you lied to me! shouts Halley.—You lied!

—Yes I did, because it was so irrelevant, says Robert.—There are some things it's better not to know.

—You told me it was instant! shouts Halley.—Why should I believe anything you say now?

—Believe what you want, says Robert. His hand is shaking but he won't put the knife down, he goes over and over the neck of the figure he's carving as if he's stroking it but it's not gentle. It's not Robert.

It's not Robert, it's someone else who met Halley at a party and didn't like her enough to remember her. It's not Halley any more, she's just gone and lost herself somewhere between the pages of Robert's diary, so now she's a girl with average looks and a solid body who sometimes thinks so much that she doesn't say a lot.

—You thought I was plain, didn't you? she accuses.

—I didn't think that, says Robert. His words fall like ice cubes, slow, hard, separate. He chips away at the wood as if he hates it.

—No, you didn't think I was anything! shouts Halley.—You didn't think about me at all!

—For Christ's sake, Halley, says Robert.—What does it matter what I thought then?

His voice is so quiet that Halley wants to smash it and now, finally, he puts down his knife.

—Oh, it doesn't matter at all, says Halley.—Nothing matters.

Her own voice is standing on the edge of tears and she yanks it back.

—Our whole relationship's built on a lie, she shouts.—You lying fuck!

—Fine, I'm a lying fuck, says Robert.—Now get out. Go on, just get out.

He picks up a chisel and tries for the wooden shoulder of his sculpture but gets his hand instead. Blood comes from the webbing between his fingers but he has no expression on his face. Or maybe it hasn't had time to get there yet.

—You *still* don't care, do you! Halley shouts.—I'll make you bloody care!

She steps forward and snatches up the small carved figure, aims it at the metal clamp on the side of the bench.

—No you don't, you bitch, says Robert.—No!

His hand grabs hers and holds it down against her side. She can't move.

—Let go of me, she says angrily. Through his wrist, up his arm, she can feel his whole body shaking.

—It's you, Halley, he says.

—What? she says.

—It's you, you stupid bitch, he says. He unwraps her hand from the carving. It's a nude. It's her. It's beautiful.

She's not going to cry but she has to look at the floor for a long time. Robert puts her smaller self back on the bench, keeps working on the curve of the back.

—I'm sorry, she says.

He doesn't answer.

—Robert, she says. She goes to him and puts her arms around him from behind. Her head presses into the dark skin of his shoulder where it most belongs.

—That's all very well, Halley, he says,—but look what you've made me do to your arse.

Claudia

There is a sometime hammering in Claudia's head which she hesitates to describe as anger, for this seems too specific a term for it. Something is working on her, though, so that she feels both incomplete and full of restless significance at the same time. Sifting through possible reasons, she settles on Diane. At least, she feels it is something connected with Diane which is making her feel unconnected. They seem to talk from opposite sides of the fence, always.

—Adrian's had it too good for too long, Diane is saying now.— He should just get on with it.

—But Diane, says Claudia,—that is so, so—

There are too many endings to her sentence, so many that she can't finish. What is it? So unfair, so narrow-minded, so simplistic, so *Diane*. The attitude that life is always worth living is beginning to seem strange to her and she looks at Diane, decking the living-room out with celebratory balloons, as if she is an alien. Diane, who deals only in the mechanics of life, who grasps babies by the head and wrestles them into the world without thinking they might be better off left where they are.

—One in five Kiwis have a mental illness, Claudia says. She had read this before Adrian's revelation, had remembered it but not registered it until now. Now she walks the supermarket aisles and looks for desperation behind every face, sees tremors in the hands that carry baskets and work the checkouts.

—Oh Claudia, that's a load of crap put out by private shrinks, says Diane.—Trying to justify their BMWs to the rest of the health service.

She continues to hang bright paper streamers that are completely incongruous to the conversation. She hammers away happily and Claudia clenches her teeth with every blow.

—And *that's* the sort of attitude that leads to people committing suicide, says Claudia. For a second the motorway opens up beneath her feet, and then it's dirty shagpile carpet again.

—Uh-huh, says Diane from the top of the stepladder.—Pass me the end of that banner, would you, hon?

Claudia looks sourly at the message about to be blazoned across the living room. WELCOME HOME! It is a lie because this is not Giles's home but then Diane has never been one for subtle nuances. In a card sitting on the mantelpiece she has written *Great to have you back Giles—we've missed you. Love Mum.*

Claudia has not missed Giles, and Diane is not his mother but only ended up with Garry who already had Giles with someone else. Claudia holds Diane's ankles steady but really she feels like shaking them, rocking Diane's eternal composure, knocking her from her complacent stepladder. Step—it's the operative word. Diane is Giles's stepmother, Giles is Claudia's stepbrother; and the whole family is out of step with each other.

She imagines the scene lying in wait for her tonight. Giles of the ginger eyelashes, hugging her and smelling of damp wetas. Diane getting teary on sherry. Giles eating with his mouth open and talking about burnt orange regions of the Australian outback and dark green regions of the South Island. Claudia doesn't want to hear about anywhere lit only by starlight. She wants spotlights on Parisian catwalks, strobes in the clubs of Berlin, and sunrises from a spire in Prague.

And there it is again, the familiar swooping lurch in her stomach, a sense of dislocation so strong it's as if she's falling. She thinks back to that Saturday night, to the whining traffic under her feet and the doors of Accident and Emergency sealing them into a nightmare. Although Diane is so close that Claudia can see the veins in her ankles, she might as well be on the other side of the world. She is no help to Claudia who sways, casts desperately around in her mind for something solid, and can only think: it is time to go. It has been time for weeks now, and she can't wait any longer for fate to take a hand.

Diane says something.

—What? says Claudia distractedly.

—Are you going to work later? says Diane from a long way away.

And amidst the slipping rushing scree of panic, Claudia can see a secure foothold. She will return to it.

—Not till Monday, she says. A smile of relief, of discovery, flickers on her mouth.

—I wish Giles was staying with us, says Diane, a bit plaintively.—He always goes straight to Elaine.

—Well, she is his mother, says Claudia, pinching her finger in the elbow of the ladder.

—So am I, says Diane indignantly.—So is Suzanne.

It is true, Giles has not one but three mothers. Elaine is his birth mother, Suzanne his current mother, and Diane his ex-stepmother. Not bad for an insignificant ginger boy. Claudia, by far the more beautiful and striking, feels far less fortunate. Still, she has one thing going for her: she is an opportunist, who has just seen an opportunity.

Monday morning

is a good time to launch a new campaign. The weekend has been full of Giles, crammed with bush tales and a feeling of mateship, a veritable Henry Lawson fest. Claudia, striding down High St, takes a deep breath of cosmopolitan air. Fumes, coffee, wet pavement, new clothes. She feels energised.

—Got a new flatmate yet? she asks Leith casually.

—Nah, the band's trying out a new drummer, says Leith,—so once that's sorted I'll deal with the flat thing.

—Well, if you don't want to advertise, says Claudia, offhandedly.

—Claudia, there are customers out here, bellows Myrtle.

—I'm looking for a place, says Claudia to Leith. Before she can hear a verdict on her domestic needs, she has to leave the kitchen and tend to other people's gastronomic ones.

—Two pumpkin coriander fritters, one vegetarian sandwich, she tells Leith.—And I could come round and have a look at the room this week.

—Yeah, well, says Leith.—Maybe.

He sticks his head in the fridge, bends his head over his fritters. Claudia leans on the bench, waiting for him to lose the preoccupied chef act and realise what she's offering.

—How much is it? she says, leaning beautifully.

—The landlord's talking about putting up the rent, says Leith in a distracted voice.

—And do you normally split bills down the middle? asks Claudia interestedly.

—Look, I haven't decided if I want a girl, says Leith. He brushes back his hair with his elbow.

Oh. But this is Claudia! Claudia garnishes the fritters with confidence and fills carafes with her clear, sparkling irresistible self. She decides to give Leith a day or two to acclimatise.

It is Monday a week on. Things appear to be the same, except Leith is cooking paua patties instead of pumpkin fritters, and Claudia is one week surer that this move is the answer. It doesn't matter what the room's like. She wants to wake up with new streets running in her veins.

The surface of the café is calm, one couple has made ripples and has been fed and subdued. Claudia dives into the topic that is currently interesting her most: her future.

—Diane's driving me crazy, she says in a confidential tone.— Have you thought any more about me moving in?

The walls of her new room are painted chalk yellow, one corner is bursting with dahlias. She is hanging her array of hats off the corners of doors.

—Oh yeah, says Leith.—That.

Claudia waits to hear when the next sector of her life will start: tomorrow, the weekend, the end of the month.

—Look, Clawd, says Leith. His voice rushes out like a petrol overflow on the forecourt.

—What? says Claudia. She feels a little bit suspicious, knows it isn't a good sign when a sentence is started with Look and then your name.

—It's not that I don't want you, says Leith hurriedly.—I've just found someone else.

—Huh, says Claudia.—OK, so you decided on a guy.

She shrugs in her best Gallic way. This is disappointing and annoying but explicable. She has lost in the battle of the sexes.

For a guy who jay-walks in front of yellow buses and dices daily with vats of boiling oil, Leith looks a little uneasy.

—Actually, he says,—it's a girl. She had nowhere to go and I thought it was the right thing to do.

—But Leith, you KNEW I wanted a room, cries Claudia. She abandons the French cool and gives way to impassioned Italian.

—Well, there are other rooms in Auckland, says Leith reasonably.—I'll help you look if you want.

Claudia doesn't want, she doesn't want him to help her into a flat where he isn't. That is really not the point at all.

Haley

Ever since she arrived, Haley has been thinking she recognises people: this is her mind trying to find a home, tricking itself, tripping itself up too many times. Now that she sees the Maori guy from the police station in her shop, she just stares at him. She knows it's him, but won't let herself be taken in again.

—Can I help you with anything? she says. Even to her London ears she sounds unfriendly.

—I met you in the cop shop, didn't I? he says.—Last Saturday?

—Oh yes, says Haley.—That's right.

She sounds very falsely English, as if she's out of a Merchant Ivory film and wearing a muslin dress. His T-shirt is ripped under one arm.

—How you doing then? he says.—Feeling any better?

She feels hot all over, would rather talk about anything than her physical state.

—But your friend? she says quickly.—Did it all turn out all right?

His calm face is swept for a moment by shadows.

—Yeah, it wasn't what we thought, he says obliquely.—She can be a bit of a drama queen sometimes.

—Oh, says Haley.—That's good. I mean that it wasn't serious.

—Though I do think there's a bit of a problem there, muses the guy, looking past her at the struggles of people she doesn't know.

Haley isn't sure what to say next, feels the familiar weight on her tongue and struggles with it.

—So what brings you in here? she says in a rush.

He looks a bit surprised, refocuses on her, and swings his pack up onto the counter.

—I'm doing the rounds, he says.—I was wanting to sell some stuff.

Stuff? Haley looks at him, waits for cocaine to spill across Kath's shining counter, waits for cops to spill into the shop. The sight of his hands with their knife-marks is linked with blue uniforms and the sound of crying. The hands pull soft leather pouches out of the pack and spread a body of bone and greenstone across the counter.

—You're a carver! she exclaims.

—Just pendants, he says modestly.—Just a sideline.

But she can tell they are a part of him just by the way he touches them, by the way he spreads them out over the glass with both assurance and respect. She has avoided looking at pendants since the hold-up, has hurried over them with her eyes, skimming the surface of memories in case the shaking begins again. But these pendants dissociate themselves from violence, hold in their form the quiet secrets of stones.

They look back at Haley and return her old self to her. Some are the colour of mummies, some the colour of sand, and some are a deep green that cools her hot mind. As she smooths one with her finger, something shifts inside her, and suddenly she's released from the desperation of her routine: shop followed by hostel followed by shop, day after night after day. Looking at the curves this guy has created, she wants to tell him how the shutter has lifted from behind her eyes but she doesn't think she can find the words. For the moment, it's enough just to feel it.

There's a small not uncomfortable silence, then

—You need to talk to Kath, she says practically.—She's the manager.

—Oh, I thought you were, he says.

—No, I'm just a minion, she says.—And Kath's in Hamilton today, buying.

—Well that's irony, he says.—When I'm here to sell.

—Is it? she says.—Irony I mean. I'm never sure.

—You sound just like someone else I know, he says with a laugh.—Ironically challenged, both of you.

—Oh really? she says politely, inanely.

—Oh well, he says.—Better get on.

He gathers the stuff up. She looks at his fingers with a feeling that is very like recognition. She feels slightly alarmed at the thought of the door closing behind him, and Queen St closing around him.

—If you want to leave some of it, she says,—I could ring you.

—Yeah? he says. He sounds doubtful.

—I can almost guarantee there won't be two armed robberies in a week, she suggests, humbly.

He laughs.

—I just don't want you to stick your neck out for me, he says.— Your manager, is she OK?

—No, she's a bitch, says Haley.—Why don't you leave some samples?

—Where are you from? he says.—Don't make me guess, I'm not that good at accents.

—From London, she says. She looks out the hot window and

sees Camden Rd in the rain. Awnings filled with water, looping like Victorian curtains.

—So you've come over here to escape the winter, he states.

Haley sees entrances to the underground plastered with red and yellow fliers. Tired feet slipping on fast corners, tripping over tramps as if they're part of the pavement.

—Yeah, sort of, she says.—When I left it was minus eight.

—Christ! he says.—Good move then.

She thinks of the chill inside her which has remained untouched by subtropical temperatures.

—I guess so, she says.

—Have you got a good place? he says, packing his leather pouches easily, quickly.

—Well, I'm in a backpackers' actually, Haley says.

—You don't want, he starts.—You don't want.

—Want what? she says.

—It's just I've got a room going, he says.—My flatmate's moving.

A possible life swings open in front of her, wide windows and all she has to do is step out. Then the hard swell of her stomach against the counter reminds her. The windows swing on their hinges, bang shut.

—But you won't want, she says unhappily.

—Want what? he says.

—The baby, she says.—Remember? You won't want a baby.

He doesn't deny, doesn't confirm. All he says is

—A baby shouldn't be born in a hostel.

His face is perfectly serious. He stands there with his hands in his pocket, offering her a foothold. She steps out cautiously.

—Well, I could have a look, she says.—And you should think.

—I have thought, he says.—I hadn't forgotten about the baby when I offered, I remembered from last week.

—Oh yeah, the Maori instinct? she says, smiling. She feels the British paving on her face finally cracking.

—Maori crap! he says.—I've got four older sisters and I could tell by the way you looked, sort of peaky and sickly.

—Thanks very much! she says.

—Come and have a look anyway, he suggests.

—Well, give me the address then, she says.

—Give me your name, he says.

—Give me yours, says Haley.

She gives him the first month's rent the day she moves in. She offers him bond as security, but he says no.

—It's OK, Haley, I know you won't do a runner, he says.—Mainly because you've got nowhere to run to.

—Oh, thanks for reminding me, she says.

She hasn't told him, but he senses, that she is dispossessed. Now at least she has a room to call her own. It's dark because it's at the side of the house, two feet away from a concrete bank. It still smells of boy's clothes. It's smaller than her room at the hostel, it's dirtier. But it's cheap. And it's hers.

She doesn't mind living in a cave, actually, and she likes Grafton's sloping valley sides. Sometimes the width of the sky in New Zealand makes her feel like an agoraphobic, she looks up for roof-lines that stretch an entire street instead of gapping like some kid's teeth. Now, for the first time since she has arrived, she feels protected. She can lie between tight night sheets and think of Russian dolls: in a gully in a street in a cottage in a room, in a bed in a Haley in a womb.

At the centre, safely, the girl-boy.

On the third morning she pulls up the blind, looks for concrete wall, comes face to face with a sun. Its painted mouth curves slightly but its eyes turn up at the ends like questions. She's never believed that people laugh when they're by themselves—her laughter is almost as rare as her crying. Now she laughs, and then she goes looking for Leith, creator of light.

In the kitchen: bowl with mosaic of cornflakes, plate with moustache of crumbs, chair without Leith. She doesn't have his number at work—doesn't know him well enough to ring him even if she did—so she can't thank him. Her English feet, accustomed to central heating, are getting cold on the bare lino so she takes them back into her room. Then she stands for a while in the smile of her private sun which is backed by a cloud of grey concrete.

Leith says he's always wanted an excuse to graffiti the wall.

—And now you can tell them back home, Leith says,—that the sun really does shine 24 hours a day here.

He doesn't ask her who she has back home, why she left them, or what she's going to do when she becomes two instead of one. He just lets her get quietly bigger and live in the present. With him she can ditch her past and forget herself.

—Leith Lethe, she says.—The river of forgetfulness.

—You gonna cross my palm with silver, then? he says.

There must be some things he doesn't know but if so she hasn't found them yet. He knows how to work a story and a loaf of rye bread, can tune a car or a guitar, can talk or be silent.

Out the back of 402B there's a square of grass like a green picnic rug, and sometimes Haley lies out there while Leith plays tunes on the dustbin lids. But she prefers sitting on the front steps where there is also bright green grass but imitation, not real.

—It's more restful, don't you think, says Leith.—We can sit and watch the grass not growing.

From these steps there is a view of Grafton Bridge. The bridge stretches over roads buildings trees like a large hand, cars speed like flies across its knuckles. When Haley's working an early shift, she gets home in the late afternoon, sits on astroturf, and watches the heads marching home from work. Though this is not so restful, because at this time the low light glints remindingly on the struts of the bridge. Rows of heads caught in concrete, necks trapped in wire, steel skeletons. And then the bridge no longer looks solid but dangles dangerously over the motorway, and the fake grass starts to scratch Haley's legs and she has to go inside.

She is getting better, though. Sometimes she can look down from a height without the ground detaching itself from gravitational forces and flying up to hit her in the face. It happens less often now that she wakes in the night with her hands clawing at the bright and useless air.

❧ *Claudia*

Recently, more and more, Claudia has felt as if she is floating. Yet it is not a restful kind of float, it is more a free-fall in which she senses a violent or tragic end. It is an eerie feeling, a mental and emotional feeling that sometimes translates itself into the physical. A couple of times she has stumbled in the street and this is not like Claudia, light of foot and often light of heart.

Is there more in a name than letters of the alphabet?

In the meantime, there are smaller thorns in Claudia's side. Remember Heath? Well, he's still around. But now he stays in her life and her mind mainly because assonance is an underhand route to proximity. *Heath* sounds like *Leith*: an aural connection that lends him a saving grace.

This is the thing: Heath's name is an echo, a nearly-but-not-quite there. Because of the seductive power of sound, he has the air of potential perfection. Heath sounds like Leith, who is perfection personified.

Heath may come second in Claudia's savage heart, but he's first in the alphabet. There are only three letters between Heath and Leith, but the chasm between them is growing by the day. Heath remains on ground level, available for walking over at certain specified times. Leith, ostensibly within reach for more time on more days, drifts further from Claudia's outstretched hands. As she watches him rise gently upwards like a hot-air balloon, she feels something approaching helplessness.

Claudia is fucking Heath, lusting Leith. She is entangled with a flawed healer of bodies, admires a maker of perfect scones.

Claudia begins to lose control

Driving through Mt Eden on her way to work, Claudia sees a wheel rolling past her. She starts to laugh and keeps laughing until she realises it's her wheel.

Next she realises the need for an immediate decision but this is taken out of her hands by the laws of physics. Her car hits the traffic island, close-shaves the grass, merges with the merge sign. The damage is major but more major still is what it signifies for Claudia. She has just become a victim.

This is a strange and transforming moment for her. Diane has always droned, *No gain without pain,* and Claudia has had gain for twenty-odd years. Now the pay-off begins. As she lurches from the car, her hair gets caught in the seat-belt, which is caught in the door. A small coin-size patch of hair is torn from her scalp. Her right leg acquires double-lane scratches from the crumpled door.

Standing there adorned with blood, she learns a couple of lessons fast. That hair the colour of a well-made latte doesn't protect you from the deterioration of mechanical things. That skin the texture of molten caramel doesn't come with a lifetime guarantee. And that, under stress, she cries as easily in front of strangers as she does in front of friends.

Phone calls, tow-trucks, and other tedious things follow so that she's an hour late for work. She anticipates Myrtle's reaction with tiredness, and Leith's not at all. But

—You OK? Leith says as soon as she stumbles in the door.

She's gratified to find that her recent disfigurements (torn hair and skin, rumpled composure) have a use after all. She props her liquid legs up against the sink while she ties on her apron.

—Had a bit of a car accident, she says.

—Clawd! Leith says.—What happened?

He comes over and touches her shoulder with his floury hands.

—It's nothing, she says. She sniffs. Leith's hand moves to her arm, leaving white comet-dust on her skin.

—D'you think you should work today? Leith says.

—God, yes! Claudia says. She's appalled at the thought of losing eight hours of Leith-time, and she's appalled that she's so appalled.

—What about getting home? Leith asks.—Is your car in the garage?

—Yeah, sniffs Claudia. Her new role has far more potential than seemed possible two hours ago, on a traffic island beside a three-wheeled Mazda.

—I thought they'd just serviced your car, says Leith.—Bit ironic.

—Is it? says Claudia, uncomprehendingly.

—I'll give you a lift after work, offers Leith.

—But it's out of your way, protests Claudia, weakly.

—It's OK, says Leith.

And it is. For the rest of the week, until she can afford to pay for a new tyre, she rides home from work behind Leith. He takes the corners so low that her feet scrape the ground. And the friction in her feet is transferred to her head, where a quiet plan is forming.

Universal truths

Let's face it. Being strong has got Claudia nowhere. Being proactive in a hot kitchen has merely left her out in the cold. As her feet swing low against dusty summer roads, she realises: it is sometimes an advantage to be vulnerable.

And so (she decides) she will sidle on the approach, will achieve through subtlety, will get what she needs through being needy.

And her feet dip and swoop, low behind Leith's, and sparks fly from the hot wheels.

Progress

Having been born with the lean muscled legs of a lioness, Claudia now tames them. She no longer strides around work but treads lightly on the lino as if it is a beach of transparent shells. She has strong, long-fingered hands but she asks Leith to open pickle jars and lift the ham-slicer. He does this for her, quietly. But he never offers. Her goal for February is to hear him offer.

Her hair is also affected by development plans. It is a convenient type for redecorating: high-gloss so it will always look finished, yet pale enough for a foundation colour. She trawls through Megan's paint charts.

—This! she says, and she points.

—Aubergine? says Megan dubiously.—But Claudia, that's too dark for you.

—You mean it'll make my skin look pale? says Claudia.

—Right, says Megan.

—Great, says Claudia.

—Can't we go with grape? pleads Megan.

—Oh OK, says Claudia in resignation.—Just don't fuck it up.

And it is a success. Even with grape, she looks successfully frail.

And regress

—Has something happened to your hair Clawd? asks Leith.

—Well, it didn't just *happen*, she said.—I wanted it done.

—Pretty big change, says Leith. He stands with his hands in the mixing bowl and looks at her.

—D'you like it? says Claudia confidently.

Leith plunges his hands into the middle of his bread dough. He kneads silently.

—Leith? says Claudia, less certainly.

—I heard you, he says.—I was just deciding what to say.

—Oh great! says Claudia. She forgets that her new voice is low and slow, hears it soar treacherously.

—Hey, don't get upset, says Leith.—I mean, it doesn't matter what I think.

—It fucking does!—doesn't, says Claudia. She begins to pace the kitchen dangerously.

—Watch out for the oil, warns Leith. He moves the open tin out of her path, puts flour on his hands, divides his dough into six strands.

—I just thought I'd try something new, that's all, says Claudia. She looks at herself in the mixing bowl and gives a start.

—Change is good, she says angrily.

—Yeah, sometimes, agrees Leith.

—You don't have to agree with me! says Claudia. She squeezes half a bottle of Palmolive into the sink, swishes the water around viciously.

—OK, I won't then, says Leith. He starts to plait his bread slowly and neatly.

—I liked your hair before, that's all, he says.—The colour of wholemeal flour.

Claudia says nothing, angrily.

—Did you know this is Challah bread? Leith offers.

—No, says Claudia.

—Jewish, says Leith.—Traditionally made on Fridays.

—Fascinating, says Claudia bitterly. As if she could care about the conventions of baking! Her hair is semi-permanent and her unrequited passion seems set to linger for an equally lengthy time.

—It's the bread of peace, says Leith seemingly irrelevantly.—Should always be broken by hand, never with a knife.

Claudia looks at him. She has never felt more warlike. But she forces herself to remain calm. Anger never won hearts.

Claudia and Leith regress still further

Even at first glance her daily stars look unpromising but she scans them anyway, out of habit.

> **Your horoscope today:** You will spend the day craving attention. Leos need an audience and often feel they exist only through other people's adulation. To paraphrase Descartes, 'I perform, therefore I am.' Keep a close eye on your insecurity.

—How's the new flatmate working out? Claudia asks. She is being deliberately mature.

—She's great thanks, says Leith. He looks surprised and Claudia is pleased. It is always an advantage to surprise someone with an enquiry, even if it is born from insincerity.

—You should come round and meet her one night, says Leith.

Claudia thinks this is taking maturity and insincerity a bit far. She smiles distantly and picks up a tray of scones.

—Found a flat yet? says Leith helpfully.

—No, says Claudia stiffly.

—Clawd, I'm sorry about all that shit, says Leith.—I just didn't think it would work out, you and me flatting together.

Claudia stiffens. She had thought it was a matter of gender, then of situation. Now she finds it's personality.

—Well thanks, she says, forgetting to be meek.—You've made it clear you think I'd be the flatmate from hell.

Leith shakes his head. His hair falls irritatingly, delectably, over his face.

—Don't take it so personally, Clawd, he says.—I just think we wouldn't be compatible.

This is worse.

—And you and That Girl are? says Claudia. (In fact she knows Haley's name, but she prefers not to.)

—She's pretty quiet, says Leith.—She's been having a rough time, I think.

—Oh, has she! says Claudia.—And I haven't?

She picks up a bread roll and starts tearing it savagely into tiny bits. Leith's handiwork, Leith's flesh. She tears, she rips.

—Well, you're OK at Diane's, aren't you? says Leith.—I know you don't like it that much, but you're not seriously unhappy, are you.

He doesn't finish with a question mark. Quietly, he removes the bread roll from Claudia's agitated hands.

—How the fuck would you know? says Claudia in a tragic voice.—No one knows what goes on behind the scenes in someone else's life.

—Honestly, Clawd, says Leith.—Sometimes you act like you're Anna Karenina or something.

—It's all right for you! says Claudia.—Growing up with all your sisters, people to talk to all the time, one big happy family.

—You would've hated it, says Leith.—Having to share everything all the time.

—Are you implying that I'm selfish? asks Claudia. She doesn't know if this is what he's implying but right now it suits her to be indignant.

—Well, you have to admit you like things your own way, says Leith mildly.

For a moment Claudia feels satisfied, then she realises Leith has actually insulted her.

—Only because I've been deprived in other ways, she says angrily.

—So you're an only child, shrugs Leith.—So you got lonely sometimes.

—*And* I'm adopted, says Claudia.

—Well, that's nothing to be ashamed of, says Leith.

—You know nothing about me! says Claudia very loudly.—All you see is the end result, you don't know what I've been through to get here!

—Maybe you should stop shouting, says Leith,—or Myrtle will make you go and wipe tables.

Although this advice has the ring of truth about it, Claudia ignores it.

—You see me as some self-sufficient chick with attitude, don't you? she cries.—With one suitably modern parent.

—Umm, not exactly, says Leith.

—Well, I've got news for you, Leif, I mean Leith! shouts Claudia.—I'm as needy as the next person.

—No kidding, says Leith. He raises his eyebrows.

—You go and live with this drifty girl just because you feel sorry for her, says Claudia.—Why the fuck don't you feel sorry for me?

—I'm starting to, says Leith. There is a half-smile on his face but he is listening politely, and this appeases Claudia.

—Well good! she says uncertainly.—Because, you know, Leith, I *have* had tragedy in my life and I really think it's messed me up.

—Claudia, there are things called tables out here, says Myrtle, putting her sarcastic head round the door.

—In a minute, Myrtle! says Claudia. She steps closer to Leith.

—I haven't told anyone this, she says in a low quavery voice. She looks sideways at Leith, but he now looks pleasingly serious so she goes on.

—I haven't told anyone, she repeats,—but I think I was a twin. I'm absolutely sure I had a twin who died at birth.

Leith looks slightly sceptical, raises a quizzical eyebrow.

—Yes, I read an article about it, insists Claudia,—and it suddenly hit me that that's what's been wrong all my life.

Leith looks annoyingly disbelieving and Claudia elaborates.

—I've had this deep feeling of loss for so long, she says.—A deep loss, deep inside me.

—Y'know what, I think everyone has that, says Leith.

—Do you? says Claudia, intrigued.

—Claudia! Get a move on! shouts Myrtle through the wall.

—Yes, it's called the human condition, says Leith dryly.

Claudia stares at him angrily. She feels like hitting him.

—Think what you like! she says.—All I wanted was for you to realise that I'm not invulnerable.

—Oh, I do realise that, says Leith.—Invincible maybe, but not invulnerable.

—But you still go and give your flat to some sad girl when you knew I needed it, cries Claudia. She has suddenly remembered what she was originally angry about.

—She does need it, says Leith,—more than you do.

He wipes his hand across his face in a tired way.

—You don't know what I need! says Claudia angrily.

—Claudia, get out here NOW! bellows Myrtle.

—You don't know what I need, repeats Claudia.

—Neither do you, Claudia, says Leith quietly.—Neither do you.

🌿 *Haley and Claudia*

There's something on at Quel Fromage on Saturday, Leith tells Haley. The place has been booked out by the French Bakery.

—They want a Kiwi-style work do, he says.

—So they go to a café with a French name! says Haley.

—And they want French bread and cheeses, says Leith.—They don't see the joke, though.

—I'm impressed that you can, actually, says Haley.—Don't New Zealanders only laugh at people falling over?

—And this from a Brit! says Leith.—Where the top-rating TV programme is *Best Home Videos of the Bourgeoisie!*

—Is not! denies Haley.—Actually it's *Supermarket Sweep.*

—What do they sweep? asks Leith.

—They run up and down the aisles of national television

hunting for toilet cleaner, says Haley severely.—It's sophisticated entertainment.

—Sounds like it, says Leith.—So why did you leave all that behind and come to a cultural desert like this?

Suddenly the joking has stopped. Leith's question sounds more serious than Haley wants and it puts her off her breakfast. She puts down her half-eaten toast, tilts so far back on her chair that she's looking at the ceiling, and back-pedals through the conversation to safety.

—OK, so maybe you Kiwis get the joke *sometimes*, she says. Her voice sounds way too quick; it's like a runaway trolley and she drags it back.

Leith says nothing.

—Maybe you're less like the Americans and more like us, she continues airily. The left chair leg is starting to crack so she rocks forward and looks at the wall instead of the ceiling. She knows Leith's looking at her hard, but all he says is

—*The Simpsons* are US-born.

—True, she acknowledges.

—*Seinfeld* was created by Americans, he says.

—OK, says Haley,—so there are at least five Harvard graduates capable of irony.

She knows this capitulation is far too hasty to be believable. She knows Leith knows she's avoiding more than a debate, and she forces herself to look at him. He leans forward, puts his arm on the arm of her chair.

—Haley, he says.

She feels tension kicking inside her, or maybe it's the baby. She hasn't said Robert's name to anyone except herself for many weeks and she doesn't know if she can do it now.

—Yep? she says nervously.

Leith looks at her finger, which is picking the side of her thumbnail. Over and over, her finger won't stop. He puts his hand on hers, holds it still.

—We need extra dishwashers, he says.—You need some cash?

—I'm desperate, says Haley.

And it's not a lie. She does feel desperate, right at this moment.

—Great, I'll let Myrtle know, says Leith.—Bit of pocket money for you. And you can meet Clawd.

—Yeah? says Haley. She's not sure if she wants to meet Clawd and her limelight but right now she's just grateful not to be in the limelight herself. Anyway, she's working on being less critical, mainly to stop bile rushing to the womb.

—You'll like her, says Leith.

Haley wonders why boys are always so definite that girls will like other girls. Especially when it's almost certain that they won't.

—Yeah, she sounds, she says.—Umm, great.

She hopes the baby can't distinguish between truth and lies yet.

Claudia gets closer

By now Leith has finished his toast but he hasn't finished with Haley.

—Have you waitressed before? he asks her.

In fact, she has been a waitress before, but a silver service one, serving born-with-a-silver-spoon types. The restaurant belonged to a friend of Sandra's, and was in Piccadilly. Sandra approved of students working part-time but didn't approve of Halley pulling beers at the local pub, which was only two blocks away, and fun. So she had fixed things with her friend Max and after that it took Halley forty minutes and two changes of train to get to work. At least Sandra was happy.

—Only she wasn't for long, Haley explains to Leith.

—Why's that? asks Leith.

—Because it turned out that Piccadilly Max would only employ white middle-class females, says Haley.—He was a racist pig.

—So Sandra told you to leave? says Leith.

—Yep, says Haley.—She's got strong principles when it comes to political correctness. Which is strange, considering.

—Considering what? says Leith.

—Well, her attitude to Robert, says Haley, blundering in where she has most tried not to.

—And Robert is? says Leith.

Haley looks at him and tries to refocus. The sun slants in the window behind him so that he's just a square-shouldered Leith-shape with no face, like a witness being interviewed on crime TV.

—My partner, she says offhandedly.—Back then.

—How long were you together for? asks Leith.

His voice is casual and masked with toast crumbs so Haley has no idea how easily he'll let this one go.

—Oh, a pretty long time, she says rapidly.—Anyway, I left the restaurant which was good because I hated it because we had to wear these gold lycra dresses for uniforms.

She's aware she's babbling but can't stop.

—Gold dresses slit to the arse, she says. She feels like grabbing herself by the hair, yanking her head back: *Shut up!*

—What a bummer, puns the Leith-shape, but its voice is serious.

—And that reminds me, Haley rushes on,—what do I wear to play New Zealand waitress?

Leith doesn't answer straight away. He gets up and sticks his coffee cup in the sink—an act of tidiness that is out of character. When he looks over his shoulder at her, his newly returned face is as serious as his voice.

—Haley, give it up, he says.

—What, says Haley.—Give what up?

—Oh, forget it, says Leith. He walks out without saying anything else, but Haley thinks she can hear the word *evasive* hanging in the air, mingling with the breakfast smells. There is also a strong atmosphere of disapproval, known to Haley from long association with Sandra and a shorter association with Kath but never until now connected with Leith. She feels the beginnings of regret, disappointment, guilt, wants to call Leith back but doesn't know what she'd say if she did.

She smashes toast on the side of her plate with her knife and thinks of the trust that has been building up between her and Leith. Smash smash. He's only half a house away but it might as well be a hemisphere.

And on with the play

To pretend to be a waitress, to pretend to like Claudia, to smile and simper when really she feels like crying. This is what she must do. She must get up from the table of memory and dust the crumbs out of her mind and head into another day and another day and another, without Robert. She has no future but Saturday, which comes around far too soon.

Myrtle looks her up and down. Haley has squeezed into her jeans, but Myrtle gives her a white lace apron to tie over the top.

—I might get her to help out front, she says, scrutinising Haley.—She's too attractive to hide away.

—Whatever, says Leith amicably. He disappears into the kitchen.

Haley doesn't appreciate being talked about in the third person when she's right beside Myrtle but she doesn't quibble. Because, although Myrtle is clearly stupid and rude, at least she has called Haley attractive. This is something Haley hasn't heard since Robert, since she was Halley. She follows Leith into the kitchen, tying the incongruous apron over the small swell in her stomach. She doesn't look at all like a French maid, if that's the idea, and from what she's heard she can't imagine that Claudia will either.

As it turns out, she's right. Claudia is about to turn up in Haley's life looking more like a French actress playing the part of a French maid. The coffee shop will suddenly look dusty and insignificant, Myrtle's manic directorial gestures will lose effect, and the real French women there will be forced to step into the wings. All Gallic eyes are destined to be on Claudia, moving between the bit players carrying her Euro-props: nonchalant petits fours, casual tapas, glamorous bruschetti. Haley, even while trying not to be, will be deeply impressed by Claudia's stage presence.

Even her entrance is effective. Haley, standing at the sink, tackling the first of a thousand greasy trays, hears the plastic curtain flick flack. She turns to ask Leith where the extra pot scrubbers are and sees an arm parting the plastic strips. Not Leith's arm, a smooth brown female arm parting the smooth red green yellow strips. The hand is long, with silver curling around fingers and thumbs. The two longest fingers make the peace sign.

—I come in love, brother, Haley hears.—I bring an Indian song for you.

Leith is putting the rubbish out the back, and there doesn't seem to be much Haley can say to this. She turns the tap on, swishes the water for some token noise, but the voice carries on regardless.

With lively feelings may I walk

Being as it used to be long ago, Haley hears.

There definitely isn't anything she can say to this.

—Does that make sense to you? she hears.—Are we *as it used to be?*

Haley can't confirm or deny, because she doesn't have any idea how it used to be between the owner of the arm and (presumably) Leith.

—Safe to come in? she hears.

This she can answer.

—Um, sure, she says.—Come on in.

—Leith? she hears,

and the owner of the Indian hand, speaker of Indian chants, bounds into the kitchen.

Haley's first impressions of Claudia

1) She's slim, she's bird-like, she's the colour of flax and she moves like flax in the wind. She knows Navajo poetry, which Haley likes.

—That was a Navajo chant, are the first words she ever says to Haley without a plastic curtain between them, without thinking she was talking to someone else.

2) She has no reserve, which Haley finds refreshing.

—Thought you were Leith, well, I call him Leif, but you're not, she says.—So who exactly are you?

3) She has eyes the colour of lime leaves, which Haley finds interesting, and turns out to be unafraid of hard work, which Haley finds reassuring.

4) She has no time for other females, which Haley immediately notices when Leith walks in.

—Hey Clawd, says Leith.

—Hey Garrett, Claudia says (for some unfathomable reason). Her oval Madonna face becomes prettier, the irises of her eyes darken to fern or just to the shadows on a late-afternoon sea.

—Have you guys met? asks Leith.

—Just now, says Claudia. Her sea-eyes flick over Haley briefly, sum her up, dismiss her, and sweep on to Leith.

—You've got tea leaves on your face, she says. She steps very close to Haley, passes her without touching her, and her slim hands go up to Leith's face.

—And in your fucken eyebrows, she says. Her use of fuck is nicely calculated, Haley thinks. It contrasts effectively with her girl-voice, just as her clompy shoes do with her slim brown legs.

—Can you show Haley the ropes? Leith says. He doesn't exactly pull away from Claudia, Haley notices.

—Sure, says Claudia, without looking at Haley. She reaches across Leith, who has started kneading dough, to get an apron hanging off the automatic tin-opener.

—Scuse me, she says.—Leif.

She could have walked around him.

Claudia's first impressions of Haley

Claudia isn't looking forward to the French Bakery day. She has a hangover that has turned her head into an overripe melon, and when she drags herself to the mirror her eyes have marijuana shadows under them. Worse, she hasn't spoken to Leith since the flatmate fight and, since he's always happy with silence, she knows she will have to talk first.

She strides to work with a Navajo chant in her head to keep her legs going. She hopes it'll be an ice-breaker, that it will erase the memory of her shouting at Leith and storming round the tables, and Myrtle telling her to keep her voice down, and a teapot breaking out of spite. But in fact the chant is completely wasted because there's an English girl in the kitchen instead of Leith.

Claudia knows immediately that it's Haley, though she pretends not to and asks who she is. This is Haley—the new flatmate, the impostor, the understudy for a role which should have been Claudia's. It is not a good start and there are other things about Haley that make Claudia look at her briefly and then not want to look at her again.

1) She's too observant and

2) she's too silent and

3) she's too at ease with Leith.

Claudia herself feels anything but easy. She feels strangely nervy, which might be the alcohol still churning in her veins or might be that she is still thinking of altercations with Leith, over trivial hair stuff and serious life trauma. She can't spare much time for Haley, will assess her properly later, must sort things out with Leith. Because of her nerves, she keeps touching her hair, though she knows she shouldn't since it will only remind Leith of how vain she is, and how grape. So she takes some tea leaves out of his face to give her hands something to do.

—You'll show Haley the ropes, won't you? Leith says. He stands like some goddam monolith when she touches him: most people display some reaction to Claudia's cloud touch, but not him. A wave of dismay merges with a wave of nausea and together they threaten to close over her head. So all she can say is

—Sure.

Actually, at the moment she has no particular feeling for Haley, who stands at the sink doing some impassive pot-scrubbing. Reaching for her apron, Claudia looks sideways at Haley, sliding her eyes without moving her head. Haley's attractive enough and her hair is its natural colour, but it's not such a great colour and her waist looks a bit thick. Claudia ties on her apron and decides with relief that there is no threat from the English impostor in the glamour stakes. Though she has to admit that Leith is strangely impervious to glamour.

—Scuse me, Leif, she says in a slightly more certain tone.

Haley looks at her with an inscrutable look: guarded, closed, as if transparent plastic curtains were still between them. She seemed to like Claudia's Navajo poem but Claudia has already decided. It is not at all likely that Haley and Claudia will become friends.

Losing a limb

Halley and Robert are in London Zoo, avoiding the attendants who are trying to flush them out. It's late afternoon and the winter sun is running over the faces of the enclosures, weaving diamonds through their wiry, wire-netting hair. Halley has this idea that she wants to stay all night.

—It'll be fucken cold, says Robert.

—We could get close to lions, says Halley.

—I'd rather get close to each other, says Robert.

Halley looks at him, feels her stomach contract and her heart expand. This is their first day together which could also be called a date, and they are about to step off the plank of friendship into the thin, bright, beautiful air of possibility. She sways towards him.

—OK, Halley! says Robert.—Get up here.

(Halley is about to find out that Robert moves with precision in a relationship: one step forwards, two sideways. It takes him most of an evening to get round to kissing her.)

'Up here' is a round stone picnic table. Halley gets up here, where space is circular and at a premium. She feels Robert's hip, hard under his leather belt, close against her side.

—Now jump, Robert says.

She looks down and around. Their small round world is floating in a crazy sea of paving stones, surrounded by other small round worlds.

—But wait! Robert commands.—There's a catch.

He looks sideways at her in the cold golden light. His skin is black overlaid with gold and demands to be touched, like a smooth carving in a gallery. She wants to run her hand over his cheek but her own radar beams are still in operation, she is still standing behind her own infra-red lines. So instead she says lamely

—There's always a catch.

—Uh-huh, and this is it, says Robert.—You've gotta jump with no knees.

And he jumps for the next table over, keeping his legs completely straight, with no bending at all.

—Ta-da! he bows from the waist, on stiff legs.

—Your legs, Halley laughs.—They look like Norfolk pines.

—Make like a pine! shouts Robert.—Jump, Halley-tree, jump!

Halley locks her legs, lurches off her table and onto Robert's. Before she can be felled by gravity, he catches her, holds her easily like an animal. For a cold sunny second his hands are warm on her waist, and her neck—a significant step forward, Halley thinks, before Robert lets go of her for his next step sideways.

—No knees! he shouts, jumping away from her.

The stone thrums under their feet as they fly, stiff-legged, Norfolk-pine-like, from table to table. The sun jumps off the top of the monkey cage and runs away towards Regents Park Rd so that Halley and Robert are left with no knees and half-light.

No knees no knees and refocus on each other every second table in the grey grey end of the day. Sharpen their eyes needle to the heart of the shadows to see what shapes can be made of this thing, this beginning.

Halley: Yeah, you did everything right.
Robert: You know the rightest thing I ever did?
Halley: What?
Robert: Meeting you.

And so it goes

Ironic, that Robert should start so well and finish so badly. Should start so surely, one decided step forwards, one deliberate step to the side. And then end by stepping trustingly onto wood that couldn't care less about him, that let him down. Ironic that he should enter Halley's orbit so slowly and exit so fast, plummeting to the black pavement in the space between Halley's breaths. So much for his perfection and his perfectionism. When it came to his method of dying, he fucked up as badly as anyone else.

So much for care time and thought. So much for supposed beginnings. Our optimism for new starts—it is entirely irrelevant, because the stars have decreed what will happen before we open our eyes from our first sleep and see their faces through the dark window.

And back to trivialities

After Claudia has ignored Haley for half an hour, the sink blocks. Haley asks if this happens regularly and Claudia tells her not too often but when it does someone has to stick their hand down it. She watches while Haley grovels around up to her elbow like some vet birthing a calf.

—Nice work, she says politely, when the sink decides to swallow.

Haley's arm is now covered in tea leaves just like Leith's chin but, unsurprisingly, Claudia doesn't wipe them off with her hand. Instead she just looks faintly disgusted and then, when Leith walks in, faintly brighter.

—Haley, there's a plunger in the cupboard if the sink blocks, says Leith,—which it does at least five times a day.

—Oh, not five times, laughs Claudia carelessly.

—Claudia's just given me the lowdown on the sink, says Haley expressionlessly.

—Good on you, Clawd, says Leith vaguely. He starts chopping peaceable dates in his corner of calm.

—Low-down and dirty, more like, says Haley to Claudia.

Claudia arches her eyebrows, is about to say something, but Myrtle shrieks from the front like a freight train.

—Gotta go, shrugs Claudia.—Sorry.

The day crawls on its hands and knees towards five o'clock. Haley washes ten lettuces stacks a hundred dishwashers heaps a thousand curses on Claudia's head. It isn't like her to feel antipathy to this extent and she feels her identity drain away with every change of the dishwater. Where's the old Halley who shrugged off insults and ignored the surliness of bus conductors? She watches Claudia skim in and out of the kitchen on slim sandalled feet and hangs on tight to her English accent. Today is not the day to lose her personality.

What she has lost, however, is the long serrated knife that Leith needs for slicing crostini.

—*More* French bread? asks Claudia incredulously. She makes sick noises.—Don't they ever eat anything else?

—Coming, doughboys, she calls sweetly to two bakers whose only English words appear to be Hello and Beautiful. Her tone pays them a compliment so they lurch at her and offer her a wine.

—Knife, Haley? Leith calls. His face is covered in sweat. He hasn't stopped for lunch, nor has he complained about not stopping. For the first time Haley realises: Leith never complains at all.

—Can't find it, she says frantically. She lifts up trays, rifles through bags of old, cold sausage rolls that will probably go on sale again the next day.

—You'd think they'd have more than one serrated knife! she says.

—Myrtle? More than one anything? says Leith.—That's a joke.

He starts telling her how the last kitchen hand left over a row about five-minute eggs.

—The element must be turned off at exactly four minutes, he says.—Myrtle's law: the heat lasts, hence the last minute's free.

Myrtle walks in. Leith buries his face in the supply cupboard.

—More crostini, Leith, she shrills.

—Yes, mein boss, salutes Leith to her back.

Claudia flies in looking like a harassed angel.

—They won't leave me alone, she says.—They keep brushing against my arse and expecting me to put up with it.

Her face is flushed apricot and she carries a carafe of wine with olives floating in it like water-lilies.

—French version of drinking games, she explains, heading for the sink.

Haley continues her desperate, tentative hunt for the knife as chaos towers around her. Any minute now she will remove something vital from the bottom of a pile and the entire kitchen will collapse like a game of Pickup Sticks.

—Shit!

It's Claudia, doubled over and screaming.

—What the hell's the matter? says Leith, leaping towards her.

—Some dumb fucker's left a knife in the sink! says Claudia.

Still holding the jug with olives like a sacrificial offering, she slides down the wall. Such are her waitressing skills that she doesn't even tilt the jug, and again Haley's impressed until she realises that, in fact, she herself is responsible.

—Oh my God! she says,—I'm so sorry.

Leith takes the jug out of Claudia's left hand and picks up her right one. The first finger is blossoming red like an exotic flower.

—Oh God, says Haley again.

—Stand up, Clawd, orders Leith.—Put it under the tap.

—I'm going to faint, says Claudia. She allows Leith to lift her under the arms and position her at the sink.

—Squeeze the edges together, Haley says, moving towards her.

—Leave me alone! says Claudia.—Hasn't anyone told you not to leave knives in the sink?

They all bend over her finger. Their breathing mingles with the breath of the cold tap. The tin-can edges of the cut fit neatly back together, jaws closing, teeth slotting into jagged teeth. Leith's fingers hold it capably together and make Claudia's flesh turn white.

—I think you'll live, he says.

—It's going to be impossible to work, snaps Claudia.

—At least it's your right hand, says Leith in a pacifying voice.

—Oh, are you left-handed too? says Haley, trying to smooth the conversation.—So am I.

Claudia doesn't answer. In silence, all three of them watch the blood wash away, deep rose fading to pink fading to the colour of water. Leith turns the tap off.

—I'm really sorry, Claud, says Haley.

—My name's Claudia, says Claudia.

No one says anything. The hum of the fluorescent tube swells and fills the kitchen, pressing on the walls of the room and the drums of Haley's ears. She doesn't know what else to say or do, so she turns the tap back on to rinse the sink.

—Band-Aids, Clawd, orders Leith.

Claudia doesn't correct him on the name issue, Haley notices. She just follows him to the first aid box and stands close with her hand out.

Haley stares downwards at the spiralling water. Does it really go the wrong way down the plug-hole? The realisation that she can't remember which way it used to go in England fills her lungs with hot panic. She rests against the dishwasher to get her breath back.

The boy-girl stirs inside her, just to remind her that it's still hanging around.

Watch your careless back, it whispers.

Too late. Instead, Haley watches Claudia's indignant back and Leith's concerned one huddled together and realises more clearly than she ever has before. There is no one but herself. No one to blame, no one to help, no one to matter to.

The many shades of pain

The pain of losing someone, Halley soon found out, is made worse by its unpredictability. If pain is constant, the body can adjust, can make provisions. The mind can lock the windows and doors and lie in hibernation until the howling is finally over.

But from the moment she was pushed into a chair and told the news, she learned: endurance is not that simple.

The first hour:

Disbelief. Something like a theatre curtain keeps dropping in her head every time she tries to understand that Robert is gone. This is natural, the psychiatrist tells her. This is a defence mechanism kicking in immediately; this is a protective mental adrenaline rushing to the front line of battle.

Knowing that it is natural is no help, however. Halley wants to get the suffering started but, because her mind is subject to determined human responses, she is not allowed to. So she feels hope every time the door opens, and answers the phone expecting to hear Robert's voice, though she is not really surprised when she doesn't.

Already in that first hour, though, she senses enough to dread the second hour. Through the muffled hope and the strange moments of almost-euphoria, she can still make out the bones of the future. And she feels sick at the thought of all she has yet to go through.

The second day:
This day, and the days immediately afterwards, are action-packed for Robert's parents (organisers of the funeral) but blank for Halley. Days of off-white paper, and no words or events to fill them. She eats because it's something to do, she sleeps only when her eyes force themselves shut over her turning brain. She can't read because such a distance has sprung up between herself and the world that other people's thoughts are irrelevant.

She feels she should do something to retrieve the situation. Although Sandra has told her not to—has almost forbidden it—she goes to the street in Fulham. The street where it happened.

There is nothing there. The scaffolding has been taken down, the building is newly blinded with squares of plywood, the chalk marks on the footpath have been washed away by rain or fire-hoses or tears.

She feels a lightness inside her and the sun glints on the clouds. This is bearable, she thinks, almost arrogantly. Yes, she will get through it, no, it is not a big thing. It is not a war or a famine, it is only one small event that is over, was already over before she even knew about it.

She is halfway back to the tube when the pain crashes in, so heavily that she almost sinks to her knees. A knowledge, more huge than anything she has ever experienced, enters and takes over her body. Suddenly she knows everything, and because of this there is no point in going on, because there is nothing left to discover. She has seen too much. And once you have seen too much, where is there to go?

The third week:
Some mornings Halley can only just get out of bed. Sandra talks about the tiring effects of grief but Sandra is wrong, just as she is

wrong about so many things. It is the lifting of grief that is tiring: its absence.

Sandra sends Halley to the clinic of a friend who prescribes antidepressants.

—They'll make you feel a bit draggy, she warns.—Maybe nauseous, definitely slow.

Halley submits passively, takes two and then three green and yellow capsules every morning. They do make her feel slow but they don't stop the shutters in her head opening and letting in light, nor do they stop those shutters then slamming shut. Shutting her, slamming her into breathless darkness when she is ill-prepared and at her weakest.

In this week she can think of Robert's face quite dispassionately. She sees his broad nose, the scar on his lip and his eyelids curving over his soul. She looks at his face so closely that she can see the pores of his skin and she feels strong, strong.

This—the feeling of strength—is the worst part because it is false. She hates her mind for deceiving itself, when really she knows she is bleeding somewhere far far below the skin where her thoughts cannot go. This internal wound, this weeping wound, is not accessible, cannot be touched or probed or made to hurt for paradoxical relief. It goes on its silent course, a course that cannot be predicted or anticipated, and when unexpectedly it makes itself felt, the impact is staggering. Halley staggers where she walks.

Leith's family: or, learning to stand

Leith's mother is huge. She is called Rose and she is just like one, Haley thinks: a huge, full-blown, aging rose sitting in a garden in Grey Lynn.

Rose has gout and can't walk well, so everyone comes to her. For conversation advice humour food, and now Leith and Haley are coming to her to pick up Leith's spare amp.

—How many sisters did you say you've got? asks Haley as they walk up the path.

—They'll probably all be here, says Leith with a laugh.

They are. There are four of them sitting round in the garden but it seems like more because they are very—*present*. That is the only word Haley can think of: present. Their minds are there and only there, they're not planning the rest of the day or thinking about what they did that morning. They're just there, every one of them, every bit of them.

—Tara Jasmeen Aroha and Jane, says Leith rapidly.

Haley sees smiles, eyes; hears Giddays and Hi Haleys.

—You're the only boy? she asks.

—Yeah, and the youngest so my life was hell, says Leith.

—And the favourite, so his life was sweet, says Tara.

—Favourite, my arse! says Rose.—I don't have favourites.

Her eyes are like bright copper domes hidden in the folds of her cheeks. Haley thinks she can detect a wink, flashing at her out of leathery skin.

—You're English, Rose states.—And you haven't been here long?

—Not long, agrees Haley.—Did Leith tell you?

—Nope, I can tell from your skin, says Rose. She touches Haley's cheek.

—Gorgeous English skin, says Jane.

—Like a baby, says Tara, who is an obstetrics nurse.

—Bit like yours, Mum! says Aroha.

And this is all the questioning Haley gets, on this first visit. Here, in this garden full of people she's only just met, she could be anyone from anywhere. It's easy, it's astonishingly easy, and she looks at Leith with a new understanding. Now she sees where he gets it from.

Although she is learning how to relax again, she is also paradoxically and constantly aware of a shortage of time. The weeks before she escaped from Sandra—living through those weeks was like wading through porridge. There was too much time, it was everywhere, grabbing at her ankles, sucking her shoes. The nights stretched out thin and clingy, like strands of wet hair she couldn't shake off her fingers. Here she doesn't have time for everything she has to do. This is her everyday:

—she has to remember who she is

—she has to walk a long way by herself to give Robert talking-space

—she has to function like a normal person, talk, eat, brush her teeth

—she has to work a forty-hour week

and, above all, she has to write.

What Robert really left her

When Robert joked all that time ago that he would bequeath his memory to her, it was partly true. He hasn't left her his own ability of total recall—many parts of the last months are frightening in their blankness. But from the moment he hit the ground, he left her with the task of recording all that they were together. Another kind of memory, and one that has become as much a lifeline as a burden.

And so, even though Haley has travelled across oceans to a new world, she has continued to write. Time goes faster when she is doing this, and is more certain. When she has a pen in her hand and paper in front of her, she can hold years in her head and not fall. She can traverse years in an afternoon and not feel tired. She will write on anything, money-machine statements or paper serviettes or the label ripped off a beer bottle. She'll beg for paper from strangers when she wouldn't ask for help. She writes. She writes.

But she isn't a writer. She would never define herself as one, has no pretensions about her occupation or the quality of what she is producing. She doesn't sit writing in cafés, watching herself

look at that interesting girl, writing there by herself, looking slightly sad but what a fascinating tale she must have to tell

nor is she waiting to be discovered by a film-maker or a publisher. It's something she must do, as essential as breathing. It's part—and only one part—of the legacy of pain, left to her by Robert.

Techniques to keep hold stay bold

She isn't interested in creating fiction. She isn't interested in promoting a story, in birthing something, in pushing anything out of her dark safe head into thin air. The story she scrawls on page after page has already been told, and she is simply reviving it.

Her notebooks are full of reconstructed conversations that are mostly in the present tense. And this, too, is logical, because she is attempting to keep her past alive. She is the only person who can resuscitate it, who can keep any small part of it breathing and living. With a wisdom more than twenty years old, she fears the human capacity for forgetfulness.

So she must move fast. Her true history, his true history, are still legible but they are sitting in the full light of an open window. (Even Haley, much as she wants to, cannot close herself to time.) So Robert's words, and the words of Halley with 2 Ls, must be transcribed before they are scorched and bleached. Before they move beyond reading beyond recognition beyond redemption. Simply, before they become fraudulent.

It is an exhausting task he has left her with because every day she must relive every scene, whether or not she is at the point of writing it. Her mind leaps forward, leaps back and sideways, to take in the entire plot. The hand of her mind stretches wide, covers his past and hers like a great spider, shields it from the devouring sky. She recalls each scene until she is sick with familiarity, retches with it, but still she cannot keep away from it. She returns to it instinctively, writes in her lunch-hour and on buses and in bed and in the time before she is even conscious that it is another day. It is a compulsion, it is an illness, it is the saving grace of her waking life.

And so here she is, spending her present writing Robert's past. Spending her current life recording Robert's too-short one. She is getting down the screenplay of an important, defunct existence: every detail is retrieved, whether it is grainy or sharp. Every detail, that is, except for the final moment when the head of the hero cracks on the bone-hard pavement, for this is too terrible to be seen.

Leith's warning
It is interesting, the way death has changed over the decades. On

one of Haley's purposeful, directionless walks, she discovers the graveyard in Upper Symonds St.

(—Don't go into the graveyard in Upper Symonds St, says Leith.

—Why not? says Haley.—I don't get spooked by graves.

—It's not the dead you have to worry about, says Leith.)

Haley ends up there as if her feet are compasses and the graveyard is magnetic. She is drawn off the loud mosaic street into the cool, grey-green oneness. Yes, things have changed as the century has accelerated. These early people went quietly and she walks quietly among them.

Capn A. Crosbie was taken from this world on the second day of February 1929 by the merciful hand of God

Mary Lightfoot, 1901–1943, wife and mother of three, departed this life to rest in perfect peace

Louisa, James, and Margaret, most beloved of children, died on the tenth day of December 1906 and are now safe at home with Jesus

Robert—Oh God, Robert—W. Dillon drowned in his schooner on the Kaipara Bar, this last day of 1913, engaged in the work he loved best

And so it goes on, and so it goes on. Husbands are put to rightful rest by wives or with wives; children are farewelled with resignation rather than anger. There is no snatching or clutching. There are no deaths by falling.

Modern deaths, you see, mirror the modern world. Births have always been bloody and loud, technology can never change that. But death, which used to hold peace—there is no peace in death any more. Taxi drivers lie face-down on motorways, their skulls crushed by bricks. Prostitutes are stripped raped taped and thrown into harbours. Children crumple like biscuit wrappers under the wheels of cars. Old women, their fingers ripped off by bag-snatchers, bleed where they fall.

This is it, this is the difference. Death is no longer private. Take the case of Robert Lilley. Exposed to the public, sprawling in the dust of a London construction site. Legs lying slack, able to be trodden on, when they should have been striding high above the street. Once only Halley Barbaud had the right to see him so defenceless but suddenly there he was, being stared at by people who didn't know his name.

She knows it was not an accident. She can trace the origins of Robert's violent death so easily that she is still amazed at the coroner's verdict. She can walk backwards along the plank that gave way beneath his size eleven feet, she can see exactly where and why, though she could never have prevented it. But to save him? She would have had to fight a foe with centuries at its back—too much for a lone twentieth-century lioness, too much even for her who, where Robert was concerned, displayed tooth-and-claw protective instincts.

Because this is the truth, as Haley sees it.

Over too many years of human abuse, the natural world has become resentful. It was natural resentment that made it hurl Robert to the ground. The wood he had been standing on, for example, had been wrongly treated. Raised on dreams, wrenched from moist black earth, shoved through a saw, dragged to a site, walked over by countless boots. No, it was not bad luck that Robert was killed. The splintering of his skull was the reflex action of the world kicking back.

There are trees here in the Symonds St graveyard, some which would also be at home in Britain. Oaks, silver birches, liquidambars, all dripping with ivy. There are many, too, which Haley has only just learnt to name: kowhai, pohutukawa, cabbage trees, and tree ferns. Together they drape a pretence of peace over this tiny part of the city but even here, even in their shade, Haley is surrounded by that human arrogance that has proved fatal.

For here, tombstones fight for supremacy. Huge marble monuments crack under the weight of urns, flowers loom in enormous jam jars. Here are monstrous cherubs, threatening angels. All have been created by men eager to stamp their personality on the soft face of the world. These very men are lying here now, even after moths have settled in their brains: settlers shipbuilders booksellers and publicans. All, still here.

So where is Robert? He is nowhere. Is this because the marrow of his bones held no arrogance and his veins ran with humility? He has left no mark on the world, has disappeared as completely as a sound. Haley stands on a bone-dry slab and strains her ears for Robert-resonance, but all she hears are relentless cicadas and the heartless throb of traffic.

So this is what it's like when the world stands still

The phone line hums like a motor. She holds the greasy receiver between her ear and her shoulder, though remembering Sandra telling her that germs can be transmitted through any orifice.

In retrospect, the phone card slid into the slot with ominous ease. Normally Halley struggles with the mechanical things so easily mastered by the rest of the general public: laundromats are tense places for her, Coke machines dispense only frustration, money machines defy her. But thinking back, how easily the card slid in! How calmly it was swallowed, and how certainly it offered her the prospect of conversation with Robert.

She is lulled into the commonplace as she hears the phone ring in Robert's house. The day outside is grey and kind. It is a kind day, and all she has to do is step out of the booth to feel its mild breath again, to be taken back into its milky mouth.

—Chilli or coriander? she is about to ask. She can't remember which Robert needs for his curry and, as she waits, she watches a tiny Indian child catching a ball of yellow bubble-gum from a vending machine. Then, in her ear:

—Hello?

It's not Robert.

—Robert? she says stupidly, though she knows it's not.

—Who's this? the voice says. It's a voice she's never heard before but after this will never stop hearing.

—Well, who's this? she says. She's caught in the uncomfortable place between suspicion, and fear of overreacting.

—I'm sorry, Miss, the voice says,—I have to know who you are.

The Miss sounds ludicrously like a detective programme and with his next line the scene turns to farce.

—This is Detective Inspector Ryan of the Brixton Precinct, the voice says.

The bubble-gum machine is malfunctioning. Halley watches the Indian child grabbing at air as the balls cascade, small yellow suns and red planets and blue moons, over the grey footpath.

She leans her forehead against the metal plate above the phone. It is very smooth and very cold and she presses her head against it so hard that her eyes close involuntarily.

—This is Robert Lilley's partner, she says, from her blind dark place.

—Where are you, Miss? Can you stay where you are? the voice says.—We'll send a patrol car to get you.

—Tell me, she says. She drops the receiver and it swings against the smeary glass, but in slow motion. Swings. Slow. She catches it and lifts it to her ear. It has become very heavy so that she has to use both hands to hold it close to her mouth.

—Please, she breathes into the receiver.—Just say.

—We'd rather come and get you, says the voice.

She whispers where she is. They say they will be there in ten minutes. They say not to move, not to panic, they'll be there in ten. Why are they repeating themselves?

The door of the phone box is covered with graffiti that she hasn't noticed before. She decides to read it all before she steps outside. *Damon sucks*, she reads. *Homeboys are all dickheads. Boycott fur.* And more and more, but not enough. Not enough to keep her reading forever, which is what she wants to do.

And the phone card. She turns to get it and finds, strangely, that she is a long way from the phone, has to wade towards it through tepid air that other people have left behind. Step. Another. Step. Take the BT card and step away, slowly, hands above her head. She will be held hostage by this moment for many nights afterwards.

After she has removed the last link with Robert and filed it away in her wallet, she swims to the door. But she knows she can't open it while the bubble-gum child is still in the gutter. This would be a dangerous thing to do, because the booth is full of an unnamed substance that the police will shortly define as bad news, and

Halley will later recognise as tragedy. She presses her cheek to the glass, as if she is trapped in a submarine that has been inadequately sealed. She stays there drowning in half-knowledge until the police car pulls up.

The perils of disregarding warnings

(Leith: Don't go into the graveyard by yourself.
Haley: Why not?)

There's a path leading down into the gully. She has to follow its promise, Pied Piper-like. Down in the gully, behind a wall of flax, she is rewarded. For at last she finds one grave that makes sense to her.

Here lies Matilda, who has been written to in faint, bewildered stone writing.

> *She bade no one a last farewell*
> *She said goodbye to no one*
> *Her spirit fled before I knew*
> *That from me she had gone.*

Haley sits beside the flat slab and lays her hand on it. Forty years ago, Matilda was forty. An oak tree has taken over her enclosure, twisting and lifting the covers of her concrete bed. Roots reach like arms over the rusty railings. There's a fair amount of anger around this grave, a lot of hurt, a small portion of resentment. Matilda's relict was very conscious of being shut out, left behind. Haley supposes she is Robert's relict, and will be all her life. At this thought she feels immensely tired and lies down on the scratchy dead grass. Her eyes close against the bright grey glare. Just for a minute.

(Leith: Don't go there even in the daytime.
Haley: Why not?)

She hears a strange noise. Tiny clatterings tiny clickings. Sits up, opens eyes. Only a few feet away, there is a woman, building a pyramid of stones. She is thin, thinner than the trunk of a cabbage tree, and her bones are clasped by a dark red velvet dress, but she has no shoes. Her feet are frighteningly thin, look skeletal, and her restless hands gather stones and move them about.

—You slut, she says conversationally to Haley, without looking up.

Haley looks at Matilda's gravestone and then at the woman's pile of stones which looks like a cairn. She gets to her feet.

—I'm sorry, she says quickly.—I'm just leaving.

—You bitch! You're always leaving, cries the woman.—Always leaving always leaving me!

She whips her face towards Haley and her eyes are red, blood red as the dress. And the skin on her face is raw.

—But I don't know you! says Haley wildly.—I've never seen you before.

—Oh, that's what they all say, spits the woman.—All the pretty sluts.

She springs to her feet and flies towards Haley. Haley tries to move but is too slow.

(Leith: Don't go there.)

—Leave me alone! screams Haley.

The woman's claw is around Haley's wrist, turning, turning. Her strength is unbelievable, it is the strength of wire, of steel, of despair.

—Don't think you can leave me, she whispers into Haley's face.—You took him with you, now I'm keeping you.

Her breath carries nights that never end, sleep that isn't, and the reek of illness.

Haley forces herself to look into the woman's eyes.

—Someone has left me too, says Haley very quietly.

The woman's fingers uncurl but stay on Haley's wrist, rubbing and stroking. She stands close and smiles at Haley and her face is now that of any woman on the street, with a life not only behind but also in front of her.

—They leave us, she says. She nods calmly.

—Yes, says Haley.

—And we lose, says the woman.—We're always the losers because we have to go on.

—Even when we don't want to, says Haley.

—But you! says the woman, and her eyes suddenly become sharp like the flax.—You don't want to be here with me either, do you?

—Yes I do, but I have to go now, says Haley. She desperately wants someone else, needs someone else

(Leith: Don't go by yourself)

but she knows no one will come this long way down into the gully.

—I can see it in your face! screams the woman.—Don't play games with me, don't trick me, bitch!

She spits in Haley's face, in her eyes, and the saliva feels hot, sits on Haley's pupils and burns like acid. Haley pushes the woman and she falls, crashing into her funeral pyre of stones, lying there screaming.

—I loved you all when you were alive, she is screaming. She screams and screams at the silent stones.

Haley runs. She runs up the path, out of the gully, running running and almost collides with a table of old men beside a huge monument.

—Hey little girl, you want to join us? they cackle.—We're having a drink with Auckland's first mayor.

They point to the monument, laugh inanely as Haley flies past them.

This is the second time that Haley has cried in New Zealand. All the way home, she cries, tears mixed with a stranger's saliva.

March

Does the comet recognise Haley? After all, they have seen each other before, though on the other side of the world. But she looks different now: is rounder, fuller in the face and breasts. And now the Comet Soho is surrounded by different stars: Southern Crosses, upside-down hunters, inverted pots.

She is looking at it now, because Leith has called her onto the roof for a gin and tonic—or, in her case, a tonic without the gin.

—Shit, I didn't bring the lemons, he says. He swings himself back through the skylight and down the stepladder.

—That's why, Haley hears him say.—Because there aren't any lemons.

—D'you know what the Chinese used to call comets? she asks him through the roof.—Broom stars, because they swept the heavens clean.

—I can't hear you Haley, calls Leith.

—Clean sweep, she repeats quietly.

—I'm just going on a lemon run, calls Leith.—Back soon.

She hears the front door close and lies there narrowing her eyes so that the tail of the comet runs like paint. Next thing she knows he's back.

—That was quick! she says.—Service station?

—Nope, neighbour's tree, says Leith.—Not lemons either, grapefruit.

—D'you know what the Chinese called comets? says Haley. They drink grapefruit drinks and lie under blankets.

—D'you know what you're having yet? Leith asks.—Baby-wise, I mean.

—No particular hunch, says Haley.—And I don't want to ask the doctors.

—Know what I reckon? says Leith.—It'll either be a boy or a girl.

—Hah, says Haley.—Very funny. For a while the comet demands her attention. Then

—You could be wrong, she says thoughtfully.

—About the baby? says Leith.—Yeah, I guess you could have an alien.

—I meant, I could have twins, says Haley.

—God forbid, think of the nappies, says Leith in horror.

—Speaking of twins, he says.—Claudia was going on the other day about having one that died at birth.

—A twin? That's sad, says Haley.—That's really sad.

—It would be if it was true, agrees Leith.

—Isn't it? says Haley.

—She doesn't know, says Leith.—She's convinced herself, I think. Says she's always had this really lost feeling and Diane clams up when she hints at it.

—Y'know I think that's a girl thing, says Haley.—Wanting a soulmate.

—Or an excuse for insecurity, says Leith.

—That's the first verging-on-unkind thing I've ever heard you say, says Haley.

—Not unkind, says Leith. He lies back and repeats himself. —Not unkind, I think Claudia's great underneath it all. She's just a bit lost.

—But why? asks Haley wonderingly.—She's so established here, her friends, her mother.

—Well, that's another thing, says Leith.—Apparently she's adopted and she's hung up on how wrong Diane is for her.

—I can see why you could get a hang-up about adoption, says Haley thoughtfully.—But that's not necessarily why she doesn't get on with Diane, is it?

—Nope, says Leith.—I bet ninety per cent of the population would exchange their real parents if they had the chance. Better be nice to that baby, Haley.

—Y'know what the strange thing is? says Leith after a few gins.

—What? says Haley.

—That Claudia actually looks a bit like Diane, says Leith.

—What are you saying? asks Haley curiously.—That the whole thing's just a big Claudia-story?

—Oh, I don't know, says Leith.—Maybe it's like the pet thing.

—What? says Haley.

—Dog owners get to look like their dogs, says Leith.—Diane-dwellers start to look like Diane.

—Ha! says Haley.

—Probably just coincidence, says Leith agreeably.

—Probably, says Haley. But she doesn't sound all that convinced.

Horoscopes are modern riddles

This morning (and almost every morning) Haley reads the paper.

Starwatch: Your Day Today
Some people think astrology can't work because it's impossible for an object as far away as a planet to have any connection with life on Earth. But scientists now believe the tiny particles that make up our bodies can be linked to stars on the other side of the universe.

So Haley reads on this particular morning, shortly after she has been locked into inexplicable antagonism with her flatmate's workmate. She chews over the particle idea with her muesli. She would have scoffed before she stepped on a raft made of metal and floated through the sky on the mechanical knowledge of others. Now? She still doesn't know why planes lift off but she's here because of them, at the top of three long islands arrowing their way to the bottom of the world. So how can she dismiss scientists?

—Leith, she says, hearing him in the hallway.

—Hmmm? he says. He comes to the door in his rugby gear that she would call kit if she were still English.

—D'you believe in star-signs? she says.

—Star schmar, he says.

—Does that mean you don't? says Haley, half-disappointedly.

—Dunno really, says Leith thoughtfully. He sees the paper open at the horoscope page.

—Not in that crap, he says, pointing.—Everyone knows they're just rotated from week to week.

—You can see yourself in them if you want to, says Haley.

—Yeah, because they're deliberately ambiguous, says Leith.

—But you do believe in some of it? asks Haley.

—I think you'd be crazy not to, says Leith slowly.—Astrology is just like modern science in a way.

—How? says Haley. Her brain seems to be moving at half-speed, mainly (she suspects) to give her heart time to decide what it wants. Does she want to hear that there is no such thing as free will? Does she want to know that, if she had stopped Robert from going to work that Tuesday, he would have died on Wednesday instead?

—Both of them are based on predicting the future, says Leith.—Physics, chemical engineering, even weather forecasting—they all rely on recurring patterns, and that's what astrologists rely on too.

—Natural causality, says Haley.

—Exactly, says Leith.

—So there's no such thing as free will, says Haley. She is questioning and stating, feels both better and worse. If there is no human freedom, then she had no choice in letting go of Robert.

And so she has no responsibility weighing her down. But does this also mean that she and Robert didn't choose each other? Does it mean that they did not weigh up, with every atom of reason and intellect and intelligent love, that they were right for each other? At this thought, every hair on Haley's head stands up in protest, and every nerve cell in her independent body rebels.

—I wouldn't say that either, says Leith,—because you always have the freedom of response.

—Too hard! cries Haley.—Too complicated! Explain.

—Take Claudia, says Leith.

(I'd rather not, thinks Haley.)

—That twin complex we were talking about the other night? says Leith.—Maybe it's real, maybe it isn't, but that's not the important thing. It's what she does with it that's important.

—So you might not have control over actual events, says Haley, —but you can control them by the way you react?

—Yep, says Leith.—Right now Claudia's holding a grudge against fate.

—Which is holding her back, says Haley, understandingly, grudgingly.

—She's got to find a new way of interpreting her life, explains Leith.—Like a puzzle that doesn't have a real solution, but you can invent one that works.

—Making a silk purse out of a sow's ear, says Haley, half-mocking, half-serious.

—Well, there's no escaping it, life's a bitch sometimes, affirms Leith.—Sometimes it just deals you a bum hand.

There's a silence in the kitchen, which Haley feels she is supposed to fill. She does this by dropping her spoon.

—Seems to me you've found that out already, says Leith, quietly.

Haley picks up her spoon, wipes milk off herself, flusters.

—But what were we talking about? she babbles.—Star-signs, birthdays, when's yours?

—It was January, says Leith.—Past. When's yours?

Haley hesitates. When is it? Has she adopted a new birthday as well as a new persona? Or should she just tell him the birthday of her old self, the old Halley she has buried back in England? Too late, she realises she has stepped onto ice and she slides helplessly, while appearing to sit still on her breakfast chair.

—I'm not really into birthdays, she says. She looks out the window, twists her hair: classic evasion techniques, recognisable as such.

—Well, I am, says Leith,—and the fact you won't tell means it's next week or something.

Haley twirls desperately.

—Don't be a baby! says Leith.—Just tell me.

Haley shakes her head.

—I'll get your passport! says Leith. He flies from the room.

Haley runs too but he's in his rugby gear and she can't compete with a winger. He's into her room, at her chest of drawers, looking straight at her document wallet, which she sees as radioactive but he doesn't notice its glow. She walks over, takes it up casually, and gives herself away. He holds it above her head, extracts her passport. She waits for her small, carefully blown eggshell of a world to shatter. She ducks her head, not wanting to be hit in the eyes by flying shards of Haley Purcell.

—It's next week! says Leith.—You should've told me, Haley, because now I'm gonna give you a party as a punishment.

Haley looks up, sees her face in the mirror. Incredibly the same, incredibly undiscovered, still, incredibly, opaque.

—No party, she says.—No way.

—Yes way, says Leith.—It's only polite and we happen to be the politest race in the world, you know. That's why we get trampled over by the big guys.

Haley can't listen to global talk when her personal world is teetering. She isn't listening, is looking at Leith's face and thinking burning thoughts about false pretexts, issues of trust, and living under someone's roof when they think you're something else.

—This is a crap photo, says Leith.—Doesn't look like you at all.

He looks at her consideringly. Haley feels a stab of panic, of guilt, but then—the photo is her, it's just the details underneath that aren't.

—Passport photos never do, says Leith.—I look like a crim in mine.

Haley looks at the strong shape of his face and his wild hair. She knows he is gentle but she also knows enough about appearances now to realise: 90% of your life is how you look. Leith could easily look like a criminal to a passport photographer, or a customs officer, or anyone who doesn't know him.

—A criminal, she echoes faintly.

—Or something out of a heavy metal band, Leith muses.

Haley's heart is heavy metal, hanging in her chest so she leans slightly forward with the weight.

—A mass murderer, says Leith.

Haley is a mass murderer. She has murdered Halley with 2 Ls: partner of the dead Robert, adopted daughter of Sandra Barbaud.

—Oh, the dangers of judging a book by its cover, quavers Leith in a pseudo-old, pseudo-worldly tone.

He goes to rugby, leaving her with the photo that doesn't look like her, but is her, but isn't her. She looks in the mirror again and again. She has to reassure herself that her forehead isn't transparent, that the life which she has coiled up tightly and stowed in her head isn't exposed.

Suddenly she notices something. There are freckles scattered over her nose which were not there before. New birthmarks thrown at her through a hole in the bright alien ozone, and suddenly she is yearning for grey English clouds.

Dear Robert,

Did you know that you never really see yourself until you've been on video? This is the only way you can know how other people see you— straight on, face to face. You can look in the mirror forever but you won't find yourself, because a mirror image is just that. Only an image of your face. Your left side is your right side to other people, and vice versa. So, in a way, other people have more of a hold on your reality than you do.

You held me, Robert. You held my reality in your eyes, you saw my left side for what it really was, and my right side.

And now here I am, on the other side. The other side of the world, and I can understand that the earth curves so gradually that I don't have to walk on a slant. But I still feel that I'm slanting, all the time. Because you're not here to give my feet anchors. When I walk down Queen St everyone else is in straight lines, not like London where they drift. Here they keep to the left like cars. Sometimes I get scared that I'll fall under their feet, under the fat feet of some businessman powering to work on an Egg McMuffin, and he'll walk right over me.

How will he know to stop? Because he won't be able to see me. No one can see me, I'm invisible without you.

I'm falling without you.

Are you understanding me?

Robert?

Haley gets up early on Saturdays to watch the BBC World News. It's not that she wants to be back in the middle of it all, it's just that recently she's found herself flicking over the international pages in the paper as if they're nothing to do with her. This bothers her.

She is living on the edge of the world which is, after all, what she wanted. But just lately there has been a growing feeling of guilt, and so she gets up at 7 am and watches world news with a rug wrapped around her. In the Northern Hemisphere, the spring is swelling like her belly, and here the leaves are turning in the domain and Haley watches TV in the early morning with a rug.

—Morning, Haley, says Leith, wandering into the room.

He looks sleepy, played at a gig last night which went till 3 am. Haley hasn't slept well herself but at least she hasn't spent hours sweating it out on stage only to face a full day's work today with Claudia. Haley knows, from hearsay and now from experience, that Claudia is more draining than her frail appearance suggests. She looks at Leith with his tired eyes and doesn't envy his day ahead.

—What're you watching out here? asks Leith.—Are you getting nostalgic?

—Not for Iraq and surrounding regions, Haley says.

Although she is not lying, she is once again evading the truth (something she hardly ever did when she was Halley with two Ls). In fact, she has not been able to wrench her mind away from

London since she turned the TV on. She is sharply aware of the clock in the corner of the screen. This broadcast is not live so the clock is counting off English minutes that have already happened, have already been lived through by Sandra.

Today (Haley thinks) Sandra will have gone to work from a silent house, first looking on the mat for a letter from the missing girl. Maybe today she will meet with a detective who will be hunting Halley down, not realising that his quarry no longer exists.

Haley feels briefly sorry, not so much for Sandra as for the shadowy detective who will draw any number of blanks and will have to face Sandra's scorn.

—You ever think about going home? asks Leith, sitting on the arm of the chair.

—I don't think of it as home any more, says Haley. This is partial evasion too; her head has deliberately decided she has no home but her gut, her memory, the marrow of her cool English self—these tell her otherwise. As Leith shifts on the chair, she hears again the swish of the crematorium curtains. It is Robert passing through to join the clammy English air.

Dear Robert,

Today I am thinking back to when you were burnt. All those parts of you that were in contact with me, either dispersed in the air or becoming heavy grey matter. What I would have liked to do was put your heaviness in a backpack and walk up a river to a vast wasteland, where I would have strewn you over the stones. I don't want to think of you deposited in one place because then there are remains. I want you—all of you—to disappear into thin air, I want to be a magician and effect a magic trick that cannot be reversed. I would like to feel the weight of a cardboard box wherein are your bones teeth skin hair finger and toenails.

Put that on my back, take you into space, let you go.

Weight into weightlessness, this you would have liked. The same contrast as in your favourite baroque music. Grave compositional rules, dense notes clustered on a stave with great conventions pressing at their backs. And then the feather sound which the music started with, that untouchable essence which wandered into a composer's head one day and stayed. Passing through a hard technical birth into other people's lives, to become effortless, beautiful, intangible again.

This is what you would have liked.

—Haley, don't you think it's time you talked? says Leith.

His eyes, like hers, are attached to the on-screen maps; he, too, pretends intense interest in potential oil cables wriggling sperm-like through countries. But this is as direct as he has ever been to her, and she is in her dressing gown on four hours' sleep, and she doesn't know what to say.

—You don't have to talk to me, he says.—But why not to my mum or Tara. Or to Claudia even.

Haley can't stop a snort escaping.

—Claudia! she says.—She probably doesn't even remember who I am.

—Actually it's strange, says Leith,—but I think she's quite interested in you.

(—Only because I'm sharing a house with you Leith, thinks Haley.)

—That is strange, she agrees.

—She asks a lot about you, says Leith.—Where do you come from, why are you here—that sort of thing.

(—Curiosity is different from caring, thinks Haley.)

—And what do you say? asks Haley.

—What can I say? asks Leith. He looks straight at her, then stands up and grabs his bag.

—I don't know anything about you, Haley, he says.—And that's OK, it's your prerogative, except you should think of the baby.

—What d'you mean? asks Haley. Panic weaves through her voice like water in sand.

—You'll be the only one who knows it when it arrives, says Leith.

—I don't know what you mean, says Haley stubbornly.

—We'll all be able to see it, we can all hold it and talk to it, but we won't know where it comes from, will we? says Leith.

—It comes from me, says Haley stubbornly,—and so I suppose its past is me.

—Don't you think that's a dangerous way for anyone to arrive? says Leith.—With the whole of their identity in the hands of one other person?

After he has gone Haley watches the TV fiercely and reminds herself that she has saved Robert. From Sandra, from all those Sandra-like people with common sense and a social conscience who have no idea. Even Leith has no idea what it is like to keep a secret for so long so that you wake up every morning not being able to take a deep breath. Lungs head chest full of stuff that you long to expel, but can't.

The wisdom or otherwise of the body

She falls asleep, wakes on the sofa with her mouth half open and her teeth jammed into a cushion so that they feel numb. Sits up and sees cartoons with the outside of her eyes, falling flares on the inside.

She knows little about her birth because she has asked little, but she remembers Sandra saying that she was born under some violent departure in space. First light to Halley was not the beginning of the day but some flickering midnight sun. A solar flare can generate enough energy, she has read, to power America for twenty years. She has never equated her calm self with such a dramatic emerging, her entrance to the world has never been as important as her continued presence there.

Never important until now and she thinks back, thinks of herself opening her new-born eyes to seismic rays miles high and shivering buildings. Has she carried this violence with her, does it hang about her head? Did she somehow bring about the manner of Robert's death? Did he, by accident, emulate her birth? Or is this arrogant?

The sofa cushion prickles her cheek like grass. She is so disorientated that she cannot remember which season it is and has to stumble to the window and look out, can't remember that it's March but sees the leaves are crisping on the trees.

—Are you hot in there, baby? she says to her stomach.—Or is it winter where you are?

She can't get it straight so how the hell is the baby supposed to know? The foetus is already old enough, she knows, for its handedness to have been determined. If it is left-handed, like her, and now it doesn't know where it is, will this cause problems? Will it be confused forever, start to stutter, will it be unable to write or paint or build a wall because it has been born on the wrong side of the world?

There is no certainty in Haley's bones any more; she swings like a broken compass and looks for familiar points and finds none. She is slipping down with nothing to grab, no way to stop herself and worse, she has chosen this. She has come to the other side of the world to find Robert, to save him, and now she is not at all sure if this is what he wanted.

Claudia and Leith meet halfway

That day they met in Albert Park. It was a coincidence, if there is any such thing. They both had time on their hands and a will to be generous, so they sat together on a bench in Albert Park under a dark red tree. Claudia wore a pink dress. The scar on her right knee, left behind by the car accident, had turned into a small white cross. (Sometimes she coloured it in so it looked like a small, hip tattoo.)

What did they talk about? The traffic roaming up and down Princes St swallowed their voices but there were a number of possible subjects: Adrian's recovery, Ben's privacy, Haley's secrecy, or just Claudia. Leith carried a book that could have been Hemingway. At one point he had it open on his ripped and faded knees, and might have been reading a passage to Claudia.

Silver planes needled the sky, the curve of the bridge looked both sublime and close enough to touch. Claudia and Leith sat for an hour talking and looking. Looking like friends?

There are many moments like this, unobserved moments that determine the ebb and swell of relationships. Even when it seems that a particular part of the world has stopped spinning, movement continues outside. People circle, cross paths, link up or sever from each other, and not always because of any conscious decision. There is no such thing as a static state, even if this is what is desired. So Claudia and Leith, who not very long ago looked as if they were heading in opposite directions, have turned again towards each other. And a few city blocks away, Haley sits yawning behind the souvenir counter, not knowing that this turning will affect her life. In fact, not even thinking of Claudia or Leith, but of how soon she can shut the shop and what she will cook for tea.

Because of their talk

Leith asks Claudia to come to Haley's birthday dinner.

—Go on, Clawd, he says.—She doesn't have many friends and I want her to feel that she belongs here.

Claudia doesn't necessarily want this—in fact, she prefers to think that Haley is just a visitor to her life. But a Haley who is needy is easier to cope with and so Claudia begins to recreate her: after all, she has only seen her once so renovations are easily possible.

—I guess she doesn't want you to arrange anything, right? she says.

—Yeah, she's been kind of quiet on the birthday front, says Leith.

—That's the Pisces in her; says Claudia kindly.—They don't like attention.

She thinks back and recreates the kitchen scene. The original Haley, who stands coolly at the sink washing cool lettuces, retreats. Another Haley comes forward, one who is shy and gets flustered over the Navajo chant mix-up.

—I don't think it's that, says Leith.—She's not shy.

Not shy. OK, then she's diffident. Claudia's mind conjures yet another Haley: one who keeps deferring to Claudia about practical matters (*where do the paper serviettes go?* and *how do I arrange the cutlery?*)

—Maybe she's a bit insecure then, says Claudia.—About having your friends around instead of hers.

—No, not insecure, says Leith.—No more than the next person.

Claudia sighs. Her seamless generosity towards this girl becomes ridged with irritation.

—Well, what is it then? she asks, slightly resentfully.

—She just didn't seem into the birthday thing, shrugs Leith.— Tried to keep it a secret.

To Claudia, who adores birthdays, this seems inordinately strange. The chance to revel in your own day without feeling selfish! Actually being expected to take centre stage! Why would anyone not want this, unless they were—

—Pisces, she says firmly.—Pisces are compulsive about secrets, even when there isn't a reason.

Enter: Haley the irrational. Her level stare lacks logic, and her eyes no longer weigh things up. Instead she has the slightly vacant gaze of one who is swayed by incomprehensible emotions. The fish, the sign without solid form.

—A surprise party! enthuses Claudia.—Just don't give her any warning or she'll try to sneak out of it.

(This will be good. Already she feels anticipatory.)

—Too late, says Leith.—I've already told her I'm arranging something. Anyway, surprise parties suck.

—You think? says Claudia incredulously. She can't think of anything she'd rather have happen to her.

Falsities and niceties

Leo: (July 24–August 23)

The Moon seems to be forcing you into a social gathering which you may find unwelcome. However, there will be a chance to discover something important to your future, so don't let secret, half-understood fears be responsible for holding you back.

On the morning of her non-birthday, Haley the Leo-Pisces lies in bed and watches the ceiling slowly descend on her. It gets closer and closer to her face. Now she can reach out and touch it with her fingertips, now it is resting lightly on her nose. Now it is pinning her to the bed so she cannot get up or turn over until night falls again and the ceiling lifts.

The alarm goes off. She sits straight up and the ceiling springs back like the surface of well-kneaded bread. Back to where it always is and so she has no excuse to lie where she is, in a compulsory womb or tomb. She has to emerge, must lie in a different way—deceive and lie, smile and deceive. She has been doing this for months, she is the Great Deceiver, but she has never felt such a specific fraud as she does on this morning, this fine March morning during the Piscean reign.

Kelly and Kath have no idea it's not her birthday so they treat her the same way as they always do: Kelly talks at her, Kath talks down to her. But at home, on the kitchen table, Leith has left a kind Leith note:

Kashmir Kitchen 8 pm and Hey Hey Haley Happy Birthday
and she knows she has to turn up.

The dilemma. She is fond of Haley with one L, she is grateful and even indebted to her. But she has no desire to be a shadow. She has never wanted to be a shadow, has always thought to be an identical twin would be the worst of all fates, and even resisted for a long time being a couple.

(*Yeah, thanks for nothing!* says Robert.)

So she is reluctant to take on the shades of Haley Purcell, is loath to jettison her old birthday, which fits into the calendar so neatly, and take on a new one, which swims somewhere in the middle of a nondescript month.

—I'm sorry, Haley, she says to Haley Purcell, and to all those people who still mourn her going. To the Purcell parents who are probably waking today still thinking of births, waking in a dim double bedroom with lace curtains and a motorway outside, still wanting to arrange parties with a magician but having to invite the neighbours over for gins instead, just to do something, just to fill in the desperate hour before the six o'clock news.

—I'm sorry, Haley, I'm not ready for you, she says.

She looks in the mirror and sees tears pouring down her cheeks. But in one hour she has to be ready, to face Claudia and Leith and

God knows how many others. She drags herself out of her work uniform, through the shower. Because Leith is going straight from work, she calls a taxi, waits out on the footpath, and practises arranging her face. She must show joy and surprise, she must be prepared for the celebration of someone she is not.

Observations

To Claudia's eyes, Haley doesn't look that good. She looks pale and unsure. But the fact remains that she, Haley, is the centre of this night. Yes, she is the reason for this fourteen-strong table: Leith, assorted family, assorted partners, assorted band members, and Claudia.

Sometimes Claudia watches herself in social situations and wonders. How she got here and how she is not paralysed by the fact that, a year ago, she knew none of these people, and a year ahead she may not know any of them any more.

Yet she goes on talking about hairdressers, where to find them, how to keep them in one place, and as she skims she watches Haley.

—No, it's nothing like curry houses in London, Haley is saying to Leith.

—Let's face it, hairdressers have the nomad gene in them, says Claudia to one of Leith's sisters.

—This is much more natural, Haley is saying to Leith.—A Western setting for Western people.

Claudia is genuinely impressed. Cultural correctness inverted correctly on itself, and on your birthday, too, when your mind should be full of yourself. Suddenly, she feels like making a connection with Haley. In the meantime—

—You need to find a stylist you trust, she says to Leith's sister.—That's the thing.

She throws a smile at Haley but Haley is looking at the tablecloth with a strange look on her face. A stranger-look.

Haley looks at Claudia, who is talking animatedly about hairdressers. She is as luminous as ever: she shines like the floors and reflects back conversation without effort. She doesn't even glance towards Haley.

They order dish after dish: Tandoori chicken (and they wipe their red fingers surreptitiously on the tablecloth), chicken korma, onion bahjees, puffy naan as big as duvets. Haley retreats into her head for a moment and looks for Robert but all she can see are the gold lines of spotlights intersecting her lids.

—What? she says.

Claudia has moved, is sitting beside her.

—Did you get much mail from England? says Claudia.—For your birthday?

Haley would rather not see it but there is real interest in Claudia's eyes. She wishes Claudia was as one-dimensional as she likes to remember her.

—None, actually, says Haley distantly.

—Why not? says Claudia. Her eyes are alight with interest.

—I haven't kept in touch with anyone there, says Haley. She drinks half a glass of water very slowly but Claudia is still there when she surfaces.

—What about your parents? persists Claudia.

Haley's head is starting to hurt.

—I don't have a father, she says,—and my mother and I don't see eye to eye.

—Really! says Claudia.—How fascinating.

Haley would rather be ignored than patronised.

—Why fascinating? she asks bluntly.

—Because Diane and I are like that too, says Claudia slightly irrelevantly.

Haley is relieved but not surprised that the conversation has swung in Claudia's direction. She raises her eyebrows, not knowing if she wants to hear more.

—Diane's my mother, explains Claudia unnecessarily.—She annoys me. A lot.

Even though she doesn't know her, Haley feels sorry for Diane. Even more strangely, she feels sorry for Claudia.

—But she'd still send me a card, says Claudia,—even if I was in England.

—Yeah, well, Sandra and I had a bit of a falling out before I left, says Haley.

—What about? says Claudia. There's curiosity in her question, which Haley finds preferable to sympathy so she doesn't mind going on.

—I'm having a baby, she says.

—Oh my God! says Claudia.—Really? You don't look pregnant! Haley shrugs.

—Everyone will know soon, she says.—I'll start to balloon any day now.

—So Sandra, your mother, persists Claudia.—Did she disapprove? Kick you out?

Her face is vivid, interest falls from it like heat from the sun.

—If only, says Haley wryly.—She wanted me to stay safely under her roof and have a tidy abortion.

—Oh my God! says Claudia again.—So what will you do when it's born? Will you contact her?

—I don't know, says Haley.—I haven't decided.

—And what about the father? asks Claudia.—Did you break up with him before you found out or after?

For a second, for a tiny tempting wrenching second, Haley wants to tell her. She has always thought she would tell Leith, if she told anyone, but suddenly all she wants is to take the terrible knowledge from behind her own eyes and transport it into Claudia's green-blue ones. But then

Robert stumbles on the scaffold, bootlace hanging into nothing, and grabs hold of Haley's words to save himself and

—He never knew, is all Haley says, distantly.

—So are you going to stay on here then? asks Claudia.—Have you got residency or what?

Haley stares at her. The noise of the restaurant booms like the sea, rolling over the bare floors, tidal waves in her ears.

—I guess that's all sorted out, is it? says Claudia.—Because of your work permit?

—Will you excuse me for a minute, Claudia? says Haley.—I've just got to go to the toilet.

—Oh sure, says Claudia.

Haley makes her long way across the shining treacherous boards, and feels Claudia's interest radiating after her, warming her cold neck, breathing on her chilly spine.

She sits on the lid and pulls her knees up so no one will see she's in there. Is she going to spend her whole post-Robert life leaving for the toilets? She used to hurry back so she wouldn't lose out on a conversation, now she doesn't know what she'd do without the excuse.

How the hell has she ended up here? In a country where no one knows her childhood, in a restaurant where no one knows how old she is or is not turning. In a toilet where there are unbleached paper towels instead of a hand-dryer.

But something worse than dislocation is making her stomach spin. She has only just realised—Claudia has made her realise—not only is she a fraud, she is an illegal fraud. She is here—to stay?—without a visa, without government approval, without a future. Ever since she has arrived her energies have gone into hiding the Halley that was. This has been her self-appointed task, and her route to survival. Now she sees, and her stomach plummets, that it is not enough to maintain her disguise. Not only does she need to hide her past, she just needs to hide.

Dear Robert,

I nearly threw up last night in the middle of a party that was given for me, but not for me. For the other Haley, whose identity I've stolen. The hugeness of what I've done, the enormity, is growing inside me like the boy-girl. And, like the baby, I can't send or pretend it away.

Yesterday was my supposed birthday. Leith saw it on my false passport and how was I supposed to explain? Impossible so I had to go out for dinner like a complete fraud. I guess my birthday will be in March now for as long as I stay here, as long as I stay in this person I've made myself into. And the first day of August will be just another day and I'll go to my illegal job and no one will know it's a special day for me.

My job. It's illegal. And even if I manage to keep it, how the hell will I support a baby on under-the-table wages? I left my qualifications at home with the rest of me.

My lying self. Just by getting up every day in this flat I lie to Leith. and Claudia has started asking questions I can't answer. Robert, I've really fucked up, I've blundered into this with the blindness of grief and now that my vision is clearing I can't even see where I came from, so I can't get back. Most of all, worst of all, I can't see you. You're not here, but are you back in London? I don't think so. You're not anywhere.

Of love and mechanics

Despite the extensive work put into it by the men from Marcus Motors, Claudia's car is deteriorating. It is twenty years old, the same age as her, but it is depreciating much faster. Claudia loves the Auckland climate, the haze and the warm rain, but it is bad for cars and hers is rusting up. It has also started backfiring so that people stop and stare. Usually Claudia revels in the stares of strangers, but not in this case. Her car is beginning to embarrass her in public, like a friend who gets too drunk too easily. She is starting to deeply dislike it.

—Any idea what might be wrong with it? she asks Leith.

—Could be the timing, he says.

Now Claudia feels even less sympathy with the car. She has always had impeccable timing, her entrances and exits are carefully considered and in general highly successful, and she has little patience with those who lack the skill, even if they are inanimate objects.

—Will it get better by itself? she asks hopefully.

—Doubt it, says Leith briefly. He is quieter than usual today and Claudia wonders what she's done.

—Leith, she says tentatively.—Are you OK?

—What? he says abstractedly.

—Oh yeah, I'm fine, he says, and his easy smile comes back.—Sorry, I'm just trying to work out a song for the band.

Oh. Claudia feels relieved that it's not her, and disappointed that it's not her.

—So I should get the timing fixed, she confirms.

—Definitely, says Leith, chopping onions with a lyrical look in his eye.

Claudia swishes the dishcloth in the water discontentedly. She has two options: spend still more money on a dying vehicle, or abase herself to Diane for a loan to buy a new car. Neither option is at all attractive. She squirts dishwashing liquid directly onto the plates which is forbidden: she draws squiggly despondent figure eights and curses technology.

—LEITH!

It's Myrtle, screaming about something. Claudia ignores, squirts, swishes.

—Leith! Your fingernails!

It's Myrtle, screaming about the black circles under Leith's fingernails.

—I can't get them clean, says Leith.—It's not dirt, it's just oil.

—It looks terrible, Myrtle says with a disgusted

(*disgusting*, thinks Claudia)

face.

—Get the brush and give them a good scrub, orders Myrtle.

Leith takes the brush, scrubs away at the sink, whistling calmly.

—What's a boy supposed to do? he shrugs to Claudia.—Give up his bike for a day job?

Claudia brightens, but not obviously. She is adept at hiding her glimmer behind a cloud of purpose.

—You do your own maintenance on your bike? she says casually.

—Wouldn't take it to a mechanic! says Leith.—They lie worse than politicians.

Claudia does great sweeping arcs with the dishwashing liquid. Her money is safe, her pride is safe: Option #3 has just showed up.

—CLAUDIA!

It's Myrtle, back again, but this time her horror is directed at Claudia.

—Claudia, look at the bubbles! she says in horror.—Do you know much that stuff costs?

—It's only dishwashing liquid, mumbles Claudia,—not fucken gold.

Leith laughs.

—What did you say? Myrtle demands.

—I said you're absolutely right Myrtle, says Claudia clearly.— Good as gold.

Leith laughs again. Myrtle looks suspicious, peers at Leith's grey fingernails and Claudia's innocent face, sighs and leaves the kitchen again.

—She's very disappointed in us, says Leith, shaking his head.

—Yes she is, cackles Claudia.—She's a disappointed woman.

If Diane knew that Leith was fixing Claudia's car for her, she would also be disappointed. Diane is a strong advocate of coping by yourself, especially if you're a female.

—They'll take advantage of you every time, she warns Claudia constantly.

—Who, says Claudia baldly.

—Everyone, says Diane.—If they think you can't look out for yourself.

Diane can. She has had one unsuccessful husband and several useless partners and still she forays forth on a Friday night to meet future potentials. But she won't put up with any crap.

—That's why I got rid of your father, she says to Claudia impressively.

Claudia suspects it was the other way around but, kindly, doesn't say anything. It's important that Diane takes some pride in herself. Sometimes Claudia feels almost motherly towards Diane.

Once, in the middle of the supermarket, Diane kicked a woman in the stomach. Claudia was only two so can't remember it. But, since the incident was centred around her, she has no difficulty in imagining it.

Most appropriately, Diane and the woman she felled had met in self-defence class. Fortunately Diane had proved the more adept at kick-boxing. Although Claudia has never managed to extract the full story from Diane, she has recreated it in great detail. In her numerous mental reruns, the woman is taken out by one swift kick from Diane's leg (sturdy and muscled from nights walking the wards). Claudia names the woman *Nova* as being close to *nouveau*; for, if Nova's wicked plan had succeeded, she could have represented a whole new life for Claudia.

The background (some true some imagined): after building up a friendship with Diane over the hard green mats, Nova had enlisted her support in a custody battle. After losing her own two-year-old daughter, she had transferred her obsessive motherly instincts to Claudia. It all began innocently, with Nova babysitting for Diane; and ended dramatically, in the supermarket, with Nova snatching Claudia and the trolley as Diane deliberated over brands of frozen peas.

In Claudia's vivid mental re-enactments, there is a lot of passionate shouting.

Nova: She's mine, bitch!

Diane: You're insane!

Nova: You stole her from me at birth!

Diane: You're insane!

Nova: I'm taking her home.

Diane: You're insane!

A high-speed but silent trolley chase ensues, during which Claudia's outstretched legs catch a display stand of chocolate wheatens. The wild whisper of wrappers falling is the only soundtrack to the furious chase, although the occasional screech of cornering trolley-wheels intrudes.

Diane vaults a chest freezer and comes face to face with crazy enamoured Nova. Nova seizes Claudia from the trolley-seat and holds her close. Through the soles of her woollen feet and her capped woollen head, Claudia can feel the pounding of Nova's possessive heart.

Diane: Give her to me, now!

Nova: Stay back! I've got a can of flyspray and I'll use it if I have to!

With a one-handed karate chop, Diane knocks the aerosol can from Nova's trigger-happy fingers. With one swift well-aimed kick, she knocks the breath out of Nova's solar plexus. Claudia flies, white woollen head first, out of Nova's falling grasp and is caught like a round fragile egg in Diane's outstretched arms.

Diane: Next time I'll get the manager!

(Never in Claudia's imaginings does Diane care enough to call the police.)

Nova (from the dirty lino floor): How can you take her from me?

Diane: Come on, Claudia, we're going home.

Although Claudia knows much of this is fabrication, she is adamant that she remembers this much. As she is carried through the checkouts, she can still feel Nova's heartbeat racing through her body.

And she knows this. Never has she been wanted, desired and coveted more than by poor crazy passionate daughterless Nova. Was there a modicum of reluctance in her two-year-old shell to go home with Diane? She suspects so.

Attention spanner

Leith doesn't have the tools he needs to fix her car. There's much more wrong with it than the timing: the fan-belt is frayed, the universal joints are creaking. Claudia doesn't even know where these parts are, let alone what their function is. She admits this happily (though Diane would certainly not approve).

—We'll go round to Rose's, says Leith, checking his watch.

—Who's Rose? asks Claudia suspiciously.

—My mother, says Leith.—She's got a garage full of tools.

The inclusion of a mechanically minded matriarch lends credence to the whole venture. Diane would approve (though Claudia should not, does not care, about Diane's approval). There is only one spanner in the works.

—Wanna come to Rose's? Leith asks Haley, who is cocooned on the sofa writing in some scrappy book.

No not really, Claudia wills Haley to say.

—No, it's OK, says Haley.

Claudia does a few dance steps in the corner of the room, twirls, fanfares under her breath.

—Come on, Comet-Girl, says Leith.—She'd really like to see you again.

Claudia stops dancing and picks at the Band-Aid still on her hand from Haley's knife-in-the-sink trick. Haley, inflictor of the wound, actually appears not to notice. She looks down at her scribblings.

—Leith, we should get going, Claudia says politely.—The traffic, you know.

—Early days, Clawd, says Leith in his most relaxed of relaxed voices.—Come on, Hale, get off your butt and come for a ride.

And of course, because Claudia has been anticipating and desiring most strongly a solo trip to Leith's family home, Haley is persuaded to come along. At the door she turns back and grabs her book, stuffs it into the back pocket of her jeans. At least

—You can have the front seat, she says to Claudia.

All the way she watches the streets out the window, and Claudia watches her. Her lips move soundlessly now and then, and she seems smaller, somehow—though she should be expanding, Claudia thinks. At the thought of Haley's pregnancy, and what she has to go through, Claudia feels far more generous.

As they walk up Rose's path, Claudia feels herself intensifying. Her personality becomes concentrated essence of Claudia, she brings herself to the forefront of her bright eyes and words crowd to the front of her tongue. Ready! She is ready to print the vivid image of herself onto a new and most important blank screen.

Haley is subdued. She walks with flat feet and her pale face is inscrutable.

They follow Leith round the side, one almost dancing, one almost plodding. The three of them form a trail like a row of pilgrims, through the side door into the kitchen, to the wise woman.

—Haley girl! It's great to see you again!

It's Leith's mother, larger than life. She sweeps Haley into her huge arms and where her flesh touches Haley's cheeks, a faint pink flush appears. Leith is rummaging through the biscuit tin, opening the fridge door. Not surprisingly, he doesn't realise that introductions need to be made. Although Haley is looking better by the moment, she doesn't seem forthcoming either so Claudia is forced to announce her own arrival into Leith's family life.

—I'm Claudia, she says, smiles, holds out her hand.

—Hi love, the big woman says.—Grab a cup.

—Just came to get some tools, Rose, says Leith.—We're gonna fix Clawd's car.

—Cars, eh? says Rose.—More trouble than they're worth. You should stay put like me, make people come and visit instead.

Haley laughs.

—You had a few fans around the last time I was here, she says.

It's the first thing she's said since she offered Claudia the front seat.

—Fans! I wish, says Rose.—They just come for the cake.

Claudia has no idea who they're talking about. She waits for someone to explain but no one does.

—One good reason to have kids, says Leith.—Never lacking for company, are you Rose?

—That's for sure. You're doing the right thing, Haley, says Rose.—You'll have a friend for life.

She gestures at Haley's stomach and looks completely serious for a minute. Haley looks back, and Leith looks on. The three of them form a tight magical circle with their eyes, and Claudia can feel her glow beginning to fade.

Hidden

Haley is writing to Robert. She is wedged into the corner of the sofa telling him how she has felt small all day. She really has, she has been shrinking since she got up and is now dwindling into the tail-end of the day.

Like a cube of ice, she writes. *Left out of the freezer. I'm disappearing.*

She hears Claudia's voice. It fills the house, drops into every corner, settles lightly on Haley's hair and on the cushions she has walled around her. It is a light green voice, full of light bubbles over rapid shallows.

—Great! Let's go to Rose's! it says.

Haley hopes they will leave without spotting her. It shouldn't be hard to avoid their eyes, she thinks, because by now she must be almost invisible. She presses back into the sofa and thinks camouflage thoughts. She is a lizard who wants no place in the sun.

—There you are, Haley!

Leith has walked into the sitting-room and somehow has seen her immediately. Reluctantly, Haley puts down her pen, puts Robert out of sight, sits up.

—Here I am! she says, trying to sound jovial.

—Well, stop whatever you're doing, says Leith,—and come see Rose with us.

Although Haley doesn't want to abandon Robert on the sofa, she knows she'll feel better after even one glimpse of Rose's rough beautiful face. But she can feel Claudia willing her to stay away. Possessive vibes are emanating from the corner of the room where Claudia dances, her supposedly careless steps tapping out a warning.

—Nah, I'll stay here, says Haley.

—The traffic! warns Claudia.

—Get off your butt, orders Leith.

Grey Lynn is cast in shadows, Haley's head is still full of her own diminishing voice talking to Robert. She doesn't want to antagonise Claudia so she has hung back, has given her the front seat in the car, makes sure she walks last up the path. At least she has put her book in her back pocket, and she traces the outline nervously as she follows the others into the kitchen.

Robert Robert stay with me through this

She's right, Rose is great. She not only hugs Haley, she picks up on Claudia's needs straight away too.

—You've got beautiful hair! she says to Claudia.—Grab yourself a cup and tell me all about yourself.

There's surface talk about cars and relations and the importance of daughters. It's like sinking into a bath of the warmest water after sitting all afternoon with numb hands and feet. Tara arrives, Rose keeps pouring tea, Claudia seems to be relaxing, and Haley can stop feeling as if she shouldn't be there. She says something about last time, and Rose turns to Claudia and smiles, preventing the blade of exclusion falling on Claudia's slender bowed neck.

What is it about this house? Haley feels responsibility lifted from her tired shoulders, she is absolved from talking or making her presence felt. She sits back and drinks three cups of tea and watches Claudia sparkle, set off by the rich dark background of Rose and Leith and Tara. She is content not to be a principal player in this pleasant, low-key comedy of manners.

—Here's Violet! says Leith.

A huge cat jumps onto her knee. Touching the low belly, Haley imagines the shape of kittens: two, four, five. They move under her fingers, tiny tails and soft claws created by her own skin. Violet stretches like a line, then curls like a question-mark. Someone says something about the shape of cats.

—And do you have any pets? Rose asks Claudia kindly.

Tara talks on and on like the restful sound of a tap running. About what she's been reading, and how did Claudia meet that brother of hers? And now Aroha has blue hair.

—She's bloody versatile, I'll give her that! says Tara.—She changes like a cat, like Haley said.

—Actually, says Claudia in a loud strange voice,—I said that.

—Oh sorry, says Tara.—I've got a memory like a bloody sieve.

Did Haley make the cat comment? Maybe, maybe not, but even if she had she wouldn't mind Claudia taking away some of her words. She has been burdened with them for too long: in her head, in her dreams, in her diary. Suddenly the book in her back pocket becomes a discomfort instead of a comfort. She can feel jagged phrases digging into her flesh and she shifts in her chair.

—Yep, Tara's memory's hopeless, says Rose.—And d'you know what she blames it on? Her star-sign.

—That's right, says Tara.—I was born on the cusp and I've been confused ever since.

She winks at Claudia.

—These girls are too smart to believe in all that stuff, says Rose.—Mercury sweeping into Gemini sweeping into a load of nonsense.

—Never underestimate the power of the heavens Rose, says Leith in a dark, significant tone.—Look at Claudia.

—Why look at me? asks Claudia, glittering, gleaming, under the battery of attention.

—Clawd was born under a solar flare, says Leith to the kitchen at large.—Which explains a lot.

—A solar flare! says Haley. She sits up and Violet jumps off her and flies out the door.

—What does it explain? says Claudia, ignoring Haley. She is shining as if she herself is some celestial body.

—Your collision course through life, says Leith.—Your sense of high drama.

—Huh! says Claudia, pretending to look offended but really looking gratified.

—A solar flare! says Haley again. The book digs warningly into her lower back.

—It's an eruption of gas, says Claudia in an instructional tone.—They happen all the time but my flare reached Earth and caused huge disruptions.

—I know what they are, says Haley. She opens her mouth to continue but Claudia, as if she doesn't want the conversation usurped, speaks first.

—Let's get going, shall we? says Claudia.

Haley goes in search of information
although she is careful not to give any away.

—Leith? she says, sitting on the edge of the sofa.

—Hmm? says Leith, who is cleaning his guitar strings.

—D'you know what star-sign Claudia is? says Haley.

—No idea! says Leith, flicking his chamois in her direction.—Why?

—Oh, I just wanted to confirm a theory, says Haley.—I bet she's a Leo.

—You know, says Leigh.—I think you're right. Because I was talking about horses' birthdays.

—What exactly has that got to do with it? asks Haley.

—Well, I was telling Clawd, explains Leith,—that all horses are aged from the same date to make it easier for the breeders.

—The things you know! says Haley.

—The birthday of all horses is August the first, says Leith, —which (Clawd then told me) is her birthday as well.

Haley is silent.

—That either makes her a horse, says Leith into the silence, —or a Leo. Or both.

—Maybe I'm right, says Haley slowly.

—I must be right, she says again.

Her ears are suddenly full of waves and her head swims on her shoulders.

Claudia goes in search of water

Claudia is seriously tiring of Heath. And she is seriously tired. For some reason she hasn't been sleeping well, and she bed-hops in an effort to get a good eight hours. Heath's place to Diane's, marital bed to single, his to hers. Neither is effective, and going to work each day is like carrying a head of lead on a very thin spaghetti neck.

Vivienne is away for a month in the South Island visiting a friend—or a lover. Claudia is surprised at the indifference Heath displays towards the possibility that his wife is screwing around.

—But you should understand, says Heath,—you don't give a damn about anything.

He doesn't know Claudia. After hearing this line, Claudia knows he obviously doesn't know her. A tiny despising shoot springs from her heart, small leaves of dislike unfurl under her skin under Heath's hands. But she needs to sleep, didn't sleep last night at Diane's, has to try here.

—Heath, I'll stay here tonight, she says, commandingly.

—Great, says Heath with relish.

—I want to sleep, says Claudia warningly, desperately.

At 2 am she is still awake.

—Try counting something, says Heath.

Claudia almost hits him. She lies on her back and puts Vivienne's pillow over her face and thinks about Leith and Haley in their house in the valley. She thinks of Haley's belly, pushes Heath's hand off her own flat one.

Haley and Leith, Haley and Leith. Deprived of sight, her eyes create their own visions on the back of her lids. Haley and Leith. Her mind slots into a deep groove that she can't stop. Chiselling into her mind, the sight of Haley coming out of the toilet at the Indian restaurant. Chiselled—the sight of Leith pushing his chair back and taking Haley by the hands. Chiselled. Haley swaying Leith holding both leaving.

The needle jumps out of its track only when Claudia remembers Leith's hands touching her own shoulder.

—Thanks for coming, Clawd, he says, and he holds the thin bone of her shoulder under its thin silver strap.

Then he leaves, with Haley. The needle goes flying across the surface of Claudia's mind until it hits the side of her head, which is resting on Heath's. She groans.

—Claudia darling, you need to sleep, he says.—Keep those starry eyes bright.

He reaches into a drawer, offers her a sleeping pill, which she scoffs at, so he offers her two.

—Don't you know by now, she says angrily,—I don't like those fucking things.

Heath throws back a couple of pills himself.

—Gotta be on top form for work, he excuses himself.

(Or top form for your new fling, thinks Claudia dispassionately. She is already suspecting him of double infidelity.)

Heath steps politely (he may be a philanderer but he is always polite) off into sleep, leaving Claudia stranded on the other side. Claudia is left counting, not sheep but dissatisfactions. Heath is dull. He sleeps too fast. And the final thing: he talks about the bones in her face. This is proof to Claudia that she means nothing to him. When guys talk about the bones in your face, they've got a boner in their pants. When they talk about your cheekbones, they're thinking about other parts of your body.

She must get up and do something. She has a terrible thirst, goes to the kitchen for water, drinks one glass after another. Her thirst remains, it is all-consuming. She doesn't want to be in the house. She pulls on her jeans, shakes the Heath dust out of her shoes, walks out into a 4 am world. The grass is bleached, the sky is blacked in.

The world is a photo negative and a pale image of Claudia walks through it by herself in search of water.

Haley the outlaw

In stepping out of her London life, Haley has stepped over many legal boundaries. Not only is she outside the law, she has broken it in many ways, smashed it irreverently on both sides of the world. (But to save herself! To save Robert.) And wait, there is worse. When she came through Customs she had something in her pocket as hot as radioactive material, though she carried it in a plastic canister instead of a lead one.

Over the past weeks, the contents of this canister have seeped inside her, have infected her blood with longing and despair. At night she feels the fever running through her wrists and ankles, can calm it only by reaching out and touching the small black Kodak container. Inside is Robert.

A part of him, an organic part. His eyelashes—more him than any other bit of his face or body. They are black touched on the end with dusky lightness like grass under a moon.

It all started as a joke, or two.

His joke: She told him she never cried. He said he didn't believe in absolutes, so she amended, *OK almost never*. He decided he would collect her tears in a bottle. By the time he and she were sixty, or sixty-five, or seventy, he might have a tiny pill bottle full of Halley-water, salt-sting, bitter-sweet. Proof that she trusted. Him.

Her joke: She was sitting on the Piccadilly line by herself wearing his jumper. A cliché, it's true, but only a cliché because it's what people in love really love to do—wear each other's clothes.

She was picking hairs off his jumper. She found one of his eyelashes, glinting against the navy wool: crescent-shaped, golden-tipped. She trapped it in a bubble of spit on one of her fingers, carried it carefully through tube doors and turnstiles and through Leicester Square.

Its owner was waiting under the Swiss clock.

—You've lost something, she said.—Other than your mind.

—You've found my mind? said Robert.—Give it back at once.

—Very funny, she said.

—I've lost my heart, he said. He kissed her and the Swiss cows came out and the bells rang five times.

—Not that either, she said.—I have found a valuable eyelash belonging to Robert Lilley.

—You know what? he said.—He says you can have them all.

And so she collected them off pillows and out of her hair, took 24 photos of Robert to use up a film, put the eyelashes in the empty canister. Him.

As Haley Purcell, minus most of her past possessions, she took these eyelashes to New Zealand. Organic matter, brought into a country with some of the strictest quarantine rules in the world. She had studied the pamphlet on the plane; she had no feathers or bone or shell but nowhere did it say eyelashes.

Now, in her Grafton Valley room, she counts them, sitting on her bed with her Leith-sun looking in the window at her. Five six seven. She was sure there were eight, feels panic rising in her. She can't afford to lose any more of Robert. Then she spies the eighth lash sitting under the rim of the container like a dark smile.

This container, destined to be thrown in a bin, instead elevated to longevity. It is a reliquary. A receptacle for relics.

Haley is familiar with these terms. Archaeological definitions of the word *relic* are several and precise: an object that survives from an earlier age; a lasting trace of a custom or practice; a part of a holy person's body or belongings kept after their death as an object of reverence.

Reverently, Haley lays the eyelashes in a row on her orange

candlewick bedspread. They are all of the above, they are the definition of Robert, they define her loss.

And what is she, looking at these tiny remnants of a former age? Add a T and there you have it. She is not a relic but a relict, she is the person who has been left behind.

Responsibility

There is no wind but Claudia walks so fast that her hair is blown straight back off her face. The cool black air streams over her forehead and she walks quickly to the waterfront.

She can smell the water, she can see it as a shifting mass, but she cannot see any surface detail. It is the sky that is asking to be watched. Out over the dark shoulder of Rangitoto is the Comet Soho: silver body, milky tail, running from the moon. But it can't streak ahead too fast because its tail is so long, it is caught and anchored by a strong star. Claudia is not the type to stand and stare at the sky, but even she puts her life on hold long enough to sit on the sea-wall and watch the chase.

After a while, out towards the heads, the surface of the sky starts to give way. It tears slowly, and slowly a long streak of lime green lining appears. The water moves restlessly, swells like a pregnant belly. Claudia thinks of Haley with a movement inside her that is nothing to do with her own volition. The thought rouses a strange envy. Claudia sits on the wall and feels envious, and exhausted, at the thought that nobody else will move any part of her body. It is up to her and only her.

She has a bizarre, an overwhelming desire, to submerge herself in water. She wants it to close over her head, enter into her eyes nose mouth lungs, fill her hair with its weight and relieve her of decisions. Instead she gets off the wall and starts to walk back towards the city. The street lights go off as she is passing McDonald's so she has a wish just in case. One light stays on, burning stubbornly, irrelevantly in the brightening morning. She is made uncharacteristically anxious by the waste of this, the redundancy, the selfish introverted act of shining on against a stronger light. She feels short of breath and there is a pain in her left breast.

She cuts through the bottom of Parnell, crosses without looking because the streets are mostly deserted, and nearly gets hit by a petrol-tanker. The bottom of Constitution Hill is wrapped in the smell of sewage and she hears a rat rustling in the bushes, so she takes the steps two at a time.

It's only when she gets to High St that she realises how early she is. The sky has been busy but the streets are still deserted. She can't get into work, she can't have breakfast anywhere because the streets are wet and swept and the doors are all closed. Even the construction workers haven't started yet. She peers through a wire-netting fence into a huge pit eaten out by the mouths of yellow bulldozers. Feels dizzy. Feels pain in her breast. Straightens.

Strung up beside her face is a Walkman headset but one half is missing. The remaining ear-piece dangles uselessly on its wire, sways in the wind. It looks strangely shocking, mutilated, and she feels compelled to reach out and touch it. Cold chrome, foam rubber like cartilage: a structure of tough, flexible tissue that has been ripped from its partner and is now dysfunctional. More redundancy, and Claudia shivers in the cool morning.

She needs coffee toilet toast. Sets off for Burger King, then halfway there thinks of Leith's, and sets off again, up the hill, out of town. On the smug emerald grass of old Government House, in front of the sign that says 'Passive recreation only', she does a wild dance. She runs up Symonds St, across Grafton Bridge, and the chilly dawn is ringing, ringing in her head, and her ears burn with the displaced air.

She must keep moving. Frenetic movement is the only way, she thinks, to keep ahead of herself and the tearing, wrenching feeling of separation. She knows she is slowing down, running down like a clockwork toy, but can't won't doesn't dare to let it happen.

(That night, Haley wakes to find that something is missing. Is she thirsty, hungry, cold? She runs through the possibilities, and as usual her mind settles on Robert like a tongue locating a toothache. But even after this, there is a nagging feeling. Something gone, something unsatisfied, unquenched.

There is a ringing in her left ear, a pain in her left side somewhere near her heart. She sleeps again, dreams of a light burning uselessly against the brighter light of day, and somewhere there is water.)

Alarm, radio, shower, painted sun, breakfast. Like any other morning in Haley's (now-temporary?) now-life. Except this morning the next thing on the list is an unexpected visitor.

—I hope you don't mind, Claudia says. She has come into the kitchen without waiting so her question is rhetorical. But what is it that Haley feels at the sight of her? In fact, it is the opposite of minding: it is close to relief.

—Of course not, but what're you doing up so early? says Haley.

—I've been out walking, says Claudia, vaguely.

—Where? says Haley.

Leith comes in trailing his duvet round his shoulders like an Indian chief.

—Clawd! Hi there! he says.—Want some coffee?

Haley wishes she could be more like Leith: less questioning, less surprised. But still she wants to know.

—Why out walking? she says.

—I was way too early for work, shrugs Claudia.—So I thought I'd come up for a coffee.

—Fantastic idea! says Leith, who's a morning person. He pours them all coffee and sits with his hair standing out around his face in black rays.

—But I thought you weren't a morning person, he says to Claudia.

—Not, says Claudia.—Unless I'm still up from the night before, which I am.

—A good night out? says Haley. She thinks Claudia looks tired.

—A crap night in actually, says Claudia.—No good TV no good conversation and no sleep.

—I haven't been sleeping either, says Haley.—So at least you've got company.

—That makes me feel better, says Claudia.—It's lonely,

feeling that you're the only one awake in the whole world.

—Yes! says Haley.—Lonely is exactly what it is.

She looks at Claudia consideringly.

—May as well make the most of insomnia, says Leith.—Wanna schedule a sleepless night for next Tuesday?

—Why? says Haley suspiciously. She is developing a complex about not scheduling things: because how does she know she'll even be around next week?

(—*Or Leith, or Claudia, or anyone,* she thinks.—*See what you've done to me Robert?*)

—Thought we could go star-watching, says Leith.

—I didn't think that was your thing, says Claudia.—You mean celebrity clubs, Hollywood Boulevard, screaming fans?

Almost, she looks conspiratorially at Haley but then seems to decide she's not ready for shared jokes yet. Her eyes slip off Haley's and fix on the rim of her coffee mug instead.

—Every year, early April, there's a meteor shower, says Leith.—Though maybe a bridal shower is more your style, Clawd?

—Ouch, says Claudia, making a face.—You're so cutting.

—Well, what do you reckon? says Leith.—It's an amazing show, better than *Star Wars* even.

—Oh well, in that case, says Claudia.

—Haley? asks Leith.

Haley looks cautiously at Claudia, wonders if this is like the visit to Rose, just played out in a different way. She has noticed the flirtatious way Claudia has been eating toast in small fingers, and so all she says is

—Maybe.

—No maybes, says Leith.—You're coming.

Claudia suddenly puts her head down on the table and Haley gets ready to remember an important arrangement. Only it's unlikely she'll have anything arranged for 2 am next Wednesday morning.

But Claudia's glossy hair is lying in the jam, and Haley knows her well enough by now to be pretty sure: this would never happen if something wasn't wrong.

—I don't feel too well, Claudia says. She lifts her heart-shaped face to the kitchen and her upper lip is lightly dusted with toast crumbs and sweat.

—Have you slept at all? Haley says. She stands up and hovers over Claudia, puts her hand out to touch her shoulder, pulls it back.

—No, I haven't, but it's not just that, says Claudia.—I've got a kind of pain. Here.

She trails her bird hand over her narrow chest. It is a typically touching performance, but one that also has the ring of truth about it.

—You'd better go and lie down, says Leith, pushing back his chair, also going over to her.

—You can have my room, says Haley diffidently.

—OK, says Claudia.—If you're sure.

Unlike her earlier question, this is not rhetorical. Even through her pain, she looks at Haley as if realising that the offer has been forced out of her. But she heads for Haley's room anyway, walking with tiny doll steps.

Haley snatches up her bag, her cardigan, thinks: what else does she need to take to work? The room looks small and dull with the curtains still pulled, and she opens them so the yellow concrete sun bursts in.

—Close the curtains, says Claudia in a small voice.—My eyes hurt.

Haley closes them. The room shrinks again. Claudia lies on Haley's bed curled up on her side, looking beautiful and frail.

—Stay as long as you want, Haley says.—Just pull the front door shut when you go.

Leith turns up with a glass of water.

—I've gotta go too, he says.—Will you be all right, Clawd?

—I hope so, says Claudia. Her face is pale against the candle-wick bedspread, a white daisy on orange-tufted grass.

—Tell Myrtle, she says,—whatever.

—Yep, I'll sort it out, says Leith.

—Thanks Leith, says Claudia. She gives him a weak smile that still manages to hold a hint of radiance. Haley and Leith hover by the door until Claudia closes her eyes and shuts them both out, and then they leave her alone.

Haley takes the bus downtown instead of walking, because she is now late. There is an uneasiness inside her at the thought of someone else in her room.

The two-ness rule

Absolutists may deny it, but there is a definite duality to life. From the moment Haley closes the front door, both she and Claudia become increasingly, acutely aware of the physical distance growing between them. Haley happens to be the agent; it is Haley who draws out the distance, who throws down behind her Grafton Bridge, and many lines of panting cars, and then a shop door and then a glass counter.

This, single-minded people would say, is an end to it. Out of sight, out of mind. So why then, during that lengthening journey, do Haley and Claudia become more aware of each other rather than less? Why does that unravelling piece of string between them seem to tighten, so that Haley finds herself working on the till with an image of her own bedroom carpet before her eyes? Why is Claudia, battling to control the hot swirling nausea behind her own eyes, counting out line after line of orderly change across a smooth cool counter?

It's a fact. Life is a dual-edged act. Sometimes it is secretive about it, pretends to be singular and simple, but the moon is always in the sky even when it isn't visible.

Where there is one, we automatically look for another. We traverse our lives by this instinct. It is there in our need to travel: across a room, a river, the world. Feeling a wall at our back, we are strangely compelled to seek the opposite wall and we will not rest until we touch the cool plaster in front of us. Whether it is resisted or recognised or ignored, this instinct for duality is always there. It never goes away. Absolutists are liars, soloists are kidding themselves.

✄

Tension may be building but life goes on

And what of Adrian and Ben? While Claudia's hold on health is slipping, while Haley waits for her paper world to fold around her, Adrian and Ben continue to weave their way through March, solving their own problems. It is reassuring for Claudia to realise that, although she may be grinding towards some kind of halt, others go on. In Adrian's case, with humour in the face of adversity.

Adrian has realised that there is a certain comedic potential in his condition. He sits in Retropolis and hurls spiky jokes about, discouraging sympathy. When Claudia herself seeks sympathy, the day after her sojourn in Haley's bed, she finds his comic armour almost impenetrable.

He answers the phone so professionally that at first she thinks she has the wrong number.

—Psychiatric Helpline! he says smartly.

—Aids? says Claudia.

—If you are obsessive-compulsive, please press (1) repeatedly, he says.

—Aids, it's me, says Claudia.

—If you are co-dependent, ask someone else to press it for you, says Adrian's disguised voice.

—D'you wanna come out for coffee? says Claudia, ignoring him. She needs to talk about Leith and Heath, her accommodation problems, her tiredness, her pain and her racing mind.

—If you have an avoidant personality, fires Adrian in a mechanical voice,—hang up immediately.

—For God's sake Adrian! shouts Claudia.—Shut up!

—Aren't you pleased I'm handling it so well? says Adrian offendedly.

—Yes yes, says Claudia impatiently,—but you don't have to be so proud of it.

—The only thing I'm proud of, my friend, says Adrian,—is pulling off the ultimate ironic stunt. The kid of two shrinks going crazy! It's huge!

Claudia sighs. Sometimes even Adrian, with all his wisdom, can let people down.

—Don't worry about it, she says resignedly. She hangs up and tries to call Ben instead but he has been particularly reclusive lately and she suspects he has his own set of problems.

It's behind you, Ben

Ben's problems? Sometimes it's hard to know what they are. He recedes where Adrian sticks his neck out, he shrinks where Adrian expands. He has a bigger mouth than Adrian but he speaks less. He is intensely private.

This extends to his living arrangements. Claudia has never once been invited into Ben's home. Neither has Ben been into Quel Fromage, obviously finding it impossible to force himself past its pretentious door.

Until now. Five minutes ago, he has walked into the café and asked his friend Claudia to come to dinner tomorrow night.

The invitation falls into the conversation like a casual atom bomb. Claudia is so startled that she drops a croquette, which explodes on impact. Hot potato shrapnel hits her smooth legs.

—Fuck! she says. She slams the right-hand door of the warming cabinet, dances.

Ben is so intent on churning out his first invitation that the marring of his best friend's best feature doesn't seem to feature.

—About 6.30? he says nervously.

—Shit! says Claudia.—Shit!

—Shit? echoes Ben.—Does that mean 6.30's too early?

—Don't you worry about a thing, honey, says Claudia savagely.—6.30's fine.

—Great, that's great, says Ben.—I've invited um, yeah, and I wondered if you could help a bit. You know, with your experience and everything.

His bony hand waves at the potato-spattered floor, at the chaos Claudia has created in less than sixty seconds. Claudia looks around and behind Ben's head for sarcasm, sees none, decides to remedy the lack.

—Well hey, after all those dinners you've cooked for me, she says.—It's the least I can do.

Ben looks surprised, which quickly turns to embarrassed.

—Yeah, well, sorry, he says, going red.—You know.

He starts playing the piano on the counter, leaves behind fingerprints that Claudia knows she will have to clean off later. Her outrage swells until it's grotesque. It sits in her throat like a giant goitre so her sarcasm can hardly squeeze past into the open.

—Have you really thought about this Ben? she says.—It's a pretty big step to take, you know, this could change our friendship beyond recognition.

Ben's fingers accelerate until they blur like the counter.

—Come off it, Claudia, he mumbles.—It's just, you know.

—Yeah, the first step down the slippery slope of hospitality, says Claudia.—Today it's just dinner, tomorrow it could be the houseguest from hell.

Her legs are hurting quite badly and there's a little red fishhook of pain on her kneecap—her second scar in a couple of months?

—Oh forget it, says Ben. He turns away. Claudia forgets Ben's part in her permanent disfigurement and remembers the way he brings her green tea in bed when she's sick.

—OK OK, she says.—I'll come.

Ben's turn is worthy of Astaire.

—Really? he says.

—Yeah, really, Claudia says.—I'll cook, serve, do whatever. So who are you trying to impress then? Some girl?

The red tide starts somewhere under Ben's rugby shirt and floods quickly up his neck.

—Um mmm um, he says.

—What? says Claudia, intrigued.

—My mother, Ben says.

—What! says Claudia.

—Don't keep saying what, says Ben.—You heard.

—But! says Claudia for variation.

As far as she's deduced, Ben has nothing to do with his family. She thinks of him leaving home at five years of age, setting off in pursuit of scientific knowledge before he could even write a note explaining to his parents where why and how.

—She's going on holiday, says Ben.—Wants to see me before she leaves.

—But how touching! says Claudia.

Ben starts to look annoyed and Claudia quickly becomes expressionless.

—Right, she says, in a business-like way.

—She's bringing a man, says Ben.

—Right, says Claudia.

—See you tomorrow then, says Ben.

—Right, says Claudia.

Of mothers, fathers and doctors

Because the blemish on her leg has faded and the pain in her left side has temporarily lifted, Claudia turns up at Ben's door with two bottles of wine instead of one. She knows the actual door quite well, having stood at it numerous times craning over Ben's shoulder to decipher the gloom. It's not knowing what's inside that makes her feel as if she's entering Bluebeard's den.

There's certainly no room for dead wives. It's tiny. One room over a garage, and every fifteen or twenty minutes the floor of Ben's room shakes.

—It's the neighbours' automatic garage door, Ben says.—They can't ever decide if they want to go out or stay in.

Today his eyes are so deep in his white dough-face that Claudia feels as if she's watching him implode.

—I thought I'd do eggplant casserole, he says.

—Sounds complicated, says Claudia.

It looks complicated. The bench is laid out like an operating tray. Vegetables lie in rows according to size and colour and Claudia looks at them with apprehension.

—You're making it from scratch? she says.

She looks hopefully in the fridge but sees only a bottle of vodka and a few rolls of film. Before they start, Ben shows Claudia his balcony: four feet by four. They look out onto a vast acreage of corrugated iron and fire escapes. Rust on grey on grey.

—Picturesque, n'est ce pas? says Ben. His mouth goes

up at one side and his shoulders hunch, Quasimodo-style.

He tackles the eggplant with a corkscrew since he doesn't have a decent knife, scores out regular wavy-edged slices, which Claudia sprinkles randomly with salt. It all takes a very long time and she pours herself a huge vodka to compensate for the boredom. Even so, she is at snarling point when, finally, the reason for all this domesticity arrives at the door.

It is the mother. The jet-setting, spotlight-netting mother. She is staggeringly beautiful in a lean hungry leopard-like way. Her deliberate walk and ravenous eyes make Claudia feel like some small mud-dwelling animal, but her effect on her son is even more dramatic. With fascinated horror, Claudia watches Ben shrink, fade, turn himself into a crack in the cracked plaster. He might as well be invisible but his beautiful mother doesn't seem to notice. She aims a kiss at him and turns away.

—Claudia? she says.—Sweet name.

Her own sweet name is Rhonda. Her black-purple hair has a sheen that puts Ben's eggplant in the shade. Claudia's legs begin to feel weak with despair, though this could also be the vodka.

Rhonda is on her way to Nepal. Claudia can see it now. Trails of Sherpas toiling over the mountain-tops, labouring under designer sponge-bags. Rhonda always one summit ahead, flying her aubergine head in the thin wind. She has to travel, can't take New Zealand for too long, has lived in Singapore on and off for a number of years.

—Doing what? asks Claudia.

—Oh, a little of this, a little of that, says Rhonda.

Claudia has never heard anyone use Oh in such a conscious way.

—A little interior decorating, says Rhonda.—And a little beautician work.

Claudia rejoices. Because she has never needed one, she despises beauticians with the whole of her easily beautiful heart.

—How *useful*, she says.—Did you start your own business?

—Oh my God, no! says Rhonda, laughing.—I just did it for close friends, it's a little talent of mine.

Claudia can feel the rage of the patronised pressing on the backs of her eyes. She throws back a necessarily large mouthful of vodka and sees the whole of Rhonda's life. Her vodka-sharp mind sums it up in two short sentences:

1) Rhonda is a woman of excess

2) Rhonda is a bitch.

As Claudia begins to see the downside of these qualities, Rhonda continues with her twenty questions.

—Where do *you* work? she asks.

—In town, hedges Claudia.

—Doing what? pursues Rhonda.

—I'm in the food industry, says Claudia.

She despises herself. She also knows that, as soon as Ben regains the power of speech, he will imitate this answer several times a day for the next three weeks.

—How *useful*! says Rhonda.

In spite of herself, Claudia almost admires her.

—My friend's daughter has just started dietitian school in Dunedin, says Rhonda.—Was that where you trained?

Claudia shifts on her uneasy chair. Ben has entered his statue state.

—I'm sorry, could you speak up? Rhonda asks.

Claudia looks at Ben. His face is white marble.

—Oh, I didn't train, Claudia says.—It's just a little talent of mine.

There's a lengthy silence. Claudia looks at Rhonda, Rhonda looks at Claudia. The silence grows. After thirty seconds or so, which seem like hours, Ben's desperation turns vocal. His voice is rusty from disuse as he addresses Rhonda.

—Where's my better half? Rhonda echoes. Clearly, the term *better* is so ludicrous that she doesn't take offence.

—He's late, mumbles Ben.

—Yes, of course he's late, says Rhonda.—His schedule's hell.

—Do? says Ben faintly.

—Speak up, darling, says Rhonda.—I'm not a lip-reader.

—What does he DO? asks Ben.

—He's a doctor, says Rhonda.

—Have you heard from, says Ben. The garage door swallows up the last word and the question-mark. Rhonda's eyes roll to the ceiling.

—Christ, that noise! says Rhonda.—I don't know how you put up with it.

—DAD? bellows Ben into sudden silence.

—Your father! says Rhonda. Her lips fold themselves into an origami sneer but not before Claudia notices that her teeth are unusually sharp.

—I wrote to him, says Ben.

—And? says Rhonda.

—And nothing, says Ben.

—Exactly, says Rhonda.—Your father turned non-communication into an art form. He only ever mastered three words. You know what they were?

Ben looks impassive. Claudia tries to look impassive.

—*The same again*, says Rhonda.

Silence.

—He got so good at that one that they invited him to rehab, says Rhonda.

—So he's still inside, says Ben drearily.

—So I would suppose, says Rhonda.—But I don't make a point of taking flowers.

She laughs angrily. Ben gets up, stumbles to the kitchen, and puts his head in a cupboard.

—Believe me, says Rhonda,—living with Ben's father was like shutting my thumb in the door daily.

—For God's sake, Mum, says Ben from the cupboard.—Why is he always *my father*? Why don't you just say his name, for Christ's sake?

—Because he's not worthy of a name, says Rhonda.—Your father isn't human so he doesn't have the right to a human name.

—My father my father, comes Ben's voice from the cupboard.—You make him sound like *my* goddam responsibility.

—Well, he's sure as hell not mine, says Rhonda. A stiff strand of designer hair springs from her head. Claudia is interested to see that even the most expensive lacquer gives way under severe stress.

—You used to love him, says Ben's cupboard voice.—Responsibility comes with love.

—I gave up on the responsibility trip the day I found out about Annie Bloody Barrington, says Rhonda.

There's a silence.

—But that was after the divorce, says Ben finally. He takes his head out of the plate cupboard and puts it in the oven.

—Or so he said, says Rhonda. She turns to Claudia.

—Don't trust a word men say, she says.—They'll screw you any way they can and then they decide to hear the call of the wild and go and screw someone else.

—If we don't eat soon this'll be ruined, says Ben's voice desperately.

—Got a man in your life, got a problem, says Rhonda to Claudia.

Claudia thinks of Leith, who doesn't even know he's in her life, let alone what a problem he is to her. Suddenly she has tears in her eyes which she hasn't even summoned.

—Shit, it's burning, says Ben from the oven.

—Though my current man's better than most, says Rhonda, with a return to complacency.

The doorbell rings.

—That'll be him now, says Rhonda with satisfaction.—Get that, would you, Ben.

The doorbell rings again.

—Get that would you, Claudia! says Ben, waving smoke off his casserole.

Claudia opens the door and then has to lean against it. She hopes her face is nowhere near as expressive as the one in front of her.

—Hi, she says, weakly.

—You've arrived at last! says Rhonda.

Her man, better than most, walks past Claudia with his head down. He stands in the middle of the expectant room.

—Ben, Claudia, says Rhonda grandly.—This is Heath.

Claudia faces things

—So then what happened? says Leith with intense interest.

—Then I got off my face, Ben got off his face, Heath got off his face, and we all sat around in a drunken haze and loathed each other, says Claudia.

—Heath looked as good as ever, she says reflectively.—Bastard.

She looks at Leith for signs of jealousy, doesn't see any. He keeps slicing his serene way through a ham.

—Sounds a riot, says Leith.—And what about Rhonda?

—She just smirked, says Claudia despisingly.—Whether or not she realised what was going on, she was just one big lamb-dressed-as-mutton smirk.

—So that's it with Heath, then? says Leith.

Claudia looks at him for signs of pleasure. None.

—Yeah, she says.—Replaced by someone's mother, for God's sake.

It is not this that makes her dispirited. After all, she had already decided to step off this particular stage and cast around for another play. Admittedly, she will miss playing the roles of huntress and temptress; she will miss dressing for the part of seductress, will miss making her flamboyant entrances into Heath's conservative world. But it is not this that is preying on her mind. No, there are darker shadows waiting for Claudia in the wings of her mind.

It is true, she does loathe Heath—but not as much as she loathes herself. For she has done something truly Othello-like, fuelled by jealousy and her instinct for intrigue. Her mind vaults back to before Ben's dinner, to before the Heath incident, which seems minor in comparison. Her mind takes her back to Haley's dim room, where she is lying in bed feeling unwell and incredibly, unbearably tempted.

From that short curtained hour she has learnt that it is sometimes better to remain ignorant. And that one rash step necessitates another, and another. She behaved despicably, and now it is unavoidable: she will behave even more despicably in the coming weeks. Her future stretches out like a thin overhead wire and she can't turn around, can only go on. Must plot and scheme, must disclose other people's secrets, even as she looks at Haley's face and feels pity.

Re-enactment

Although she cannot make time return, her mind does so again and again. Inescapably. Now she is crouching at Haley's chest of drawers, now rummaging through piles of paper, now looking under the bed. She is feeling nauseous, though whether from illness or guilt she has no idea. Now she is lying back in bed, curiously disappointed, curiously relieved. Now, she spots what she was looking for all along, in full view on the bedside table.

And her heart is pounding, and her hand is reaching out.

Stop Claudia stop.

I can't.

Providential?

What made Haley snatch up the phone and ring her own number? With each waiting ring, the vivid image of Claudia muddied until she was only aware of a rushed chaos. This chaos was not Haley's own—the shop was empty, the carpet smooth and newly vacuumed, the counter clear. But as she listened to the phone ringing back in Grafton, as she sat perfectly still and waited to speak, all she could feel was frantic movement.

—Hello? she heard, in a voice that was Claudia but not.

—It's Haley, she said.—Just calling to see how you are.

—Fine! said that strange, rushed, frantic voice.—Thanks! I'm just going to head home.

—Is everything all right? said Haley.

—Of course! said Claudia.—Why shouldn't it be?

—No reason, said Haley.—You sound strange, that's all.

—Of course, said Claudia again.—I'm sick, remember? That's why I'm here.

Haley put the phone down but even Claudia's rudeness hadn't

reassured her. She thought she had heard movement in the background, a drawer opening, shutting too fast.

Predestined?

Very often we hear what we most don't want to, as if by imagining the worst we actually make it happen. Claudia's ears first interpret the phone as a siren, shrilling her guilt through the house. When she snatches up the phone in a reflex action, it is with a sense of inevitability that she hears Haley's voice. For this, too, is what she has most dreaded.

Why has Haley rung right at this moment? It is as if she has X-ray eyes, can see through streets and over pylons and through the windscreens of crouching cars, through the closed curtains of her own room into Claudia's guilty, sneaky heart.

—Just checking up on you, Claudia hears her say.

—You're *what*? asks Claudia. She can hardly believe it, yet she has expected this from the moment her treacherous hands began rifling through Haley's possessions.

—Just checking on you, repeats Haley, sounding slightly surprised by Claudia's strong reaction.

—Of course I'm OK! says Claudia, forcefully. She is not; she is covered in sweat and her hand slips on the receiver, and her other hand reaches quickly, quickly, for Haley's bedside cabinet, clumsily opens the drawer, shuts the drawer.

—I'm going home, she says, and it is true. Although she still feels weak, she cannot wait to leave the scene of her crime and she hides the evidence in the drawer, closes it up in darkness. She is perversely glad that Haley has suspected her and interrupted her— whether by prescience or by guesswork, she doesn't know. But she also knows, with a sinking feeling, that she has gone too far to turn back.

For already, as she looks around Haley's tidy room, the snake of knowledge is stretching through her veins. As she smooths the bedspread, it uncoils itself slowly into the very tips of her fingers. By the time she closes Haley's door behind her, it has already poisoned her blood and infected her mind.

She looks back at the house and marvels that it is intact. For the destructive impulse that has entered into her makes her feel that she should be seeing flames, eruptions, crumbling walls. If she has her way, the lives contained in that house will soon be changed beyond recognition.

She feels elated at the prospect, and also sick. Sick with stolen knowledge.

Falling towards an answer

Haley dreams

she is walking along a flat ribbon of blutack, which is part of a medical test to see if she will be a fit mother. what will happen if she falls or fails? they haven't told her but there is a nurse way back at the start of the blue road cheering her on

you must reach the top of New Zealand, the nurse shouts

the blutack is getting thinner and is stretching. Haley reaches down and starts using her hands but sees she has thick mittens on and cannot grasp the line

i can't make it, she shouts, *you'll have to let me off*

she doesn't know if she has made a sound

you've left your wallet behind, the nurse shouts. her voice sounds strangely familiar, like the sound of a voice calling down a Croydon road. Haley looks back. the nurse has turned into Claudia but she has Haley's hair and Haley's clothes, and she is holding Robert by the hand

give Robert back to me, screams Haley

not until you tell the truth, laughs Claudia, with tears streaming down her face

the blutack swings dangerously, swings and loops like an insecure cradle. Haley screams again but can't hear anything. she looks down and sees the ground is very close, only a foot beneath her

i'm getting off, she shouts, *i have to leave*

she tries to step off. her feet are tangled in thin sticky blue spiderwebs and she falls forwards

puts her hands out to save the baby and herself

wakes.

Her wrists are braced against the headboard and aching, and she has pins and needles in both her hands. She flexes her fingers, lies there breathing hard, reaches out for her Robert book but it isn't there.

She sits upright. Her hands scrabble desperately through the darkness by the bed.

Where are you Robert where

Somewhere far away, inside her head, a drawer opens and shuts. Her fingers relax, fish inside the cabinet, find the book. Mechanically, she begins to write.

April

April is cruel. Eliot said so. Everything is false—appearances, expectations. Every aspect of life is being swept towards some kind of ending, while instinct is crying, Stay, look back, only hard ground lies ahead. Yes, April is cruel, Eliot said so and now Claudia is about to prove it.

In Auckland April is more treacherous than in any other place. Days are warm as the wolf's breath, so that the bite of night is like a betrayal. The sun rocks slowly through the sky but the dark comes unexpectedly early. The trees turn gold and look radiant but hidden in the leaves the tuis croak of sadness.

With the falling away of the sap, with the hastening of winter, Haley's and Claudia's stories quicken too. In fact, their lives have become so entwined that their story has become one, and it begins to accelerate under the combined weight of two pasts. Looking back, Claudia wonders if this absolves her of guilt. Because events have been set in motion that are too heavy for her to stop, even if she wanted to. There is no such thing as an accident of birth. Her part in this was decided before she could speak.

It is the first hour of the first day of April. In the darkness of this early morning, the Comet Soho, the crescent moon, and various falling meteors will witness without interest the intensifying of human emotion. The quickening of Claudia's anger, and of Haley's fears.

No avoiding it

Haley is sunk deep in sleep. Her mind wants to see the Perseid meteors but her body wants sleep. And if there's one thing she's learnt in the past months, it's the supremacy of the body.

She gives in to cravings constantly, is always in pursuit of physical comfort. She, who always disapproved of Sandra taking her electric blanket on holiday. The London Halley used to insist that the intellect can overcome all. The new Haley has been forced to admit—because of grief, because of pregnancy—that humans are essentially animals. When the flesh says it's time for warmth, when the tongue demands salt, when the eyelids fall with the weight of a Negro spiritual, that's the time to listen. There is no choice.

Story within a story

In the middle of a downtown plaza was a shopping centre, with floors stacked like a many-layered gateau. In the middle of the shopping centre was a sweet factory. A jewel in the bowels of the earth, it held a myriad of tiny jewels within its form. Ruby and amber and emerald globes shone, and pastels beckoned with husky aniseed voices.

The girl was drawn here, at first once or twice a week, then every day. As if to a magic well, she found her way through slanting glass walls and sloping floors. She was drawn to black, this girl. There was black in her mind and her heart, and in her bruised eyes. Using a plastic shovel, she would mine those barrels filled with black. For a small sum, she could carry away all that her body called for, and her black treasure would sustain her through that day until she returned the next.

(—Liquorice, says Haley to Leith.—It's all I want to eat.)

Black has always had a bad press. It is associated with foreboding and death. Black flags, Victorian mourning clothes, stormclouds, and bottomless lakes housing weed-ridden bodies. Black moods black looks black dogs on shoulders and black sheep in the family.

But there is something positive about black, too. For it cannot be changed, cannot be diffused or stained or mixed into something different. It is what it is, and the girl knew that. She nourished the child inside her with certainty—quite something in such an uncertain world. She fed the child on the traditional colour of death so that it would grow strong and sturdy with no false expectations.

This is what her body told her to do and she obeyed.

(—Dutch liquorice, she says to Leith.—Strong and salty and you can chew it for hours.)

Ever afterwards, no matter where that girl was in the world, whenever she smelt that curiously pungent black smell she would remember humid air, tuis creaking in the trees, and the flat nasal voices of people who could have been her own.

(—Yuk, says Leith,—sounds revolting.

But he begins to bring home small paper bags for her, full of her craving.)

Yes, by now Haley's appetite is like the sea, roaring up on her as she stands at the shop counter or watches TV. Just when she thinks she can turn her back on it for a while, it launches at her again, rearing its huge head, opening its demanding mouth. It is fathomless, bottomless, and she finds the best way to appease it is with bread.

—Just as well you live with a baker, says Leith. Obligingly, he puts away his musician personality and his bone-carving self, dons his baker's cap. Inside Haley, the boy-girl breathes to the sound of eggshells cracking and the soft fall of flour.

Every now and then, Haley stops at the Greek foodstall halfway down Queen St and buys a square of baklava. Scattered with nuts, packed with sunshine and the song of bees.

—You have a sweet tooth, no? the middle-aged Greek guy asks her.

Actually it is not for the teeth but for the soul.

Falling stars and rising antagonism

Midnight is here, Claudia is here, and Haley is dragged from sleep on a blanket of nausea.

—Go without me, she says through her hair.

Leith bends down to pillow level.

—You'll never forgive yourself if you stay in bed, he says seriously.

Claudia looks as if she'll never forgive Haley for getting up. The look she gives Haley is strange, so strange that it penetrates Haley's daze. It is a look swollen with resentment, distorted with dislike.

Haley pulls her hair back from her face.

—You shouldn't use rubber bands in your hair, says Claudia disapprovingly.—It splits the follicles.

This is more normal. Haley relaxes.

—OK kids, we're outta here, says Leith.—Be prepared to be amazed.

—Be amazed, be very amazed, chants Claudia. She spins round the kitchen and ricochets off Haley's stomach.

—Oh sorry, she says. But she doesn't look it, and she keeps twirling.

Bastion Point. It has a safe sound to it but Haley feels more and more vulnerable as they drive in Claudia's car away from the city lights and up towards the sky. The threat seems to be felt only by her; Leith is unchanging as ever, and Claudia glitters and reflects off him. She is as luminous as Haley has ever seen her, and her talk devours the silence just as her car devours the dark miles.

Quasars are super-massive black holes that can swallow up whole stars the energy surrounding them is brighter than a million billion suns

The gates are closed so they have to leave the car on the main road and walk up the hill. The obelisk stands above them like a tooth, and under it (Leith tells them) are the remains of the one-time prime minister Michael Joseph Savage.

—*Savage*, says Claudia, striding over the dark grass.—A good last name, couldn't be better if he'd invented it. What's your last name, Haley?

Haley trips over a clump of grass and Leith catches her, sets her on her feet.

—Careful! he says.—You're walking for two, remember.

Claudia's beautiful profile is as stony as the obelisk. She stalks ahead, leaving Leith, Haley and the boy-girl to follow. At the top, she sits in the moonlight and tries to start an argument with Leith about when the land was occupied by Maori protesters.

—It was 1978, she says definitely.

—I think it was 1977, says Leith, equably.

Haley knows little about it but she can feel dissidence in the very ground she is sitting on. She closes her eyes and hears hammering, sees rough wooden shacks; hears shouting, sees police batons falling.

Hears Claudia.

—Bloody English, she is saying.—Always marching into places that aren't their own, taking over.

—Claudia! says Leith, half-laughing, half-reproving.—Christ, you overstate things.

Haley can't even retaliate, is starting to feel that she will never have anything to say again. She hasn't felt this excluded from humanity since Bangkok airport, and God knows there have been some grim moments since then. She huddles down into her blanket, arranges it in a hood around her face with just enough space for breath. Still she doesn't feel secure, and the chill wind of Claudia's meanness makes her ears ache.

—D'you know what causes this meteor shower? asks Leith. He has a beer in one hand and a beanie on his head, but he sounds like a professor.

—God? says Claudia glibly.

—Go to the bottom of the class, says Leith.—Flippancy always fails.

Claudia laughs and her eyes spark through the midnight air. She is so hard and bright tonight that she is outshining the stars, and Haley wishes she could ask her to dim her lights.

—Next pupil? says Leith kindly, drawing the mute dunce out.

—Don't know, Haley manages.

—No point in asking *her*, says Claudia.—Haven't you heard of pregnancy brain drain?

—What a load! says Leith.—Didn't you tell me your memory gets better when you're pregnant, Haley?

—Well, I hate to disillusion you, says Claudia,—but last time I looked at Haley she was a shop assistant, not a medical expert.

In fact, she has hardly looked at Haley since they left the flat, and that seems so long ago (Haley thinks) that Claudia probably doesn't even remember what she looks like.

—A shop assistant with an archaeology degree, muses Leith.— I kind of like that. Selling modern artefacts, plastic things that will never decompose.

—So anyway! What causes the meteors? interrupts Claudia. Her voice slices the flow of Leith's conversation like a scalpel, but still she tilts her flower face to the moon.

—Umm, says Leith. In thinking about Haley's career (or lack of), he has discarded his didactic act and it takes him a minute to pick it up again.

—Umm, he says,—it's something to do with a comet.

—Comets! says Claudia.—It's all we ever hear about now.

—Swift-Tuttle, that's its name, says Leith.

—You'd think they'd give them good names, says Claudia.—Or at least pronounceable ones, like cyclones.

—Haley's a comet name, says Leith.—If you had 2 Ls in it, that is.

He turns to Haley with such deliberate casualness that she feels worse. There is only one thing worse than being left out of a conversation and that is being kindly forced into one.

—Yep, she says,—but that's not the way I spell it.

She hasn't spoken for so long, and has had so many thoughts dammed up in her head, that on this lie her voice nearly breaks.

—Haley's a comet girl in more ways than one, says Claudia. Her voice is slick, oiled, coated with a foreign substance that Haley can't identify.

—What ways? says Leith. He lies back against a bush and drinks his beer.

—Oh, just the way she arrived, says Claudia airily.—Out of nowhere.

Haley shivers.

—And maybe she'll disappear that way too, continues Claudia conversationally.—All of a sudden, boof! Comet-girl's gone.

—What are you babbling about, says Leith idly.

The sky is almost orange, reflecting the sinister city: glow of a nuclear aftermath.

—What's this thing we're waiting for called again? Haley asks in a small voice.

Most meteors are no bigger than a grain of sand

—Pregnancy brain drain, says Claudia in a low voice.

friction heats them

—Perseid, says Leith quickly.—After the constellation Perseus.

until the air is incandescent with fire

—Think you can remember that, Haley? says Claudia.—Or do you think you should write it down?

—What the hell's the matter with you, Clawd? says Leith, who is starting to look annoyed.

Claudia ignores him and for the first time looks directly at Haley. Her eyes are shadows on white canvas skin.

—You're always writing, she says to Haley.—You just don't ever talk, do you?

Haley looks back. She is sick of having tiny needles of conversation inserted under her fingernails and skin, and is scared to think what they might signal. Most of all, she is ready to fight back.

—Some people talk too much, she says.—Some people spend their lives talking and acting.

Irritatingly, Claudia retreats.

—Look, there's a meteor! she says sweetly.

Silence falls with the shower of meteors. Bright streaks fall across the sky, landing behind Rangitoto so Haley cannot see the moment of their death.

The fall of meteors is directed from one area which is called the radiant

Now, her attack over, Claudia is mostly quiet. She speaks only to Leith, and then she lights up, her voice glows, the whites of her eyes shine silver. Towards Haley she is like a black hole.

Haley keeps her eyes on the north-eastern sky and watches the particles plummet at a rate of forty miles per second, falling from glory to extinction.

European starwatchers named the meteor shower after a Spanish martyr who was killed close to the time. They called it the burning tears of St Lawrence.

The streaks merge and blur until the sky is running with gold, and Haley has to wipe her eyes with the corner of her blanket.

Haley is losing her way

—What exactly was that all about last night? asks Leith.

—Fucked if I know, says Haley, shrugging.—Claudia's obviously got over her brief liking for me.

She realises how bad it has become: that even Leith, with his instinct for avoiding conflict, has noticed. All day she has been walking around blind with depression, it has weighted her head as the baby is weighting her stomach. At work she has had to lean on the counter, feeling as if she will fall back or sideways if she tries to stand unsupported.

—Try not to worry, says Leith.—She'll get over whatever it is and if she doesn't, well, it doesn't really matter, does it?

She supposes not, supposes she could cut her losses and just leave. Get out of these lives she has crashed into, which is so obviously what Claudia wants her to do. But partly *because* this is what Claudia wants her to do

(Robert: *You always were a stubborn bitch Halley!*)

and mainly because there is still unfinished business here, she knows she will not leave yet.

It is hard and getting harder, though. Claudia's needling, knowing voice has been filling her head, filling her with fear. What does Claudia know and how long will it be before she blows Haley's life sky-high? Even in daylight, it is terribly real: the huge bright endless night, raining sharp stars into Haley's eyes. She longs for the safety of low English cloud. How often does this happen, she wonders: that you get to the end of an escape route and suddenly have a perverse desire to retrace your steps.

—Why are you so late home? Leith asks now.

She is late home because, after leaving the confines of work, life lost its bearings. She walked random streets, turning and turning somewhere down near the wharves. When she saw certain signs on certain corners more than once, she was slightly reassured. Her inconsistency had some pattern to it, at least, and she clung to this as evidence that she still existed.

(—*Security through insecurity*, says Robert out of the roaring space.)

In a wasteland of oil drums and huge coils of wire, she had climbed onto a concrete pipe and had sat incongruously in her work clothes with her head between her knees. When she looked out past the harbour to the open heads, the space wasn't roaring quite so loudly.

—Claudia is only flesh and blood, she had said, slowly.—Flesh and blood.

Claudia is losing her grip

Last night was terrible. She couldn't stop herself, her feet slithering on sentences and her hands grasping at words that fly out her mouth anyway.

There is no turning back, either. She is now committed to her course, she is heading at top speed towards some kind of collision with Haley. Worse, she is taking a bizarre pride in her work, making it as smooth as she can, turning destruction into an art form.

She can't exactly see how this will all end, and when. But it will end, and violently, because of something she did recently that is entirely her fault, and something that happened to her a long time ago for which she cannot be blamed.

Once, Claudia and Adrian talked about it all

Very often, Claudia thinks of Diane with something approaching hatred. If she wants to, she can track most things wrong in her life back to Diane.

—If she hadn't adopted me, Claudia said to Adrian,—who knows where I could have been by now.

—Probably on the streets, says Adrian.

—I could've been adopted by some rich British couple, grown up in London, said Claudia wistfully.

—Lucky escape, said Adrian.—You'd now have chronic chilblains.

—But think where I could've ended up working! said Claudia.— Paris, Prague, Palermo!

—Paramatta, said Adrian brutally.—Face it, Claud, life's mundane wherever you are.

—It doesn't need to be this mundane, said Claudia stubbornly.

Always, she wants to step back and alter Diane's decisions. At different times she enters different real-life scenarios, twists their outcomes and feels the world open up to her like an egg cracked over a basin. If Diane had only lived differently, made different choices.

—If only she'd MADE SURE, said Claudia.

—Made sure what? said Adrian, lost.

—Made sure I wasn't an only child, Claudia repeated sternly.

—She probably couldn't have kids, suggested Adrian.—I can't believe you haven't asked her.

Claudia looked cagey.

—I don't want to pry, she said.

—Well I bet that's it, said Adrian.—She adopted you because she's barren.

—That's no excuse, said Claudia dismissively.—She could have adopted again.

—But you wouldn't have liked that! said Adrian practically.—Because you know what you have to do with brothers and sisters, Claudia? You have to Share.

—Yes, exactly! said Claudia.—I could share the responsibility for bloody Diane.

—Haven't you got that the wrong way round, sweetie? asked Adrian.—She's the parent, remember?

—Not the wrong way round at all, said Claudia darkly.—Diane's neediness is legendary.

Adrian raised his eyebrows slightly sardonically.

—Like mother like daughter? he suggested.

—Not my mother, said Claudia automatically.

There is no one to help when she looks at Diane and suddenly sees her neediness as vulnerability. This is even harder, this kind of seeing. When Claudia sees the skin around Diane's eyes collapsing from too many cigarettes and too many late nights, then she feels as old as Rip van Winkle and as guilty as Eve. At times like this she wishes she could just accept Diane—even like her—instead of feeling compelled to disown her.

Claudia's pain, explained

In the shower, of all predictable places, Claudia discovers she has a lump in her left breast. She thinks this might be irony—the fact that a doctor has recently been on intimate terms with her breast and hasn't even noticed.

—Is this ironic? she asks Adrian.

—It is, he assures her.

They sit back on the Shrinks' leather sofa and look pleased: the master of irony, and his diligent disciple who has finally cracked the code. Then, simultaneously, they realise that the reason for Claudia's success is nothing to be pleased about. Adrian looks concerned, Claudia tries to look unconcerned.

—You'd better get it checked right away, Claud, says Adrian.—And not by that useless family fuck of yours either.

—Are you kidding? says Claudia indignantly.—I wouldn't let him near me or my family.

—If I had one, she adds.

—And now Ben, the poor bastard, has got him for a father figure, says Adrian gloomily.

—You'd think Heath was a poor bastard too, says Claudia,—if you'd met Rhonda.

—You know he probably caused your lump in the first place, don't you? says Adrian.

—How? says Claudia.—And don't call it my lump, I don't intend to have it long.

—Too much mammary manipulation, says Adrian.

—It's more likely to be that witchy wife of his, says Claudia.—Putting a hex on me.

—That's a bit imaginative, says Adrian, cackling.

—Well, she could have a talent for modelling clay as well as clothes, says Claudia defensively.

Voo-doo Vivienne. Suddenly Claudia is aware of a throbbing pain in her left side.

—Ahh shit, she says.—She's at it again.

She jumps up from the sofa and the pain stops.

—Oh, that's where my Rubik cube got to, says Adrian, seizing it up.

Claudia rubs her left hip and sits down again. She looks at Adrian, he looks at her. They listen to the antique clock ticking towards another night.

—You going to be OK? Adrian asks.

—Look on the bright side, says Claudia.—At least death is a hundred per cent guarantee against turning out like Rhonda.

Claudia is being surprisingly mature about the possibility of having a life-threatening illness. She doesn't cry when she is examined by a female GP and referred to a specialist. She doesn't rage after a needle biopsy reveals she must go to hospital for an operation to remove the lump. In fact, she remains quite calm and discusses the whole procedure in a detached way with Diane, who annoys her intensely by getting teary-eyed every time they speak about it.

The truth is, Claudia is preoccupied. A brush with impersonal death is relatively insignificant compared with what is going on in her personal arena. For she has lions with human faces to conquer, has bears with complicated human personalities to wrestle with, has bulls to bait and snakes to charm. She, the golden gladiator, strides towards her battle, and hospital appointments, mammograms, and hovering cancer are relegated to the shadows.

But there's still fun to be had

and Ben still comes round to play. He summons Adrian to join them.

—Adrian! he orders down the phone.—I've got baked goods.

In the high-floored, low-ceilinged gloom of Diane's living-room, he opens his backpack and brings out a tupperware container.

—A little play-lunch, he says, rubbing his hands.

The cookies inside are the neatest Claudia has seen, so she knows Ben has baked them himself. They are beautifully oval, like the orbit path of a planet, and are smooth on top. The cornflakes are well-crushed, with no jagged bits to scrape the roof of your mouth. But

—Just be careful Claud, warns Ben.—They're pretty strong.

—I can handle it, says Claudia in a deep voice.—I'm no girly.

She breaks one in half to start with, chews and swallows, sits around waiting. Nothing happens so she picks up the other half.

—Rather you than me! says Ben, blowing out his cheeks.

Adrian strides into the room and the ceiling lowers still further. Ben holds out the container, house-husband at a kitchenware party.

—Want one? he asks politely.—If you wanna catch up with Claud you'd better have a whole one, but you'll be off your face.

—I'm not! says Claudia but suddenly Diane's living-room looks very spacious. And Adrian appears to be a long way away although, when Claudia puts her hand out, his arm is actually right beside her.

—Are you all right there, Claudia? he says.

His voice sounds as if it's on an answerphone tape that has stretched.—Youuu roight theeere Clauudeea???

She thinks she'll lie down and does so. But once she's lying down she still feels as if she's falling. Ben says something. Adrian says something. She thinks it's interesting and that it is probably directed at her, but a second after she's heard it she has forgotten it.

—Sorry, I've forgotten, she says.

—I said, how's that flatmate of Leith's getting on? says Adrian.—She looks kind of sad.

Claudia's body is a bank of snow, deep deep with inertia. Her hands and feet are numb and then they start to tingle, she loses them again and finds them. She has something important to say about Haley but she can't move anything except her eyes, and even that's an effort.

—We should ask her out a bit more, says Adrian.—Get to know her better.

Claudia makes a supreme effort, because somewhere she knows that this is supremely important.

—NO!! she says.

Both Adrian's head and Ben's head swivel towards her with one slow movement.

—What exactly is your problem with Haley? says Adrian.

Claudia swoops in her mind, tries to stand upright on the surface of it but it sways under her feet like a hammock. Right at that moment she can't think why she has a particular problem with Haley, but NO is still resounding in her head with conviction so she says it again, several times.

—Is it a threatened only child thing? she hears Adrian say wisely to Ben.

—Is it jealousy over Leith? she hears Ben say uncertainly to Adrian.

—Whatever, it's definitely a turf thing, says Adrian.

—You mean, Stay off mine? says Ben.

—Exactly, says Adrian with emphasis.

Claudia can't retaliate because she's concentrating on keeping her balance. Her mind freefalls sideways, hits the side of her head, and by the time it's upright again she's forgotten what they said anyway.

Thinks of Haley. Feels sick. Groans. Wishes it was twelve or twenty-four hours later.

Aftermath

She wakes up late. Cookie crumbs in her hair, nausea in her stomach, rocks in her head. With the return of reality, memory also returns, and she remembers the path she has committed herself to.

She has to wear dark glasses into work, because the fluorescent lights in the kitchen are brighter than they have any right to be.

—What happened to you? says Leith.

—I overindulged last night, says Claudia with dignity.—And consequently will be less than my usual effervescent self today.

—So I'm safe? says Leith.

Claudia takes a deep breath, feels it grate past the nausea sitting in her throat, and her muscles tense.

—Depends on your definition of safe, she says. This is it and, now she has started, she stops thinking and leaves it up to animal instinct.

—I don't want to scaremonger, she says,—but there's something you should know about Haley.

She whips off her dark glasses, fixes Leith with a compelling stare.

—What? says Leith.—Is she OK?

He looks inordinately anxious and, if Claudia was faltering in her stride, this is exactly the encouragement she needs.

—Depends on your definition of OK, she says with skilful repetition.—I know things about her, things you should know.

—Clawd, if this is gonna be a bitch session, says Leith, shaking his head,—I don't want to hear.

—I wouldn't bitch about Haley! says Claudia glibly. (She is adamant that she is telling the truth.)

The swish of plastic curtains makes them both jump.

—Hey, you guys! says Myrtle the magnanimous.—Why don't you take a break?

—I've only just got here! says Claudia, startled into honesty.

But it appears that Myrtle also wants to adopt an unfamiliar guise today—that of benevolent employer. Claudia, after twenty years of only-childhood, is quick at recognising gift horses and not looking them in the mouth. Without another word she leads the way out the back door, winces in the sunshine, puts her glasses back on. She sinks down on a bread crate.

—I wonder what's happened to Myrtle, says Leith.—Maybe she's won some money on the horses.

—Leith, don't change the subject, says Claudia sternly.

—I wasn't! says Leith looking surprised.—We hadn't started talking about anything, had we?

—Haley? says Claudia loudly, as if Leith is retarded.

—Oh yeah, says Leith.—Well, get on with it then, if you have to.

—OK, says Claudia, taking a deep breath. Suddenly, she has a fleeting image of Haley standing at a glass counter, and a Japanese tourist fingering kiwi badges as gold as any New Zealand sunrise. Then, just as suddenly, she is back looking at rubbish skips and a concrete block wall.

—Haley, she says firmly.—She's not what she seems.

—As if you'd know what she's like, says Leith.

Claudia sways on her crate. The tourist is shaking his head—he doesn't understand—Haley is helping him put the pin through his jersey. It slips, Haley sucks her finger, and—

—Ow, says Claudia.

—You haven't exactly spent quality time with her, says Leith. He is closer to sharp, closer to sarcastic, than Claudia has ever seen him. This unnerves her but she tries to stay calm.

—I know things about her, she says.

—Yeah, like how to get under her skin, says Leith, looking at the wall.

—No! Like she's not who she says she is! says Claudia indignantly.

—What are you on about? says Leith wearily.

—I don't think her name's Haley, for a start, says Claudia.—
And I think she's here under false pretexts.

Leith raises his eyebrows in a disbelieving way, which infuriates
Claudia.

—There's a partner in England, she says icily.—The father of
the baby.

—You sure? says Leith. He narrows his eyes against nothing,
shifts on his bread crate.

—I have this feeling that her partner is dead, he says.

—She still writes to him! says Claudia.

—Well, she never talks about him, says Leith.

—Exactly! says Claudia triumphantly.—Does she ever talk about
anything?

—I guess not, says Leith shortly.

—Well then, says Claudia.—That's what I'm saying.

—I'm not sure what you're saying, says Leith.

—I'm saying that she could take off at any moment, says
Claudia.—She's homesick and she writes to her partner and sooner
or later she'll take off leaving a trail of bills behind her.

—But I trust her, says Leith.

—You'd trust anything! says Claudia angrily.—Do you even
know where Haley's from?

—Yes, says Leith,—London.

—You're too literal, says Claudia, realising too late that she's
assassinating Leith's character instead of Haley's.

—You know, where she's From, she elaborates.—Where she's
At, where she's Going.

—I get the feeling she doesn't know herself, says Leith.

—Aha! says Claudia.—That's exactly what she *wants* you to
think, when what she's actually going to do is have a great holiday
at your expense and then skip back to the UK.

Leith looks sceptical.

—Do you really think she's having a good time here? he says.—
I think she's pretty down to it, actually.

—That's exactly what she wants you to think! says Claudia
again. She kicks her heel against the plastic crate in frustration.

—What she really wants to do, she invents rapidly,—is have the baby and leave it here, piss off back to Britain free as a bird, and marry Robert.

—You know his name? says Leith slowly.

—I told you, says Claudia impatiently,—I know all about her.

—How do you know? says Leith.—Has she told you?

Claudia looks dismissive—an expression perfected over years of living with irrelevant Diane.

—I can't disclose my sources, she says in a dignified way.—Let's just say I think you should get rid of her before she dumps on you.

—Why should I believe you over her? asks Leith. He has a curious look on his face.

—Because I've got your best interests at heart! cries Claudia.

—Do you know what I think? says Leith.—I think you've got *your* best interests at heart.

—What? exclaims Claudia.

—At the risk of sounding like Adrian, says Leith,—I think it's the only child syndrome rearing its ugly head.

—That is so untrue! cries Claudia.

—Oh, I forgot, of course, you're a twin, says Leith.—But bereft at birth, right?

He is sounding more sarcastic and more human by the minute. Claudia looks at him and doesn't know if she even likes him any more.

—Look, Clawd, says Leith, and he stands up.—You like attention, you wanted to move into my flat, you don't particularly like other females, so you want Haley out of the way.

—That's not true! says Claudia. She wants to cry but she's terrified Leith will add this to the list of things wrong with her.

—For God's sake! she says.—I just thought you should know the truth about the person you're living with.

—So you have no particular attachment or antipathy towards Haley? says Leith disbelievingly.

—No! says Claudia.—Of course not.

Strangely, she still believes she is telling the truth.

It's a two-way street

—Haley you're not thinking of moving on, are you? says Leith casually.

—Why, do you want me to? says Haley in alarm.

—Of course not! says Leith.—You want some of this curry?

—OK, says Haley.—But where did you get that idea from?

—Oh, nowhere really, says Leith. His face is slightly flushed, which could be from stirring one of his lethal curries over a high heat.

—Tell me Leith, demands Haley. She has no right to demand anything from him, especially the giving away of information, and she is aware of this as she hugs her baby and Robert and London and her real self to her deceiving chest. But she needs to know.

—Just something Claudia said, that's all, says Leith, opening a random drawer and looking for nothing.

—What did she say? says Haley suspiciously.

Leith rummages in a vague way that suggests he wants to avoid conversation, but the truth is forced out of him by Haley's steely stare.

—She just said, he says reluctantly.—She's just got some crazy notion that you might be here on false pretexts and that any day now you'll be hitting the road.

Panic envelops Haley like the hot mustard smell of the curry. Threaded through her panic is the faintest of admirations for Claudia, who has seen beyond her own beautiful nose. Rage is often the best way to cover up fear, and so now rage takes over.

—Why the fuck can't she leave me alone! shouts Haley, reaching in front of Leith, slamming the drawer shut on her finger.

—Ow shit! she says.—Ow bloody Claudia shit!

—Why can't she just live and let live? she says.

—Why's she getting hung up on me? she says.

Then she thinks she should stop and let Leith say something.

—I think she's jealous, says Leith seriously.

—Well, that's a laugh, says Haley, not laughing at all.—Of what exactly? My figure? My future?

—Your focus, says Leith.—I think.

—My *what?* says Haley. She does laugh at this. She has come halfway around the world to find someone who no longer exists, she is selling postcards of a country she should be seeing, she has no money no identity no idea of what to do next—but she's focused.

—The point is, you live without looking around you, says Leith.—You do. You just go on, whether people are watching you or not.

—Christ! says Haley, wryly.—Only through necessity.

—No, says Leith.—It's in you. It doesn't matter who you are or where you are, you'll always be you. But Claudia, she's different. She needs to be watched all the time or she'll fade away. She thinks. And you, because you don't need that, you threaten her and you take attention away from her. That's what Claudia thinks.

This is the longest speech Haley had ever heard Leith make. It is also, she thinks, one of the most ironic. Because, since the fall of Robert, since the curtain of blood descended over his eyes, ever since that moment she has been deliberately shrinking. She has checked her being for natural fibre and then hurled herself into a hot dryer, she has melted herself down to the smallest pool of Haley-material possible. She has gone to such great lengths and travelled such great distances to avoid attention and lose herself, only to be blamed for attracting attention and being too much herself.

—Shit, she says. She shakes her head.—Shit, I'll have to have a word to Claudia.

—Look, I don't think it'll do any good, says Leith.—If it wasn't you it'd be someone else.

—But to tell her! says Haley.—To tell her that I'm not interested in stuffing up her life.

—It's her problem, says Leith.—Here, have some curry and forget it.

But Haley cannot forget it. She eats curry and feels the hot cardamom pods explode in her mouth, but she cannot forget. The problem is not solely Claudia's, and Haley has known this and not known it ever since the two of them met.

This is the thing. She would prefer not to believe it, but her eyes have been taped open for some time now and, though her lids are stretched and aching, she cannot close them. She looks at the truth directly, just as her tongue correctly deciphers cool coriander and the smokiness of cloves.

The knowing. It has been mixed with curiosity, muddied with disinterest and dislike. But it has always been there, on both sides.

Operation Leith

When it comes to the chemistry of people, Claudia is remarkably clued up. Now she realises: to deflect the Comet Leith from its course, and then to place herself at the centre of its orbit, she must first understand where Leith is coming from.

The facts are simple. Leith refuses to believe Claudia, who has proof that Haley is not Haley but cannot reveal how she came by that proof. To reveal that would destroy any remaining shred of any possible liking that Leith has for her, and Claudia is not one to burn bridges.

Leith is not simple: is more difficult, in fact, than any male she has come across in her twenty years. He is particularly multi-sided, which makes it hard to identify where he is coming from; he is particularly focused, which makes him impossible to deflect from his course. He is like a dark brother of Soho, with an impenetrable coma and a nucleus steadfastly centred around a number of things. His career in music, his bone-carving, his sport, his family. And now, it seems, the preservation of Haley.

How many projects has Claudia undertaken since spiky, troublesome Haley has spun into her cosmos? Several, and perhaps they account for her growing tiredness, the recent pain in her side. Claudia now feels like a general, worn out from successive campaigns against an unwitting enemy. She feels like a detective, exhausted from exhausting all leads on an unwelcome intruder.

What's in a name

Claudia has always wanted a last name like Blahnik. Something exotic that conjures up feather boas and doormen and the money to take cabs all the time, not just when your shoe is broken. She resents Diane for lumbering her with Saunders, always introduces herself just as Claudia-without-a-last-name. She would like to be a phenomenon: known around Auckland by one title only, like a drag queen or a rock star.

So it's the name of the psychic that first attracts her attention. Leaving work one day, she notices fliers have been put up all along the street. They glow gold in the gold autumn sunset and, as Claudia passes each lamp-post, a name flicks at the edge of her vision repeatedly, like the shadows of railings seen from a moving car.

ROSENBLATT gap ROSENBLATT gap ROSENBLATT

She steps out of the flow of foot-traffic, gets her ankle kicked her elbow banged, gets a few scowls and gives a few back. Then she stands close in the backwater of a postbox and reads the paper promises of Dr Rosenblatt, psychic and healer.

1) He is an experienced aura reader and compassionate counsellor

2) He can help with love/ health/ career/ decision-making and life transitions

(and best of all)

3) HE CAN TELL YOU HOW SOMEONE TRULY FEELS ABOUT YOU!

This is certainly enough to make Claudia brave the current of fast walkers again and to borrow a pen from the most approach-able. Despite the fact that Dr Rosenblatt also has a website, she takes down only the phone number. She doesn't want to know too much about him. Mystery is almost always good—except when it comes to Haley.

The paradoxical art of lying

While sitting on her indignant bread crate, talking to Leith about the deceitful Haley, Claudia was disguising exaggeration and wild surmise as concern. In fact, during her supposed 'revelations', she came to tell the truth without realising it. Or did she, perhaps, cause a lie to become truth?

Because, as Claudia sat down to lie to Leith—*she's going*

to skip back to the UK—the very same thought came to Haley.

It seems to have been decreed: Haley will leave. Even as she goes through the motions that would enable her to stay, she feels as if she is climbing in socks up a highly polished slide. She must get out of Leith's kitchen and think this through, unclouded by Leith's friendship and concern.

—I'm going for a walk, she says to him after tea.

—Don't emigrate without saying goodbye, he jokes.

Haley manages to smile. She is beginning to feel transparent, and wants to draw the curtains in her head.

—See you later Claudia, she says.

Leith looks surprised. Haley also looks surprised, wrenches her mind back to the here and now.

—Oh sorry, she says.—I mean, Leith.

She walks fast up Symonds St with rain spitting in her face. She reaches the bridge. Leith has told her that, a couple of months ago, they thought Adrian had jumped to his death from this bridge. Haley cannot see this desperation in Adrian. To her he has always been wise, kind, and detached in a way she appreciates.

—Hail Haley, he says to her. And

—How goes it in the tacky-tiki land?

Questions that aren't questions, that are more like small, non-intrusive handshakes. Once they bumped into each other in Vulcan Lane and went upstairs into a huge warehouse for coffee. They sat in a vinyl booth and talked about playing pool, and he bought her a plate of nachos without making her feel indebted.

—D'you miss England? he said to her.

—I don't know, she had said.—Sometimes I think I miss the smell.

Adrian had told her that, when he got back from overseas and stepped out of Auckland airport, the different smell was the first thing he'd noticed. Warm earth and diesel, he'd said.

—Compared with cold earth and diesel, Haley had said.

—You're right! said Adrian thoughtfully.—So maybe it's not that different after all.

They have spent time sitting in a booth, he and she, talking as if they knew each other. Even though by then she'd known it was there, she had seen nothing of the despair shrieking in his head. But why would she have expected to? He didn't even know her last name, real or pretended, knew nothing about her except the face she presented to him under the Chinese lightshade, and the gently swelling belly she was feeding with nachos bought by him.

Now, she tries to imagine him right where she is standing, putting one long leg up on the rail, bringing the other one up, crouching above the tails of fast lights. Would he have slid from a crouch, or stood to his full height and tilted forward? She can't say. Still, she can only picture him with his usual sardonic smile and his beret, cannot make tears appear on his cheeks.

He stands on the rail, he wavers, he is a tall scarecrow of a figure outlined against blurring motorway dazzle. But it is not Adrian, he never jumped and possibly never even thought of this method of release. Haley leans by herself, looking at green signs in the grey light. She could go to Western Springs Helensville Whangarei, to Nelson Street or Auckland City. But she doesn't want to go anywhere. Except back. And now the tears are Haley's, cold and colder with each rush of air from the trucks passing below.

The tedium of daily routine, the trauma of loss, the aftermath of grief. She wants none of it, yet can't escape any of it. This is what she learns, standing on the Alex Evans bridge. That deliberate exclusion of the self is no easier to cope with than any other kind of exclusion, because the result is still the same. You still end up standing on an overbridge by yourself, the dark falling fast on your head.

Doubling back

This is the feeling that Haley has, these days. That she has arrived somewhere new, has arrived in a new room and has spent a long time, a long hard afternoon, learning the position of the furniture. That finally she has fallen asleep, knowing where the window is and which way to walk to the door. That she has woken suddenly to absolute darkness, so complete that her feet and her head have spun 180 degrees around each other. Some larger hand has lifted her, has turned her so that the room has altered and the layout is no longer as it was when she went to sleep.

It would be easy to panic. But just as Robert loved the orderliness of numbers, so he appreciated the quiet dogged way Haley operates. Now, quietly, she asks Kath if she can leave work early.

—What for? says Kath sharply. She is like a needle, Haley thinks, standing there on her thin high heels. Her words jab into conversations and just as quickly withdraw.

—I've got to get my eyes tested, Haley says calmly and deceptively to Kath the Needlewoman.

—You need glasses? flashes Kath.

—I don't know, says Haley patiently.—That's why I'm going.

She stares hard at the display of shiny platinum plates, so that the reflected sun burns the whites of her eyes. She looks back at Kath and blinks weakly.

—In shop time? reprimands Kath, out of habit.

—It was the only appointment I could get, apologises Haley. She doesn't mind abasing herself when she is lying, though she would rather die than apologise to Kath for real.

—Is it really necessary? asks Kath grudgingly.

—Well, I'm finding it hard to read the price tags, confides Haley the non-confider. This is a master stroke.

—We can't have that! says Kath smartly.—Just make sure you adjust your time sheet.

The buses are bloated with school children, and so Haley decides to walk up Queen St. She doesn't look around her at all until she reaches the top end, where the Asian stores and sushi bars make her feel that she isn't the only outsider.

Encouraged by this, she goes into a superette, buys an overpriced apple from a Chinese guy who is reading an Asian newspaper. But when she smiles at him he stares at her with opaque eyes.

—Have a nice day, she says weakly.

Still, he stares at her expressionlessly. She turns away from the counter and hits her head against the swinging carcass of a duck. As she walks out into the glaring street she puts her hand up to her head and her fingers come away covered in grease. She throws her apple untouched into a rubbish bin.

ATC Immigration New Zealand. She has seen it before as she has walked along K Rd but she has turned her face and mind away. Until now, until she knows that it is irrelevant and useless but that she is going to go through the motions anyway.

She remembers a time long ago. Lying on her back in Kensington Gardens, on a picnic rug, at the feet of her favourite Peter Pan statue. She has patted the squirrels and rabbits clustered around his ankles, has stroked his iron-grey sleeve.

—Why is it streaked with gold? she asks Sandra wonderingly.

—Because other children have touched it too, explains Sandra.

Halley looks at her hands, inspects them for gold flying dust. She still doesn't understand but she doesn't really want Sandra to take away the mystery in that kind instructional voice of hers. So she just lies down and sniffs her palms: metal with a hint of blood, the statue smell.

—Tomato soup? asks Sandra without really asking. She hands Halley the top off the thermos. Halley puts out her left hand, which isn't used to dealing with things, especially on this angle. Her left arm wobbles and the white plastic burns with red soup. She knows without looking that it is homemade—they never have tinned soup like other families.

—Better sit up, darling, says Sandra. She's not saying this would be better, she's saying it's the only thing to do. Halley lies disobediently, holding the cup on a strange angle, looking at Peter Pan's nose from underneath. The sky tilts crazily, English clouds loom against a pale sun.

—Darling, don't spill it, says Sandra warningly.

Halley knows she is going to spill it. It is just going to be that way. She will try to drink it lying down, it will pour out of the cup on both sides and run down her face and onto the rug. Sandra will be cross, Halley will feel stupid, they will take the bus home in silence and Halley will stare out at her reflection and open her mouth wide and Sandra will tell her not to make faces at the people and Halley will look at the floor.

She can't help it, doing things that she knows are a waste of time or won't work. She doesn't know if everyone is like this or just her, but there is a need to feel the hot sting of homemade tomato soup on both sides of her chin, so she lies on the rug on her back and tilts the mug. There's nothing else to do.

ATC Immigration is a blank building. No potted plants inviting your feet to step up to the doorway, no open door when you get there. No information about opening times, no chance of looking through the mirror windows to see if there are other immigrants in there. Haley recognises these tricks with admiration and with loathing. The tricks of a friendly government that is becoming less friendly; of an open, open-minded nation that is deeply suspicious; of a country made up of recently arrived mixed races that nonetheless feels threatened by foreign blood.

She puts her hand on the metal bar, pushes on the door and then stops pushing before it has even opened a crack. She steps back on the footpath and reads the windows.

Residents Students Workers Visitors Appeals Citizenship

There are no other options. Haley doesn't even know why she is there. Yes, she is a worker, yes, she is a visitor, yes, she is full of appeals and she could do with being a citizen of anywhere. She is all of these but none. What exactly is she going to ask for?

—The bastards! she hears.

A Pakistani woman is rushing out the door in a blaze of gold and purple. She is half-carrying a child by his wrist: a little boy, who is holding a Coke can and wearing a huge Nike cap over his face.

—Those bastards, the woman says angrily to Haley.—I've been waiting three hours and they still don't want to know.

Coke slops out of the kid's can onto Haley's shoe. She shrugs sympathetically at the woman.

—I've heard you've got to wait for a while, she says.

—Yeah, says the woman. Her voice is sarcastic and is already overlaid with a Kiwi accent.

—You have to wait forever, she says, marching her son off down K Rd.

Haley hovers on the footpath, stands on one foot and wipes the Coke off the other with the back of her leg. She stands like a lone heron in the midst of a grey tarseal swamp. Then she turns away from the blank-faced building and walks to the dairy to get her own Coke. Now, suddenly, she knows what she wants and what she doesn't, and it's not ATC that will help her.

She doesn't want to officialise the New Zealand side of Haley Purcell. She does want an identity, but one that she's already had.

Of dark women over water

Up on K Rd, Claudia thinks she sees Haley hovering outside a dairy. Quickly she crosses the road to the bus-stop, scrunches down beside a huge Samoan and asks inane questions about the breadfruit he is carrying. Where what and how do you cook it? she babbles stupidly. She would rather be thought stupid, she thinks, than be caught going to see a psychic. Although, in Haley's opinion, this would probably amount to one and the same thing.

For some reason, Claudia feels that if Haley sees her, her mission will be exposed immediately. Because Haley, although no Dr Rosenblatt, is certainly intuitive when it comes to Claudia. She sees straight through that shining exterior of Claudia's which so often blinds other people. She doesn't need to stoop and snoop. So thinks Claudia, with a mixture of guilt and panic as she talks about taro.

She is transported undercover by a yellow bus to Rosenblatt's house. It is interestingly mundane: a bungalow in Kingsland complete with a gnome and an ornamental pond. A suburban front? thinks Claudia confidently, as she walks up the path hooped with white-painted tyres.

Unfortunately, Rosenblatt seems to be composed of a number of fronts that extend well beyond his chiming doorbell. He stands in his low-ceilinged living-room and there are beads of sweat at his receding hairline. His eyes—advertised as accurate and all-seeing—slide off Claudia's as he tells her that he charges on a sliding scale. Per minute.

Claudia is undeterred and eager to start. She makes for a chair, but is stopped in her tracks and instead is ushered into a sunroom stuffed with driftwood and hot air.

—The vibes must be right, says Rosenblatt vaguely. He has an accent that doesn't seem to have any convincing country of origin.

They get straight to the heart of the matter. Relationship questions, as the posters insisted, are a specialty here. Claudia describes Leith, his star-sign, his talents, the lines on his forehead as he kneads his dough and the scars on the tips of his fingers.

—And he gives you no encouragement, right? says Rosenblatt in a thoughtful way.

—Right, says Claudia. Her excitement at being close to an answer wanes at this reminder, as if turned down by a dimmer switch.

—No encouragement, she says flatly, honestly.

—But no *dis*-couragement either, I sense, says Rosenblatt wisely.

Claudia feels the first flickerings of impatience.

—No, she says. Anyone with half an eye would know this just by looking at her, she thinks. As if her attentions would ever be actively discouraged! She shifts in her basket chair, looks at her watch, calculates the dollars she has already spent listening to her own voice.

—I am sensing that you are impatient, says Rosenblatt slowly.—You must wait while I tune into this Leaf.

—Leith, corrects Claudia loudly.

There is a pause during which Claudia hears some of the five o'clock news on a radio next door. The sky (she hears) is to be particularly stunning over the next two nights, as the comet will reflect off the earth and light the dark side of the moon.

—You should forget him, says Rosenblatt decisively.—You could get someone more worthy of your attention.

Claudia sits back, her own light momentarily extinguished by disappointment. Then she realises she has heard a statement that could apply not only to herself but to almost anyone. She decides to disregard it.

—But what does he think of me? she persists.—Does he think of me at all?

—He thinks of another, says Rosenblatt, waving his hand.—Maybe a female, maybe even himself.

His fingernails are bitten to the quick—probably, thinks Claudia savagely, due to the boredom of bringing out the same lines day after day while constantly maintaining a vacant stare. She pulls a tattered yellow poster out of her bag, points to it.

—You know, she says warningly,—I'm entitled to a free palm reading if I'm not satisfied.

—If you're not satisfied with the *validity* of the *information*, says Rosenblatt, quick as lightning. His stubby chewed finger highlights the out-clause.

—If you go to Leith and ask him, he elaborates,—I think he'll confirm what I've just told you.

—Of course he will! cries Claudia angrily.—Instantly! Would you be attracted to anyone who goes to a phony goddam psychic for romantic advice? For God's sake!

Suddenly Rosenblatt stands, holds up his hand, stares out the window.

—Wait! he says commandingly.

Claudia has already decided she won't be handing over any money, so it doesn't matter how many more minutes she stays around for now. She sits with a sardonic look on her face, watches him intently scrutinising the neighbours' concrete block wall.

When Rosenblatt looks at her again, however, there is something different about him. Maybe it is just that the late afternoon light is behind him, but his body seems to have grown taller and Claudia squints against its silver edges.

—OK, you're right, he says in a straightforward voice. The sing-song lilt has deserted him, and has been replaced by a strong Kiwi accent.

—I'm not getting anything on this guy, he says bluntly.

—Who knows, maybe he likes you, maybe he doesn't.

Claudia feels relieved, annoyed, certain, uncertain.

—The thing is, says Rosenblatt slowly,—something's coming from somewhere else. There's a girl. Dark, kind of stocky.

Claudia shifts uneasily.

—D'you know who that could be? asks Rosenblatt.

—No, says Claudia immediately.

—Maybe you don't, says Rosenblatt speculatively,—and maybe you do.

His eyes are invisible in his shadowed face so she can't see if he's looking at her, but she thinks he is.

—You don't know her as well as she knows you, he says,—but there's a real connection there, and it's going to get stronger.

He stands in front of the burning window. The embroidered tassels on the curtains sit over his head like some absurd kitsch tablecloth but he doesn't seem to notice.

—And the sun, he says.—Something to do with solar energy, the sun.

—It's in my eyes! interrupts Claudia rudely.

Rosenblatt ignores her.

—She's come from a long way away, he says.—Over long distances.

—For God's sake don't start talking about travel over water, says Claudia loudly.

—She's going to give you some very important information, says Rosenblatt.—Which will change your life.

Claudia leaps to her feet, stuffs the poster in her bag and then takes it out again, throws it on the highly polished coffee table.

—I won't be needing *that* again, she says pointedly.—Thank you for nothing, and goodbye.

Diane has a theory that she voices to Claudia every now and then in a mildly reproving way.

—You're always rude when you get rattled, she says.

—Rattled? What's that supposed to mean? quibbles Claudia, always.

—You know, Diane always explains patiently.—Scared.

Haley surprises herself and everybody else

So they're round at Leith's with all the sisters and Leith's Auntie Kira, who isn't really related to the family at all but seems to be known universally as Auntie.

—Now don't forget, Haley, says Tara with her mouth full,—that I'm around to help at the birth if you want me.

—It'll be painful enough without you there talking your arse off! says Aroha, whose hair is now yellow.

—Don't stress poor Haley out, says Rose reprovingly.—It'll go like a dream, Haley girl, you'll see.

Haley sits silently. The thought of the birth doesn't worry her, she thinks. What worries her is the fact that, by the time of the birth, she doesn't even know whether she and Tara will be in the same hemisphere. Her silence gives Auntie Kira the chance to say even more than she would usually.

—Will the father be at the birth? she asks interestedly.

—There is no father, mumbles Haley.

—What's that girl? says Auntie Kira.—Did you say, Where is the father?

—I don't think Haley wants to talk about it Auntie Kira, says Leith.

At this point Haley realises an atmosphere is brewing up—after all, this is Leith, who hardly ever intervenes. Her face closes.

—The father isn't important, she says woodenly, as if by saying it she will make herself believe it as well as everyone else.

—Not important! cries Auntie Kira.—The whanau is a baby's lifeblood, its lifeline, its life!

—I don't know what a 'fanoh' is, says Haley stubbornly,—but my baby isn't Maori anyway.

—A child should know who its father is, says Auntie Kira reprovingly.—Whatever race it is.

—Auntie Kira! says Leith.

He looks as anxious as Haley has ever seen him look, but still it isn't enough to make her stop. She has become one of Robert's volcanoes, and the lava that has been pulsing through her ever since he plummeted out of her life has finally reached the surface. She is sick of being calm, she is sick of suppressing rage, she is sick of supposition when there is no bearable reality to counter it with.

—OK, you want to know who the goddam father is? she shouts.

Everyone looks at her and for once they are completely, unnaturally, silent.

—Haley, don't, says Leith quickly.—It's none of our business, you don't have to tell.

—Oh, I'll tell all right! shouts Haley.—Just to get you all off my back. He's dead, OK? The father of my baby is lying in a tiny box in the garden of some hideous crematorium in Edgeware, England. OK? Are you satisfied now? Will the baby be satisfied hearing that?

The faces around her look anything but satisfied, which makes her feel worse. She has not made herself feel any better, all she has done is make other people feel as bad as her. The only people who have come anywhere near close to her since she sealed herself off from the world, and she has hurt them.

She must leave immediately because she is going to cry. She walks out of the blurry room, hits her shoulder on the door as she goes, steadies herself, and lurches into the side of the glass porch. Christ, anyone would think she was drunk instead of just reeling, reeling with grief.

All the way home to Grafton, Leith drives beside her. Cars hemmed in by double yellow lines pant angrily behind him, drivers shout at him, pedestrians laugh at him. A tramp tells him he'll regret it if he doesn't leave the girl alone. Leith ignores them all.

—Haley, please, he says politely.—Please get in.

He drives slowly, slowly, steering with his right hand, leaning over to the passenger door and holding it open a slit with his left.

—No! says Haley. She still can't see very well and she's not sure if it's because she's blinded by the reflection of the low sun, or blinded by shame. She stumbles on a crack and her anger increases.

—Fuck off, Leith, she says.—Go back to your fucking family and be pleased that you've got one.

—Haley, I just want you to get in so I can take you home, Leith says over the roar of the traffic.

Haley's rage is intense, it spikes the grey sky like the casino tower behind her.

—I haven't got a fucking home! she shouts. Even as she shouts, she realises her anger is misplaced anger. Then she realises that, if she's still thinking in jargon like that, Sandra is still in her head. This enables her to shift the focus of her anger to Sandra and the Northern Hemisphere, and her steps slow.

—You're being stupid, says Leith.

She is, she knows she is, but she wants to continue because it's like having a rest from herself. So she keeps on acting out of character, being stupid, stupidly walking, and Leith drives in first gear with one wheel nearly in the gutter, politely waving people past.

When they get back to Grafton, he parks the car in its normal illegal place on the footpath and throws the keys to her. He sets off down the street without a word. She sits on the porch because she's not ready to go inside, and soon he comes back with a carton of milk.

—Might feel like a cup of tea later, he says. He sits beside her with his back against the post.

They don't say anything for a long time. Then

—Can't you go away, says Haley sullenly.—Go inside.

—Well, I could but you've got the key, he says.

—Oh yes, she says.

—My key, he says,—but your home.

She doesn't give the key to him because she doesn't really want him to leave her, and he doesn't ask for it. They watch the sun burn filthy orange in the west and then they both say sorry at the same time. Haley's is an apology but Leith's? Well, Leith is looking at the sunset, and the tears in his eyes are orange and gold.

MAY

As the air starts to smell of leaf mould, Haley realises that she has missed the rain.

—But it rains all the time in Auckland, says Rose, —even in the summer.

—Only showers, says Haley. —And the sky stays high.

Rose doesn't ask her to explain this. Maybe she doesn't understand what Haley means: she has never been to England and so has never known a sky that hunches over the roof for seven months, resting its shoulders on the chimneys as if it has some degenerating bone disease. But whatever Rose doesn't understand in conversation, she sails right on through and Haley can walk in the draught-free space she creates, sheltering behind Rose's floral tent dress.

—Yep, we got crap weather here, girl, says Rose comfortably. She sits in the sunporch that her sailor husband—Leith's father—has propped up at the end of their house on one of his weekends home. Haley likes to hear Rose complaining. She has had twenty years of stiff-upper lips, and of witnessing pale English sun-haters travelling stoically to European beaches.

Sandra condoned no complaining. (Haley's mind, as we know, has been returning frequently to Sandra.) Sandra would stride into the sort of day that would be better not commented on, and proceed to comment.

—At least you know you're alive! she'd say heartily, as the wind sliced into their cheeks and knifed deep cracks in their hands.

—Makes you appreciate summer, she would say, as the tyres of a black cab scooped up dirty water and threw it over their legs.

It is hard to grieve around someone like that, hard to see the bright side of a death that you secretly hoped would happen after your own.

—At least you've known great love, Sandra had said.—No one can take that away from you.

But, after saying this, she had tried to take it away and now Haley sits on the other side of the world and listens to Rose complaining peacefully about rain.

As the days burrow deeper into May, Haley rigs up a washing line in her bedroom. The outside clothesline has become a thorn in her tired side. She is tired of coming home to find the pale shapes of her washing dripping in the dark, tired of picking shirts out of the mud after the pole has given in to their dead weight.

When she first puts up her inside line, she takes it down the same day. This is what Sandra would have advocated because routine is good for the soul, and tidying before sleep guarantees a restful night. But soon Haley realises that she doesn't mind sleeping with sleeves brushing the air above her face. She leaves the line up one night, and then every night.

—It must remind you of home, does it? says Leith.

—What's that? says Haley, sitting on her bed eating an apple, peering at Leith through the branches of her fabric forest.

—You know, all this rain, all this washing hung round the house, says Leith.—Does it remind you of winters in London?

—Actually, no, says Haley.

It doesn't, because Sandra had both a separate laundry and a clothes dryer. She would sort clothes and handwash jumpers without being asked and—without asking—would take anything with holes in it to Oxfam. Now Haley can lie in bed with her wardrobe waving gently over her. She can wake up in the half-light and notice, with a sense of relief, gaps in seams and the glint of safety-pins.

Now she can get up every morning and pick what she wants to wear out of the air. She has become happy in her own routines, although increasingly unsure about where she wants to perform them.

Claudia dreams

The night before Claudia goes into hospital for her operation, she has a dream

the sky is full of movement. clouds jerk around on cosmic strings, and the comet shoots back and forwards as if a huge hand is tipping the sky. stars spill over and back like balls on a bagatelle board. the milky way is one huge bar of splintered white chocolate

claudia is standing in the middle of a night desert. at her feet is snow instead of sand. she calls for adrian ben leith even diane but the flatlands stretch further than she can see and there is no one

suddenly a lion appears. well, it has the head of a lion but a human body, its mouth is open in a kind of snarl and its eyes are dark spaces into nowhere. it begins to dance, no ordinary dance but a ritualistic swaying rhythm with arms to the sky

claudia is mesmerised, doesn't know if it means harm for her. there is a foreboding inside her but her legs begin to walk towards the lion-human. just as she draws close enough to see that there are lights inside its cavernous eyes, stars begin to fall like hail on her head hurting like hail and the lion turns and opens its mouth

and claudia runs with her head down into a cave lined with moist warm walls and lies in a small, very dark space with her knees curled up to her head and someone takes her hand

listen the someone says

all i can hear is the sound of stars falling, says claudia with her eyes closed

it is a heartbeat, the voice says, and it says *look up*, and *you're safe*, it says

the light grows through claudia's eyelids and she lifts her head and sees it is the lion who is holding her hand, left hand to left hand. it lets go and reaches up, and starts to pull its face away and underneath it is a girl after all, a girl with familiar dark eyes but before claudia can say who it is

she wakes

and she can't remember very much at all, except that she has had a very strange dream about shooting stars and lions, and that today is the day of her operation.

The force that is Claudia

Is there really such a thing as the calm before the storm? Perhaps it is only ever scraps of memory pasted together later by nostalgia. Certainly in hindsight, Haley comes to see these grey days, these quiet May days drifting with rain, as some kind of lull. As if the world was holding its breath before at last releasing the truth.

The day Claudia goes into hospital is also soft and blurred with mist, looks like any number of days before it. But in fact this day summons an end to all deception, and Haley is finally sucked into the vortex that she has been pretending is avoidable.

In cartoons or space posters, comets are great golden stars with substantial curvy tails, and often they have smiles on their faces. In real life, seen from the earth, they are round solid spheres of light: serene, mysterious, impenetrable. But in truth they are neither. Up close, in truth, they are huge roaring clouds of ice and dirt, rocks, dust and frozen gases. The haze around them, giving the deceptive appearance of calm, is actually a spinning halo of chaos called a coma.

Claudia is put to sleep for her operation. Although her personal coma lasts only a few hours, the hidden energy roaring beneath it—a rapid current under the surface of a frozen river—has been there for some weeks. Even under anaesthetic, lying in supposed peace, she is seething with her secret. As her breast lies still under the surgeon's light, her mind continues to whirl.

Afterwards Haley will think of Claudia as a comet. A steadily brilliant exterior. A bright tail streaming away from the sun, deflecting attention from her purpose. And then the reality: masses of unseen, unforeseen energy hurling its way into Haley's life, speeding towards Haley at 27 miles per second. Tons of pouring, roaring gases that Ben would name as methanol, formaldehyde, carbon monoxide, hydrogen cyanide, but Haley would call by other names: jealousy, insecurity, fear, desire.

Threatening, yes. Dangerous, yes. But also essential for life. For collisions, Haley remembers—also in hindsight—collisions are what the earth was born of.

Just visiting

She walks along the hospital corridor to see Claudia in a slightly diffident way. She knows that, personally, she would hate being trapped in a bed unable to abandon conversations when she wants to. She is ready to pick up on non-visitor vibes, is ready to leave after five minutes or ten.

She is ready for anything, she thinks.

Her feet move on the shiny lino and her eyes keep pace with the doorways, scanning the lists of patients inside. Faith Fitzgerald Allison and Hall. She finds herself making law firms out of the neat typeface, the names falling neatly into rhythms. Jacobs Jefferson Cooper and Co.

But then there is Claudia, and she is out on her own. It isn't hard to spot the name after all. *Miss Saunders* has been neatly typed by some misguided administrator, who has been corrected—not neatly at all—by Claudia. Over the *Miss* is scrawled a huge *Ms* in violent, violet felt-pen.

(Haley smiles. She has a clear picture of Claudia being wheeled back into the ward: drugged, nauseous, but wielding her purple pen determinedly.

—*I am not a Miss*, she is shouting, brandishing her weapon of independence and political correctness.)

Haley sees Claudia before Claudia sees Haley. Lying back against a hill of pillows, hair like moon-dust against the dull metal bed. She looks pale but she is still starry. And still, when she sees Haley, she has that curious look in her eyes: animosity masked by curiosity, or is it the other way round?

—Hi, says Haley awkwardly.—How are you feeling?

Awkwardly, she pushes some daisies at Claudia.

—Daisies, says Claudia distantly.—I thought I smelt a strange smell.

Haley sticks her nose in the bunch and realises that they do smell very strange.

—Sorry, she says, and she takes them out of Claudia's drip-fed arms and places them on a trolley by the door.

—So how are you? she asks again.

—Minus a lump of breast tissue, says Claudia dismissively.— Apart from that I'm much the same.

—You're looking good, but then you always do, says Haley lamely.

—So that's no different either, she adds inanely.

She sits in an uncomfortably slippery chair, casts around for something to do.

—Want me to peel you an apple? she says, seizing one off the fruitbowl.

Claudia shrugs, watches Haley's left hand slicing red skin off white flesh.

—No fingernails, she says, as Haley quarters it.

—What? says Haley, surprised.

—I don't like those hard fingernail things left on the apple, says Claudia.—From the core.

Meekly, Haley examines the slices one by one and hands them to Claudia, who holds them in her right hand and nibbles them suspiciously from her left. Then

—How's Leith? asks Claudia abruptly.

—He's fine, gabbles Haley.—He sends his love.

—But no daisies from him, says Claudia with her eyebrows raised.

—I guess he's not really the flower sort, says Haley.

—Well, you'd know about that, says Claudia pointedly.—You know him so much better than I do.

—Oh, not really, says Haley hastily, trying to bolster Claudia up like a hospital pillow and make herself smaller and less important in the sphere of Leith.

—Sometimes you can live with people and not really know them at all, she expands.

—What exactly do you mean? says Claudia. She rises from her white bed like a snake, eyes glittering.

Haley presses back in her chair, unaccountably nervous. She hasn't really meant anything, particularly. She has thought before this, several times, that she is glad she and Robert didn't have to talk over a hospital bed. There is something about the situation and setting that seems to turn people into fools.

—Just that even when you see people every day, she improvises,—you still don't know what's going on behind the scenes.

Claudia stares at her intently.

—Unless you have some secret route to them, continues Haley rapidly. Claudia's snake eyes are making her nervous.

—Like, I don't know, she says.

—Like you might overhear a conversation or something, she says.

—Or read something about them, she says.

Her palms are sweating.

—For Christ's sake, Haley, cut the crap, says Claudia suddenly.

—What crap? says Haley, startled. She looks out the window at the grey May sky and could swear that, for a second, she sees a flare of white light heading straight for her.

—You know what I did, don't you? says Claudia. She lies back on the pillows but not in a vanquished way. Her drip catches the overhead light with a steely glint, and throws it back in Haley's eyes.

—I really don't, insists Haley.—I don't know what you're talking about.

She doesn't, but she knows she is about to. There is a roaring in her ears like some natural disaster—an earthquake or a tidal wave, from which is it impossible to run.

—Your diary, says Claudia clearly.

Haley stares at her.

(Robert's voice, echoing in her head: *You what?* he is saying. *You read what?*)

—I read your Robert book, says Claudia, and she stares back at Haley. Unrepentant but expectant. Unrepentant—but with fear in her eyes.

—My Robert book, says Haley expressionlessly.

—The day I was sick, says Claudia.

—The day I let you stay in my room! says Haley.

The blood is whirling in her ears and she feels very sick herself. She sits like a stone on her hard hospital chair, wonders if it is clichéd to put her head between her knees.

—That's right, says Claudia.

(*I don't believe it*, says Robert slowly.)

—Look, just believe it! says Claudia impatiently. She looks at Haley as if she wants to shake some reaction out of her.

—I'm not lying! Claudia says.—Unlike some of us whose whole life is a lie.

—So now you know, says Haley slowly.—More than you should.

Her face feels as if it is covered with a layer of bandages, immobile, and only her mouth opens a slit and pushes out words.

—So now you know, she repeats with difficulty.

(*Feel good, does it?* sneers Robert.)

—Don't think I'm proud of myself, says Claudia defiantly.—But I had this feeling you were hiding something and it turns out I was right.

—You were *correct*, says Haley the pedant.—But you weren't *right*. There is nothing right about what you did at all.

She speaks with the conviction of the experienced. Only those who have sinned and repented can preach with such certainty.

—You were lying to my friends! says Claudia.—You told us a load of utter crap!

—But I wasn't harming anyone! says Haley.—I'm still not!

—Maybe not yet, says Claudia.—But what about when you walk out on Leith and your workmates and all those people who think you're here to stay? What about when life here gets too hard and you want to go back to Robert?

—Go back to Robert, repeats Haley stupidly.

—Yes, Robert, says Claudia with killing sarcasm.—Remember him? You should, you write to him enough.

—What the fuck do you know about Robert, says Haley. This is not a question, it is a contemptuous dismissive statement but Claudia, wrongly, chooses to answer it.

—I know he's the father of your baby, she produces triumphantly.—I know you broke up in a bad way, and you regret it.

Haley's lips part incredulously but there is nothing to say. These tangled assertions are both right and so terribly wrong that she doesn't know where to begin unravelling them.

—So you're harming him too, says Claudia accusingly. The drip in her arm swings faster as her outrage at manipulative Haley gains momentum.

—And all those people you ran away from at home? she goes on.—That Sandra you told me about? I bet that was a lie too. I bet Sandra wants a grandchild and you're just too selfish to share it.

The mention of Sandra is just what Haley needs. Suddenly she can speak again. She raises her eyebrows in Claudia-fashion.

—Exactly how far did you get in my private book? she asks pleasantly.

Claudia shrinks momentarily.

—I only read a few pages, she says defensively.—And not all of it, I just skimmed.

—Just dipped into it, did you? says Haley, still in an even tone.—And how could you bear to put it down if it was such a good read?

—You rang to check up on me, remember? mumbles Claudia, looking away.—Pretending to be concerned about me.

Clearly, the reminder that Haley is a pretender gives her back her confidence.

—Yes, pretending! she goes on emphatically, and she looks straight at Haley again.—I got as far as your birthday, or should I say your false, pretended, unreal, deceptive birthday.

Strangely, Haley is swept with relief.

—So really you know nothing, she says quietly. She has a sudden image of Claudia crouching in the dim room, book in hands, holding enormous knowledge about herself in her very hands but not turning to the page that would unlock it. The phone rings. Shock! Claudia drops the book into Haley's bedside cabinet.

(*So that's how it got there*, realises Haley.)

—Nope, you still know nothing, she says almost to herself.

—I know plenty! cries Claudia.—I don't have to read your whole goddam book to know that you reek of guilt! I could smell the guilt the first time I met you.

Haley looks at her, feeling more pity and more desire to protect than she has ever felt towards anyone. She looks and wonders: how should she tell Claudia the rest of the truth? But Claudia seems unsettled by the look rather than reassured, and she almost spits at Haley.

—It turns out I was right, she says with enormous contempt. —I was right, AND HOW.

(*Americanism!* scolds Sandra.

Not now! says Haley.)

But the Americanism slips between her protective bandages anyway, slides into her skin like a needle. Although it is only a small jab it hits a vein, and suddenly her arms and legs and head are flooded with anger.

The balance of power swings

and turns upside down like an old-fashioned egg-timer. The coloured sand pours into Haley's hands. She discovers the paradoxical strength that comes from being criticised and laid bare. Suddenly she is the attacker, and Claudia is the defenceless.

—You stupid cow, Haley says slowly and coldly.—You're forcing answers out of me, and it would have been so much better another way.

—Better? Oh sure! Better to keep us all in the dark, says Claudia in a small, sarcastic, childish voice. Her righteous rage has shrunk in the face of Haley's. She is petulant while Haley is possessed.

—OK, you want the truth? says Haley.—I'll give you some truth. She is starting to talk like an American lawyer in a movie.

—I'll give you truth, she repeats. She stands up and moves to the bed, touching the cool flat sheets with her fingertips.

—First, let me tell you that Robert is dead, she says. She feels a kind of pure white satisfaction at the look on Claudia's face.

—Oh, says Claudia.—Oh my God.

—Yes, says Haley. She begins to stride in a measured way around the room.

—He smashed his brains out on a London footpath, she says in a conversational tone.—I wasn't there to see it but they say his head was split open at the back, cracked like an egg.

—Haley, stop, says Claudia. Her own voice is cracked, it is a tiny eggshell voice, brittle in the bright room.

—I only imagined I saw the blood on the road, proceeds Haley matter-of-factly.—I imagined a strange shape, almost like a map, with Robert's hair matted into roads.

—But you write to him, whispers Claudia.—Like he's alive.

—Dead! says Haley brutally, spinning round suddenly so that Claudia flattens against the pillows.

—Killed in a scaffolding accident last year, she says, leaning towards Claudia.

—So did he know? says Claudia. Her whisper floats and dissipates before she can finish the sentence but Haley knows what she was going to say. She knows so much about Claudia that she could virtually answer her before the questions are asked.

—No, he didn't know I was pregnant, Haley says directly.— Well, perhaps that's why I moved in with Leith, d'you think?

—Stop, Haley, please, says Claudia. She turns her face away towards the cracked basin but Haley strides to the other side of the bed, pushes her face close to Claudia's.

—Why doubt my manipulative abilities now? she says.—I need a ready-made family, after all, to kid the authorities and all that.

—What, you mean you can't stay? says Claudia.—You're here illegally?

Her voice has the most bizarre shades to it: tinged with hope, tinted with what could be regret.

—Yes, you could easily expose me, says Haley.—Dob me in, get me deported, make Leith hate me, give me away as a liar.

Claudia turns her face on the pillow, from side to side, in what could almost amount to a shake of her head.

—No, you won't do that, will you, because we liars must stick together, says Haley softly.

—What d'you mean? says Claudia. Her hands suddenly look very thin and pale as she pulls at the cardboard edges of the hospital sheet.

—Why are you bothering to pretend? I've got a lot of experience with liars, says Haley.—As you know, I'm quite a good one myself.

She feels the ruthlessness of a surgeon about to slice open a reticent swelling and expose a seething cancerous tumour.

—What are you, says Claudia, —talking about?

Her voice comes like water from an unevenly pressurised tap.

—Are you talking, she says jerkily, —about Diane?

—Very good! says Haley the surgeon.—That's exactly what I'm talking about.

She feels the power of waiting and pauses with her lancing instrument above Claudia's head.

—Haley, please, you can't tell, says Claudia intently.—Please, you mustn't tell anyone.

—Why not? says Haley, in a cold, flat voice.—I don't owe you anything.

—Not for my sake, says Claudia.—For Diane's. She looks tough but she's got to be protected. She'll be so hurt if she finds out.

Haley sees the shiver of the overhead light reflected in Claudia's eyes, which are suddenly full of tears.

—And speaking of which, says Claudia in a voice that is halfway to crying, —how did you find out?

Haley looks at her consideringly. Behind the tears she can see someone else crying, someone older than Claudia, with more lines on her face, but there is a resemblance.

—Not from Adrian! says Claudia.—Not from Ben. They've believed me forever, I've told them that story ever since I met them and they still believe it.

—Huh! Talk about living a lie! says Haley. With this childish jibe she feels more human, and she feels the fierce power seeping out of the soles of her feet, through the bottoms of her shoes, onto the cold floor.

—How did you find out? says Claudia, almost beseechingly.

—I don't know if you're ready for this, says Haley. She sits back in her chair and looks up at the fluorescent light, which is flickering like some instrument monitoring the atmosphere in the room. Her rage is ebbing, it will not carry her through, it is diffusing and her stomach feels weak.

—No, you're not ready, she says, although whether it is her or Claudia who isn't ready, she can't be certain.

—I'm going to go, she says.

And she does. She leaves Claudia and she heads out onto Grafton Bridge where the traffic lights run into one long blur in the early dark. She sits down in the gutter by the bus-stop though she doesn't need to catch a bus, and she throws up there in the dark with strangers walking past and Claudia lying weeping in the labyrinth of rooms behind her.

Disclosure in a distinguished setting

There was the Ivy restaurant. She knew about it when she was thirteen from reading *Hello* magazine and the society pages of *The Times*. It was an integral part of the mythology of glamour, which was in turn a part of growing up in London.

This mythology peopled the streets for Haley—not the fawn prosaic streets of her home territory, but the starry terraces of South Ken and Knightsbridge. Although she never actually saw anyone significant, whenever she walked these terraces to meet Sandra at the clinic she always felt as if she was on the verge of an encounter. She imagined the tails of famous raincoats whisking round a corner in front of her, caught the tiny trail of expensive perfume that could only have come from the wrist of an actress. Once she found a bright turquoise pill box that appeared empty but was in fact full of discarded, invisible glamour.

They were all—the raincoat-wearers, the actresses, the gilt-edged invalids—they were all, always, on their way to the Ivy. To eat chicken livers and oysters, to drink from round ruby wine glasses or long ones full of lengthy gold bubbles.

—I think we should go out for dinner tonight! says Sandra.

It is Tuesday and Halley has homework waiting for her, stacked up on the coffee table. She is allowing herself half an hour of cartoons before she starts in on the maps, the graphs, the paragraphs, which are so important tonight but tomorrow night will be completely irrelevant.

—But it's sausage night, says Halley.

She is startled. This is so unlike Sandra, who is only spontaneous on very rare occasions and, even then, is so in a calm and measured way. *Let's be crazy tomorrow*, she will say, *let's drop everything and go to Brighton, I'll just make a few phone calls first and reschedule things and then we'll check train timetables and weather forecasts, oh and pack a few sandwiches and we can be back by six.*

—Darling, is your life really that dull? says Sandra. She laughs and her laughter falls to the floor where Halley is lying, and gets caught up in the cartoon cackles in a disturbing kind of way.

The afternoon outside is pretending to be older than it is. Only 4.30 pm, but as Halley looks out the street lights flick on and so she can close her eyes and have a wish. She wishes for—oh, excitement, and something out of the ordinary and a new self and a new bike.

—What are you doing darling, says Sandra absently.—Are your eyes sore?

Halley opens her eyes and propels her wishes out into the lighted street with a few blinks of her eyelashes.

—Where d'you want to go? she says. She and Sandra often talk like this, like dutiful netballers, sending well-meaning sentences back and forwards but failing to catch them. Their questions and answers cross clumsily in mid-air and sometimes collide.

—Put your coat on, says Sandra, walking to the window. Halley sees that round circles of rain have been slapped on the glass by a careless wind. Sandra seems strangely uneasy and this makes Halley suddenly long for sausages cooked with onions in a comforting brown gravy.

—It's OK, she says quickly.—I've got heaps of homework anyway.

—Funny Halley, always so serious! says Sandra.—There'll be plenty of time when we get home because we've got an early booking.

The mention of a booking reassures Halley instantly. This is no random ill-advised whim, it is a decision that Sandra has made earlier that day or maybe even the day before.

—I booked weeks ago actually, darling, says Sandra.—Because I thought we'd go to the Ivy.

—You're kidding! says Halley.

—Americanism, says Sandra automatically.

—Sorry, says Halley automatically.

—Well, we've both been working pretty hard lately, says Sandra.—We could do with a treat.

(Ever since then, the word *treat* has sat uncomfortably in Halley's vocabulary, its semantics quite different for her than for any other person. *Treat*—since then the word has pinched at the base of her spine, hovered behind her head. It fills her with a profound unease.)

They must be the only people in the restaurant to have travelled by train, tube and then on foot. Even when Sandra is extravagant she is sensible; her frivolity is chained and restrained by the iron links of common sense.

But once they are inside—well, then they could be anyone. Pretending to be a child star, Halley sits upright in a dark red chair and looks around. She spots a film director and someone who looks a bit like Isabella Rossellini. Sandra orders a glass and a half of wine.

—You're growing up, after all, she says to Halley.

Halley stiffens as the wine waiter brings her a ridiculously depleted glass but he is extremely polite and there is no detectable smirk on his face. He repositions her gleaming knives and forks, of which there are several.

Every table has its own lamp, and every glass of wine on every table casts its own circle of gold on white linen. Suddenly Halley and Sandra are quite companionable, and their comments catch onto one another's threads like caps screwing neatly onto bottles. They chat through consommé and ham steaks garnished with red and green, and they end up in harmony at the dessert menu.

—We'll have mango and kiwifruit sorbet, decides Sandra.

—Kiwifruit! says Halley happily.—Wow!

(Looking back, years later, Halley still remembers the first sharp taste of kiwifruit, and is still unsure as to how this particular touch had been orchestrated. Had Sandra phoned ahead to check on the menu? Studied it on a special trip in her lunch-hour? Or was it a happy chance of the sort that always seemed to happen to Sandra and never to Halley, so that Sandra always seemed prepared while Halley stumbled behind? Whichever, it was strangely, uncannily, cannily appropriate.)

So it was over pale green ice, which made Halley's teeth ache, that the revelation began. The entire evening had been spearheaded towards this, she realised, though cleverly blunted by sweet wine and dark deferential waiters.

—Do you remember anything about New Zealand? asks Sandra conversationally. She raises a spoonful of sorbet to her mouth with seemingly more attention than she has paid to her question.

—It's hard to say, says Halley. It is so unusual to have Sandra's full attention that she feels absurdly flattered and compelled to expand.

—You know, I'm not sure whether I remember it or just think I do from photos, she explains.—And from the stories you tell.

—Yes, I know, darling, frowns Sandra.—It's called reconstructed memory.

—I feel as if I remember that beach where you were holding me and I peed in my swimming costume, says Halley. She flips through the photos in her head: Sandra in a hideous trousersuit eating an ice cream, herself hunched on a giant concrete toadstool like a deformed gnome. Real or imagined? She doesn't know but she feels the pressure of keeping the spotlight of attention, so she takes another breath.

—Then there was the time when we went shopping in a little village by the sea, she recites.—And you left me behind in a bookshop.

Sandra laughs rather forcedly.

—And when you nearly got arrested for shouting at the Prime Minister, expounds Halley. She leans back on her chair like a juvenile professor.

—Don't tilt, says Sandra sharply.

Halley sighs and relinquishes the reins of control.

—But those are what we call shared memories, says Sandra in her patient work voice.—They've become part of our family legends, they've gone into the annals of family history.

Annals? Halley hasn't heard this word before, thinks of *Girls' Own* annuals instead. She imagines brightly coloured, round-faced Sandras and Halleys, wielding hockey-sticks, flanked by huge menacing kiwis and curly silver ferns. Meanwhile Sandra sweeps on professionally.

—What I really wanted to know, she says in the voice that Halley thinks of as her young-delinquents delivery,—is whether you can recall any other faces? Or any times when I wasn't there?

—Oh, says Halley uncertainly. She stretches her mind experimentally, easing it out of its London shape, pulling it away from the everyday surface of school and bus and Sainsbury shopping trips. But the tentative edges disintegrate like old stamps and she is left empty-handed, empty-minded.

—No, she says to Sandra in a wavering voice. Her spoon falters on her plate, avoids the kiwifruit seeds that have refused to disclose their origins to her.

—Are you sure, darling? insists Sandra.—No houses, for instance? No living-rooms or bathrooms?

—I was only two when we left, says Halley defensively.

—Some of my patients can remember the first time they saw sunlight, says Sandra wisely.—Or their first taste of solid food. It's amazing what comes back.

Well, I'm not some of your patients, thinks Halley angrily, squeaking her spoon around the side of her bowl. *I'm your daughter and I thought we were here for dinner, not a rebirthing session.*

(Later, she spies ironic glints under the dull surface of these thoughts.)

—Don't look so sulky darling, says Sandra mildly.—I'm not criticising, I'm just checking.

Checking? For what? thinks Halley. *For faulty memory? For poor recall skills? So you can return me to the shop?*

(Later, with perfect recall skills, she sees these thoughts as prescience.)

—So there's really nothing there? confirms Sandra.—No voices, no faces? Another little girl, another woman?

—I remember nothing! Halley almost shouts, theatrically stressing the negative. The next table looks sideways at her while pretending not to.

—It's OK, sweetheart, says Sandra quietly.—It's OK not to know.

This compassion is almost worse.

—Why the interrogation? hisses Halley.—Are you thinking of emigrating or something?

—Look, says Sandra. She lays down her spoon and dabs her mouth with a serviette so stiff that it leaves V-marks in her lipstick.

—Look, she says again.—There's no easy way to say this.

Halley glances around her in alarm. She envisages Sandra at work, using this phrase with frequency: *there's no easy way to tell you this, Mister or Mrs, you're completely mad, you're stark raving, barking, pillow-bitingly mad.*

—Halley? says Sandra.

Halley's head snaps back to attention so fast that she feels her neck could be a rubber band. Zing, pow, ping.

—Yes? she says snappily.

—I think you're at the right age to cope with this, says Sandra.—Darling.

The wine waiter hovers. Halley holds her glass out to him, eagerly, desperately, but Sandra waves him away as if he is an annoying gnat.

—The thing is, says Sandra, reaching for Halley's hand.

The thing is, thinks Halley:

a) Sandra is dying of cancer

b) Halley is being sent to some hideous rural boarding school

c) they have lost all their money and will be moving within the week to a halfway house.

—You're adopted, says Sandra.

The chair under Halley whirls and swoops as if it is a swivelling office number instead of an elegant deep red plush one. When it steadies itself,

—You're kidding, says Halley inadequately.—You're having me on.

—Darling! Americanisms! says Sandra.—No, of course I'm not, I'm telling you the truth.

—You're not my mother, says Halley. She doesn't know if this is a question, a statement, a plea, or a cry for help.

—Your real mother lives in New Zealand, darling, says Sandra. She reaches across the table and lays her hand gently over Halley's hot one.

—You took me away from her? says Halley.—She didn't want me? Or she wasn't fit to have me?

—These are all perfectly natural questions, says Sandra.—The answer to all of them, of course, is no.

Her hand caresses Halley's, around and around in annoying circles.

—What then? demands Halley stupidly.—What's the yes question, why did I end up here with you in the wrong country?

—Don't be silly, darling, says Sandra, caressing.—This *is* your country now, we just thought it would be better for everyone concerned if I took you.

—We? Who is we? says Halley.—You mean you and my real mother, do you?

—Your Birth Mother and I, says Sandra, as if it is the name of a musical.—I like to think of myself as your *real* mother.

She draws her hand away just in time, before Halley bites it. Halley looks at the tablecloth. Sandra's bracelet has left a dirty smudge on the white linen. She looks at her own hands and notices the tiny whorls on her fingertips, the tiny hairs on the backs of her hands. Everything zooms into focus, clarifies, magnifies. She feels as if her eyes have been in training up to this point and have now reached an unbearable state of excellence.

—We met through the hospital, explains Sandra.—She was a midwife there the year I was in Auckland on sabbatical. You were only two then.

—And she foisted you off on me? interrupts Halley rudely.—So you could cart me back to London and bring me up as one of your sociological experiments?

She knows this is an exaggerated suggestion, but she can't help feeling that Sandra would be more likely to have adopted her through curiosity than affection.

—Don't be silly, darling, says Sandra again.—She loved you very much, just as I did as soon as I saw you. But she was struggling financially and worried about doing the best for two children, and I'd been wanting to adopt for a long time, and it just went from there.

—So were you friends? demands Halley.

Sandra looks as if she is struggling to be honest.

—Well, we didn't have much in common, she admits.—We agreed not to keep in contact.

—Why? cries Halley.—Because she wasn't interested in what happened to me?

—The opposite! cries Sandra.—Sometimes the only way birth parents can cope with giving up their children is to sever the ties completely.

—And the other one? says Halley suspiciously.—You said there were two of us. Does that other kid know about me?

—Darling, I couldn't even say, says Sandra.—That's up to Diane.

Suddenly, they are no longer talking in generalities, which are Sandra's specialty. They are talking names, which will lead to faces, which will lead to cracks appearing in Halley's life and other people's roots stretching out to take hold of her.

—That's enough! says Halley quickly.

—But it wasn't exactly closed adoption, muses Sandra,—so if you really wanted to, I guess we could find out where she is now and you could write to her.

—No! says Halley in a suddenly mature voice.—No, we should leave her in peace.

Sandra smiles at her.

—You're being extremely adult about all this, she says encouragingly.—We can talk about it later, when you've had some time to think. It's a complicated thing.

She reaches for her purse and Halley notices that the world has slowed right down. The purse sways on its chain in slow motion, Sandra gestures for the waiter with a hand that moves like a lead weight. A credit card, a silver platter, a pen, and Halley sits motionless. She has no real desire to move on from the deep red chair. This is enough.

She swings her eyes up and across the table, her pupils rock towards Sandra slowly like chairs on a moving ferris wheel. They watch Sandra consideringly as she smiles and signs and folds. Sandra's neck is blotchy.

Because the world has considerately slowed for her, by the time Sandra has paid Halley has had all the time she needs to think. Sandra is wrong: it is not so complicated after all, and Halley will make it even simpler. She doesn't want to know any more than Sandra has already told her. Suddenly, after years of shuttered sheltered living, she has been handed independence and she is not about to relinquish it that quickly.

Yes, this is the truth. Halley doesn't really mind where she has sprung from, from whose loins or whose womb. It is enough to know that, now, her feelings towards Sandra are OK. She no longer has to feel guilty about disliking her own mother.

Sandra, who is not her mother but only a chance acquaintance, shepherds Halley out of the restaurant. They move towards the tube station, but still in slow motion so that by the time they get there, Halley expects, the last tube will have long gone, and they will sit on the platform all night in unrelated silence.

—Nice meal, darling? says Sandra.

—How much was it? asks Halley.

The night air bites and nips at her hot cheeks.

—You're a funny thing, says Sandra.—It's my treat, you don't need to worry about it.

And this is true too. Halley does not need to worry ever again, because Sandra is no longer her responsibility. The umbilical cords that have been threatening to choke her ever since she was conscious of thought have fallen away, the clotted blood ties have dissolved. Far away, standing on their heads in some upside-down country, an unknown mother and sibling live their thankfully unknown lives.

Halley no longer has any hostage to fortune. Loneliness is always there but it is small enough, and remains crouching in the shadow of freedom. There is no one to lie awake and worry about. (And it stays that way for many years, until Robert.)

—You could have told me over sausages, she says.

To the present

Once Haley has wiped the vomit from her mouth and chin with the shreds of a tissue, she props herself against a lamp-post and looks back at the hospital. Lit up like a huge liner, it floats in the hollow of the valley. She imagines it gliding down the motorway, slipping down to the harbour and taking to the open sea. With Claudia in it.

This is Haley's birthplace. She has no doubt that this was where it happened, her arrival into the world under that violent solar flare. Suddenly she can picture the scene of twenty years ago easily:

fewer lights along the streets, barbed wire running the edges of Grafton Bridge to stop the jumpers, and suddenly the huge explosion rimming Rangitoto with fire. She has been living so close to her place of origin: she has been sitting on Leith's steps looking at its outline for weeks and weeks, but it has taken Claudia to get her through the doors. This is no surprise. Whatever Claudia's past might be, she is shaping Haley's present.

Haley's current picture of Claudia lying in her white bed weeping is correct. Claudia doesn't cry until Haley has walked deliberately out of the room (where Claudia would have stormed, Haley walks with measured tightrope steps).

But she is crying when Adrian and Ben arrive to entertain her.

—My beautiful Claudette, you can't cry now, says Adrian.

—Why not? cries Claudia.

—Because it's far too predictable, says Adrian.—Everyone cries in hospitals, the tears being shed as we speak on all these floors would, would . . .

—Would make a grown man weep, finishes Ben.

Adrian throws himself into the shiny chair that Haley has recently vacated.

—You're too original for this, he proclaims.—You may be a human tap, Claudia, you may cry often and leak secrets occasionally, but you're a tap with style and so you must stop now.

Claudia knows he is talking to give her time to recover. The kindness of this makes her cry more.

—We're going to come and kidnap you tomorrow, says Adrian.—Pick you up from the front doors and take you somewhere to recuperate for a night.

Claudia can't wait. Already she feels as if she has been incarcerated for several weeks instead of one day. She longs for autonomy, for her own lights to switch off and a fridge to wander to and unexpected faces on the street which she will never see again.

—Where are you taking me? she sniffs.

—It's a surprise, they say.

—We've squared it with your ma, adds Ben.—She's longing to have you back under her eye but she agreed to the abduction anyway.

—She's not my ma, says Claudia automatically, then falters, looks out the window for a minute.

—Anyway, I bet she's relieved, she finishes.—She'll probably be working.

—When will you ever learn, Ben? chides Adrian.—She's not Claudia's real mother and she's always working.

(With unwelcome clarity, Claudia has a flashback to Diane dropping her off at reception, kissing her goodbye.

If Adrian can't pick you up, Diane is saying worriedly, *make sure you let me know and I'll swap my shift.*)

—In fact, she'd probably rather Claudia wasn't around, says Adrian cheerfully.—She can't stand the sight of you, isn't that right, Claud?

Claudia tries to laugh, starts to cry.

—Christ, Adrian! reproves Ben.—I think you're past your quota of bad jokes for the day.

—She knows I don't mean it, says Adrian. But he passes the tissues to Claudia and brushes her hair back so she can blow her nose.

—And now present time! says Ben, reaching into his old vinyl bag.

—Yes, this is true friendship for you, says Adrian gravely.—We risk our reputation bringing you this token of our love.

—Nay! We risk our young lives, says Ben, handing over a crumpled bit of tinfoil.

—Is this what I think it is? says Claudia.

—For after lights out, says Adrian, laying his finger against his nose.

Claudia snorts.

—In the toilet or the shower, advises Ben.

—Don't share it with the nurses or you'll get them sacked, says Adrian.

And so they leave her with the joint, and with a pillow of talk on which she can rest her head, thereby avoiding the bare bones of an earlier conversation. But she knows that tomorrow, or the next day, or the next, she will be forced into action. Not by Haley or by any threat that Haley might represent, but by herself.

The knowledge is there, has lain there under Adrian's chatter and Ben's occasional remarks. She has had a pleasurable flirtation with the edge of reality. But the situation she has created for many years has drawn too close to the edge, could easily tip over and must be righted. She realises that she is in danger of becoming a stranger in her own life and that she must become acquainted with it again.

Despite her capacity for deception, Claudia is at heart a realist and has a realist's passion, a realist's respect, for truth.

Haley goes to a lighted pay-phone, calls her own home.

—Just off out the door, Leith says.—Good timing.

—I need Claudia's address, says Haley.

—Hmmm, that's a tricky one, says Leith.

He is undecided as to whether he knows it or not. Has he got it written down? The jury's out on that one too.

—But I know how to get there, he says.

By the time he has described every significant side street and every memorable building, the pay-phone display is flashing 0:00 at Haley. She holds the connection button in desperately, pretending that she is about to feed the phone another card. This ploy gives Leith enough time to get to the description of Claudia's house.

—Sort of that pinky-grey stone block, he says in a leisurely voice.

—With a big tree outside, he recalls.

—But Clawd's not there! he remembers.—She's in—

His redundant last word is lost somewhere in the darkened valley, left behind unclaimed in some phone-line in the shadow of the great hospital where Claudia (he has just remembered) is lying.

Haley is lying too, though more by intention than word. She did not really want Claudia's address from her vague, helpful flatmate. The address she really wanted was Diane's.

She must find Diane as the crow flies: that is, not by street maps but by landmarks. She catches a bus from Khyber Pass to Dominion Rd, trying not to be distracted by anything so that Leith's word-map stays clear in her head. It is hardest when the bus passes through clusters of shops: Indian cafés, Chinese grocery stores, boxes of fruit, chattering children. Haley's insides forget her head and twinge with London neighbourhood nostalgia. Yet

I remember nothing!

She gets off the bus in an area which the driver tells her is Mt Roskill. Luckily her head has not betrayed her, has remained in the present and is able to lead her past a furniture warehouse and three blocks of brick houses and under a huge spreading fig tree.

I remember nothing!

It was not a lie at the time, when she almost shouted it at Sandra over green sorbet. Even though, as a two-year-old, she would have been carried over this dip in the pavement that she now stumbles over aged twenty—no, it was not a lie then. Impossible that, at the age of thirteen, she could have sat in the Ivy and cast the sinker of her mind back into these dark warm waters. Impossible that she could have fished up this small brick house with a rectangular lawn.

But, now, it is proved a lie. *I remember—something.* Because after their initial trip-up, Haley's feet walk reasonably certainly up to the gate. They walk through the gate and up the path and take the two steps to the front door in one. The compass inside her quivers and shifts.

She knew that the door would face this way. The only things left to discover are how the past eighteen years have changed Diane. And exactly how much Haley will be tempted to tell her.

In the end, there are no decisions to be made. As soon as Haley sees Diane's lined eyes and sees her kind, tired smile, she knows what path she will take. She introduces herself without a name, as Leith's flatmate and Claudia's one-time workmate.

—Is Claudia home? she asks, as if she hasn't just left Claudia a couple of hours ago lying with tears in her eyes in a hospital bed.

—I suppose you wouldn't know, Diane says.—She's in hospital, just overnight.

—Nothing serious I hope, says Haley.

—Well, probably not, love, says Diane.—But I'm still worried sick about her. You know how it is with kids.

She looks in an understanding way at Haley's stomach, and invites her in for a cup of tea.

—Gotta look after yourself, love, she says.—Now you're eating for two.

They sit together in the front room, which is like most other living rooms, with ferns and magazine racks and a piano that no one ever plays. They talk companionably about the public transport system and the public health system, and where Haley is from.

—London, says Diane wistfully.—I've always wanted to go there, ever since . . . Well, for a long time.

—It's not that different from here, reassures Haley.

—How long are you in Auckland for, dear? asks Diane.—Just a working holiday, is it?

—Yes, I'll be going back pretty soon, says Haley.

She looks around the room, and again at Diane's face, and feels like the glass bird she had when she was little, which rocked up and down and dipped its beak into a pot of coloured dye. She is dipping in and out of a sensation that is too vague to be called memory, yet too real to be called déjà vu. It is unsettling but not unpleasant and soon she gives herself up to the motion, and to Diane, completely.

She tells Diane about the baby she is expecting and she listens to Diane talk about Claudia.

—You shouldn't have favourites, Diane confides.

Haley waits for her heart to lurch but instead finds herself listening quite dispassionately.

—I've got a stepson called Giles, says Diane.—And he's a gem. But there's something special about daughters, they become your friends.

Haley sits back, realises that, for all her dispassion, she has been sitting on the edge of her seat.

—Friends, she says consideringly.—I suppose they could be that.

Over the second cup of tea Diane tells Haley about her other, lost, daughter: Claudia's twin.

—I adopted her out to an English woman whose marriage had broken up the year before, she says.—I was really struggling and this woman, well, she seemed like she could do with a friend.

—Did you know her well? asks Haley carefully.—The woman, I mean.

—Just well enough to know that my girl would have a better life with her, says Diane.—But in a way I didn't want to get too close. It probably seems strange to you.

—No, says Haley.

—Once you give a child a new life, says Diane slowly, —you sort of owe it to them to stay away.

—Yes, says Haley.—I suppose you do.

—Not that I wanted to, says Diane.—I had to pull her out of my heart. Two years with her, and then she was gone. But it was for the best, I still believe that.

There's a silence, and then the clock tings on the mantelpiece.

—Have a biscuit, dear? Diane asks Haley earnestly.

—Oh, says Haley.—Thanks.

Diane has never told Claudia about her twin.

—She's always been too vulnerable, says Diane.—Just a bit needy, our Claudia. I don't think she could handle hearing that she's got a sister somewhere.

—What exactly wouldn't she handle? asks Haley.—The competition aspect?

—Partly that, says Diane.—But more that it would complicate her view of herself, I think. She's used to seeing herself as an only child, you see, and she likes it that way.

Sometimes you can live with someone and never really know them. The words are in Haley's head before she realises they are her own, and she has said them earlier to Claudia in a hospital ward. Is there something about tonight, she wonders, that is making her speak the truth without knowing it, and tell lies without intending to?

—Do you really think so? she says doubtfully to Diane, this

mother who has only ever seen the tip of the iceberg that is her daughter Claudia.

—Well, she's certainly never talked about wanting brothers or sisters, says Diane.—She seems to resent Giles.

Haley thinks of the look on Claudia's face when she saw Rose and her noisy daughter and her quiet son all talking at once in the kitchen, and the phone ringing and the voice of another noisy daughter on the other end. Hadn't that been envy?

—And if she'd ever found out she had a twin . . . ponders Diane.

Haley is interested to notice that Diane speaks in the past tense, as if there is not even the remotest possibility any more.

—Well, then her whole life would feel like a lie, wouldn't it? asks Diane.

—Maybe, says Haley slowly.—But maybe the opposite, maybe it would fill in the gaps. You hear about twins separated at birth who don't know they're twins but just feel lost all the time.

—Lost, you say? echoes Diane, looking slightly lost herself at this.—I hope I haven't done that to her. I thought I was protecting her.

(Robert: *Back away Halley my darling, you've done right, but back away from the edge now.*)

It is reassuring to know that Robert would approve of what she's doing, but she doesn't need advice. Sometimes there are moments when your seeing is so clear, it is as if windscreen wipers have swept away rain; when a truth is heard so sharply it is like a blocked ear unblocking. This sort of omniscience lasts only for an instant—cannot last longer or the burden would be unbearable. But this is one of those instants, and Haley looks at Diane's uncertain face and her understanding goes beyond mere certainty or conviction. Claudia was right: it is Diane who must be protected.

—I'm sure you've done the right thing, she says quickly.—And d'you know what I think?

—What? says Diane.

—She's really lucky to have a mother like you, says Haley.

The lines on Diane's face fall into a huge smile. Hospitably, she offers Haley a third cup of tea but Haley smiles too and says she must go. Diane sees Haley to the door and says Claudia will be sorry to have missed her.

—She's going to Waiheke Island tomorrow with some friends, just for the night, she explains.—I'll tell her you came round as soon as she gets back.

—If you like, says Haley.

—But I don't even know your name! realises Diane.

—Oh, I'm sorry! says Haley.—I'm Roberta.

(Robert: *God, you're unoriginal! And what a terrible name.*)

—It's been lovely to have someone to talk to about it all, Diane says.—It's really made my night.

Haley kisses Diane goodbye—an action rare for her on a first meeting. She hears the front door close and then the slow beat of blood in her ears as she walks steadily away from her mother.

Claudia? Yes, she is vulnerable, she is sometimes needy, but these are only part of her surface and, as such, are partly created by design anyway. Claudia is not weak, Haley knows as she treads the shadows of the fig tree and passes the warehouse on her left. Claudia has an integral strength that mirrors Haley's, a dignity that deserves to be recognised. And so Haley will tell her what Diane never needs to know, and their secret will finally be shared, halved, in two.

Island in the sun

Rhonda the beautiful, Rhonda the callous, Rhonda the begetter of Ben and the snatcher of Heath, has a beach house.

—On Waiheke, says Ben.—Which we'll use.

—How come we've never used it before? says Claudia.

—Because until recently I had this illusion, says Ben,—that independence equated with freedom.

—And now? says Adrian.

—Now I've realised you're never free from blood ties, says Ben.—So you may as well cash in on the assets.

—Spoken like a true child of the new millennium, says Adrian approvingly.—Embrace your tiresome mother along with her holiday accommodation.

—It's all right for you, Claudia, says Ben.—Did you realise that 'adoptee' rhymes with 'free'?

Claudia shifts uncomfortably in the front seat of the car.

—You OK? says Adrian.—Need more pillows?

—You need a good dose of Waiheke air, says Ben.—And two old friends.

—Well, make that one, says Adrian, slightly apologetically.—I might have to drop you kids off at the ferry and leave you to it.

—Why? chorus Claudia and Ben, disappointedly.

—I scored a cancellation slot to get my head read tomorrow morning, says Adrian.—And to get back to the mainland in time I'd probably have to swim.

They consult the ferry timetable, and he's right. But at the last minute, as Claudia and Ben are about to walk through the ticket barrier, he decides to come anyway, for the day.

—For the wine, he says.

They sit outside under pale May sunshine and taste pale wine. The leaves on the vines hang like huge hands and the rich earth steams.

—Oh, to be a winemaker, says Adrian, longingly.

The owner of the vineyard tells them that he has been putting in fourteen-hour days for the last two months because of a record vintage. He has huge bags under bloodshot eyes.

—Oh, to be a shopowner, says Adrian, gratefully.

—Yeah, much less pressure, agrees Ben.—At least fashion doesn't demand urgent attention.

Adrian and Claudia look doubtfully at him. The collar of his rugby jersey is rucked up at the back and one leg of his jeans is tucked—by mistake, they hope—into his sock.

—That's a matter of opinion, says Adrian in a restrained-for-Adrian way.

—You run a shop? says the winemaker in his kind German accent.

—Yes, a retro shop, says Adrian.

—Your own kind of vintage, says the German, patting him on the back.—A great achievement for one so young, no?

—I wish Chris and Gerry could've heard that, says Adrian, preening.

—Look out, Aids! cries Claudia.

—What! What? says Adrian in alarm. He looks around, bats at the air for swarming wasps.

—Your head's swelling! says Claudia.

—Better go back to the mainland and get it shrunk, hoots Ben.

—Should I even be drinking? says Adrian meditatively.—They say that lithium and the devil's drink don't mix.

—You'll be fine, says Ben with the assurance of the chemically trained.—It'll just take effect faster.

—Which means I'm cheaper to run, says Adrian happily.

—We'll take you out anytime, says Claudia, raising her glass. She feels the stitches in her left breast creak but it only serves to accentuate the brightness of the day and of her friends' conversation. There is something to sort out back in the city, she knows, but the prospect is sweetened by the swirl of her glass and the gold on her tongue.

This could be the way back anyway. Whichever way you look at it, the starting point is her.

Claudia and Ben talk about lies

When Adrian leaves on the 7 pm sailing, the early dark has already sat down on the island, spread itself over the olive groves and the rocky hills. From being three they become two, and the atmosphere shifts in Claudia's head like tectonic plates. As she walks away from the ferry terminal, turning in case Adrian's looking back to wave at them, her feet readjust and find a new footing. Sitting on the bus to Oneroa Beach, she feels herself settle into her Ben-self, which is a quieter and more peaceful self to be.

Ben leads the way up a winding path and switches on lights in a polite deprecating way.

—My God! says Claudia.—There's no way this can be called a bach.

—Well, you know Rhonda, says Ben slightly awkwardly.—Never one to settle for second best.

—Yeah, so what's she doing shagging Heath? wonders Claudia.

—Your detachment never ceases to amaze me, says Ben.

They put on coats, pick up gin, and lie on deckchairs on the balcony. The air smells of cold water untainted by anything else. Claudia and Ben turn their faces away from Auckland and the dark sea offers them any number of possibilities.

—D'you know, says Ben,—I don't think I've ever been here with Rhonda.

—Would you want to? asks Claudia.

—Not really, Ben says with a crack of laughter.

There's a silence, broken by a ship's plaintive horn. Perhaps it is this that prompts Claudia to start towards her new life.

—Ben, do you ever lie? she says slowly.

—Umm, says Ben.—You know what? I don't think I do.

He sounds surprised but at the same time quite certain.

—You don't even lie to protect yourself, do you? Claudia says slowly. Her footsteps along this line of conversation are as slow as her voice, but not exactly reluctant.

—How do you mean? says the dark shape that is Ben.

—Well, take Rhonda, says Claudia.—You must want to pretend sometimes that you and Rhonda are closer than you are.

There's a silence.

—Don't you? To yourself? Sometimes? says Claudia hopefully. Her hope is as much for her own sake as it is for Ben's.

—Not really, because I know it'll hurt when reality crashes in, says Ben.—Self-deception is always self-defeating in the end.

—Hmmm, says Claudia slightly dejectedly. Then she remembers something.

—But the eggplant night when Rhonda was leaving, she says.— She said she loved you when she was leaving.

—When she was leaving with Heath, corrects Ben.—She always loves me in front of other people.

—An act? says Claudia interestedly. She doesn't mind being

sidetracked down this path which is, after all, linked to where she has committed to go.

—I don't know if it's that deliberate, says Ben.—Maybe it's subconscious.

His voice is so calm and objective, he could be reciting the periodic table instead of dissecting a mother's love for him, or the lack of.

—Apparently seventy per cent of kids have learnt to lie by the time they're three, he says.—I would say Rhonda was what they call a born liar.

—And now it's become instinctive for her? says Claudia.

—You just need to look at the woman, says Ben.—Fake hair, fake tits, fake farewells.

—So why do you even bother to see her? asks Claudia.

—Because she's my mother, I suppose, says Ben.—For what it's worth.

—But she doesn't treat you like a son, argues Claudia.—She picks you up when she wants and then puts you down again.

—Which I guess is one way of proving I'm her son, says Ben.—Don't get me wrong, it's a crap way, but some people just treat their family like that.

—A sort of taking for granted? says Claudia in a small voice.

—Yeah, but more than that, says Ben.—Taking them so much for granted that it's like a denial of possibility.

—I don't understand, says Claudia, not knowing if she wants to.

—Well, why should anyone you don't know be more interesting than someone you're actually related to? says Ben.—If you discount them just because they've made your dinner for ten years, you could be missing out on the best thing you'll ever have.

—I see, says Claudia. She sinks into her creaking canvas and spills gin down her front.

—Shit, she says.—OK, Ben, I've got to tell you something.

—You're finally pissed? says Ben with courteous rudeness.

—But if I tell you, you might not like me any more, says Claudia with sudden panic, rising out of her canvas cocoon.

—I like you sober drunk stoned half-cut, says Ben.—I even like you hungover.

—I'm not talking about the state of my liver, says Claudia desperately.—I'm talking about my, well, my moral fibre.

Ben snorts with laughter and gin goes up his nose. He ends up hanging over the balcony, his eyes streaming, which is slightly better for Claudia. Even though it's too dark now to see faces clearly, it's somehow easier to talk to a back.

—Here goes nothing, she says rapidly.—This is it. I'm as bad as Rhonda.

—Surely not! coughs Ben.—You haven't had multiple husbands or been recreated by a cosmetic surgeon, have you?

Claudia has no time for jokes. She is well and truly back on track and she rushes towards her final destination: Truth with a capital T.

—I've been living a lie, she says.—I've been using and abusing family relationships. I'm guilty of pretending things are what they're not or not what they are. I've been keeping secrets from my best friends.

—Phew, you have been busy, comments Ben.

Is he being deliberately kind? Because he keeps his back to Claudia.

—And I can't make myself be nice to Haley, adds Claudia quickly.

—Yeah, I have noticed that, says Ben non-judgementally.—Why, exactly?

—She threatens me, says Claudia.—I don't know what it is, it's just a feeling of general *threat* and I've had it ever since I met her.

—Anything else about her? asks Ben.

—Yes, says Claudia.—She knows what I've just told you.

—Which is, what? says Ben carefully.

Claudia prepares

She takes a deep breath. She straightens her mind, smooths her doubts with slightly damp hands, looks into the huge darkness. She is about to launch herself out of her old persona towards a new one, not knowing if anyone will be there to catch her. It is possibly one of the most frightening moments of her life.

—I'm not adopted, she says. She free-falls into the silence.

Ben is there

—Diane is your real mother? Ben says.—Is that what you're saying?

His voice sounds quite normal and holds no hint of incredulity/loathing/reproof.

—Yes, affirms Claudia.

—Yes, she's my real mother, she says with something like despair.

—Ever since I was little, she adds.

—Ever since you were conceived, I would imagine, says Ben, with a small laugh.

—I mean I've *lied* about it ever since I was little, says Claudia.—I've made a point of lying to everyone about her. Saying she adopted me.

—But why? says Ben.

—Because I didn't like her, says Claudia, swinging again without a safety net.

Second time also lucky

—That's OK, says Ben.

—Is it, though? says Claudia desperately.—I don't know if it's her or just everything she seems to stand for. It's all so hideously, horribly, deeply boring.

—By boring, says Ben, turning round,—do you mean normal?

—I suppose I do, says Claudia.

—Do you like her now? asks Ben.

—I don't know, says Claudia.—I don't think I've looked at her properly since I was ten.

—Well, that'll be something interesting for you to do when you get home, says Ben.

—I suppose it will be, says Claudia.

—You might think it's strange, says Ben,—but some people would sell their souls for a bit of normality.

There is a thread of wistfulness in his voice that Claudia reaches for but it slips through her fingers, leaving her empty-handed. She feels inadequate, but then it is hard to swap instantly into the role of comforter when you have just cast yourself voluntarily as the fool.

—I'd sell my grandmother if it meant I could be exotic, she says, reverting to herself.

—Other people see you as exotic, says Ben.

—Do they? says Claudia doubtfully, hopefully.

—You bet, says Ben.—You're no dull green native fern.

—But I'm not foreign, says Claudia.—Not like Haley.

There is a note of longing in her voice, now, as she thinks of the advantages that Haley has and she doesn't. Such as: a different accent, a right to be lost, and a never-ending supply of newness.

—Aha, says Ben wisely.—So that's why you can't handle her. You feel supplanted.

He takes a swig of gin.

—Haley couldn't be exotic if she tried, he says.—Which she doesn't. You don't dislike her, you just envy some things about her.

—She makes me uneasy, mutters Claudia.—She knows things about me and she makes things happen to me that I can't understand.

—She does see a lot, agrees Ben.—But I think that's just because she's been through a lot, don't you?

—I think it's more than that, mutters Claudia.—She sees *me*.

—So for some reason she can read your universe, shrugs Ben.—But she can't realign it. Think of her as an astrologer, not a god.

—Hmmm, says Claudia, sounding unconvinced.—Well, tell me then, how does she know about Diane and the disownment scheme? Because she does.

—Have they talked? muses Ben.—Haley and Diane?

—God no! says Claudia with horror.—They haven't even met. And I hope they never do.

—Would it matter that much? says Ben, turning his head on its canvas backdrop to look at her.

—More than you know, says Claudia.—I may not want Diane as a mother but I don't want her hurt either.

—Well, that redeems you, says Ben. He sounds as if he is only half-joking.

—It's just that I don't want to end up wearing a uniform every day and eating poached eggs! cries Claudia desperately.

—Well, you won't then, says Ben.—She's your mother, Claudia, she's not your destiny.

—How can one so young be so wise, says Claudia.

—Certainly not by emulating his mother, Ben says.

Relevant and irrelevant summaries

The night curled around them like a comforting white lie. The slightly frosty air pierced like a truth. Both co-existed in Claudia's head but now they sat more comfortably together and she settled back into her canvas womb with a little sigh.

The pockets of the hills were studded with lights. Houses clustered together, massing against the dark bush.

—Don't you think it's strange the way that humans hang out together? said Ben.—When they don't even like each other all that much?

—Strange but necessary, said Claudia.—It's a matter of survival and I don't mean just physical.

—Emotional survival? Yeah, you're right, said Ben.

—Ben, said Claudia in a small voice.—What do you think of me now?

—Well, said Ben.—Are you ready for this?

—I don't know, said Claudia in a smaller voice.

—I think what I always have, said Ben.—Which is, if you weren't my best friend . . .

Claudia thought she heard him taking a deep breath but it could have been a wave brushing the beach below.

—If we weren't best friends, said Ben,—I'd fall for you like a dying star.

There was a silence.

—It's the truth you know, said Ben conversationally.

—Really? said Claudia incredulously.

—Yup, said Ben.

—Even now you know I'm the Great Deceiver? said Claudia.

—Even now, said Ben.

There was a silence but inside Claudia was singing. There was a cold autumn wind rising from the harbour, but inside Claudia was glowing like a live coal.

—Thanks Ben, she said casually.—Thanks a lot.

—Anytime, said Ben casually.

Hello

They wake up when the day does. Their deckchairs are weighted with dew and the sky is washed white.

They say hi to each other, exchange insults about how hungover/tired/ugly they look. Then they head inside for toast and powdered orange juice, and mattresses that are ten times more comfortable than canvas but not as conducive to confidences.

Hello again

When it happens—the final showdown—it isn't planned but relies instead on a chance meeting. It so often happens this way. Think of Diane and Sandra, Haley and Leith, Leith and Claudia. The threads of their acquaintance began as gossamer and could just as easily have been broken as followed, but from them lives have been woven and have formed webs of their own.

While Claudia and Ben have been lying on deckchairs, Haley has been doing a lot of thinking and planning. About Sandra, about Diane, about Claudia and herself. She has decided she will invite Claudia round for dinner on Thursday when Leith is at band practice. She also practises: what to say to Claudia, what emphasis to put on what words, even what Claudia's responses will be. She doesn't anticipate an easy night but she isn't nervous. Why? Because she expects nothing.

This is something Robert has taught her, not in living for he was an incurable optimist

(*Expect the best, Hale! The world's our oyster!*)

but with his falling. Haley will be prepared for anything for the rest of her life, but never expectant.

On Tuesday a wind blows. A pointed wind straight from the summit of Rangitoto, which arrows into the base of the city. All day people complain of the cold, but after work Haley steps out into the world and the salt scuffs her face with a rough affection. She thinks she can smell ash in the wind, and honey from the beehives still kept on the island.

She walks down to the ferry terminal to post a letter. It is addressed to Sandra and has taken many hours to write. As easily as the written word now comes to Haley, there is a raw quarry inside her from where she has hacked and hewn the right phrases.

She posts her sentences through the airmail slot, hears her explanations her apologies her plans land lightly on a pile of others. She intends her words to begin building a new structure, into which Sandra will be allowed access but not input. The last twenty years have been razed to the ground, and this time round Sandra is no longer the master builder.

Leaning on the rail, Haley watches the ferries lumber into the wharf. Much further out in the gulf is a huge luxury liner, looped with a thousand lights. Behind the dazzle, she thinks, will be tennis courts, casinos, restaurants: in the midst of the dazzle will be dancing, flirting, deception of others, deception of the self.

There is a disruption on the wharf. The Quickcat has appeared out of the half-dark, passengers are pouring from its mouth. And there, in the middle of the flow, is Ben, and there is Claudia.

Haley's heart lurches.

—Hi there, Haley! How're you doing?

It's Ben and he looks pleased to see her.

—Hello, Haley.

It's Claudia and she is far less certain. She looks narrowly at Haley, as if suspecting her of loitering, lurking, lying in wait in the Fullers Cruise Centre for the past 24 hours.

—What a coincidence! says Haley, trying to reassure Claudia (and herself) that this meeting is pure chance. She ends up sounding both patronising and panicky, rushes on.

—How was Waiheke? she gabbles.

—Illuminating, says Ben, for some reason.

—How the hell did you know we went to Waiheke? asks Claudia immediately.

—Chill, Claudia, says Ben.—She just saw us getting off the boat, remember?

—That boat stops off at other places too, says Claudia. Her eyes are as wary as a cat's.

—Look, I'd love to stay and quibble, says Ben,—but I can see my bus about to leave. Are you gonna be OK to get home, Claudia?

—I'll ring Diane, says Claudia, answering Ben but looking at Haley.—After all, what are mothers for?

Ben gives Claudia a kiss on the cheek.

—Talk to you soon, he says.—I'm proud of you.

He bobs his head slightly awkwardly towards Haley and lands a kiss on the side of her nose before scurrying off, an ant with large boots carrying an oversized backpack.

Claudia picks up her bag as if she is about to leave too, then puts it down again.

—OK, how did you know we went to Waiheke? she says again.—I didn't tell Leith.

—I didn't ask him, says Haley.

—You've spoken to Diane, says Claudia flatly.—Haven't you?

For some reason Haley is not surprised that Claudia has got there so fast. They are on a collision course, and their minds are racing ahead of them.

—Yes, I have, says Haley quietly.

—Right, says Claudia.—You just couldn't resist getting on the phone and letting her know what a bitch I've been all my life.

—I didn't tell her, says Haley quickly.

—Well, thank you so much for that, says Claudia, the sarcasm in her voice almost hiding the shake.—She's actually quite vulnerable and I don't think she'd appreciate hearing that her daughter's been going round disowning her.

—She is vulnerable, says Haley.—You're right, she really is.

—And you know this from one phone call, says Claudia, with

scathing disbelief.—Oh, but I forgot, you're an authority on every-thing aren't you, even other people's mothers who you've never met.

All Haley wants to do at this moment is to walk very, very fast away from Claudia and what is about to come, but her obstinate, dutiful, rational mind forces her to stand still. She stands like a wooden post, but when she speaks she almost winces.

—Actually, she says,—I have met Diane. I went round to your house the other night.

Claudia stares. Her light green eyes look as if they are changing colour, darkening to stormy black. Surely, Haley thinks in almost-fear, it is the light?

—You *what?* says Claudia in a very low voice. Her voice is so unexpectedly untheatrical, is so true and raw, that Haley's fear increases.

—The night you were in hospital, she says quickly.—There was something I had to check out.

—Something you had to CHECK OUT? says Claudia. Her voice suddenly rises as if someone has accidentally bumped a volume knob with their elbow and continued walking.

—You stupid, stupid fucking HALEY! she shouts.—What could you possibly have to check out, whoever you are? I wish to God you'd just check out of my fucking life and leave me alone!

—Claudia! Please! I can explain, says Haley, in the best tradition of soap operas.

—No, THAT'S ENOUGH! shouts Claudia, stamping her foot.—You've done too much already!

Haley steps forward to put her hand on Claudia's arm, but it is like trying to stop an avalanche or a tsunami, which sweeps on over and around her.

—Moving into my life! Claudia shouts.—Taking over my friends and my workplace and ruining everything, nothing's been right since you got here, I've been sick and I've got sicker and my affair has finished and I don't have another one and now, NOW you've sneaked around and found out that I've lied about adoption and mothers and just get out of my face would you just GET OUT OF MY COUNTRY!

She pauses for breath.

—Shut up! shouts Haley, putting her hands over her ears.—Just shut the fuck up!

She is vaguely aware that both she and Claudia are behaving as if they are in some badly directed play: foot-stamping, ear-covering, melodramatic half-sentences. People are looking at them and sidling away from them, and the space around them is growing. But for once Claudia is so much herself that she is oblivious of being watched.

—**Shut** up, Claudia, Haley says for a third time. But this time it is **an** entreaty, not an order. She steps close and feels Claudia's **emotion** resonating through her body like music through a wall. It is so uncontrived, so instinctual, that she hardly recognises Claudia. Suddenly she doesn't know if she can bear this much longer.

—You don't have to worry, she says in a tired voice.—I am going to leave.

—You have to leave, whether I tell you to or not, says Claudia.— You don't belong here.

Her eyes are darker than the shadows crouching under the wharves.

—But I do, says Haley.—If you'd just listen to me.

She stops to take a breath. Her lungs hurt. People call and clatter around them but the short space between her and Claudia is solid, bricked up with silence. She runs against it.

—This is my country too, she says.

—I was born here twenty years ago, she says.

—On the first day of August, under a solar flare, she says.

She looks at Claudia, waits for recognition, sees a slow slow change in her face like the turning of night into day.

—What are you saying? says Claudia, in a voice that is blown in from some distant horizon. Her sea eyes hold no fear.

—I'm your twin, Haley says.

The coming together

They talk for a long time, the faded golden girl with a hole in her breast and the dark sturdy girl whose belly curves like an apostrophe. Their long chain of talk has slipped through the cracks of planning, has dropped into time before it was due. It takes place not over candlelit pasta on an intended Thursday, but on a tired Tuesday evening in the coffee shop of a ferry terminal.

Yet maybe this is the only way these two sisters could have come to it. In a sense their whole lives have been preparation for this moment. But humans are adept at avoiding their destiny. There are always distractions, and the distractions are always justifiable: trips to take, tragedies to surmount, grievances to grow out of.

At first the two sit stiffly, facing each other like prisoner and visitor. The tabletop might as well be a vast prairie, and them gesturing uselessly from each side of it. But gradually the formica surface becomes smeared with hands and weak tea, sprinkled with crumbs. It shrinks—though slowly—until the two are close enough to shuffle their explanations and questions together like a pack of cards, examine them, pool them, re-deal.

First, there is the Diane hand: this is put back gently, face down, and will remain undisclosed for the duration of the long game.

(—But I don't understand, says Leith later.—Why shouldn't she know?

—Because the mother should always remain the mother, says Claudia cryptically.

—Because she must be allowed to keep protecting Claudia, says Haley.)

Then there is the Sandra hand: to be considered carefully, discussed at length, and played with assertion.

(—I'll talk to her but I won't let her take over, says Haley firmly.

—Won't she drive you crazy analysing the whole thing? says Claudia.

—She can analyse forever, says Haley,—but I won't let her drive me crazy.)

And their strategy when it comes to each other? This will be worked out over time. Tact is required, and patience, and a measure of tolerance and forgiveness, all of which they now make a start on. Voices are raised, fall. Stars and suns, striding lions and upside-down hunters, northern and southern lights, throng about their heads. And the long light fades.

—So you're really going back to England, says Claudia. There is an odd tone in her voice: admiration, mixed with uncertainty.

   —Yes, but not to the way I was, says Haley.

   —No, well, you can't ever go backwards, says Claudia.

   —Even if part of you wants to, says Haley.

   There's a pause.

   —You're like the comet, says Claudia.—You arrived here at the same time and now you're both disappearing.

   (There is something like regret in her voice.)

   —If that's the case, says Haley,—you won't see me again for two thousand years.

   —Really? says Claudia.—Are you saying you won't ever be back?

   (There is definite sadness in her voice.)

   —I was joking! says Haley.

   (There is remorse in her voice.)

   —So you might come back this way again? asks Claudia, casually.

   —Would you want me to come back? says Haley, tentatively.

   —Yes, if you wanted to, says Claudia.

   (There is hope in both their voices.)

   —In that case, says Haley,—I think I might.

They sit for a long time, these two, until the tired teenager mops the floor from under their feet. Then, like schoolgirls at the end of the day, they put their chairs up on the table and walk out looking entirely different from how they looked when they walked in.

   That is, they look more the same.

∝

RECONNAISSANCE

Kapka Kassabova

Nadedja is backpacking around New Zealand, in the surreal haze of summer. Her encounters are comic and revealing—and often sexual. But Nadejda's tour is a deep and personal one; it is a journey into memory and family myth.

Faded memories of happy times conflict with more disturbing pictures as her determination to uncover the truth is diffused with an immigrant's yearning to belong and a young woman's longing for love. And who is the mystery narrator who 'talks' to Nadedja as her travels lead her to him.

Set against the turmoil of present-day Bulgaria and the sweet simplicity of her new country, *Reconnaissance* is a grand, sweeping novel of family secrets, dislocation and ultimate reconciliation.

A powerful and sensual debut novel.

Kapka Kassabova's book of poems, *All Roads Lead To The Sea*, received a Montana Award.

Believers to
the Bright Coast

Vincent O'Sullivan

The infamous Dr Crippen's mistress finds a new life in disreputable Auckland in the early decades of the century. A French nun, Marie Claire, gives herself to working among the disabled and the poor . . . Young Spicer, a slow-witted lad who looks great in a chauffeur's uniform, finds himself deeply involved in the lives of both. Together they form an unlikely threesome.

This is the setting for Vincent O'Sullivan's brilliant new novel, an intricate story steeped in the early decades of the century that leads us through an astonishing array of perversion, kidnapping and violence. Awaiting its moment is the mystery of 'the Chow', as the North Island is criss-crossed at gunpoint . . .

Vincent O'Sullivan's best-selling novel *Let the River Stand* won the Montana Book Award in 1994.